Immodest Creature

by

Christine Tripp

The Black Swan Saga

Immodest Creature

Cover Art by *Tina Lynn Stout*

The Wild Rose Press, Inc.
PO Box 708
Adams Basin, NY 14410-0708
Visit us at www.thewildrosepress.com

Publishing History
First Edition, 2023
Trade Paperback ISBN 978-1-5092-5016-5
Digital ISBN 978-1-5092-5017-2

Published in the United States of America

"Is it not romantic?" Serena asked. Such poetry from a man was alluring, even though it was a bit demonstrative.

"No. In the tales, the ladies are married to kings or dukes but in love with the poet or troubadour. I cannot think of a worse fate for a woman to be in love with one man but married to another. How is that romantic?" he asked.

She couldn't adequately cover her feelings; they spilled forth in a dour turn of her mouth. He made particularly good arguments. "I suppose it is better to love a man you cannot have than not to love at all. A life without love seems tragic and hollow."

There was a noise, similar to a gulp. Serena looked to Frederick, who looked equally confused. She looked to Lord Vincent, but he had vanished. The air where he should have been was empty. But immediately below that air was an open manhole cover, leading to a shallow, rocky tunnel with Lord Vincent inside. All his smugness hadn't stopped him from falling prey to an obvious peril.

All his viciousness could muster was "I believe I have wrenched my ankle."

Dedication

To Christine, from everyone that ever knew and loved her. We live in the world made from your beauty and love, and I will never stop loving you. I will see you soon.

"Immodest creature, you do not want a woman who will accept your faults, you want the one who pretends you are faultless—one who will caress the hand that strikes her and kiss the lips that lie to her."

George Sand, *The Intimate Journal of George Sand*

Prologue

April 14, 1876

Lady Serena sat up as straight as a pawn on a chess board in the downy carriage. The ride was kinetic and chaotic—more of a tumble down the road than a calm rural jaunt. This was not her father's finest carriage. Her parents had taken that one. They had decided that Serena would ride in this carriage from Cornwall to Oxford, as it would be overwhelming for her to ride a train and then find a cab. Of course, this meant it would take at least a day's ride and her party would have to stop at an inn. Under different circumstance, twelve-year-old Serena would have been over the moon to make this trek. Today she could not stop the tears from flowing.

Mr. Brooks, the butler; Mr. Michaels, her father's valet; and Mrs. Stone, the housekeeper, traveled with her. At least five of the servants had fled as soon as the news hit the house. Her mother's lady's maid stole over half of Serena's mother's jewelry when she left. The stable master stole two beautiful, proud horses. The two footmen and maid merely stole a myriad of silver pieces that had been in her family for over a hundred years. Her eagle-eyed defenders had changed to ravenous locusts overnight. They had picked the house clean of anything of worth and left only the bones and her sad memories.

Serena had found her parents' bodies. They had not returned home after a ball, which, by itself, was odd. She had ridden her horse, Luna, as she did every morning before her studies. Her governess was never far behind on these mornings, and Serena had heard her faint echo just a few paces behind her. The first thing Serena saw when she came across the wrecked carriage was her mother's golden hair falling out of the broken window. It shone like a puddle of spilled sunshine that caught her eye even though it was far away. Serena's bones had chilled, and her throat had swelled, but no scream ever came. She was terrified. Her governess left Serena to find help while Serena stared on. Not a single part of this made sense. Not in the cosmic sense, but in the simple, visceral, logical sense.

The clearest thing in Serena's mind was the fact of her parents' murder. Surely, it had been made to look as though a wreck occurred. But it was tidy—almost curated. An accident scene with no blood. Even if every person had snapped their neck upon the wreck, the shattered glass would have cut her father's loving face. His placid, closed eyes and unblemished face looked slumbering, not fearful. And although the carriage wreck killed her mother, father, a coachman, and two footmen, their horses were alive and well. Not a scratch, every blinder intact, every knee and hoof unscuffed. This was a literary accident, possessed of all the components of a tragic event one could describe, but none of the anguished details. This was all wrong. Deep in her hidden heart, she felt a wound more complex than mere sadness forming. The tears began to fall on her cheeks. But they did not feel like her tears. It did not feel like her body. This did not feel like her world. For a second, her tiny, lonely body wanted to lie down next to them in the darkness. But her feet were too heavy to move.

Someone decided that they would tell Frederick, her older brother, in person. Serena did not remember or care who. But one should not send a telegram to alert a man that his parents were dead and that he was the new Marquess of Berkeley. Even though Frederick was at Oxford University, Serena received a letter from him every week to recommend books to read. Every week her father (who Serena still called Daddy even though she was nearly a woman) bought her whichever book Frederick recommended and read it with her. Who would buy her books now? Who would read with her and help her understand? When Serena thought, sometimes it was in her own voice, and sometimes it was her father's. How long until the memory of that voice disappeared, and she was alone?

The Percys were used to being chided and mocked for their "common" traits. Much of the ton believed they were far too middle class for a ducal family. They sincerely loved each other, and their most treasured moments were with each other. That was decidedly out of step with much of London society, for whom a solitary handshake and sparse compliment around the holidays was sufficient kindness. Daddy had believed that the Percys were cursed. He would tell Serena and Frederick that they were doomed to marry only for true love or spend their lives alone. This seemed like a very romantic variety of doom. Her father married the most beautiful Swiss milkmaid who had ever laid hands on a cow, Frederick and Serena's mother, Regina. Although he was ostracized and insulted for it, he never regretted it. Serena knew from living with her father that the true curse was having feelings in a world built to destroy them. Or to privilege commerce, station, or duty above them.

The staff and Serena rested in Exeter and again in Bristol before finally arriving in Oxford. Mr. Brooks solemnly walked to find Frederick while Serena waited outside of his lively dormitory. But there he was, directly across the lawn, jabbering and strutting in the center of a large group of students. Frederick was laughing, and the boys listened while cocking their heads toward him. He smiled too glibly, like he knew half of what he said was not true but understood that his gentle fibbing made for a better tale. She hated that she had to hurt him. Why should she have to be the one to tell him their parents were dead?

Her cheeks were wet, and her eyes felt red and raw. The tears had not stopped running, or perhaps they had simply begun again. Frederick saw her and smiled broadly as he jogged over. He clearly had not observed the details of her grief or was choosing to ignore them to make her less self-conscious. "Serena, is Mum with you?"

One of his friends chased him. "Lyons, where are you going?"

Serena shook her head. No, Mum was not with her, and Mum would never be with her again. And, no, Frederick was no longer the Viscount Lyons but the new Marquess of Berkeley. Everything was wrong. Dead wrong and terrible and Serena hated every bit of it. She desperately wanted the world to return to the world of a week ago, when things seemed good and decent.

"Pet? What is wrong? Where's Mum?" Frederick asked as he came closer to her. He was close enough for her to know he was holding his breath and waiting for her to speak. He must know already.

She shook her head violently. If she did not say it, maybe it would not be true. He deserved a few more seconds living in a distant, happier world.

"My lord, I must speak with you," Mr. Brooks said as he exited the dormitory. Such a noise would have been startling if she cared about people sneaking up on her anymore.

"What is it, Mr. Brooks?" Frederick asked, although his lips barely moved. He must know something was very, very wrong.

"I regret to inform you that your parents were in a carriage wreck and have died." Mr. Brooks blurted out the sentence in a flat monotone without a single pause. It was the tone of an indifferent vicar officiating an irresponsible wedding—no love, no judgment. He had been rehearsing it completely differently during the journey but most likely became nervous at the time.

Frederick's face was like an eclipsed sun—everything light became dark. Serena saw the tears in his eyes. He pulled her violently in to him and hugged her tightly just below the shoulder. He pulled her up so high that she felt the empty air between her feet and the ground. She was weightless, like a sad feather. "I'm sorry. I'm sorry. I'm sorry," he whispered. Every sorry was different. One was formal—it was expected and sympathetic. The second was pure empathy for her and was more plaintive and tearful. The last was a raspy scared thing. Like he didn't know if he could be the

5

person she needed right now.

The next moments and days were chaos. While Frederick gathered his things and said his goodbyes to his peers and friends, her cousin Benedict Cooper—the Viscount Melgum—joined them. They did not return to Cornwall. That was where they took holidays. They had lived in their estate in Bedfordshire. No, instead they took a train to their grandparents' estate in Berkshire. The news of her parents' deaths began to trickle around. Strangers suddenly began expressing forced and formal sympathies whenever they stopped during their journey. Serena knew the small circle of friends that had journeyed to visit throughout her life. It was a sick, sick thing to see a tragedy twisted into an opportunity for performance.

At her grandfather's insistence, an inquest was performed. The conclusion was that, in fact, the marquess and marchioness had been murdered. The coachman had been poisoned, which in turn had led to the deaths of her parents. The details were deemed too grave and disquieting for a female child to hear. The murders caused an enormous scandal—after all, it was an assassination. Suddenly her parents were beloved. Each story or memory of them, no matter how trivial, became a bright gem to be shown off at a party or written about. At the funeral, those same people who had caused her mother to cry with judging looks and vorpal words suddenly spoke of her as though they had been friends for years.

Serena felt a rage beyond words at her parents' funeral. These people, the so-called gentry, had terrorized her mother. It was disgusting to watch them coo about her beauty and how lovely her mother was in death when in life they called her a whore and a usurper. What strange, repugnant illness overtook them all to make them kind to her in death but punitive to her for falling in love while she was alive? Had she changed by dying? Was she no longer a mere bumpkin who exploited her feminine wiles to seduce a marquess? Serena could barely suppress a scream. It echoed and spasmed in her like a sputtering fire. She gripped tight to her dress, feeling the fabric yield and rip under the stress of her anger.

After the funeral, there was a great deal of discussion about Serena's future. Or, more pointedly, what was to be done about the child? Her grandparents wanted her to live with them, but Frederick was concerned it would overwhelm Serena to live in a duke's home. The required events and callings were a full calendar for an enthusiastic and composed young woman. She could not make the appropriate pretenses in her current state. So, as the Percy family was wont to do, they compromised so all parties could be happy. They would let a home in Oxford, and Mr. Brooks and Mrs. Stone would care for Serena. Frederick would visit every weekend without fail. For holidays and summers, the siblings would journey to their grandparents.

The aspiration was that Serena might speak again. She had not uttered a word since she found her parents' bodies. But her mother had taught her to only speak pleasant words. Serena could now only vacillate between sorrow and rage. So, in order to honor her mother's memory, she would not speak until her words would not be gasps of venom and fire. She was a perfect porcelain doll full of unspoken rage, staring unblinkingly and seeing nothing but a broken world. She would not speak for another year.

Chapter 1

There is a strange magic to the month of September. It begins with the last of Summer but quickly transforms to the beautiful harvest season. I once attended a lecture, where a man spoke on butterflies. According to him, in the countries of Mexico and Texas, at this time of year, the monarchs begin their long journey South. The lands are absolutely littered with the butterflies. And when it is dreary, and I haven't seen the sun in days, I dream of such a beautiful place.

Aunt Penny's Advice for Living—September 1885

Philadelphia

"You will meet a man from a far-off land," Madame Olyenska said, her ominous voice filling the emptiness around her like smoke from an angry fire. Her eyes did not drop from Serena's, willing and hypnotizing her to believe the words hanging in the air between them.

But instead, Lady Serena Percy fought hard not to roll her eyes. This old yarn, again? Every fortune teller and mystic had some version of this—a vague promise of hidden love. Honestly, did women need nothing else? On the other hand, if the mystic had observed Serena was twenty-one with no marriage prospects in sight, it was a reasonable inference that Serena would care about men. Since Madame Olyenska had not been proven wrong yet, Serena exhaled quietly and steeled her temper. This charade would continue until she had evidence she was dealing with a charlatan. Plus, the seat was comfortable.

"This man is from far away from here, or far away from where I am from? I too am from a far-off land. And so, every man I meet here is a stranger from a far-off land," Serena said. Her studious English and minor accent had betrayed her already, so revealing that she wasn't a local was not giving the fortune teller additional information.

"Far away from me. I am the one the spirits speak to. Great love comes your way." Madame Olyenska looked upward and gestured emphatically, thrusting her hands in the air and closer to Serena's face. The table shuddered and tilted as it began to float, nearly bumping her chin. This was an old and petty trick, perhaps a version with a hidden pedal and extendable base attached under the flat top of the table.

Serena sighed. It was a relief to be disappointed and to feel right in that disappointment. Men were always falling in love with her. Frederick once joked that because she had the body of a world-class mistress and the mind of a fellow at Oxford, she would equally enrage and arouse any man she tempted into an argument. This was only half true. Men confused her shy demeanor with meekness. Her quietness was framed as docility. And as soon as she was comfortable enough to speak her mind, men regarded any strong opinion as evidence she was a bluestocking. If any man got close enough to argue with her, all of a sudden, she was opinionated and stubborn, the opposite of the silent, pretty girl they first desired. She had grown close to one man who had endured a single bout of argument, but he suddenly became unavailable upon discovering she was an atheist. How difficult it must be for men, to discover that under her beautiful visage there was something deeper, and on occasion that depth needed acknowledgment.

"Lovely," Serena said evenly. Better not to inform Madame Olyenska of anything. The less she knew, the more objective Serena could be about her "mystic abilities."

"But the strange man. He will help you in solving a mystery. I see the number nine. When did your mystery begin—nine days, nine weeks, nine months, or nine years ago?"

"Nine years." Serena breathed out carefully, measuring both words before speaking. Not one mystic had ever even hinted at her parents' deaths before. A slight pang of hope shook through her for the first time. That was dangerous and a bit painful. It had felt better to be disappointed.

"Yes, yes. I see the wreck now. This man, his heart is heavy, and he feels the weight of his past, but you can help him." Before she didn't blink, but now she would not meet Serena's gaze.

"Forget about him!" Serena snapped. "The mystery...what light can you shed on it?" Desperation clawed at her skirts. For nine years she'd sought to know more, but it had been like chasing a ghost in a graveyard, always something in the corner of her eye, too quick to vanish, never fully seen. She needed to find the man who killed her parents, or she could never know peace.

"The man you seek is far away. From both of us. He still maneuvers to make men act in England and…New Orleans. I see a menagerie of shadowy men. A dark society."

"New Orleans?" Serena asked. She had heard of the city, of course, but how could it reveal anything about her parents' deaths?

"Yes, I see money flowing in and out of the city. Silver and gold, like a molten river. Find where your wealthy lords hide their greatest troves, and you will spy something familiar." Madame Olyenska paused as smoke filled the air. She pulled her chin up and stared again at Serena, her mouth askew. There was something she was omitting. She was chewing her words but not spitting them out.

"What of this society? Anything there?" Serena asked. Better to seem conversational. Appearing too serious would cause the madam to escalate. These cheap tricks were likely effective to the credulous rubes who lined Olyenska's pockets, but positively incensed Serena's skepticism.

"They are wrapped in shadows. This man, however. He carries a bitter seed that has taken a lifetime to bloom. He will not intend to hurt you, but his intentions are not relevant. Be on your guard and be strong. You must heal and help him. He is a cynic, so only a believer like you can prove him wrong."

Serena sat back dubiously against the tattered velvet chair. She wanted to laugh so hard it almost bubbled out of her closed mouth. Her, a believer? Every bone of her body was buttressed with cynicism. But for every single mystic she sought out, she held tight a secret hope that they would prove her wrong. They were all frauds and charlatans of the first order. At least, that was what she told herself whenever she was disappointed. What she knew was every cynic had a heart that had been betrayed. A heart that desperately wanted to be proven wrong. Including her own buried heart. Madame Olyenska was giving her hope. She wanted to abandon her fear and just believe. How easy would it be to lay her heart naked and do that? A choice between constant pangs of disappointment and overwhelming hopelessness wasn't a choice at all. It felt like deciding between false light and utter darkness.

She paid the woman and gave a tip in a series of large crisp bills that added up to twenty dollars. Was that generous or stingy? American money didn't make much sense. Especially with their economy being so unstable, having only recently come out of a devastating depression. She hurriedly left the room without letting her poised face slip to unveil her anxiety. Her lady's maid, Martha Swinton, waited outside with a pensive smile and climbed into the carriage right after she did. The horses clopped a loud path to the Continental Hotel along the bright Philadelphia streets. Serena rested her forehead against the window.

Philadelphia was like a charming friend. It was easy to be passionate about its history, even though it was relatively young. Whimsical little things always had a measure of innate charm. Like a book with an exciting first chapter. She loved the vibrant adolescence of the city. It was as though a collection of German and English villages were stacked on top of each other. Perhaps it was simply that it was fall and autumn held a certain romance to her, so she fell in love with a city.

Serena had been enjoying America; she could breathe here. They did not have nobility. If Serena made a social faux pas, the press did not write about it. No one insulted her. Women were far too busy falling in love with Frederick to be aggressive with Serena. Perhaps in a country without a strict social hierarchy, there was more room for one to grow. Or perhaps Serena being a lady intimidated the people she met.

Serena was considering following her cousin Benedict's suit and moving to America, perhaps Philadelphia. Frederick would be marrying soon, and there were no men worth having in their homeland. Not to mention the ton, who had picked apart her insecurities like layers of a warm croissant. She was paralyzed by the idea of an even greater ridicule if she entered society. She desperately needed to break free from the expectations and histrionics of London. Perhaps America was the path for freedom.

"Madame Olyenska seemed to be a genuine mystic," Martha offered.

Serena smiled at her maid and confidante. Martha Swinton was the daughter of the pharmacist who aided her grandmother and had become Serena's maid when Serena was fourteen and Martha was fifteen. They instantly became good friends and had been inseparable. Martha was *thin.* Her angular face and sharp golden eyes were framed by oak-brown hair. Men, even gentlemen (even Serena's suitors), liked Martha, but she met them with indifference and propriety.

"Yes, but she should quit the theatrics. She doesn't need to embellish on her talent," Serena agreed.

"Do you believe her?"

Serena considered it. She could trust Martha with an honest opinion, but she still whispered. "*If* we find something related to my parents' deaths in New Orleans, then she will have convinced me."

"Truly? What will we do for fun? If we are no longer testing fortune tellers, that is."

"I don't know. Perhaps I will begin debunking hauntings or sea monsters," Serena said with a smile.

"Not God? I know you don't believe," Martha asked.

"I refuse to take away something that is more good than bad. The church helps the poor and funds a great many artworks. If the church were to become greedy, where vicars lived in mansions wearing furs and jewels while the poor still suffered and their parishioners needed food, then they would need to be exposed. But for now, I seek to disprove only the harmful. The medium who tells a grieving son his mother has a vague message, and she may be able to repeat it for enough money—that, to me, is evil," Serena lectured.

"What would it take for you to believe?" Martha asked.

"Proof. God has sent angels to speak for him, but no more. Perhaps once a century he could send a worldwide message, in every language, and simply update his edicts. Why stay silent while his creations kill each other in his name? Why must children become sick and die? Why do hypocrites flourish and the faithful starve? God has much to answer for," Serena said. Her temples pulsed—had she said too much?

Martha sat up uncomfortably fast. Her eyebrows knitted, and she looked guilty. But she always knew when to change the conversation. "She also mentioned that you will meet a man. Should I begin choosing dresses for you that showcase your…talents?"

Serena laughed. She could not imagine the man who would tolerate her mouth. The craven suitor who courted her would have to endure her distaste for the ton while also being attacked for her opinions. What man would enjoy spitting fire at the upper classes and be free of the heavy water of their opinions?

"Best to discourage rather than encourage," Serena said.

"He might love your mind. You could wear a veil or don a set of trousers and go by Samuel," Martha suggested.

Serena snickered. "I doubt that it is my face that attracts men. If my corset cannot contain my bosom, then I shall always be besieged."

Chapter 2

As I flee New York, I must apologize to the city of Manhattan. I am certain that a great many of fine restaurants exist within the city, but I was drawn to Delmonico's for every meal. If we lived in pagan times, Charles Ranhofer would be the god of cooking. The man has an extraordinary gift to transform the mundane into the exquisite.

However, the laundry service in New York is simply miserable. All my clothing no longer fits as comfortably as it once did. Even the things I did not have laundered. The cheek.

A Curmudgeon's Tour of America, September 1885

Vincent jaunted into the Continental Hotel, which was decent enough by American standards, in the way only a wayward son of London could—his shoulders back in an affected swagger, his gaze even and confident over the laborers and tourists rumbling through the lobby. Hopefully, this hotel hosted Berkeley and his family. His search for Berkeley had been a disaster. His sister-in-law, Lily, continued to wire Vincent to let him know where their group was meant to be, but when Vincent arrived, Berkeley was nowhere to be found. Lily wrote that the wayward party was in Philadelphia while Vincent was in New York, and he took the next train. He hoped to finally find

Berkeley, because as much as it pained Vincent to admit, he was lonely.

He had never been alone this much before. He, even when he did not want it, always had company. At school he had Christopher or Sebastian nearby. When the brothers went on their tour of Europe, he never wanted for company. At home he had friends and his club to provide good conversation. Even during a scandal, when the papers were reporting his various misdeeds, he always had people near him.

But America was different. He had no connections here, and the few people he had met were not his sort. The men fawned over him like a new invention. They took his title and the fact that he was the son of a duke to be novel and interesting but took no interest in Vincent as a man. He could not help but wonder—was this what women were forced to endure? Lily and Lady Olivia confirmed this to be true.

American society both frustrated and annoyed Vincent. They had the ability and the tools to build a great society. However, the wealthy were not taught to be stewards of the lower class. They lorded over them, enriching themselves along the way. Instead of a land of freedom, it was peopled in tiny tyrants. Oddly, many of the people living in America had ancestors who hoped for a better life—yet they disparaged the immigrants and gave little care for the poor. Of course, this was a nation that had begun a war due to a lack of representation but kept and maintained slavery for nearly a hundred years. It was rather like seeing a friend, who was brilliant with potential, drifting away when you knew they could be better.

He approached the desk clerk, his polished shoes

stomping lightly to announce him. "Good afternoon. I am Lord Vincent Mandeville. I am seeking Frederick Percy, the Marquess of Berkeley, and his party. Is he residing at this establishment?"

The clerk, a young man, checked the registry. "Yes, sir, he is staying with us."

Vincent let out a sigh of relief; finally he had found Berkeley. "Excellent! I would like to have a room near him as I hope to join his party. Would that be possible?"

"Yes, sir." The clerk waved for a porter to fetch Vincent's trunks.

Once Vincent was in his room, he ordered a coffee service and removed his coat. He began to unpack his clothing, regretting allowing Ralph to keep the valet they once shared. Vincent was particular about the order of his clothing, and without a valet, he had much more work upon his shoulders. Once his clothing and room were set right, he sat down for coffee and to reread the letter from Lily.

My favorite brother, Vincent,

How are you enjoying America? Is it as great as they say? Are the streets paved with gold or with indifference as they are in London? I miss you, and the British Empire misses your wit. Come home soon.

I have a bit of news, and I need your help telling Ralph. I believe I am with child (the doctor is coming by to confirm this belief later today). Will Ralph be happy? Some men do not like children and will use pregnancy as an excuse to get a mistress. I am both excited and afraid. What if I am horrible to the child? What if I am my mother reborn? I had hoped for more time before children, but if I am with child, there is no turning back.

I am sorry that you have not found Lord Berkeley yet. I am certain he will be in Philadelphia for the last week of September. Lord Melgum is invested in a play which opens late September (I believe September 29, but I am uncertain). My father enjoyed the Continental Hotel, and I believe Berkeley will be staying there. B. is fiercely protective of his sister. It is in your interest to be pleasant and charming to her.

I have been observing Sebastian. Miss Haverford must have misunderstood him. He never speaks of her and only escorts her when she asks. You are hurting, but the fault lies in Miss Haverford's ambitions and not Sebastian's actions. Please let the facts rule your passions. If she is using an ancient grudge to break to new mutiny, she should not be forgiven. Verify Miss Haverford's allegations. Please remember he is your brother, and he loves you. He has never betrayed you before. This would be a profound treachery. Sebastian is many things, but profound is not one of them.

Write me soon. I adore the gifts from Boston, but I miss your words. Ralph greatly misses you. I tried to wear your clothing and insult him, but alas, it was no replacement. I suppose it was as effective as you wearing my clothing and attempting to seduce him.

Your family loves and misses you.

Always your favorite sister,

Lily

Vincent's heart soared high above the American stars. A child he could teach to curse? To buy gifts for, spoil, and teach to refer to Sebastian as "the old man"? A little baby made of Ralph and Lily would be a blend of the things Vincent loved most. Lily was being silly, however. Of course, Ralph would be excited for a child. Lily was always afraid of her shadow. That shadow carried her past with it, and no one thinks they can outrun their shadow. Vincent would have to tease her until she was more irritated with him than afraid of the shadows.

As for Sebastian, the longer Vincent stayed away from him, the better. He spent his sober nights writing Sebastian long, angry letters. Demanding letters. Why had Sebastian wooed Marlene knowing that Vincent intended to marry her? Sebastian never replied. Neither did Marlene. Their inaction, their burning neglect, demonstrated what they thought of Vincent. Being ignored was an insult that fanned the flames in his heart. He burned deeply with anger and pride until all that was left of him was a deep, ashy sadness. Again and again, he died inside and returned. His heart was a bleak phoenix.

Some days were better than others. He'd never loved Marlene; she was fun to be around and a fantastic cocksucker, but he had never confused that with love. But in the maudlin hours (often when he was a little drunk), she was the only woman he could love. And so, Sebastian's competitive urges had made a wreckage of his perfect life. Vincent loved her, he hated her, he was indifferent to her. In his most honest moments, he realized she'd wounded his pride and shattered his precious ego. It was a wound that could never heal because the person she'd spurned him for was his rival, and a man he was bound by blood to love—his brother. A brother whose distance had waned and faded and whose closeness had grown, until the fateful day of Lily and Ralph's wedding.

To rub salt in his wound, his mother was silent. This was the only time he had been truly grieved by Sebastian. She should be in his corner, chastising Sebastian for this violation of familial obligation. She should be disavowing Marlene and forcing Sebastian to apologize. But Lily was an apt spy. Seraphina has invited Marlene to tea and to supper? Her silence supported Marlene and Sebastian's match, forever forcing Vincent from her home. The rejection stung like a fighter's punch even though it came from a lace-gloved hand. When would this succession of betrayals end?

His melancholy rose hard, from his feet to his outstretched fingers. Of course, the only path out was to torment Lily.

Lion Tamer,

Dear God, woman! Ralph hates children—I once saw him try to eat one. Oh, to be sure he will claim he was cooing and cuddling it, but I know the truth. Oh, my poor Lily. He will cast you out and disavow the child.

As for your fears of being a terrible mother, worry not. I have seen you tolerate that wretched fluff ball you call a cat. That thing has broken precious figurines and clocks while scaling your dresses and curtains. Yet you have never raised your voice or thrown the beast out of your house. Your mother would have had a butler drown it once it stopped being a sweet little kitten.

If I may be serious (a rare moment for me, I know), I am excited to be an uncle. Ralph will be euphoric to be a father. You will be a wonderful mother, because (according to my grandmother) you will love your child more than the person you made it with. Imagine the amount you love Ralph and double for how much you will love that baby (perhaps Little Vincent?). Unfortunately, you will become a mother before Ralph will become a father. You will have longer to love your child, and you also have more time to fret about it as well. Relax and be calm, if for no other reason than worrying won't do anything.

I am sending gifts from New York. I hope you enjoy them. And be prepared for a deluge of baby gifts. Currently, I am in Pennsylvania (I have not found Lord Berkeley, but we are staying at the same hotel). Apparently, this is Amish country, and I am certain I can find a quilt for the little one. Or coal. Lots of coal.

I miss you and Ralph. But I am full of bitterness and bile. I fear I would spit venom at you and hurt you accidentally. This trip to America is for the best, and I will return home when I am certain I can hold my tongue. Or find a woman strong enough to pluck it out.

Always,

Vincent

Once he had finished the letter to Lily, he drank his coffee and enjoyed a small repast. He still didn't taste anything. As he read the paper with news from London, a heavy hand squeezed his lungs. Lord Hume had died, so Miss Hume, the brown woman with eyes the boring color of her boring hair, had no mother to protect her. Surely, she needed someone. He broke the seal on the letter he wrote Lily to add a postscript.

P.S Send my condolences to Miss Hume. And take her on, Lily. She needs someone to help her flourish with her studies, and I do not trust anyone else to assist her.

Vincent sealed a new envelope and sent his letter

off to Lily. He was homesick, but with Sebastian and Marlene courting, Vincent did not have a home. All of London was unwelcoming, as well as Norfolk or anywhere in the countryside. Europe, North Africa, and the near East were close enough for him to be pressured to attend Sebastian's wedding. No, America was the best place for him on Earth.

If only there was something in this great forest of a country to entertain him.

Chapter 3

When the wind gusts and is thick with leaves, that is the announcement of autumn. There is a scent that only autumn has, brimming with warmth and heavily spiced. I am a firm believer in cinnamon being the premier spice of autumn.

Aunt Penny's Advice for Living, September 1885

"Oof!" Serena cried as Martha cinched her corset too tight. She knew her body was made for tight lacing, and so of course Martha laced her extremely tightly. Her natural twenty-four-inch waist (as measured in American standards) became a twenty-inch waist. That by itself was not exceptional, but when combined with her large breasts and round hips, she resembled an hourglass. An hourglass that had no time and less patience for corsetry.

Martha helped her put on a light blouse, the color of a cloud on the sea. Serena fastened the buttons with nimble fingers while Martha slid on the peacock-blue skirt. Serena grabbed the waistband tightly, and behind her, Martha draped the complicated folds over the bustle frame. The clock sat comfortably on the wall, ticking in judgment. She was already late. She slid into her matching velvet peacock-blue jacket and sat straight at attention at her vanity. While Martha fixed Serena's bun, she wiped her face with a damp cloth. The adorable matching hat was fixed to her head painfully—the hatpins scratched her scalp—and Serena rushed to the restaurant.

She was late again for lunch with Frederick and Benedict because she had snuck out in the morning to meet with a fortune teller. The worst she had seen. He predicted she would marry Frederick, but Benedict would always hold her in his heart as his true love. The fool probably didn't care if he was referring to her brother as her future husband. He had already been paid his fifty cents and most likely wanted to finish quickly. However, the one thing that Benedict and Frederick agreed on was that Serena should not visit male fortune tellers without them. After all, as a woman she could be mesmerized into corruption. She always wanted to ask what form of corruption she could entertain. Would she be an outlaw, an opium dealer, or just another fallen woman? But she humored them.

She approached the table where Frederick and Benedict sat. And of course, they were arguing with one another. "I apologize for my tardiness, as I was consumed by my book."

"Pet! You are just in time to tell Benedict that he is a fool." Frederick grinned at her. Frederick was a perfect cameo of their father with his deep mahogany hair and dark blue eyes. He even wore a beard as their father had, but that couldn't obfuscate his handsome face. How she adored him, her other, prettier half.

"Yes, Serena, please tell your brother how incredibly wrong he is." Benedict seethed. Benedict Cooper, the Viscount of Melgum, was Serena and Frederick's cousin and close friend. After the death of their parents, Serena and Frederick had cleaved closer to their grandparents and aunt and uncle. Benedict became a brother to Serena and Frederick, so she treated him like one. This did not always sit well with Benedict. He was not as charming or persuasive as Frederick, so he lost several petty arguments that he should have won.

Serena sighed. "What must I settle today? Are we debating the Catholic doctrine versus the Anglican church? Or perhaps we are litigating the battle of Waterloo? May I request that you argue as to who makes the best cake, just once? We could have a taste test?"

"No, although I do enjoy finding the best cake. Perhaps we could make that a quest for our lives. I was telling Benedict about my scheme with Adrian to buy estates and convert them to resorts or neighborhoods with shopping at the center. Benedict finds this traitorous." Frederick reached for his tea.

"It is a fool's errand. What kind of person would wish to stay at a house in the country?" Benedict pushed the sugar toward Frederick. Even in anger he still showed proper English etiquette.

She frowned as her lunch was served. Eating in a corset was not a simple matter. "Benedict, darling, I love you, but we would. We retreat to our estates when the season ends and have house parties on the weekends. Why would the middle class or the poor not desire a break from the heavy soot of London? Why would they not wish to hunt our grounds, fish our waters, and be waited on for a few days? What Frederick and Mr. Rose are offering is a glimpse of the life in the upper class."

"But you are profiting from this glimpse. How can

you speak endlessly about helping the poor, and yet you will charge them to visit a home?" Benedict always tried to argue every side so long as it was contrary to Frederick.

Frederick smiled. "Why, I am so glad you asked. Young man, could you please come here?" Frederick gestured to the young man in a crisp monochrome uniform who had served Serena her lunch. "Tell me, I am considering opening a hotel similar to this one in England. My cousin is concerned that the positions available at a hotel will not attract workers. How do you like working in a hotel?"

"It is wonderful, sir," the young man answered. They were isolated enough from other workers to give him an aura of frankness; one would hardly expect honesty if his colleagues were observing.

"Decent wages and at least one day off?" Frederick asked.

"Indeed, sir. And I get to meet people from all over the world." The young man's eyes went wide with a demonstrable awe.

"And if this hotel were not here, where do you suppose you might work?" Frederick led.

The young man frowned. "I reckon I would go to the steel factories or the mines. Dirty work."

"Thank you very much." Frederick shook his hand, slipping him a silver coin. Once he was gone, Frederick turned fast and resumed the argument. "There you are. A hotel will offer jobs and with that, choices. If a man does not need to work in the mines, the owners of mines will have to raise wages and safety. More employment opportunities are essential to create an environment where the worker demands are heard. If workers are easily obtained, managers will take advantage. But if jobs are readily available, workers will have the advantage."

And this was the cue that the argument was about to take a turn to the labor movement. It was better to avoid such a heated subject. "Isn't Philadelphia lovely? I am pleased that we are spending a fortnight here." She sought to interrupt with a mix of aloofness and authority. Certainly they would read this as a signal to stop. Certainly.

"Yes, I very much enjoy it. However, I am having a difficult time finding a wife. Perhaps I should let a wife find me." Frederick laughed thickly with amusement.

"Frederick, I would like to visit New Orleans. Is it on our itinerary?" Serena asked.

"I don't recall, but our trip is flexible and can be altered. Why do you want to visit New Orleans?" Frederick hadn't considered this destination, apparently.

Serena's first thought burst from her mouth. "Birds. I am given to understand there are exotic birds there as well as alligators. Besides, I am considering following Benedict's lead and moving to America. I like Philadelphia, but I may enjoy New Orleans more."

Benedict smiled at this idea, and Frederick scowled. "You cannot. This country is far too large, and we have no connections. Even if you were to find a husband here, I would want you to be in England. I need you, pet. You are my closest friend and wisest advisor. I would be lost without you. Imagine the sheer trouble I would inflict on the women of our homeland without you there."

She couldn't suppress a heavy sigh. Frederick would never understand how difficult it was to be a lady in the ton. The competition for a husband created an atmosphere of ferocity and arm's-length friendships. It was nearly impossible to share confidences with other women, though Serena had Honoria, her closest friend. Serena choked down terror before every event she attended. Inevitably one of the ladies or their mothers would make some nasty remark about her. She was truly her mother's daughter, bullied by the ton, and as alone as a hanging tree.

"Frederick, if Serena made a home here, she would have me for a connection. I find the best cure for a new life is to experience it. I am certain Serena will prefer Britain to America," Benedict said.

"Besides, you will have to marry soon. You will have a new friend and advisor. Your wife may not like me, but she will have to come first," Serena softly reminded Frederick.

He rolled his eyes. "I will be patient and wait to wed until I find the perfect wife. And she could not be perfect for me if she didn't love you."

"I promise not to make a decision until I have discussed this with you, thoroughly. Perhaps I could help you find a wife, as Miss Rose appears to have refused you for the umpteenth time," Serena offered. Frederick had a habit of proposing to women he knew would refuse him.

"Honoria believes I should marry for love, but I will be a duke, and so we must have ulterior considerations. Money, family connection, or prestige. Boring things. I simply wanted to marry my good friend," Frederick lamented.

"But the curse…" Benedict began.

Serena giggled. "Curses aren't real, and certainly not for our family. Some distant relative created the curse to justify a bad marriage."

"Pet, isn't life more fun believing in magic? I love the romance of fairy tales and ghost stories," Frederick offered.

Sometimes she wondered if he was her twin after all. Serena smiled. "As do I! But what about when people use superstition to enrich themselves or control others? I love fairies and the Tuatha Dé Danaan because it is fantasy without profit. If someone were to sell a sip from Cerridwen's cauldron for a price, I would have to debunk it."

"Ugh. Why must you two think it is your job to fix the world?" Benedict complained.

"If not us, then who? I don't know of many who are lining up to fight these battles. The world will not change itself, and we must fight for what we believe," Frederick answered. "I am tired. Would you like to have a lie down, pet?"

"Yes, thank you," Serena responded. She was exhausted from running about and arguing. She loved her brother and cousin, but they had very strong opinions and were not shy about sharing them.

Serena was at the top of the stairs when she realized she had forgotten her handbag.

Chapter 4

I have arrived in Philadelphia, which I am told is the city of brotherly love. Of course, I am weary given that I have two brothers. The people here have been having race riots, and that feels completely accurate of "brotherly love." The older brothers of the world are consummate brutes. They will take much and give little. Younger brothers of the world unite. They must be knocked down, and we all shall take what is ours. I stand firmly with Philadelphia's second sons.

A Curmudgeon's Tour of America, September 1885

Vincent told himself that he did not intend to eavesdrop, but he had been. He was seated for lunch when he heard Berkeley behind him. No one, outside of Vincent's father, could be simultaneously so sure of themselves and so deferential to his wafer-thin blonde mother. After half standing to make his presence known, Vincent froze in place when Berkeley and Melgum began to argue. He stayed uncomfortably in that posture, waiting for an opportunity to interrupt, but then Berkeley's sister arrived and changed the dynamic once more. The conversation started off interesting, then a man selling what was clearly counterfeit art had started his sales pitch to a nearby businessman at the closest table, and before Vincent knew it, his quarry had left. But luckily, the lady had forgotten her handbag, and Vincent snatched it. Damn, the thing even smelled good. How frustrating that such an illusory thing was now overwhelming his senses.

What was Berkeley's relationship with his sister? Vincent's own love of Ralph notwithstanding, he knew few people who enjoyed their siblings. But the Percys seemed to genuinely love and like each other. Berkeley was one of the most popular men in London, but by his own admission he needed his sister, both as his closest friend and wisest advisor. It was all very peculiar to Vincent. Envy stirred with a discernable heat inside him.

"Pardon me, sir. That is my bag."

A voice, smooth as honey, broke into his thoughts. Vincent realized he had been staring at the handbag, fingering the embroidery, and looked up from it. Before him stood an angel, or possibly Venus in disguise. But in his shock at the sight of her, bright and bold in her blue skirt, surging like lightning into his electric heart, he knew he had never loved any woman before. She had honey-blonde hair neatly twisted into a bun. Her heart-shaped face held round eyes the color of sapphires. Her mouth was adorable, with a thick lower lip that gave her a permanent pout. The cherry on the cake was her body, a clear hourglass with massive breasts spilling out. Her high-necked blouse clung to her like a disapproving mother, trying in vain to suppress something it could not control.

The electricity turned to panic. How did one make a woman like him? He had to impress her and make her like him. Of course, he couldn't possibly be himself. What had he heard about Lady Serena? She was the object of his friend Barton's affection and...well, that was awkward. But Vincent could surely falsify himself enough to earn her affection for perhaps twenty or thirty years. After that, Barton could attempt to woo her. Anything else he might have heard about her was not helping him. His memories, like everything else in him, were reduced to joyous and frothy nervousness.

"Are you certain, my lady? The bag matches my waistcoat perfectly," Vincent answered with a grin.

To Vincent's shock, she laughed. Full throated and hearty. "Indeed, it does, but nevertheless it is mine. May I have it, please?"

Vincent reluctantly handed her the bag. "Of course, I knew it was yours. But that means we match perfectly too." Surely that was witty enough. "I am Vincent Mandeville. I am friendly with Lord Berkeley."

Her eyes grew wide. "How wonderful! He will be excited to see you. I know he longs for more company. I am Lady Serena Percy."

"A pleasure," Vincent said with a bow and a kiss at the air above her glove. "I am eager to see him as well. America has been a bit isolating for me. It is so loud but so empty. I have always enjoyed Berkeley."

"What serendipity for you to have found us. I am afraid that I tend to waylay our party frequently," Serena explained with a sigh. How would her sighs sound after she found her pleasure?

"I am certain Berkeley does not mind, as it is widely known how much he regards you," Vincent flattered.

"I do hold you in high regard, pet," Berkeley bellowed as he approached them. Clearly, too much of her scarce attention had strayed from him. "Mandeville! Lovely to see you again. What brings you to

Philadelphia?"

The woman I planned to marry is spreading her legs for my brother, Vincent thought. What a corrosion jealousy works, even on a cynical mind. "My brother is recently wed, and while they are finding their way as married people, I thought I would see more of the world."

"Lord Ralph Mandeville? Did he marry Miss Snowe?" Lady Serena asked. The name Serena suited her. She was like the spring sun, gentle and warm. And Vincent would love to mark the birth and death of every day with her.

"Yes, my lady," Vincent answered. Had Lily ever mentioned Serena? He was unsure.

"Ah, felicitations. And how are the duke and duchess? Have you resolved that little conflict?" Berkeley asked casually, but the words were a probe. What Berkeley really meant was "Are you still under a cloud of scandal? Should I allow my angel of a sister near you?"

"They are well. You must have departed before the trial, but the accusing man was fresh from an insane asylum. Poor soul, but all's well that ends well," Vincent explained, hoping this was enough to let him be near them. However, he noticed Serena in deep thought. Deep consideration of Vincent's reputation could not bode well for his ambitions with her.

"You're the Malicious Mandeville!" she cried too happily. Berkeley smiled and Vincent sighed.

"Oh, yes, pet. Perhaps he will sign your fan," Berkeley teased. How confusing.

"Lord Vincent, I am a great admirer. I adore your columns as well as your humor." Serena blushed. What was so admirable about being an insufferable dinner companion who could not keep a single insult to himself? Was it his immature need to see every person that preferred Sebastian laid so low they could not get an invitation to a letter opening?

"It's true, Mandeville. She keeps a book where she writes the cleverest quotes in it. One morning she laughed so hard at one of your barbs, she spit her tea." Berkeley could see his sister's red cheeks and pursed lips, signs of mitigated embarrassment. "Don't be shy, pet. It was a very charming and graceful spitting. You weren't a camel about it. But you were amusing all the same."

Lady Serena blushed prettily. "I did not like the moniker, however. It makes light of the word 'malicious.' I don't feel you have mal intent. Perhaps 'Merry Mandeville' or 'Musing Mandeville' would be better suited."

"You are too kind, pet." Berkeley shook his head. But he was right—she needed to be disabused from any notion that Vincent was a decent person. Low expectations were easier to overcome than disappointment in failing to meet high ones. "Mandeville may make *you* merry, but he has never aimed his tongue at you. Were we to be the subject of his quips, we may become hurt. Therefore 'Mocking Mandeville' is the ideal name."

Lady Serena sighed. It was a strange thing to see her irritated with Frederick. Maybe he was dreaming. Maybe he had died and seeing her, in her fullness, was his heaven. And *friendship*! The Percys had not judged him but welcomed him. How very unlikely that he would find both a friend for companionship and a beautiful woman to court in Philadelphia. But the rotund woman with a hat that vaguely resembled a goose striding past them would not be found in heaven.

"Oh dear, Frederick, you must make Lord Vincent join us until we can find the perfect nom de guerre for him," Serena opined.

"Yes, Mandeville! You must join us. My sister is naturally shy but seems herself around you. Besides, America is too large to be alone in. And I am desperate for conversation. My sister is lovely, but we agree on nearly everything. Whereas, much to my amusement, Benedict and I agree on nothing," Berkeley invited.

Vincent smiled. His original intent before he was distracted by the gorgeous Serena was to find traveling companionship. How pleasant and unexpected that he was receiving what he wanted. Surely tragedy was lurking in the wings. "I would be delighted."

"Brilliant! You can help me plan the remainder of our tour," Berkeley suggested. For someone so certain of himself, he surely enjoyed asking others for their opinions.

"Excellent, I will leave you gentlemen to your plans. Please, do not forget to arrange for us to visit New Orleans." Serena nodded to excuse herself before leaving.

"I am thrilled that you will be joining us. I was hoping to visit some of the American whiskey distilleries. They call American whiskey *bourbon*."

Vincent snickered. "A bit presumptuous for a former English colony to name alcohol after the royal family of France and Spain."

Berkeley smiled. "I believe they call it bourbon after Bourbon Street in New Orleans, which was once a

French colony. So, perhaps not as presumptuous as one might assume it to be. However, I was told this by a ninny, so you may be correct as well."

Vincent grinned. Berkeley's gentle correction was perfect. Some would have let Vincent simply insult Americans. Others would have delighted in his foolishness, but not Berkeley. Vincent wondered how Serena might correct him if he were to rip off her dress or some other minor social blunder. "I always wondered what the difference between Irish whiskey and Scotch whisky was. Aside from the taste, color, and spelling. And now this bourbon is another curiosity."

"Ah. Serena once asked me the same question, and it was my practice to answer any questions that came to her mind. Apparently, the Irish invented whiskey, a grain mash alcohol aged in a wood barrel. The Scots use a barley mash and age the whisky in oak barrels. And bourbon is made with a primarily corn mash in charred barrels. It's interesting to me. If I had a distillery, I would experiment with different grains and woods and chars. Perhaps a rice mash in a pine barrel or an oat mash in a charred mahogany barrel."

Vincent shook his head. Both ideas were dreadful, but so was corn in a charred barrel. "I heard Annadale has a distillery in his land, and he makes an exceptional whisky. By he, I mean countless others involved in the production of the thing that he takes credit for. Perhaps he could guide you in your interest."

Berkeley nodded. "Annadale is a neighbor to my uncle, Benedict's father."

"When did her ladyship ask about whiskey?" Vincent tried to be casual and light in his questioning. He couldn't tip his hand about his interest in Lady

Serena.

Berkeley smiled. "She was ten and the most curious little creature to ever walk the earth. Father couldn't hire enough tutors or invite enough experts to teach her things. So, to satisfy her curiosity, Father and I went to Ireland and Scotland to see the distilleries and drink deep the offerings. It was the best summer of my life; he would have dragged us to every distillery in America, were he with us."

Vincent returned Berkeley's smile. He knew the former Marquess of Berkeley had been beloved, much like the current one, until his death. Vincent could not recall when or how the late marquess died, but he could sense the sadness still lingered in his son. "Well, we will have to visit a few. And perhaps bring home a few barrels, for remembrance. You can take your son to Ireland and Scotland to see the distilleries when he is of age, as well."

Berkeley brightened. "I should take all of my sons; it could be the Percy rite of passage. Years from now, sons and fathers will journey to Scotland for the whisky. Of course I will have to think of some way to adventure with my daughters as well."

"Dear God, man. How many children do you intend to have?" Vincent asked.

"As soon as I find the ideal wife, which is becoming a Herculean task, as many as it is healthy for her to have. If she is unable, so be it. I would like ten, however," Berkeley mused. This man casually wished to inflict ten childbirths on his unsuspecting, hypothetical spouse?

"Why so many?" Vincent asked. One would only want several children if they had girls. After all, they would not compete or feel like spares. Given his history, that seemed the most ethical assessment.

"Why not? I can have a little army of people who will care about the poor and working people. Think of the charity and good works we could accomplish," Berkeley rhapsodized.

Vincent visualized a uniformed child army and stifled a giggle. "And what if your children should not want to do good works?" Vincent asked.

Berkeley frowned. "Of course, I will want them to follow their hearts. If their hearts lead them away from making the world better, even in a small way, then it will be my failing as a father."

Vincent shook his head and grinned. How very sincere. "Does your sister also want a dozen children? And Melgum? Is this a family trait?"

Berkeley laughed. "No. Serena is weary of children, rightfully so, as women can still die from childbirth. Benedict does not want to ever wed. He has never offered an explanation, but I am not entitled to one. Come, let's sample some bourbon while we make our plans. I have a list from Lord Snowe of cities and sights we must see."

"Absolutely," Vincent agreed. As they left to find bourbon, a strong wind hit him with a raspy howl. It sent a delightful chill up Vincent's spine and smelled of deep autumn. In his heart, a fire grew at the hope that this would be the winter, or perhaps late autumn, of his discontent.

Chapter 5

If you are able to, I urge daily walks in the woods during autumn. Nature has truly boughed herself in beautiful golds and reds. You will see the critters all busy for the upcoming winter. Surely a more beautiful canvas has never been painted.

Aunt Penny's Advice for Living, September 1885

In Serena's dreams, Lord Vincent came to her room. He ripped her nightgown from her with an innocent violence that had no malice and delighted in her naked flesh. While she was willing, he remained rough with her, slapping her bottom and nipping at her neck and breasts. He was something ravenous, and he wanted her too bad to be a man instead of a beast. She ached with wanting and needed him inside her. She was near her pleasure, half awake to her reactions, but it was hard to stop. And while she danced close to the edge of a forbidden release, of course, a booming noise interrupted her half sleep.

Her eyes fluttered open like angry hummingbird wings, and she sat awake. Shame roused her quicker than the loudest horn. As she lifted the bed clothes from her body, she felt imprisoned in her hot and sweaty blankets. She put on her dressing gown while searching for Martha, but she must have gone to fetch warm water for Serena's morning rituals. Serena opened the door, secretly hoping it was Lord Vincent but finding Frederick instead.

"Good morning, pet. Fancy a walk before breakfast?" Frederick asked as he entered her room. Thank God for his obliviousness.

"Certainly," Serena mumbled as she brushed the tawdry sleep from her eyes.

Martha entered and began to assist Serena in preparing herself for the day. After she had washed and had her hair brushed behind the screen, Serena felt more herself, not the brazen succubus she had dreamt herself to be. As Martha began to fasten her loosely into the rose-colored day dress, she gazed at Frederick in the mirror. He had reclined comfortably and crossed his legs leisurely in a chair while reading one of Serena's magazines.

"Frederick, Martha is more of a companion than a lady's maid. Charm her into taking the position," Serena called.

"My charms have no effect on Martha, pet. Rather, they annoy her. However, Martha, you have been with us for nearly eight years. Why will you not be Serena's companion? It would make her life and yours much easier." This was clearly all academic to him. He did not even bother looking up from his magazine.

"I went into service to be a lady's maid; I love it. And her ladyship allows me to make perfumes and lotions that one day, when her ladyship is married and settled, I will sell in a little shop," Martha revealed. Her eyes went wide for second. She even smiled. For her, that was a grand vulnerability.

"Fabulous! I had no idea you were so ambitious," Frederick said, standing up with great effort from the deep cushion of the chair. "I support this idea of yours, but I cannot deny Serena her request. Therefore, a compromise must be struck. While we are touring America, you will have to act as a lady's maid. But you will no longer receive wages but instead an allowance. You will no longer have a pallet in Serena's room, but a room of your own. And I will assist you in your endeavors. Honoria would be happy to help, I'm sure. And little Aurora's face could launch a thousand ships. I am certain it could sell some potions."

"My lord, I-I…" Martha stammered.

"When we return to London, we will find a new lady's maid and begin to get into details. In the meanwhile, take the morning off and see what the Americans offer in terms of perfumes." Frederick walked closer to Serena and held her hand to softly turn her body in front of the vanity mirror. "You look stunning, pet."

Of course, Frederick wanted to change the subject and leave before Martha could refuse his generosity. Serena sensed the urgency and chimed in. "Thank you. Have a splendid day off, Martha!"

"Yes, enjoy yourself," Frederick said as he closed the door slowly behind them, the sort of slow motion that prevents the knob from making a sound when it clicks into place. It was adorably childish. He grinned at Serena. "I am sorry we had to be so forceful, but her middle-class sensibility requires acts of kindness to be foisted upon her."

"I brought the subject up for discussion. Martha is more than a lady's maid. If she requires that be repeated until she believes it, I can do so. Are you certain we should leave? What if Lord Vincent or Benedict wake and break their fast without us?" Serena asked. She attempted to hide her true intention—she wanted to see Lord Vincent again.

Frederick frowned and knocked at a door down the hall. After a loud thump and a few minutes, Lord Vincent yanked the door open. He looked alluringly wild with his dark hair mussed, and his brilliant blue gaze darted about until it met hers and then floated to Frederick. He was pulling a dressing gown over his shoulders while his bare chest was exposed. An unwelcome twinge swelled in her mouth and breasts, as if they longed to be touched by him.

"My apologies, I am accustomed to my brothers waking me. But this is just as good," Lord Vincent muttered as he covered himself.

"I apologize for waking you. I am taking Serena for a walk. She was concerned that you may assume we have left for the day. We will be eating breakfast in one hour and would welcome your presence," Frederick explained.

"I shall be delighted," Lord Vincent said.

"Excellent!" Frederick led Serena down the hall and stairs before they left the hotel. What was this strange determination he had in him? Serena had never seen it before. He crossed the street too quickly and stayed silent as they walked down Chestnut to Washington Square.

"Frederick, what is troubling you?" Serena asked as their feet hit the bouncy grass of the park. He finally slowed down.

"You, my darling sister, are what is troubling me. I am a magician with a single trick—detecting when my sister is scheming," Frederick announced, turning his head to look at her.

She swallowed fast, and her thoughts cluttered up the edges of her mind. He knew something, but was it the male fortune teller or the bawdy dream she had? If it were the latter, she would find a train to throw herself in front of. "Scheming is essential to a well-thought-out life," she deflected. A platitude was a sort of answer, right?

Frederick snorted. "Be forthright. Why are we going to New Orleans? And if you say, 'birds,' so help me, I will throttle you."

"Oh! Is that all? Oh, well, dear," Serena babbled. She had to explain everything, but at least he did not know her shameless harlotry. "This will require some explanation, and I will need to speak uninterrupted. That is undoubtedly the hardest thing I will ask of you."

"Please go on. Oh, excuse me, I am supposed to be mute," Frederick grumbled.

"You are aware that I see mediums. Until two days ago, not one was truly gifted with any sight. However, I spoke with a medium who relayed the message that the key to Mother's and Father's deaths is in New Orleans," Serena began. Please let him stay quiet.

"Good God. Is that what you have been doing with those frauds? Trying to find their killer?" Frederick asked. His tone was too rough, his eyes were large enough to hold a whole sun, and his head coiled back from her like a pensive snake.

Serena nodded. Only her articulate explanation could defuse this matter. "Yes. They always guessed wrong. Drivel like Mother wants me to marry a duke or Father is concerned about money. But I must find their murderer. I need to know why and who before I can find peace. The medium said we must find an English investor in New Orleans."

Frederick inhaled deeply before exhaling. "Very well, but the rest of this nonsense must end. You are twenty-one, and it is high time you find whatever will make you happy in life."

"Don't you mean find a husband?" Serena asked.

"If you can find a man who will make you happy and treat you as you deserve, then all the better. But if you decide you want to retire to Cornwall and tend to your books for the remainder of your life, I will support you. There is only you and I left of our family. I will be your champion." He drew a hard breath and wound up. This wais the part where he would say what he really thought. "But you have to stop living in the past, buried by nostalgia," he lectured.

Serena nodded. "I know. I just loved them so much. It has been a void, growing ever more. I will start slowly, perhaps give up mediums during the remainder of our tour...until New Orleans. I hear they have voodoo kings and queens."

Frederick laughed. Her skepticism had infected him too, it seemed. "Ah, yes, the voodoo. Pet, I loved Mum and Dad as well. We will never forget them and will always honor them. Now, do you want me to put off Mandeville whilst we run about solving murders?"

"No. Madame Olyenska predicted that I would meet a man who would help me, and we met Lord Vincent the next day. Besides, you like him, and I know it has been difficult for you without friends," Serena offered. After all, Vincent's presence would be a kindness for both of them.

"I do like Mandeville. He's witty and fortunate. If I

were courting a lady, I think she would be remarkably angry with me for visiting another continent," Frederick mused.

Serena's stomach lurched. "Lord Vincent is courting a lady?"

"Quite seriously. Miss Haverford has been entangled with him for a bit. Although she has no appeal to me, she has captivated Mandeville. She appears to be very understanding. I wonder where I might find a lady to have such a relaxed disposition," Frederick intoned, amused by the prospect of this hypothetical indiscretion.

Serena stayed quiet during Frederick's thoughts on understanding women. She fought feeling sad and a little frustrated. Lord Vincent having an understanding with Miss Haverford or being engaged was disappointing, as she found herself intensely attracted to him. Serena was not the type of woman to interfere with a well-crafted courtship and would have to end her attraction. Serena had never been so intrigued by a man. How could she simply end an attraction? She certainly could.

Perhaps if she knew why she felt such a pull to his lordship, she could simply seek another with those qualities. He was a welcome distraction from her parents' murders and the frustration that caused Serena. However, something could only be distracting if it were interesting. Serena could discover what attracted her to him while pushing him away, and nothing repelled gentlemen quite as much as when she was opinionated. It would be simple, and she would not be burdened with maintaining a pretense for weeks on end. A quick walk back to the hotel was good—the angry rumble of her ever-dwindling stomach was an unhappy friend.

Lord Vincent and Benedict joined them for breakfast among clinking flatware and morning conversation. The men immediately began discussing rugby and the newly formed football association. Serena spent the time trying to determine what men found annoying about her. Depending on the account, she read too much, or asked too many questions, or had the habit of persisting in the behavior of simple curiosity. Four gentlemen had complained about Frederick's politics, which was convenient for her purposes—she shared her brother's ideals. She would always have her atheism and familiarity with the tricks of mediums to truly repulse them. At this point, she began to understand why people spoke of her beauty, yet she had never received a proposal of marriage.

"Oh dear, pet, we have been neglectful to you, haven't we?" Frederick asked, jolting her from her plans.

"Worry not. I was trying to plan my day," Serena reassured.

"Ah! Wonderful. I gave Serena's maid the day to herself and will be escorting her around," Frederick explained to Lord Vincent and Benedict. "What shall we do today?"

"I was planning on shopping," Serena answered.

"Do you need some new dresses? Or perhaps a hat or gloves? I should marry a fashionable woman who will take you shopping every day," Frederick wondered.

"Books, darling brother. I have read all of the books I have with me." Serena pouted.

"May I join you?" Benedict asked. "I saw a woman

reading a pamphlet I wish to send to a friend."

"I would like to come as well," Lord Vincent offered. "Perhaps her ladyship could assist me in finding gifts for Lily and Ralph."

"Well done, pet! You managed three bachelors into spending a day shopping. I weep for your future husband," Frederick teased.

"Ah, I am so cunning, simply wishing to shop and voicing that desire in front of men who also wish to shop. Behold my feminine wiles!" Serena spread her arms as though she were a sorceress summoning a storm.

Frederick laughed, followed by a soft chuckle from Lord Vincent and a smile from Benedict. She hoped to overcome her desire for Lord Vincent and simply see him as a friend. After all, the mere fact that he overwhelmed her senses and made her dizzy with wanting did not mean they were meant to be married. Serena did not believe in true love or happily ever after, which was fortunate because if she did, she would only settle for Vincent.

Chapter 6

Philadelphia is growing on me. I have never beheld such beauty in the gentle sunrise. As I strolled the streets in the Autumn morning, I feel as though I am beginning to see what America has to offer. Of course, I vaguely recall Boston and New York, but the hedonism they offered overwhelmed my senses. However, Philadelphia has clean and tidy streets and allows the Pennsylvania elegance to shine through.

A Curmudgeon's Tour of America, September 1885

For the first time in an awfully long time, Vincent felt happy and excited about his life. There was no cloud of scandal above his head. Ralph and Lily were in love with a tiny human that Vincent would indulge and spoil. He had joined his friend for a tour of America, and he knew there would be an endless supply of conversation and comradery. And he was utterly smitten with Lady Serena.

She was as beautiful in the morning as she was yesterday, and he welcomed her being the first person he saw. The idea that she worried for him was eternally endearing. Serena needed more books—he should marry her now. Of course, he needed to know her better, much better before he declared himself. A shallow attraction would be insufficient to convince her and her guardian. This was particularly true as they were traveling with her brother. He simply needed to find a way to learn everything about her without interrogating her.

As the party walked to the bookstore the concierge had recommended, Vincent allowed Berkeley and Melgum to bicker. After all, that let him walk next to Serena. "Tell me, my lady, what books strike your interest?" Vincent asked.

Serena smiled brightly, her curved eyebrows giving a heart shape to her face. "Oh, all kinds. I love novels but tear through them. I must read philosophy or science to slow myself. I will balance a penny dreadful with a history of gin or the sugar trade. One must keep one's mind active."

Perfect, Vincent had little patience for anything but history, literature, and art. She would always have new topics to discuss, and he would never grow bored. "Ah, yes, I recall your brother mentioned a curiosity in whiskey production?"

Serena nodded. "And gin, beer, brandy, and all of the alcoholic drinks. It fascinated me, as a child, that some enterprising person stumbled upon the idea to drink fermented juniper berries or barley. Women used to be the brewmasters but now are not encouraged to drink wine without water. After studying the brewing arts, I spent the next seven months utterly consumed with butterflies."

"Butterflies?" Vincent asked, curious as what she could be consumed by. Butterflies were pretty and flew about. One didn't need seven months to understand that.

"Mmmm, yes." Serena licked her plump lips. "They begin life a little caterpillar and munch on leaves to form their cocoon, then far away from prying eyes, they become beautiful butterflies. There are no two the same, much like people. It is a mystery and may remain so, what exactly happens in the cocoon."

Vincent smiled at her and decided to woo her using Ralph's technique. "My estate is in Norfolk with lavender and saffron flowers. Perhaps you could help me with which flowers might help the butterflies."

"Certainly!" Serena beamed, leaving Vincent shocked that his gambit was successful. "But I may need to know about your house. Would it be able to withstand ivy?"

"Pet, I am certain Mandeville will be willing to show you his house. I know you will adore it. It is a former vicarage that may have hidden treasure from Cromwell," Berkeley teased. "However, that can wait as you need to choose which subject you will next become obsessed with."

Serena's face lit for the mysteries of Vincent's house, but then she quickly moved on to the bookstore. Vincent watched her excitedly peruse the selection of books. Vincent and Berkeley leaned against the wall near the door, while Melgum pestered the shopkeeper and Serena loaded herself with book after book. After nearly an hour, Serena heaved a few books at Berkeley.

"I have decided to read the entire works of Washington Irving," Serena announced.

"And what subject will you conquer?" Vincent asked.

Serena smiled. "Irving wrote five volumes on the life of George Washington, and I believe that ought to keep me occupied."

After Berkeley paid for the books, Melgum

approached and gave him a delicate pamphlet. "Once you have returned to Britain, will you make a visit to my mother? This is a gift for Lady Penelope, and my mother will deliver it."

" 'Advice for Marrying A Lord'! My God, even in America?" Berkeley looked aghast at the tiny pages adorned with flowing script and fancy corners.

"Lady Penelope has been tending to her sick mother and has not been introduced. My mother will take her this next season, but my mother knows nothing of marrying off a daughter. I hope this will aid Penelope," Melgum explained.

Something pricked Vincent's mind. He would have to explore later.

"Very well, I delight in Aunt Louise's company. Are there any other shops you wish to visit, pet?" Berkeley asked.

Serena licked her lips. "I heard tell of a cunning little cane shop."

Both Berkeley and Melgum groaned. Of course, he needed to ask why. "Oh my, what is the matter?"

"My darling sister collects gadget canes. We have to purchase more and more displays for them," Berkeley bemoaned. This shopping excursion, while widely agreed to, seemed to inflict a variety of complaints on poor Serena.

"And every time Frederick accompanies me to even look at them, he must purchase an expensive art cane," Serena finished. Her sanguine grin told the story of past excursions.

Vincent had heard of gadget canes, canes that could become something else. He had only seen two, a gout stool and an artist had one that could become an easel. Of course, art canes were prominent in his world, beautifully carved or gilded with intricate designs. Vincent personally fancied the bawdy art canes that had hidden drawings of carnal acts.

As they walked, a cool breeze blew past them. The dark clouds were threatening to rain and made a deep contrast between the bright orange leaves of the trees that dotted the Philadelphia street. Vincent loved autumn and the touch of mystery it possessed. He was happy to walk alongside Serena once more, her dark pink dress setting her as a feature in the landscape. This was a scene he would like to see every day.

As Berkeley and Melgum began to discuss a recent riot, Vincent turned to Serena. "Shall we play a game? I will ask a question, and you must answer with complete honesty."

Serena smiled as though she was the cat that caught the canary. "I am sporting, but you may dislike my answers."

Vincent shrugged. "So be it. Where would you live if you could live anywhere in the Empire?"

"Hmm, before I can be truly certain, I must see the Empire. However, with what I have seen as a restraint, I would say there are three places. I love the cliffs of Cornwall and the moors of York, and I was rather fond of Nova Scotia," Serena answered.

"I did not visit Nova Scotia. What did you like about it?" Vincent asked.

"I like the fog and cold. Nova Scotia made my peculiar preferences seem pretty and quaint," Serena explained.

Perfect, she was perfect for him. It was as though God decided his suffering had been long enough and led him to her. "Interesting. And have you ever met my brother, the Earl of Coningsby? What did you think of Sebastian?"

A smile flickered across her lips before disappearing. "I prefer not to reply as you may dislike the answer."

Vincent cringed. It appeared that his reputation for not getting along with his brother was known by nearly everyone. What a terribly small world he lived in. Serena had met Sebastian, and he had won her over with his pretty face and bewitching words. Happily, Sebastian was going to marry Marlene, so he could not woo Serena away from Vincent. (And for the first time Vincent was happy Sebastian would marry Marlene.) "You agreed to the game. You must answer honestly."

Serena sighed. "Very well. I found Lord Coningsby to be very polite and decent. However, he may be the most pretentious man I had ever met. Now I am certain that you no longer wish to speak with me, and I do apologize for the insult."

"No need for an apology. I have said much worse. In fact, I think Sebastian would be pleased if my only criticism were that he was pretentious. He is pretentious," Vincent reassured her. What a relief that she did not like Sebastian but did not insult him either. If she had called Sebastian stupid or rude, Vincent would have to defend his brother as he was neither. However, Serena merely observed that Sebastian was pretentious. Even Sebastian would agree.

"You have?" Serena seemed disappointed in his response—perhaps she was merely surprised.

"Pet, I am giving you a limit of two canes per city we visit. You bought eight in Boston, and we cannot keep accruing them," Berkeley lectured as they entered the cane shop.

Vincent watched Serena play with the gadget canes while Berkeley and Melgum carefully inspected the carved art canes. As Vincent perused the canes, he came across one that took his breath away. It was a mahogany cane with an ivory handle carved to look like Venus. Venus was nude, lying with her arms behind her head, her hair flowing around her. She appeared satisfied while looking off to her right as if her lover had moved in that direction.

"Have you found something you like, my lord?" Serena asked from behind him.

"Yes, I have." He held up the cane for her inspection. It was the devil in him that loved to shock a lady. Even one he admired. "Do you like it?"

"It is very well crafted. Who is she? The artist's lover?" Serena asked as she studied the cane, without a hint of embarrassment.

"I believe that she is Venus." He leaned in to whisper in her ear. "This is how I imagine you would look in this state."

Vincent could see the blush rise up her neck, but she frowned. "Close, my lord, but my face does not resemble hers. Perhaps you could find an artist willing to alter it."

"I thought you were shy. I am certain it was told to me." He was still close enough to whisper, while the cane rested in her open palm. It was his homunculus, and he rubbed his thumb on the knee striking up the thigh. He could see her arousal building as her lips parted and her pupils dilated.

"It does not go against my shy nature to state

facts." She breathed in sharply. Her voice was dry and professorial.

"It would reveal you, with your pretty face, as you would be in this pose." His thumb traveled along the figure's stomach and teased its breasts. He heard her breath catch as her blush deepened.

"Indeed, it would, my lord, but I would be in your hands alone." Serena was close to him now, and he could smell her.

"What scent is that?" Vincent asked, immediately regretting the words as Serena stepped back from him. "It is lovely, but I cannot place it."

Serena nodded. Was she being restrained or disgusted? "My maid, Martha, makes soaps and perfumes from excess flowers and whatnot. You cannot place it because it is entirely unique and made only for me."

"Pet! Which cane do you want?" Berkeley called.

"I am partial to the ladder cane, please," Serena sang as she sauntered toward him, leaving Vincent desperate for her nearness once more.

"And you shall have it. Look at this beauty." Berkeley displayed an art cane with an ornate hunting scene carved into it. "Mandeville, are you ready to leave?"

Vincent shook his head. "I want to purchase a few things, and I have to send a few telegrams. I will see you for dinner."

After paying for the canes, the Percys and Melgum left the shop. Vincent was paying for the Venus cane when he decided he should know more about Serena's passion. "Tell me, sir, which is the rarest gadget cane?"

"Most canes are special made for a man based on

his profession. I made one for a doctor last month, but those are rare. The lady appeared to collect them," the shopkeeper answered while buffing a cane carefully crafted to conceal pens and ink.

"She does, and I wish to gift her with a rare cane," Vincent explained. Although, he didn't have to. What was this strange chattiness?

The shopkeeper thought. "I suppose a lady's cane would be rare. Because women have handbags, they often do not want a gadget cane, and canes are not fashionable for ladies."

"Yes! We are travelling across the country but will be in New Orleans by October 26. Could you fashion a lady's gadget cane and have it sent to New Orleans by then?" Vincent asked.

"I believe I could, if you decide what you want the cane to do," the shopkeeper answered.

"Right." Vincent tried to think about what Serena might like. "Perhaps a concealed perfume bottle, and a mirror and a fan?"

The shopkeeper nodded. "That is possible. Do you have any design preferences?"

"Butterflies," Vincent answered.

As Vincent left the shop, he was overcome with odd warmth and excitement. He had the most wonderful secret, and he wanted to tell everyone. As if he had drunk too much coffee, he was delightfully agitated with a thousand ideas of their future together. His blood sang—how oddly euphoric! So much so that he had trouble putting his thoughts into phrases. It was a foreign but addictive sensation, one he wanted to indulge in for as long as he could persuade Serena that he was not the wretched creature he was. Vincent noticed even his wrath had subsided in her presence.

If only Ralph and Lily were here to advise him! Or at least listen as he explained how perfect Serena was. Sadly, the only people he could talk with about Serena were her brother and cousin. Humbug. They would be biased and might not appreciate Vincent's love of Serena's breasts. However, this was the modern age, and bragging was merely a telegram away, if you were wealthy enough to afford it...and Vincent certainly was. But he should only tell Lily. Ralph was close to Barton, who might not enjoy the idea that Vincent would marry Serena.

Barton did present a problem. Betrayal of a friend sat even lower in him than he had assumed. However, Barton was more Ralph's friend than Vincent's. And of course, Serena would not suit well with Barton, but such reasoning was a bit pedantic, and she might have suited him quite well indeed. He could also explain that he wanted Serena more than Barton did, which was evident by his pursuit. But Barton had tried to get a proper introduction and had not had the opportunity. In truth, Vincent wanted Serena more than he cared about Barton's tendre.

Of course, Lily was just pesky enough to be his conscience. If she thought Vincent was in the wrong for pursuing Serena, he might listen. Vincent walked to a public telegraph office to send the telegram to Lily. Writing telegrams was an art. One had to communicate volumes in a short burst, which rarely left room for wit. Vincent spent a few moments contemplating the perfect words to send to Lily before writing them down.

Chapter 7

With the railway, our world is smaller than ever! I love to take little visits to villages and towns that I would have simply passed by if not for the train. For example, two weeks ago I found the most charming village that housed a wonderful woodworker. With the season over, I recommend we all take a day to discover the hidden beauty Britain has to offer.

Aunt Penny's Advice for Living, September 1885

Serena needed to get away from Lord Vincent. Her attempts to discourage him had only tangled her into him. She liked him and was well on her way to an attachment. If he impressed her any more, she would be in love with him. She was not the sort of woman to interfere with a man intended for another woman. However, the purpose of courtship was to see if two people might suit, and if Lord Vincent favored Serena more than Miss Haverford...no! She would never have a friend again if she behaved so underhandedly.

Serena had decided to venture off to Pittsburgh for the day under a flimsy guise. Once there she would concoct a reason for staying until Benedict's play opened. A couple of days alone would give her time to think of ways to discourage Lord Vincent forever. She might have to simply belch in his presence, but could her ego withstand that level of humiliation? Either way, she needed to humble herself.

As they met for breakfast, she waited for a lull in the conversation. "Frederick, I wish to visit Pittsburgh."

"Absolutely, pet. When would you like to visit?" Frederick asked. How very pliable of him.

"Well, I thought I could go today. Lord Lake has business holdings there, and I believe the building hosts some of his artwork. We did not suit, but I remain friendly toward him," Serena said. It was true. Lord Lake was kind to her even though Serena knew the only reason he had courted her was to irritate his father. In the beginning, being used for fodder had burned immensely, but it was refreshing to be courted without pretense.

"Lake? That man is a specter that haunts me. May I join you?" Lord Vincent inquired.

Serena was a fool, quite possibly the least intelligent creature to walk the earth. It was a miracle that she did not drool on her dresses. "Of course, although I am certain you may find it boring."

"This suits me very well. I need a day to focus on the play," Benedict offered, clearly happy to be rid of them and the distraction.

"Yet another victory, pet. We shall take the next train and return to Philadelphia on the last train. Once again, you have managed us well. Your talents are going to waste," Frederick said cheerfully.

Serena should stop trying to make plans, she thought as she sat in the train car with Lord Vincent and Frederick. Her original plot was to simply discourage Lord Vincent, yet she had somehow become attracted to him. Her brilliant method to cure herself of this conundrum was to get distance between them, and yet now he was accompanying her. She was tempted to try to seduce him and watch that have the reverse effect, but that was a dangerous position. She was essentially a character in *Macbeth* at this point, and she knew she needed to stop fighting fate.

Serena liked Philadelphia. It, in her memory, was a modest London with tree-lined streets and a Quaker sensibility. Pittsburgh was a cleaner and more genteel Manchester. It was obvious that Pittsburgh was a city of industry, but with a nod to civic responsibility. An iron-hearted city. Pittsburgh was tidy and neat but not ornate. After all, it is plainly true that cities, particularly cities with several factories, required public art. It could be disheartening to have to work in the factories, and a little art could cheer one's soul, to make the drudgery less painful.

"Lady Serena, may I ask when Viscount Lake courted you?" Lord Vincent asked, intruding upon Serena's internal critique of the lack of Pittsburgh art.

Serena smiled. "I was just introduced, so four, nearly five years ago."

"He must have made an impression to remain so close to your heart after so long." Lord Vincent had a bitter tone; was he jealous?

Frederick laughed. "Well, Lake's artistry had more of an impact than the courtship. He painted Serena as Cerridwen the fairy queen."

Serena shook her head. "She was not a queen. She was something much more powerful: a sorceress. She brewed a cauldron which concocted all poetic inspiration. She held knowledge and gave it in doses only to the worthy."

"And that is why we are visiting his art? He

painted you, and now you are a supporter?" Lord Vincent inquired.

"Well, he felt terrible for courting me and desired to make amends. There are worse ways to make a friend. I like his ideals, so near to a bohemian, but practical," Serena explained.

Frederick snorted. "Practical *haute bohème* is nearly our philosophy, pet."

"Precisely." Serena grinned, and if they were not in the street, she would have stuck out her tongue in jest.

"I apologize for my misunderstanding, but why would Lake feel a debt for courting an esteemed woman like you?" Lord Vincent asked. Was this a gentle compliment or sarcasm in sincerity's mask? How very unusual.

Her pretty mouth slid into a smile as Lord Vincent fell into a quiet cadence behind her. "Lord Lake is the Earl of Castleton's only son. The earl hated my mother and would publicly call my father a class traitor."

"A nickname I inherited, proudly," Frederick teased. "And one I will earn."

"Indeed. Lake hates his father and wished to get at him by courting me. Castleton, in retribution, spread rumors about my loose morals and even that I am a hermaphrodite." Serena sighed. Since no man had "confirmed" her ladyship, this was a challenging debasement to argue against. "Lake knew his childish game had cost me dearly and wept an apology for me. Sadly, the damage had been done, and Lake left England vowing to never return unless his father had apologized or I had wed."

"Castleton has refused an apology for four years? I can hold a grudge, but even a spiteful bastard would desire to see his son," Lord Vincent stated and then paused until his smile resurfaced. "Also, why would he wish everyone to think his son was enamored of a hermaphrodite?"

"Castleton is an ass," Frederick declared. "Someday, when I find a cunning way to do so without harming anyone else, I will make him pay for every bloody tear he cost our family."

"Castleton will be dead soon, and no one will mourn him. That is punishment enough. Men tend to want to make an impact on the world, and he has, as a legacy, a mountainous pile of nothing. We built schools and hospitals in the name of our parents. Do not waste your intellect on scheming elaborate revenge against a man who does not deserve it," Serena blathered.

"Ah, pet, you are too kind. I still want to see Castleton penniless and broken. But for my beloved sister, I will restrain myself." Frederick grinned.

They had arrived at the offices of Lord Lake's steel-manufacturing company. "Lake inherited the company from his mother's family; she was a wealthy American. Apparently, his father had treated her very badly, and that is why Lake despises his father," Serena said as they entered the building.

"Sadly, being in America has made me decide against an American bride. I do not need more money, and that appears to be chief among the qualities elevated by their newfound gentry. I want a woman who understands the poor and wants to help them, but I will not allow a woman to be humiliated the way Mother was," Frederick explained, trying to keep his tone even.

"This is one of Lake's." Lord Vincent gestured to a

painting of a garden.

Serena surveyed the painting. "I believe Lake is moving toward impressionism. This work is less of the neoclassical style he painted when he did my portrait. I like it, though, as the soft brush strokes lend themselves well to natural settings. I would like to see another portrait, however, as this may have been an experiment."

"I declare that I would like to marry your sister, Berkeley," Lord Vincent teased, causing Serena's cheeks to blush like perfect carnations.

"See, pet? Men enjoy the breadth of your knowledge and are impressed. Mandeville, as an art lover, professes a desire to marry at your understanding of art." Frederick grinned at her.

"Lord Vincent is very kind, but I am certain he will retract such flattery later," Serena said as she whisked herself to find Lord Lake's other paintings. She had to lean closer to better see the art. "I believe Lake is the next Frederic Leighton. Well done, Devlin."

"Leighton or Waterhouse. He is not as idealized as Alma Tadema or as interested in symbolism as Rosetti," Lord Vincent added.

"Rosetti was mad and delusional. I do love his work, however," Frederick bemoaned. "Shall we have lunch and a walk by the river before we return to Philadelphia?"

"I think that will be lovely," Serena said as she walked out of the dusky light of the office lobby. As Frederick examined the map he had brought for the restaurant, she continued the previous conversation. "I don't believe Rosetti was mad, but he was following a code of chivalry that only he understood."

"I agree. However, any fool believing himself chivalrous is mad," Lord Vincent offered. His tone was not deadpan; it harbored enough warmth to be a sincere statement.

Serena had not yet heard the Malicious Mandeville make a controversial statement, but this held great potential. "How so, my lord?"

Lord Vincent shrugged. "Chivalry is ludicrous. Men, living in the modern age, fantasize about living in the ages before hygiene, the renaissance, and the age of enlightenment. They all believe they would be knights, but there were not that many knights. Why is it all men believe they would be heroes if not for the conveniences their lives offer them? If we were living in the age of chivalry, I would have to be a priest. Do you believe that I could be a priest?" he asked Serena.

Serena envisioned Lord Vincent dressed in priest's vestments, which was oddly arousing but completely wrong. "No, my lord."

"Indeed not. At least vicars can marry. Furthermore, think of the women in these chivalric fantasies. They are beautiful but empty vessels where the man, this high chivalrous being, pours *his* thoughts and ideas for a bygone age. Are these women ever favored because of their talents or intellects? No, they are merely dolls in a play," Lord Vincent lectured.

"Is it not romantic?" Serena asked. Such poetry from a man was alluring, even though it was a bit demonstrative.

"No. In the tales, the ladies are married to kings or dukes but in love with the poet or troubadour. I cannot think of a worse fate for a woman to be in love with one man but married to another. How is that romantic?" he asked.

She couldn't adequately cover her feelings; they spilled forth in a dour turn of her mouth. He made particularly good arguments. "I suppose it is better to love a man you cannot have than not to love at all. A life without love seems tragic and hollow."

There was a noise, similar to a gulp. Serena looked to Frederick, who looked equally confused. She looked to Lord Vincent, but he had vanished. The air where he should have been was empty. But immediately below that air was an open manhole cover, leading to a shallow, rocky tunnel with Lord Vincent inside. All his smugness hadn't stopped him from falling prey to an obvious peril.

All his viciousness could muster was "I believe I have wrenched my ankle."

Chapter 8

I will never speak of my time in Pittsburg, apart from a warning. Do not go to Pittsburg. If you are a fool and somehow find yourself in Pittsburg, please watch your step.

A Curmudgeon's Tour of America, September 1885

This ordeal was humiliating. Berkeley had to lift Vincent out of the sewers and carry him (as if he were a lady) to a nearby hotel. Once ensconced in a room, Vincent removed his soiled clothing so he could wash off what he actively chose to believe was mud from him. It was not mud, and he knew that, but his ferocious cleanliness demanded such small deceptions. The prospect of being covered in refuse was too much to bear. Finally, he rested the bulk of his sorry ankle on a settee, dressed in a dressing gown far too scratchy to be comfortable. There was, however, tea to make things better. How quaint.

Vincent could hear Berkeley and Serena arguing in the hall and strained to hear. Luckily, Serena entered the room, holding a bandage. "This is nothing like the riddle with the pig, the fox, and the grain. There is but one logical conclusion. I must stay with Lord Vincent, and you must go to Philadelphia to fetch Martha and some clothing."

Hours alone with Serena? Vincent loved this

notion.

"It is precisely like the riddle," Berkeley began to argue.

"No, it is not. In that riddle I would be the tasty pig," Serena bit off. She was more porcelain than porcine.

Berkeley paused. "Point taken. Serena, if you stay alone in a room with a man, people will assume the worst, and your reputation will be destroyed. I will remain, and you will take the train."

Vincent did not like that idea, at all.

"Well, darling brother of mine, that may be the stupidest notion I have ever heard. To take a train without a maid is an invitation for my rape. At least with his lordship, you could be assured that I would be a willing participant. He is injured, and I could easily fight him off. His decrepitude shall be my shield, as I know precisely where to kick him. Observe as I avoid his seductions." Serena stepped across the room. "And were anything to happen, you could bully him into marrying me. As for my reputation, we are in Pittsburgh. No one will know unless we tell them, and we will not be saying anything to anyone."

"I vow not to seduce your sister. I apologize for this inconvenience," Vincent added. It was hard not add a customary jibe, like "I cannot be liable for your sister's conduct, though."

Berkeley sighed. "Very well. If anyone should discover this, we will claim that you two had a maid from the hotel stay with you."

Vincent rolled his eyes. "Or, Lady Serena, will you marry me? No one truly cares about an engaged couple's poor behavior."

"Brilliant! You can cry off later, pet." Berkeley kissed his sister's forehead. "I will run to the shops and fetch some necessities before I catch the train."

After Berkeley left the room, Serena sat close to Vincent. She grabbed his naked ankle and pulled it onto her lap. Vincent struggled to keep the itchy and too-small dressing gown closed but saw Serena take a peek. She began to wrap the bandage around his ankle, not too tightly but firmly. It felt much better in her caring hands.

"I hope Frederick thinks to buy a plaster. I also hope he doesn't realize that I did not accept your proposal." Serena smiled at him. There was a common bond of sarcasm that united them. Shared derision was the most powerful of bonds, at least to Vincent.

"Where did you learn to wrap an ankle?" Vincent asked.

"My uncle Benjamin, Benedict's father, is a doctor as well as an earl. He taught me to wrap as Frederick was constantly falling from horses and trees and his falcons would bite him," Serena explained as she stacked cushions under his ankle and stood. His ankle was on display, but it felt better.

"Berkeley keeps falcons? Whatever for?" Vincent asked in passing, wishing she were close again. Sadly, she was writing something across the room.

"Frederick enjoys playing at chivalry." Serena smirked.

Vincent groaned. His mouth had gotten him into trouble again. "Do you think I must make amends to Berkeley?"

Serena rolled her eyes. "No. You made valid points, and if Frederick did not enjoy hearing opposing viewpoints, he would not be around Benedict so often. Frederick has always thought well of you; I am certain he still does."

"Thank goodness. Berkeley is one of the few men I admire." Vincent sighed.

Serena smiled. "I am going to order tea. Is there anything you want? Perhaps some almond biscuits or a particular cake?"

Vincent shook his head. "I would like to know what you like. After all, I plan on making you my wife."

Serena shook her head. "I know those jokes are meant to be funny, but if Frederick should take you seriously, there might be trouble. Besides, you would be furious if Miss Haverford refused to see you because of these jests. I shall return soon."

Vincent frowned at the door. Serena had heard about Marlene, which complicated Vincent's plans. He needed to know what Serena thought, if she thought less of him for having been jilted. She appeared to be laboring under the notion that he was still courting Marlene. He needed to disabuse Serena of this notion without slandering Marlene. Such a task would take tremendous effort, but women rarely enjoyed hearing a man speak ill of a lady.

The door opened, and Berkeley stepped inside. "I brought a plaster and had the pharmacist concoct a pain remedy."

Vincent took the green bottle from Berkeley and shook it with as much manliness as his crippled form could provide. "Thank you, I will wait for Serena before I apply the plaster so as not to interfere with her handiwork."

Berkeley surveyed the bandage. "Ay, she is skilled at helping men when they fall."

"I am sorry that I have caused so much acrimony. I also apologize for insulting your philosophy," Vincent expressed with deep affect.

Berkeley grinned. "Do not think on it. To be honest, I never considered chivalry as a philosophy. I simply enjoy sport, and jousting, archery, and falconry are great fun. Other people have decided to assume I believe in some long-ago romantic code. I am much like the ladies in the tales; others place their ideas upon me because I am so beautiful."

Vincent laughed at Berkeley's jest. "I am pleased. I would hate to offend you."

Berkeley smiled. "You will offend me, and unfortunately that is your nature. I will overlook the offense, as unfortunately that is my nature. Unless you are so odious as to make Serena cry, in which case that cannot be overlooked, and you will pay dearly. I know your secret weakness is manhole covers."

"I shall do my best." Vincent hoped he could, but women cried at nearly everything, be it happy or sad.

Berkeley handed Vincent a square and thick parcel. "I know my sister. If you should vex her but still need her, give her this."

Vincent opened the parcel to see chocolate candies. "Chocolate?"

Berkeley nodded. "So many of her quirks are my fault. When she was five, I told her that if she ate sweets, she would become a fairy. Fairies eat fairy cakes, and all that. Now, she does not eat sweets often, but they are an excellent bribe."

"If she loves them, why does she not indulge every

day?" Vincent asked. He was the sort that always wanted what he liked. Unlike Frederick, he did not question the luxuries of his existence with philosophical rigor.

Berkeley shook his head. "Have you met Mrs. Bannon? She is an unpleasant woman, the sort to spout her own predilections as if they were universally true. Her first postulate appears to be her own superiority. She made a spectacular show at Ascot, where she called Serena fat for eating a solitary piece of chocolate cake. Serena knows she is not fat, but now she refuses to eat sweets in front of almost everyone."

Vincent needed to meet Mrs. Bannon and spend an hour or so critiquing her appearance. In the same way athletes needed their calisthenics. "Why would Mrs. Bannon attack her?"

Berkeley shrugged. "I believe her granddaughter was introduced but not getting sufficient suitors. Our society makes little sense. Forcing men into a bizarre competition to be arranged by importance. I am high ranking and liked, therefore I am prized. If I snub a woman, she does not attack me, but she will begin a campaign against Serena, which is much more dangerous for that woman's reputation. My poor sister has borne the brunt of every woman who desired me for any particular end and harbors unrequited designs. And I will confess to you, it makes me hate them."

Vincent nodded. "I understand. The newspapers attacked Lily because of our family. It drove me mad with fury. Fury makes me a creative man; I have no shortage of ideas for punishments."

Berkeley nodded. "Perhaps you can understand more than most. But Lily is strong and willful. She was popular and confident before the attacks. They may have set her back, but she will remain strong. But for Serena, they poisoned the well before anyone drank. Serena was attacked at her introduction. What's worse, she believes her critics. She keeps trying to accommodate their criticism while making herself small. And I can do nothing to defend or help her."

"Can you not ridicule the people who have attacked her?" Vincent asked. He was prepared to have choice words for Mrs. Bannon as soon as he found her. She would have the breath of a goat and twice the beard.

"I must wait until she is wed, if she weds. If she is twenty-eight and unwed, I will give her my estate in Cornwall and let her live her life in peace." Berkeley stood as the door swung open and Serena entered without a whisper. "Pet! Did you order tea?"

"I did. As well as supper. I trust you like goose, my lord," Serena said as she entered the room.

"Absolutely, and thank you for taking care of me. I am pleased to be marrying you." Vincent winked at her.

"Ah! I had forgotten that I am to return to Philadelphia! Mandeville and I were talking sport. You know how I can babble," Berkeley lied as he checked his watch. "I missed the train by a few minutes. I will take the next train to Philadelphia and will join you for tea."

"Wonderful. We can pester Lord Vincent for stories of his youth so we can all be on equal footing," Serena said with a crooked smile at her brother.

"I am eager to know what being pestered by you would resemble." Vincent returned the smiles.

Vincent needed to marry Serena, not only because

she was beautiful and he liked her, but she would give him purpose. For years, the vorpal edge of his sarcasm and sharp point of his cruel wit had been a burden to himself and his confidants. As Serena's defender, he would not have to hide himself. He could use his venom to help a profoundly good lady. And if she became grateful and aroused, well that would be even better—significantly better. He needed to find a way to fool her for a few short months, potentially more, but once they were wed, he could have her for the rest of his life.

Chapter 9

Last week, I received a letter from a reader inquiring as to whether one could be prepared for every possible calamity. After thinking the matter over, I have come to the conclusion that no, you cannot. To be prepared for every possible calamity, one would have to imagine every possible calamity (giant squids and men falling from balloons included), always prepare, and have the preparations with one. This would be a paralyzing breadth of knowledge that no mind could hold without the specter of madness overtaking them. The best advice for every situation is this: stop, breathe deeply, and be calm. Hysterics never helped anything.

Aunt Penny's Advice for Living, October 1885

After tea, Serena said goodbye to Frederick. If he caught only the best and most fortunate circumstances, he would return that night. However, Serena doubted that luck was on her side and mentally prepared to care for Lord Vincent all night. She was terrified of what she might do.

It was an itch that Serena could not scratch, knowing he was naked under the god-awful dressing gown. She felt a desperate need to know what he looked like. She imagined he was hairy, perhaps with a scar from some youthful misadventure. Her terrible curiosity had flourished uncomfortably. She wanted to know what his staff looked like. Several men had told her of theirs, and she understood longer to be better.

"We are alone in a hotel room; should you not entertain your fiancé?" Lord Vincent inquired.

"It is remarkable that no one noticed I did not agree to marry you, my lord," Serena countered.

Lord Vincent guffawed. "You will, though. I have decided to marry you."

"No, but thank you, my lord," Serena retorted, annoyed at his presumption.

"Why not? I can provide a nice life for you," he argued, appearing genuinely angry when Serena had assumed he was acting in jest.

"Well, we don't know each other nearly enough. And I don't believe that your mother likes me at all. Miss Haverford also presents an issue."

"It is distressing for you to be reasonable. Can't you cry and tell me I am a mean, nasty man? Very well, tell me everything about you, and then I will return the knowledge." Lord Vincent reclined, his eyes half open in a sleepy seductive fashion.

"My lord—"

"Call me Vincent! My future wife cannot be so respectful," he chastised.

"My lord, this is foolish," Serena rebelled.

"See? You cannot call me by the name I request. Terribly disrespectful." He grinned at her open mouth and the shocked wideness of her eyes. "There is nothing else to do; humor an invalid."

Serena giggled. He was dreadfully charming. "Very well, what do you wish to know?"

"Everything, absolutely everything. You can begin by importance or chronology. Lady's choice," Vincent declared.

Serena thought for a moment about trying to impress him, but recalled he still was tethered to Miss Haverford. "I am an atheist."

Shock besieged his gorgeous face. "That is a scandal. Why? What event occurred to lead you to atheism?"

Serena rolled her eyes. "I read the Bible. That is the event. I tried, upon my life, I tried to believe, but there was too much wrong with it. I drove the vicar mad with questions. Yet he could only give me platitudes and evasions."

"I don't really spend much time thinking about God. I don't believe I have read the Bible, but I cannot be a sarcastic prat and an atheist, so I will not. What questions could the vicar not answer?" Vincent asked.

"Why babies must die? Why there is not an abundance of food and shelter to ensure children will survive? What mad God allows wee babes to get cancer? The Bible instructs a woman to marry her rapist; that is not the workings of a just God. The vicar tried to tell me that Jesus rid the world of the Old Testament, but then I ask why homosexuality is an abomination of the church? It is given the same punishment as eating a lobster, which is what the vicar was eating at the time." Serena lectured; she knew her words were offensive, but they were her own, and she was tired of keeping them to herself.

"If you do not believe in God, will you honor our marriage? What of morals? Will you lie and cheat because there is no judgment?" he asked.

"I will uphold my marriage vows, to whomever I marry, if I marry. And of course, I have morals. I do not require any god to tell me not to lie, cheat, or steal. I know if I lie, I will forever damage my credibility as all lies see the light of day. If I steal, I am harming the livelihood of another person. I would not kill as I know the immeasurable pain of losing a loved one. And the Bible is far too lenient on rape," Serena bit off.

Vincent cocked his head. "That is the second time you have mentioned rape."

"Is it?" Serena asked. They did vex her, the rape sections.

"Yes, why does it bother you?" Vincent asked.

"How does it not bother you? If a woman does not scream while being raped, she should be stoned to death. A god with complete knowledge would know that fear can choke you and bite your tongue. And if it was the work of men that were so shortsighted, then why did God allow it? Why does he care more about menstruation than child prostitution? Why does he care more about cooking than telling people not to empty their chamber pots in the drinking water?" Serena's voice had grown unnaturally loud and beyond her control.

"You are absolutely correct, or at least I assume you are. I don't recall my vicar ever mentioning menstruation, but you would not be so passionate unless you were certain. I will ask that as my wife, I be the only person you yell at, however," Vincent said with a smile.

Serena chuckled. "I am certain that you no longer wish to marry me at all."

Vincent shook his head. "On the contrary. Tell me more. Something no one else knows."

Every night I dream of you doing bawdy and

degrading things to me, and I love it. Since the day I met you, I wake with a wet pincushion and aching breasts. It makes me hate myself and adore you.

"If I am to tell you a secret, I must tell you something nearly no one else knows first. I expect to know your soul by morning," Serena offered.

"I refuse; you will not marry me if you know me. But I will tell you things that will make you like me." Vincent grinned at her.

Serena sighed. "Very well. After the death of my parents, I refused to speak. For an entire year, I would not utter a single word."

Vincent frowned. "What was wrong? Was it a medical condition?"

Serena shook her head. "No. My mother had told me, countless times, never to speak ugly words. After she died, I wanted to scream. I wanted to tell everyone what I honestly thought of them. But out of respect for my mother, I kept silent. I loved her so much, I still want to scream, but I have gotten better at controlling my thoughts."

"What would you have said?" Vincent asked.

"I was so angry. The ton ridiculed my mother for being Swiss, and then they discovered she was a milkmaid. Even my father, a war hero and marquess, was fodder for their mockery. Cruel hearts have bitter tongues, and miserable people want to infect others with their misery. After my mother had died, she was the Cinderella of London. I hated them for even pretending to love my parents when it no longer mattered," Serena explained.

"I cannot find the words to express how terrible I feel. I am so sorry," Vincent said as he hung his head.

"Why should you feel terrible? You were a child. I assume you were not hurting my mother at the age of ten?" Serena asked.

"No, but I am the Malicious Mandeville. I have clearly hurt people, with little thought to their lives," Vincent explained.

"Yes, but even the worst quotes from you were not personal. You may mock a man's beard or a lady's hairpiece but not who they are. You insult their choices, but you do not insult things they cannot change. I have never read of you insulting a person because of their birth or their finances. If you insult my hat, I will simply never wear that hat again, but I still thrive," Serena explained.

"But what if you adored the hat? Perhaps it was your mother's or a gift from your favorite aunt?" Vincent asked.

Serena shook her head. "I cannot explain the difference, but there is one. However, if my tale helps you be mindful of the repercussions of your words, then I will be happy. Enough of my silly tribulations. It is time for you to tell tales."

"Very well, but you are under a misconception that must be cleared. I was about to propose to Miss Haverford when she jilted me. Although it may not have been a jilt in a literal sense, as we were not engaged, it felt unduly jilty," Vincent babbled. Was he truly this flustered?

"Ah, is that why you came to America?" Serena asked.

Vincent nodded. "Lily suggested that I might join Berkeley on his tour. I was trying to find your party for weeks, but I am pleased that I had a few months by myself. I was tremendously angry with Marlene and needed to get away from the incident."

Serena could not imagine what sort of mad fool would reject him. Perhaps Miss Haverford was insane. "I apologize that you spent time on a fruitless endeavor."

Vincent waved his hand. "We have been far too maudlin for the week. I shall now tell you of the incident that resulted in my never being able to visit the Vatican again."

Serena and Vincent talked until the early morning hours when Serena finally fell asleep in her dress. It was uncomfortable, and her corset dug angrily into her ribs, but she was exhausted. The corset appeared in her dreams, with Serena being tight-laced as Vincent had his wicked way with her. Tonight, her dreams were less licentious and more loving and intimate. How sensual and frightening.

"Pet," the voice whispered while Vincent was deep inside her.

Serena's eyes flew open to see her brother's face. She exhaled and realized that she needed to wake before him to prevent this uncomfortable feeling. "Is it morning already?"

"Yes, well, six in the morning. I made Martha travel by carriage overnight. She will dress you, and you can take the first train to Philadelphia. What occurred in my absence?" Frederick asked as he helped Serena stand.

"Worry not. We were only within arm's reach when I handed him his dinner." Hopefully this explanation would dispel any suspicion. When she and Vincent's hands had touched, waves of excitement raced and swooped up her arm and to her heart.

"Thank God. I was terrified. We are not taking another detour without Martha again. I don't believe my heart could stand another night like that again. You have aged me, pet," Frederick said with the sternness of a doubting father.

"I apologize, but I do wish you could trust me and your friend. Vincent values you and your friendship; he would not cross any boundaries," Serena said as she walked into the bright room where Martha was waiting. "Good morning, Martha."

"I do trust you and Mandeville. However, you are beautiful, and he is a man who is gifted with words." Frederick was lethargic and whiny from behind the screen as Serena was undressed.

"Don't lace my corset tightly. I need to relax," Serena whispered to Martha quickly and low before speaking to Frederick. "We spoke of religion and family. I cannot imagine more innocent topics of conversation."

Frederick laughed. "Oh, pet, you told him of your beliefs, didn't you? Well, how did Mandeville react?"

"He understood but did not want to think on it. Then we discussed Mum and Daddy." Serena opted not to tempt Frederick's curiosity any further.

"I am pleased that all's well that ends well. I would have seen you wed if he had so much as held your hand," Frederick declared. "I like Mandeville, but I love you."

Serena rolled her eyes. "And so, if he grabbed my hand, you would force me to wed. That is hardly a loving act."

"I did say 'held,' not 'grabbed.' Holding hands is

the sweet beginnings of infatuation. Besides, I must assume you are mitigating the events. Holding hands would be actually kissing. At most there was a bit of foot play, last night." Frederick smiled as Serena stepped out from behind the screen, newly dressed and refreshed. "I know you value your independence. You are not a fool and would downplay any physical interaction."

"Ah but what if I diminished the events by not twofold but four? Or eight?" Serena challenged.

Frederick threw up his hands. "Pet, the only way I can be certain of your virtue is to trust you and your own self-interest. I cannot lock you in a tower; none of our houses have one. I blame the architects for this."

Serena laughed and kissed her brother's cheek. "Very well, I am off to Philadelphia. Vincent's laundry should be done by eleven. If it is not, I recommend pestering the desk clerk. I will see you when you arrive."

Serena slept on the train ride to Philadelphia. She was exhausted. She was eager for a hot bath and a lie-down in a proper bed without wearing her corset. She also desired time to contemplate the events of last night. Vincent had not touched her, but she felt as though he had become intimate with her. Without Miss Haverford blocking her way, perhaps she could have her depraved dreams come true.

Upon arrival of the Continental Hotel, she was handed a telegram. Serena feared something was wrong with her grandparents but hoped it was simply Honoria. Inside was the message:

V

Miss you dearly. Return home so that we may

announce our engagement. Love you always.
    M

Her confusion and betrayal boiled and churned. Vincent had mentioned that Miss Haverford's Christian name was Marlene. Why would he lie to her? What was he playing at? Did he hope to use their intimacies to mock her when they returned to London? Or perhaps he merely hoped to seduce and ruin her.

Even her enlightened imagination could not conjure the circumstances leading Vincent to be so cruel. The air had emptied from her lungs, and she was filled with lead and frankly too tired to care. He was trying to achieve some goal, and she needed to figure him out before he discovered any more Percy family secrets. It hurt, to have hope stolen from her. Serena slipped the offending telegram under Vincent's door before returning to her room.

Chapter 10

Everyone continuously asks me to stop judging people, but how can I? All old women are judgmental and critical. All actors are Casanovas. All barmaids are humoring you until they can be rid of you. All children are delightful. Until I meet a person who challenges my assumptions, I am simply correct.

A Curmudgeon's Tour of America, October 1885

It had been three isolating days since Vincent returned from Pittsburgh. His ankle was nearly healed, and Vincent had used the time to write two columns for Osborne. Serena had not visited him, and it would not have been proper for her to do so. But her absence was an unbearable strain in his harsh condition. It was a subtle thrill to have his cane in hand as he strolled to the restaurant for breakfast.

Serena was a vision he had been longing to see. She wore a robin's-egg-blue morning dress without a hat, allowing her blonde hair to shine in the morning light. She did not smile when he approached. What a disappointment. Berkeley and Melgum both grinned, childishly telegraphing their planned jibes.

"Mandeville is finally walking once more. Your cane makes you look like a dignified old lecher searching for a new wife. Are you happy to join the rest of us in the pedestrian world?" Berkeley asked.

"You may not be as smart as me, but I would never call you pedestrian. But indeed I am. What have I missed?" Vincent queried.

"Not a great deal. Benedict has been perfecting the play. I have been introduced to several of the young ladies of Philadelphia, and while they are nice, none of them strike me with love. Serena, however, has an abundance of admirers." Berkeley grinned at her.

Serena was clearly annoyed at Berkeley's words while Vincent seethed. "Truly? What constitutes an abundance of admirers?"

"Four. Macbeth and Banquo as well as Mr. Arnold and Mr. Rodgers," Berkeley listed. Was he secretly delighting in this light torture?

"It is causing a rift between the actors. Serena, I wish you had not done this." Melgum frowned.

Serena's face was pure shock, and her mouth fell open into a round *O*. Berkeley, however, grew red and had a murderous expression. "What is it that you accuse her of? I was with her during the entirety of her interactions with these men. She was polite but distant with the actors. I believe they are unused to such behavior and found her a considerable task. Men like a challenge. Mr. Arnold was not terribly interested until he realized Serena was a lady, and if he married her, he would have a rare prize. I do not like Mr. Arnold. Finally, Mr. Rodgers has a great deal in common with Serena and is respectful. Do not blame Serena for merely being herself and others behaving poorly."

"Thank you, Frederick," Serena muttered. How queer that she was not speaking up more loudly.

"I believe you owe Serena an apology, Benedict," Frederick ground out.

Melgum nodded. "I do apologize, Serena. I had only seen the rivalry of my actors and Frederick's amusement at the situation. I thought, perhaps, you were practicing flirting. I apologize deeply for thinking you were the start of the trouble."

Serena smiled at her cousin. "Of course I forgive you. I do apologize for the inconvenience. Perhaps I should abstain from the party to celebrate the play."

"Or perhaps we ought to move on in our tour tomorrow, and Benedict can meet us in Chicago. We will, of course, attend the opening so that there will not be an empty seat. Would that suit everyone?" Berkeley asked.

"I feel terrible, as though I am running you off. And if Serena likes Mr. Rodgers, should she not stay?" Melgum frowned.

"Mr. Rodgers and I have agreed to exchange letters. Besides, men forget attractions so quickly. If it is formed the moment a woman is seen, it often fades when the woman is out of their sight." Serena gave a brief but pointed look toward Vincent.

She was angry with him! That was delightful and intriguing. He returned her anger. How dare she encourage another man when he was so clearly in love with her? Vincent needed information, and he knew exactly where to find it. After breakfast he sought Serena's maid.

"Swinton... It is Swinton, is it not?" Vincent asked. He had heard Serena call her maid Martha, but it is possible that familiarity would not resonate well with the adroit young woman.

"Yes, my lord," Swinton replied with a sneer as she refused to meet his eyes.

"Tell me why lady Serena is angry with me," Vincent demanded. That might have been the wrong approach, but he did not really care why the maid was cross with him.

"She has not confided in me, but if I were to guess from her mumbling, it would be about the telegram she received intended for you," Swinton informed him. She wasn't curt, or mean, but she danced along the edge of outright animosity.

"What telegram? Lily is the only person who regularly telegraphs. Lily is fond of Serena and supports my courtship." Vincent's befuddlement defused his anger.

"It was not from Lady Lily Mandeville, but from Miss Haverford. I believe she confessed missing you and a desire to announce your engagement to her." Swinton seemed smug in her declaration.

"Oh my, that is interesting. Miss Haverford would never send such a telegram as she is certain she will marry my brother. But it begs the question as to who would try to alienate Serena from me and why? Only Lily knows I wish to marry her, but Lily supports this goal," Vincent contemplated aloud. His hand instinctively searched his jacket pocket for an answer but came up empty. Last time he had fallen prey to a conspiracy, they had informed him in advance.

"You intend to marry my lady and not Miss Haverford, my lord?" Swinton asked, reminding him of her presence. What an incredible trait, to fade into the background so astutely.

"Of course, she is perfect. How serious a threat is this Mr. Rodgers?" Vincent asked.

Swinton smiled. "None at all. He is a deeply

religious man, but they both enjoy history. Her ladyship has offered to exchange historical stories she finds in her travels for an American view of history. Their friendship is not romantic."

"Excellent. I need your help, Swinton. There are people who hate my family and want to see us suffer. I believe they sent Serena the telegram. It's rather petty I think, but it is the only explanation. From here on, will you check her telegrams for this trickery?" Vincent asked.

"Why should I help you when you have enemies that could hurt her ladyship? And I am deeply uncomfortable with spying on her ladyship's mail." Swinton frowned.

"Not her mail. I don't believe they could arrange a deceit of a letter as it would be difficult to fool her into reading a letter meant for me. No, the telegram is perfect. If the ploy is to send it to Serena's room but keep the message as though being for me. And, Swinton, Serena will be happy with me. Enemies and all. I am the villain you should be rooting for," Vincent concluded.

Swinton's perfectly still doll eyes fixed on a point just past his head as she considered his proposal. "Her ladyship does not receive many telegrams, so I will treat them as suspicious. But I must know about these enemies. Why do they wish to disrupt a courtship of her ladyship? That seems bizarre and farfetched. You are hardly a villain worth that much intrigue."

"Yes, yes, disruption of a romance does seem anomalous. The Shadow Society must miss me. This move is perplexing, but at least I know the telegrams are not to be trusted," Vincent mused. He would have to write letters, which took forever, but at least he could recognize the hand of the writers. "I am sorely offended at your unwarranted belief in my good nature." He tapped his hands firmly to emphasize, although he was only half serious.

"A society clouded by shadows? Madame Olyenska…" Swinton mumbled.

He might be able to convince her to help him, but he doubted she would ever like him.

"I beg your pardon?" Vincent asked. What was she going on about?

"You must tell her ladyship of this. I believe this society has attacked her family before," Swinton replied.

"I shall, when I have discovered their motives. But the Shadow Society has only attacked one other family, and it was not the Percys," Vincent explained. The first family attacked by the Shadow Society was extorted of their fortune, so much so that their only daughter delayed her introduction to society.

Swinton nodded quickly. She understood too quickly for a mere maid; she was clearly an ancillary guardian for Serena when Frederick could not be there. "I must attend to her ladyship."

Vincent watched Swinton walk away, happy to have won an ally. How amusing that his lusts and yearnings were the subject of the Shadow Society's newest vendetta. How utterly ridiculous that they cared if he married Lady Serena. Of course, it might have been a means to separate him from Berkeley or Melgum. It was through misplaced and delayed telegraphs that he had kept missing their party for weeks. There was a mystery afoot, and he felt more like himself as he was mired in the intrigue once more.

Vincent had been mistaken to think the Shadow Society was done with the Mandevilles. Their interference showed persistence, but to what end? The fact that they felt the need to meddle in his love life was fascinating and childish. But the dynamic had changed; they did not know he was aware they were tampering with his telegrams. He needed to figure out who was spying on him. There was certainly a spy in Lily's house, perhaps his mother's as well. Discovering the spy would involve a truly devious campaign of deception and chicanery. It should be illegal to have so much fun.

After spending his day scheming, Vincent readied himself for the theater. Vincent genuinely enjoyed Shakespeare, and of course Melgum, the son of a Scottish earl, was financing the production of *Macbeth*. Serena looked lovely, draped in pink that highlighted the extra color her complexion had acquired as a result of travel, but she still refused to meet Vincent's eye in the carriage.

During the play, Vincent was able to discover his rivals. They were not much of a threat. The two actors preened from the stage for her; she was unmoved. Mr. Arnold was a man of at least fifty years and at least two hundred pounds of rolling fat with a beard so unkempt it was embarrassing. Mr. Rodgers was unfortunately what most women might find attractive, with a very blond beard and a youthful face. Rodgers was dressed modestly and was sitting with a woman Vincent guessed to be his mother.

Vincent leaned over to whisper in her ear, "Pretend to have a headache after the play so I may escort you to the hotel."

Serena frowned and gave a quick shake of her head.

"Do you wish to attend the supper after the play? The actors might be in attendance, as will the other gentlemen who find you so desirable. Would you not rather be escorted to your hotel room by a man who found you desirable before it was fashionable? Also, I promise to leave you at your room and return to Berkeley," he whispered.

Serena's eyes cast about the theater, and she sighed. She gave a resigned nod, and Vincent knew he had won.

After the production—which was well done, much to Vincent's chagrin, as he would have loved to lampoon the actors, but he was happy for Melgum— Serena pulled Berkeley aside. The two discussed his plan, with Serena clearly winning the argument. Vincent felt a tinge of guilt that he had connived his intended to persuade his friend so that Vincent could be alone with her, but the guilt of such actions was not greater than the weight of his wanting for Serena, so he pushed his guilt aside. He would make amends with Berkeley once he had wed Serena.

"Mandeville, thank you for offering to escort Serena to the hotel," Berkeley said as he helped Serena with her cloak.

"Of course. I noticed her ladyship was not feeling well, and I know how you enjoy a fete. No one will miss my presence for the short time to escort Lady Serena to her room, at least compared to how much they will miss her." Vincent smiled.

"Ah, are you not attending the party, Miss—er—

Lady Serena? You must allow my mother and me to take you in our carriage." Ah, this must be the bastard known as Rodgers.

"Thank you, Mr. Rodgers, but Lord Vincent has offered to escort me to my maid." Serena smiled sweetly at Rodgers.

"He may join us, but our conscience will not allow us to leave you alone with a bachelor," interjected Rodgers' mother, henceforth to be known as Old Hag (although she probably had an equally repulsive name such as Meredith).

Serena sighed and nodded. They all piled into the small carriage designed with the calculable benefit of placing Serena terribly close to Vincent. Suddenly, Vincent was thrilled to have had the Rodgers' interference. "Thank you for sharing your carriage with us. Have you met Lord Vincent?"

"We have not, but Lady Serena speaks glowingly of you." Rodgers gave a forced smile.

"Thank you, my lady. It is a bit of a problem; her ladyship is constantly fawning over me." Vincent grinned at Serena's scowl. "And what is it you do, Mr. Rodgers?"

"I am a professor of history at the university of Pennsylvania," Rodgers announced.

"Ah, my good friend Oliver writes historical novels about the ancient kings and queens before the conqueror," Vincent said. He really did know enough history to hold his own, which was coincidentally enough to be entirely skeptical of all humankind.

"I will look for them," Rodgers said noncommittally.

"I read his latest on the ship from Britain. I can

send it to you before we depart tomorrow," Serena offered. She was not backing away from this *actor* quickly enough.

There was a pall of silence over the carriage. Vincent realized Old Hag did not approve of Serena but instead felt she should be desperate for Rodgers' attention. Rodgers appeared to have affection for Serena but did not have the backbone to fight for his intentions, or even render them clear. Serena practically leapt from the carriage when it stopped at the Continental Hotel.

"Thank you very much, Mrs. Rodgers, Mr. Rodgers. It was lovely to see you both once more, and I hope you have a lovely evening," Serena said halfway over her shoulder before she entered the bustling hotel.

Vincent hustled to catch her. She was moving quickly, or as quickly as a woman could move with customary delicacy. She was ignoring him and trying to escape him. This infuriating woman! Vincent dropped his foot brutally on the train of her gown, stopping her so fast she kept attempting to walk without moving a single step farther toward her room. Serena stopped, turned, and gazed down at her dress. She raised her eyebrows at him. Was she more annoyed or amused? He smiled playfully at her. After all, it was better to have her focus, regardless of the attached feelings.

"This gown is delicate, my lord. I fear you will leave a boot print," Serena announced calmly. She was loud enough to invite attention. Maybe she wanted to avoid the appearance of an intimate conversation.

"I shall have to have a new one made for you." He lifted his foot and walked toward her, close enough to touch if his arms were outstretched. "I must have your sizes." He assisted her with the door—what a true gentleman.

"Frederick loves to spoil me, and he will be happy to oblige," Serena muttered as he grasped her waist.

"Gentlemanly honor would never allow it. I despise the bustle fashion. How do you sit in this dress? Or is the intention to make it just uncomfortable enough to make woman pine for nakedness?" Vincent asked as he allowed his hand to wander down her waist to firmly grip her hip.

"Gentlemanly honor?" Serena breathed.

"Indeed," Vincent mumbled as he began to kiss her neck, breathing in deep her perfume.

"Please...oooh...please explain," she moaned. Only Serena would ask for a clarification during a brilliant seduction.

"I shall." He leaned in to kiss her. She tasted of sweet honey and luscious pears. Her eyes beamed articulate and immense surprise as his tongue explored her mouth, but soon she began to mirror his actions. Their kiss was so deep and soul exposing, every inch of him was spent as he pulled himself from her.

Serena ran her finger along his jawline. "You will ruin me."

And with that she abandoned him.

Chapter 11

Alas, I bid adieu to Philadelphia. As I reflect on my time here, I recommend the city to all who visit America. I found much to warm my heart and fall in love within the charming city.

A Curmudgeon's Tour of America, October 1885

You will ruin me.

Serena's last words had rung like unwelcome church bells through Vincent's mind in the hours since she uttered them. He was going to ruin her? The audacity of this woman; she was destroying him! She was his angel, offering the sweet balm of her company, but today she was silent. Couldn't she understand how she soothed him, how he needed her? The situation was plainly infuriating and entirely her fault.

One would think that she could not avoid him in a train car with nowhere to run. Serena proved to be a formidable challenge, plunging her nose deep in a copy of *King Solomon's Mines* and feigning interest in the tome. Berkeley was reading a collection of essays regarding the American revolution, while Swinton was embroidering silver flowers on black silk. The situation was a comedy of silence that none of them dared disturb, and Vincent needed Serena's attention. He unbent his knee and kicked her subtly. When that evoked nothing, he feigned adjusting himself and kicked her fully.

Her eyes fluttered to meet his, and he froze. The attention had been desperately required, but he had not thought of what he would do once he obtained it. His instinct was to shock her, but with Berkeley present, he could not be adequately rude or vulgar (and he wasn't feeling witty). How does one keep a woman's focus without being offensive? This was new territory—new and boring territory. He settled on deceit. Lying was often the best option.

"I do apologize, my lady. I suffer from a leg twitch. A result from a polo injury." The goal of this game was to tell the most outlandish lie possible without being caught.

All eyes in the car were suddenly on him.

"Are you an avid polo player, Mandeville?" Berkeley asked, with a pause pregnant with doubt. How dare he remain skeptical of Vincent's polo prowess.

"No, sadly. I kept mistaking the mallet for a riding crop. The horse kicked me in reprisal, the obtuse and misunderstanding animal. I did apologize, though. I even brought flowers, but the horse ate them after she kicked me." There was an awkward silence in the car, yet Serena held her book just below her cheeks to hide her smile. Vincent switched legs and kicked her again.

"And what ails that leg, my lord?" Serena asked. She might have tried to appear annoyed but could not scrub the clear amusement from her tone.

"A similar injury, but this time it was a goat. After I was removed from the polo club, I tried to join the pygmy polo league. Unfortunately, I made the same error, and the goat was as misunderstanding as the horse. Do you think the horse slandered me to the goat?" Vincent asked.

Serena clapped her hand over her mouth and shook with laughter. Berkeley smiled but shook his head and returned to his reading. Vincent had won a great prize. He might even purchase a tiny mallet to win another smile. In the brief train ride to Baltimore, he managed to kick her three more times. On the fourth, she moved her legs but winked at him.

Once in Baltimore, they went quickly through a labyrinth of rough streets to the hotel. Vincent had a difficult choice to make. Should he unpack all his clothing to prevent wrinkles for a one-night stay in Baltimore, only to repack them again? He was truly a modern Sisyphus. Ultimately, he could not bear his clothing sitting in his trunk and spent the time unpacking. As he placed the last pair of trousers on top of his bed, Berkeley entered the room behind him.

"Would you like to walk about the city with me? Serena is having a lie-down and said her legs hurt," Berkeley invited.

"I would love a walk," Vincent announced as he found his most fashionable coat.

"Yes, stretch your legs so they stop twitching," Berkeley mumbled as they started down the stairs. A striking woman with black hair passed them, causing Berkeley's gaze to linger. "I came to America for a wife, but I cannot find one who fits my criteria."

"What are your criteria? Do you insist on a love match?" Vincent asked.

Berkeley shrugged in pure dubiousness. "I want a woman who understands our class and would not be uncomfortable in society. I want a woman who cares for the poor and working-class people. I want her to be egregiously fashionable and incontrovertibly beautiful. I feel it is most important that a wife realize the difficulty in her life, to see the shackles around her, and to despise them. I will not treat my wife poorly, but she should be aware of her rights or lack thereof, and I want it to agitate her. And my family is cursed, so I can only marry for love."

"Lady Olivia is a suffragette. And she is absurdly beautiful." Vincent watched an oyster fleet come into the docks. The black soot of high industry and whipping breeze of salt air. It almost made him miss his nation.

"Lady Olivia is gorgeous, and I adore her passion for women's rights. However, both she and I have sharpened our tongues on our enemies. Were we to disagree, we would kill each other and salt the earth. I don't know why you disagree more ardently with your friends than an enemy." Berkeley narrowed his eyes, watching the ships. "We should buy a great deal of oysters and let Serena try to find a pearl."

"Oysters can be vicious and may bite her, or at least she may cut her hand. We could simply buy her some pearls. Hairpin, a necklace, the lot," Vincent answered. He might have said too much.

"What of you, Mandeville? Do you insist on a love match? Do you have one with Miss Haverford?" Berkeley asked as he pushed on the walk.

Vincent snickered. "I insist on wedding a woman who loves me, but Miss Haverford loves another man."

"Ah, so you are interested in my sister." Berkeley spoke plainly. It appeared he had suspected this all along.

"It would be difficult to know Serena and not take

an interest." Vincent tried his hand at diplomacy. Berkeley probably didn't want to hear how much Vincent was interested, the aspects he was most eager for, or the sordid details Vincent had conjured in his mind.

"Indeed. However, if Serena should return your interest, please speak with me. I am responsible for her. I must protect my sister. Also, if you hurt her, even unintentionally, I will show you just how skilled a pugilist I became over five summers of boxing." Berkeley gave Vincent a terrifying stare—too constant, too contained, possibly even kind.

"Jesus, Berkeley! I will hurt Serena, especially if I marry her. It is in my nature, but I will not hurt her maliciously and will always apologize. I am a sarcastic and terrible man, but I am not a rake or a rogue. If I hurt her and am unable to persuade her to forgive me, then you may harm me after a month. And I will show you just how skilled a pugilist I have become after three summers mocking debutantes." Vincent negotiated with high confidence. "You may bruise me. You may break my bones. But only I can compose a limerick that rhymes the word whore in four languages and deliver it at a coming out, yet still be invited for tea."

Berkeley nodded, clearly discounting most of what Vincent said. "That is fair. Serena is the most important person to me, but she is sensitive and can be hurt easily. You make her smile, so much so that I was worried of her having a broken heart when you married Miss Haverford."

Vincent breathed a sigh of significant and happy relief. "I pray you find a lady without a brother. It can be terrifying."

Berkeley brightened. "As do I! Do not mistake me, Mandeville. I support you in this endeavor, much more than any other suitor Serena has had. I cannot abide her living in America. The telegrams would nearly bankrupt me as I enjoy hearing her opinions to help shape my own. I very much like that we were friends before you met Serena. Far too often gentlemen try to become my friend to garner her goodwill. I do not have to doubt our friendship or the subjects we agreed on, and I know you are a decent man."

Vincent smiled. "I do value our friendship. Hopefully Serena will fall deeply in love with me, and we will be brothers. If not, I would hope to maintain our friendship and even one with Serena, but I fear I would be terribly jealous of her husband."

"Then you must be successful in your courtship. I refuse to aid you. If Serena is to marry, it must be to a man she genuinely likes and not someone I help cheat. It is her life after all. I must tell you something of grave importance; it affects me and our tour," Berkeley began.

How annoyingly principled that Berkeley would not help him, despite his stated support. He was fine with telling people how to run their affairs and whom they could judge, but he wouldn't steer his sister in this most obvious of ways? However, Vincent loved intrigue, so the notion that Berkeley should have a secret was riveting. "I am all ears."

"You are aware that our parents died. I do not know if you recall, but they were murdered. It was a scandal at the time, but after nine long years, I am sure most have forgotten," Berkeley began evenly. How queer to adopt a controlled tone when discussing the murder of loved ones.

"You have my deepest sympathies," Vincent mumbled. Murder was a shocking event to any person. But a marquess and a marchioness? How unspeakable and horrifying. No wonder why Serena could not speak; she must have been traumatized by the notion that not even the son of a duke was safe. That no one was. Vincent recalled himself at twelve. The subtle realizations of the world's cruelties and indifferences came slowly into light. Losing the joys and freedom of childhood was difficult, even without the loss of family. If only he could find her immediately and crush her into him until her chilling insecurities gave way to the warm safety of him.

"Thank you. It was more difficult for Serena as she found them, poor little pet. She has become obsessed with their murders, going so far as to seek mystics and mediums to speak to them. I believe the whole process is somewhat ridiculous, but the mystery of their deaths haunts her. She visited a woman in Philadelphia who told her we must seek a man in New Orleans," Berkeley explained.

"And so, we are going to New Orleans?" Vincent asked.

Berkeley shrugged. "If someone told her the answer lay in Shangri La, she would ask me to take her. And I would fund an expedition."

Vincent shook his head. There would be no clearing her head of this fixation; she was far too independent for that. "And what is she going to do when she finds this man? Confront him? Ask the Americans to detain him? Perhaps kidnap him to bring him to English courts?"

Berkeley smiled. "I have no idea, but she will not let this go. Perhaps it will involve a creative use of one of her canes. She will not move on until she finds whoever did this and sees them punished."

Vincent sighed. "Well, regardless of whether I can convince her to marry me, I will help her in this mad errand. Although I am keeping my cane."

"Excellent. This has been a distressingly heavy conversation. Let's find a pharmacy or a pub and discuss something wholly innocuous. Perhaps the Indian Removal Act or something equally light."

As they talked into the evening, Vincent hoped that this would be his future. Spending days with Berkeley and Serena and his nights with Serena in his bed. Vincent might even be able to tolerate his mother if he had Serena as his wife. And as a complete aside, how delightful to envision Marlene and Sebastian writhing in jealousy at the sight of his lady wife. Vincent simply needed to trick and connive Serena into marrying him. Luckily enough, this was America, where the soil was rich with trickery.

Chapter 12

October has a magical ability to make the scary and macabre intriguing. Whereas in November, the creaky step is but an annoyance and reminder of my childish fears, in October it is evidence that my house is trying to conjure the Halloween spirit.
Aunt Penny's Guide to Life, October 1885

There was a raven tapping at Serena's window, and an icy thrill raced up her neck. The raven tilted its head quickly, then flew overhead to a monument for George Washington in the center of the square. Serena was titillated at being in Baltimore; this was where her favorite author wrote some of his best works and died. He probably preferred the writing to the death, but who could be sure? And now, with a raven tap-tap-tapping at her door and a full sky blossoming with dark and gloom, perhaps she would catch a glimpse of a woman named Annabel Lee who resided in a kingdom by the sea.

No one understood the Percy siblings' obsession with death. Frederick seemed to be taunting him, like he was immune to fear and wished to terrorize the Grim Reaper himself. Serena, meanwhile, flirted and danced with death. She had begun her dalliances into mysticism as an earnest pilgrim, and even now she wanted to be wrong. Her adopted custom was a festive

Halloween, and she could tell a hundred ghost stories. She was not necessarily frightened by the darkness, but she lightly touched it instead of rushing headlong into it. All things eerie were comforts to her, and she had an acquired taste for danger.

Vincent was emblematic of the Percys' fixation. He was dangerous; his tongue was sharpened and ever ready to insult or spread gossip. Yet, Frederick befriended him, and Serena flirted with him. If either of the Percy siblings had an ounce of self-preservation, they would have been polite but distant to him. But like the naughty children they had grown into, instead they invited him in. Perhaps her adoration of dangerous things made her want him to ruin her. But she did, she wanted him to take her every time she saw him.

The raven had done enough tap-tap-tapping to bother Martha, so she had gone out the door to see the front desk about removing him. Serena sat and stared in the mirror for far too long. Her face began to look odd to her. She was too white, too composed. Like a manor painting instead of the wild landscape she felt inside. How long would Martha be? Perhaps Serena could fit in reading a chapter of her book on Washington as she was in Mount Vernon square. She was nearly dressed, already wearing her all-in-one, stockings, corset, petticoats, and even her lobster tail. Serena wondered how on earth she could put on her own dress. How did girls without lady's maids dress themselves?

There was a knock at her door. She hastily put on her plain dressing gown before opening it; it was probably Frederick. Of course not. Vincent stood in the hall. "Good morning, my lord."

"Good morning, Serena. You look ravishing,

but…someday I would like to see you without your bustle," Vincent announced as he inappropriately entered her room and closed the door behind him.

"Martha has just gone to see about the ravens. They are building a nest near our windows." This was textbook babbling, but it was hard to not be slightly overwhelmed by the impropriety of the situation, which unfortunately compounded her own desire.

"What is a group of ravens called? I know it is a murder of crows."

His question made Serena smile. He seemed to always speak about the strangest things, which cut any erotic pretense to the bone. Like most men's wagging tongues, it protected her virtue every time.

"It is a conspiracy of ravens. Or an unkindness of ravens," Serena answered.

"Conspiracy and unkindness, it should be called the Ravens Society. What are swans called?" He stared at the window to find the ravens, his light smile making him seem amused by his own thoughts.

"A ballet of swans," Serena said wistfully. She found the group names for animals to be utterly charming. A charm of finches or a sleuth of bears, though birds had the better terms, obviously. Also, since when had bears solved any mysteries, besides where to find delicious bee larvae?

Vincent chuckled, like he could read her mind. "We should marry."

"I beg your pardon?" What? Was he truly that impressed by her knowledge of group names?

"We suit very well. I prefer your company and conversation above all others. And I want you to be mine." Vincent reached for her hand and touched her claret-colored dressing gown. "You look lovely in burgundy. You should wear it often."

Serena sighed. "Yes, we do get along very well, and I will not deny that there is an attraction between us. I feel as though I am a magnet, and you are steel, and so I am pulled to you. However, there is the person that I am and always will be. I will not interfere in a courtship and betray someone innocent. I saw the telegram intended for you, so I know you are engaged or soon to be engaged to Miss Haverford."

"I know of the telegram, and I know it was not from Marlene. Please understand, Serena, she did not merely jilt me. She jilted me for my brother. You are being honorable to a woman who does not deserve compassion. I do not know who sent that telegram, but I vow, on this life, or anything else you will accept, it was not Marlene," Vincent pleaded. His eyes filled with despair and a faint candle flame of distant anger. If only she could embrace him and comfort him. But her doubts kept her as still as the statue of Washington in the distance.

How dreadful a predicament. If Miss Haverford was truly intended for the Earl of Coningsby, it changed everything. There were no barriers between her and Vincent. It would be forever awkward to be family with them. "That does change things, but I still do not know you well enough to assent to such a match. Any man can be witty and charming for a week."

"Oh Lord, that is an overstatement. I am neither witty nor charming, but I suppose that is evidence of your point. And of course, we spent the night together, only talking, which I found frustrating. I can only hope it is equally so for you. But it is not unheard of to marry after a weekend house party," Vincent argued. He really had made up his mind, hadn't he?

"It is not unheard of to be forced to marry after getting caught in flagrante delicto at a house party. I am not only protecting myself with my apprehensions. You may not like what you learn of me." Was it really necessary to shoot back?

"I can only hope there is more. I accepted that you are a heathen with a history of seeing mystics. You may already be married to the devil, but I still want you. Devil be damned." Vincent moved close enough to touch her, close enough to kiss her.

"I forbid my husband to have a mistress!" she cried in self-defense. Make him stop; his lust was a contagious thing, and she could not afford to catch it. If he kissed her, or even simply cuddled her, she would eagerly let him ravage her.

Vincent cocked his head. A few seconds of relief was all she needed. "What would you do if he did have one? And why does it bother you?"

"I would leave and be estranged from him. It is unfair to be the wife of a man with a mistress. He is permitted to have a house with her, and she may entertain his friends. What becomes of the wife? She manages his house and raises his children while her hopes of love and happiness diminish. I would rather live with my family alone than with a man who thinks nothing of me." Serena finished her riposte, knowing it might be fatal to their courtship. It was not fashionable, but her family believed in love above fashion.

"Sadly, I have a mistress, but if it means having you as my wife, I will release her. Her name is Olga, and I shall mourn her loss for the remainder of the day."

He moped, his head hanging and shoulders slumping. What an actor he was, in more ways than one.

"Olga?" She only knew of one woman by such a name—Miss Snowe's chaperone. Serena somehow doubted Vincent had tupped a seventy-year-old woman. But if he did, she would have taught him some amazing things.

"Hmmm, made you jealous, have I? Of course, I understand; she is a temptress. She is worldly and exotic, but sadly, she speaks no English. I have confessed my love so many ways, but she rebuffs all my attempts at seduction." He blubbered on purpose.

This was actually funny, but she needed to tease back.

"How can she be your mistress if she refuses you and cannot understand you?" Serena giggled. It was mildly infuriating how difficult it was to maintain a cool demeanor in his presence. She constantly found herself smiling and laughing whenever he was near. How terrible.

"Olga remains the mistress of my heart. When we have children, she could be their chaperone, as she was Lily's. On second thought, never mind. She was a terrible chaperone, so Lily was forever unattended. And you did not want me to have a mistress, nor do you want children immediately, so Olga may not survive." Vincent had been holding her hand but had now laced their fingers together and stood with his shoulder touching hers.

Serena shook her head and focused on the discussion. She must not swoon. His mere presence did something to her that left her dizzy and light-headed. This must be why they referred to it as "falling in love," though it felt a bit more as though she were tripping. "You may have a mistress as long as you are miserable with her."

"Would it be suitable if I made her miserable? Perhaps we could make her life wretched together. Some couples play badminton, but we could torment my mistress." Vincent offered his compromise and leaned closer, allowing her to smell him.

Serena shook her head. How sadistic; he always tried to shock her. "I do not seek another's misery, particularly some poor woman who shares my taste in men. You seem to be under the impression that I bear the taint of jealousy toward her. I do not. I simply want my husband to be happiest with me."

"If that is what you require of a husband…" Oh no. Suddenly, he was leaning in so close she could taste him. That magnetism overwhelmed her once more, and she was entirely at his command. Fortunately, the door opened, breaking the spell of desire.

"Are you mad?" Martha hissed, bringing to mind an angry weasel coming home to a foul squirrel. "Your brother is on his way to escort you to breakfast!"

Serena jumped from Vincent and dashed behind her dressing screen. She peeked out to see Vincent crawling under the bed before Frederick entered the room. "Good morning, pet! I am famished. Are you ready? Obviously not." Oh, thank goodness for his oblivious, single-minded devotion to her. A less focused or more skeptical Frederick would ask why she was still not ready.

Serena poked her head out to smile at her brother, but also to see Vincent belly crawling to the door. He was too skilled at this; had he done it before? "I

111

apologize, darling. The laundry was late. It won't be but a moment. I have plans to walk about with Martha today. Perhaps Lord Vincent will keep you company."

Vincent had left, and Frederick appeared not to have noticed. "Very well, but we need to decide if we will delay by remaining in Baltimore or extend our stay to Charleston, Lexington, or Chicago? Benedict will be three days behind us, so we have an extra three days."

Serena nodded as Martha buttoned her into her dress. "I have been thinking about this. My courses are due, and I thought I would go to Chicago early and allow everyone to arrive in five days."

Frederick blanched. "Can you not use a euphemism? There are some things I truly did not need to know."

Serena shook her head and smiled. "Referring to menstruation as my courses is a euphemism. Every woman spends roughly one sixth of her life doing it; why must we never speak of it? We are willing to discuss sleeping and eating but not a necessity of a woman's existence? I digress, I simply did not want you assuming any other reason for my departure and decided to tell you the truth."

"I like this idea. Mandeville and I can tour some of the distilleries at our leisure. And I would like to test him a bit more, as he has expressed interest in marrying you." Frederick tried to sound aloof. He was almost convincing too. Almost.

"Has he? I thought perhaps he was in jest when he asked me." She attempted to match her brother's attempt at disinterest.

"He is serious, pet. How seriously should I treat this situation? Would you like me to frighten him off or to tell him about how lovely you are?" Frederick asked.

Serena had already tried to frighten Vincent off. She had been blunt to the point of embarrassment, and yet, unexpectedly, still he wanted her. "I have to know him better, but I think we suit very well. I have told him my faults; perhaps you could sing my praises?"

Frederick smiled. "Wonderful! This will solve all of my problems. If I can befriend your husband, we will always be in each other's lives. And I will not have to fret over your reputation any longer; your atheism has aged me. Mandeville will be so in love with you by the time we reach Chicago, you won't know what to do."

Serena returned her brother's smile. "I love you, but I do not think even you can charm a man into loving me."

Frederick frowned. "I am not persuasive enough, but you are loveable enough."

Chapter 13

I often wonder which brilliant mind decided to invent pickling. How did one decide to concoct a vinegar brine and soak various foods in it to make a wholly different and longer-lasting food? It simply would not occur to me that if I put vinegar, salt, and cucumbers in a jar, it will be delicious. Sadly, we will never be able to praise this brilliant mind.

Aunt Penny's Advice for Living, October 1885

Serena leaned against the hot-water bottle and attempted to find comfort. Her courses were not extremely painful but rather uncomfortable. More than anything, she dreaded the unclean feeling that took hold of her. She dreamt of a day where a woman could function happily during her courses and not feel the cramping and moist heavy rags settled between her legs. Of course, for progress to advance, someone would have to care about a woman's displeasure and be able to overcome the natural aversion to the subject.

She sat in a lovely suite in Chicago as the wind rattled the windows. Serena had chosen to travel to Chicago as the hotel advertised an en suite bathroom. The architects were not thinking of a woman in her predicament while designing the hotel, but it was a massive advantage. A hot bath every night and a flushing toilet were the ultimate luxury to her in this moment. The hotel offered other amenities and a pretty view, making it an absolute dream for Serena.

"Good morning, my lady," Martha called as she entered the suite rolling a massive dinner cart. "I must say that this is the perfect city for you at the moment. Behold!"

Martha lifted the silver cloche to reveal a colossal amount of pickled and soured vegetables alongside cured meats. Serena was unable to prevent the "ooooh" from escaping her lips.

Martha beamed with pride. "Indeed, my lady. Pickled cucumbers, beets, and your favorite green tomatoes. I found sauerkraut and a bevy of meats. I know how these ease your pain. I was able to locate the book that you requested. Is there anything else that I can fetch for you, my lady?"

Serena shook her head. "This is the perfect amount for me. Perhaps too much. Would you care to join me in this abundant breakfast?"

Martha surveyed the spread and quickly shook her head. "No, thank you, my lady. I have never shared your love of pickled foods."

Serena giggled as she chewed a piece of pickled garlic. "Only during my courses. I enjoy pickled food constantly, but they truly help during my courses. I truly cannot explain it, but my mother swore by pickles every month. I shall have to instruct my daughters and Frederick's daughters to eat pickles during their courses as well."

"Yet another Percy family tradition. Will you also teach them to be oddly rebellious to their peerage as well? Is the new tradition for them to disdain the class they were born into?" Martha teased.

"Of course! Besides, I do not merely disdain the upper class. It is much more than that," Serena answered, her mouth half full of pickles and but overflowing with cheer at the notion of her children hating the aristocracy.

"No?" Martha asked, distracted as she poked the fire and tidied the room.

"No. I hate the upper class. I seethe with rage toward them. I long for a revolution to come and liberate their ill-gotten golden castles and boot the entire upper class from the spires of esteem and wealth. The so-called great men of our country make me sick at the sight of them," Serena spat bitterly.

Martha frowned a decidedly middle-class frown. "What has changed to make you so churlish toward gold and castles? You were not always so full of acrimony."

Serena sighed. " 'The Maiden Tribute in Modern Day Babylon.' I read the article, and sadly everything began to add up. It lifted the veil from my eyes."

"I did not read the article, but I fail to see how the unfortunate events would lead to your shift in perceptions," Martha argued with a pointed tone as she poured the tea.

"Allow me to explain. The exposé revealed that for perhaps eight to thirty pounds a man can purchase a child virgin for fornication in London. Because there are desperate and starving people, they feel they must sell their children into prostitution. It is shocking on its own merits, but I contemplated it further. Most of the working class and poor earn under a hundred pounds a year. I would wager fifty pounds is a decent average, although there are of course lucky men or destitute men. Do you honestly believe that any man might spend one fifth of his yearly wages on a child prostitute for one night? It would be absurd with the rents as high as they are. He would have to forego the warmth of a fire or the comfort of a roof for one night's pleasure. No. The men purchasing these children were wealthy."

Martha gave a little squeak of unease and set the tea aside to stare at Serena directly. "I do recall the general idea was that they were villains."

"Indeed! But honestly think about the predicament. Has any man been prosecuted for these crimes? No, but they have arrested Mr. Stead, the man who reported this tragedy. There are two sets of justice in the world. One is lace and one is iron. One for the wealthy elites and another for the poor and working class. One can be manipulated with social calls, bribery, and the veneer of privilege. Another is enforced with rigid batons and the metal bars of workhouses and prisons. The notion that a titled person can simply claim privilege is disgusting. Even without claiming privilege, our judges are the neighbors of these villains. They share their garden parties and attend their card games. Imagine being of such low character as to have your ethics purchased for a twelve-course meal."

"But surely someone will call for justice?" Martha asked. Her low voice and hurried whisper were obviously uncomfortable with all this, but it appeared she still had hope left in the system. Serena missed her own optimism in the world. But in truth, any hope in that system was twisted and mangled in the debris of her parents' carriage.

"No, not one man has any interest in uprooting this system that has enriched them. Power corrupts. It does not matter how noble your intentions are in the beginning. Over time comfort seduces even the noble, and their interests as rich men, or simply men, become the lens through which they see their world. Suddenly, the competition of which family has the grandest house or which man has the fastest carriage overrides their desires to create a better world. When you start your crusade with the idea that you can use power for good ends, you become fixated on the power and not the good. And especially now, wealth is a disease that infects the mind. To believe that you can make ten pounds off a person's work and pay them three, and that is somehow justice because they agreed to take three instead of the whole ten. And that missing seven is because you are special and clever. Even within the wealthiest, there are tiny groups of elitism," Serena explained. How could Martha not see? How could she be surrounded by these popinjays and not know how petty they were?

"I have never known your ladyship, nor Lord Berkeley, to be terribly concerned with having the largest house or fastest carriage," Martha rebutted.

Serena sighed. This was a clever trap; she would have to say she was different and better, and in doing so, be guilty of the same illness she had spent the past minutes diagnosing. "Frederick and I are unique. We are endlessly aware of our situation. Did you know that our mother was a milkmaid from Switzerland? She was not exactly cunning in her courtship with Daddy. She allowed herself to be seduced and very quickly. She was with child when they wed. My father had every opportunity to simply flee or make her his mistress. Our lives could have been vastly different. If he had fled, I would not exist, and Frederick would have been the bastard son of a Swiss milkmaid. He would have been uneducated, and his life would have been drudgery. So the choice, however romantic or arbitrary, of the person with the money and power made all the difference. Alternatively, if my father took my mother to London and made her his mistress, our lives would not have been much improved, but I would have existed. We all know how bastards are treated in England, right? We choose to treat those innocent babes are lesser, even though they have done nothing to earn that designation. We do not treat people well in our society. I fear we never will."

Martha kept her chin level and considered Serena's speech. "Why don't others recognize the slippery nature of their situation?"

"Why on earth would they? They are catered to from birth. Imagine being told from the day you are born how special and important you are. An empire of delusions fueled with money and gilded with titles and lands rich for taxing. Each man in Parliament—hell, each member of the ton—genuinely believes that their own merit is the reason for their wealth and position. They are waited on by servants who are instructed to treat them as though they are royalty. They attend schools who teach them that the English are so great and so noble that their power should reach out and seize the raw material of civilization and rework it in their own image. And we do colonize the world, but for what purpose? We steal rich silks and fine teas, and we deliver English sensibilities and brutalities. I am fairly certain that Kenya or India or China were quite all right before we taught them the proper order for the silverware. However, when your education system is an endless propaganda for how eternally wonderful you are, the only rational implication is that you must conquer the world."

Martha giggled, maybe out of discomfort, or maybe at the sight of a woman riding on a high horse with a forkful of pickled ginger. "So the Percys are angry at the English education system, the entire class system, colonization, the justice system, the peerage system, and spoiling children. Is that all?"

Serena smiled back. She enjoyed this venting greatly, but Martha was probably at the far end of her tolerance. "Sadly, no. However, I will not begin to rant about the conditions and wages for laborers or the need to abolish landlords. Honestly, eliminating all inheritance would solve a great many ills, but too many people think the pittance they will receive is more important than the greater good. I do apologize. The injustice simply wells within me like a fire. It is not that I want to scream about it. But the fire does. Typically, I simply speak to Frederick until we both feel better, and then the burning starts again. I will try not to exercise my indignation upon you in the future. You are my friend and not a whipping boy."

"Worry not. It was enlightening. I had always wondered why your lord and ladyship were so animated, but now I see. Although his lordship often speaks about his frustrations in public."

Serena laughed. "Yes, lucky Frederick. He is the man, and he has the title and wealth. He can change the world, hopefully. I am expected to be quiet and find a nice husband so I can make babies and fulfill my duties. It is most likely for the best as Frederick is a terrific orator and I ramble in my emotions. I have witnessed far too many men proclaim that one has lost a debate by yelling or becoming passionate. I think if one can witness the deadly issues in our society and not become excited to the point of exclamation, something is deeply wrong with that person. How can you know that people are hurting without proper food or hygiene and not feel the fire? I feel ill-suited to the world I must live in, but I have no choices."

Martha smiled and handed Serena a box of chocolates. "We could run away? They have a land program here. We could bugger off to Wisconsin and begin a utopia."

Serena's tongue tensed with the tremendous effort it took not to spit out the chocolate truffle. "I love the notion! I truly do. I have read a great deal about the various American utopias. My personal favorite was Fruitlands. I will think on the notion. Perhaps if I read enough and think on it long enough, my children could form a utopia. After all, reading and thought are the best stewards for such a grand design. I have decided to marry Lord Vincent, so I do not believe he would care to move to Wisconsin and begin anew."

Martha stood. "I shall inquire with the booksellers to find some books for you on the subject. My lady forgives my boldness, but you should not despair. You are correct that his lordship is very persuasive, as are you. I have never met a more tenacious family, and I know that someday the world will be much improved by you."

Serena let the silence linger as Martha left the room. Some truths demanded a hard silence in their wake. She did not feel hopeful, but she did feel better. It was easy to feel overwhelmed by the sheer volume of difficulties that lay within the world, but explaining and enumerating them made her realize that solving some of them would bleed over to the others. Once progress began, it would never stop. She might never live long enough to see a general strike or justice for the Chinese or Indians, but it would come. Someday. She had to believe that it would.

These pangs stirred within her, and she knew it was beyond her to resolve them. She must move quickly from her dissatisfaction. So she decided to write Honoria a letter.

My dearest Honoria,

Oh, my beloved friend, I have missed you so! I truly wish that you could have ventured to America with us, though I understand why it would be inappropriate. I miss our readings. There is no one for me to solve mysteries with, and I long for our endless talks.

I have decided, just this very moment, to marry your cousin Lord Vincent. I have been so wary of him due to his reputation, but he is the only man I would like to marry out of the many prospects we are mutually acquainted with. My darling, I am afraid I am overwhelmed with longing for his company. Before I departed for Chicago, he asked me in earnest to marry him. I thought perhaps he was teasing, but he asserted with actions and eloquence that he was serious. I have thought of the notion for countless hours since that day (well, it was only three days ago, so I suppose I could count the hours), contemplating a marriage to Lord Vincent. I have imagined the very worst result, but even the most treacherous nightmare seems much less likely than the possibility of a pleasant life with a man I very much admire.

I do keep trying to imagine him as a monster, but the hope of sunny Thursdays playing chess and bantering over the newest play intrudes upon every thought. We are simply too well suited not to wed. I genuinely enjoy his wit and adore our conversations. I could see us being quite great friends after the whimsy of youth has worn thin. I am aware that too many husbands grow bored of their wives and seek out the maidens in their clubs or mistresses, but even when he has abandoned the romantic with me, I believe we will maintain a friendship everlasting. But I will confess that the day he takes a lover, such a trespass will break my heart. For all my cynicism, I still hope for a perfect love that will last beyond the stars and shine brightly when they have stopped their light.

Oh, my dearest friend, I am terrified. The prospect of regretting a marriage haunts me. But should I not take my single heart's worth of risk, just the once? I have been forever timid, so afraid that one wrong motion will cause everyone to laugh and jape at me with such potent gravity that I will never recover. As the wife of the Malicious Mandeville, no one would dare laugh at me. Is it not virtuous to achieve a transformation because of love? Did Eros not change from the base attraction to a more elevated god when he fell in love with Psyche? I wonder what I shall become, or perhaps what the Malicious Mandeville will be. I'm afraid I am rambling, but you are the only person on earth that I may bare my soul to and expect perfect understanding.

I hope to marry whilst in America. I would so love to have you by my side on such a beautiful day, but I am certain you understand the necessity of a quick and quiet resolution of our courtship. My station (truthfully Frederick's popularity and title) would require an extensive guest list, and I would be unable to enjoy any moment of my wedding were I to wed in the Empire. A swift and quiet elopement in perhaps New York or on the ship home is perfect for me. I truly hope that Lord Vincent will agree.

Aside from all the hullaballoo of weddings and the philosophy of love, things are rather dull. I have been reading and enjoying the history of America. It would appear that the English arrived and that is when history began in America. Is that not the English way?

Sadly, Frederick has not found a wife, nor has he found any woman who can hold his attention for more than two days. Honestly, I fear Frederick will never find his bride as the list of requirements grows longer with every flight of fancy. Thus far he seeks a beautiful woman who is fashionable and clever. She must be of proper station but also have a great many interests. She must be able to tolerate his hatred of the upper class and the aristocracy but also be educated enough to argue with him. Where is this imagined creature? I don't believe she exists.

Benedict persists in his surly demeanor. I simply cannot understand what plagues my cousin, and I shall let that be.

We will be in San Francisco by October 15 if you should wish to write a return letter. Please extend my salutations to your mother, brother, and sister. I eagerly await our day of reunification.

Your friend,
Serena

As Serena melted the wax to seal her letter, she exhaled. She felt tremendously better, as she had gone far too long without a confidante to simply know her thoughts. These reflections had been bouncing in her mind and grown irritating. Exorcising them on poor Honoria had done Serena a world of good. She quickly read her letter before pouring the wax and pressing the seal. For the first time that she could recall, Serena was excited for the future and could not wait to see Vincent.

Chapter 14

I promise that I remain a proud member of the British Empire. However, Bourbon is a better after-dinner drink than Whisky. It is sweeter, which I crave after a heavy meal. And while I have never tried with Whisky, there is nothing better than a bit of Bourbon poured over vanilla ice cream.

A Curmudgeon's Tour of America, October 1885

Loretto, Kentucky

Vincent fell into the carriage and tumbled on the seat until he righted himself to the exact position he would have been in, had he been sober. He was foxed. Hell, he was drunk. He wasn't a mean drunk, yet, but the happy drunk of a night well spent. He and Berkeley were having a wonderful time touring the distilleries of America. They were sampling half the inventory. Not that the owners seemed to mind two solvent Englishmen drinking until their pockets were dry. Tonight, Vincent had purchased five barrels, which was but a pittance to Berkeley's fifty barrels.

"Do tell, Berkeley," Vincent began before reminding himself that he was not, in fact, a patrician schoolmarm. "What do you plan to do with all of this bourbon? Fifty barrels here, and then another twenty at the last distillery? I don't know much about your intended bride, but she cannot be that bad."

"Come the revolution, I am certain to be hanged or beheaded. I know my death might hurt the brave men and women who liberate fair Britain. I hope that they may have a drink in my honor." Berkeley grinned as he fetched a basket from the carriage. The remark captured him perfectly; he was a bizarre amalgamation of optimism and fatalism.

"Surely the Duke of the Workers will not be hanged," Vincent murmured. He did not want to be hanged, and if an affiliation with Berkeley did not spare him, nothing would.

"Oh, but I hope they would. God forbid they make me their leader and my heirs become *petite bourgeoisie*. Then my grandchildren might revert to capitalists entirely. The entire serpent's head must be cleaved lest the cycle begin again." Berkeley handed Vincent a toasted cheese sandwich as he spoke. It was cold, but it somehow was also exactly what Vincent wanted.

"Could you not simply bribe them to run off?" Vincent asked as Berkeley handed him a flask. Weary of more bourbon, he stuttered as he drank. He was in luck; it was a relatively sharp pear cider. He only half recalled the suggestion to get into a carriage. Good luck neither of them was driving.

"Ah, always have a backup plan. Yes, should I be able to flee, then I will take to the sea and become a pirate." Berkeley smiled as he tore into some fried oysters.

"You want to become a pirate?" How credulous must one be to think a sailor's life would suit a man with his lifestyle?

"I think that I would make an excellent pirate. I can

shoot and am a decent archer. I can sail, and I think I could find a crew to follow me. Pirates were the early communists. All for one and one for all." Berkeley gave a halfhearted cheer.

"That was the three musketeers." A gentle correction.

"Bootlickers. But the point stands. Bounty was always shared by the entire crew. And there were lady pirates. I am not romanticizing it, but as a useless noble I must do something with my life in a post-aristocratic world. I would be terrible at most professions, but I think piracy may be my path. This is of course with the aspiration that a revolution will come soon. It may never come," Berkeley argued. He seemed to understand he was mainly arguing with himself, as Vincent was transfixed on the cider and the toasted cheese, both of which were more appealing than expected.

Vincent chewed his sandwich. Berkeley was not wrong, but piracy seemed to be so outdated to his English mind. "Well, I may have to join your crew."

"Ha! I already have my first mate. But tell me, what about you?" Berkeley wagged a finger toward Vincent. "Why are you alone in America? And so soon after your tour of Europe. You were in London for all of three months?"

"I was going to marry a girl who prefers my brother. I take it that I have your confidence?" Vincent waited for Berkeley's nod. "She was eager with me. She seduced me on several occasions. It was she that initiated the first kiss and she that unbuttoned her dress and placed my hands on her breasts. I never expected a marriage-minded miss to suck my cock, but she did with wild abandon. I cannot believe she did so hoping to marry my brother. But the notion plagues my mind. And knowing her, she is seducing my brother as we speak."

"Even I knew you were courting Miss Haverford. Do you honestly believe that Coningsby would easily pick up your cast-offs?" Berkeley asked.

"Yes. My mother likes Marlene. Sebastian could not imagine a world wherein which he does not marry a young lady that my mother likes." Vincent spat the bitter truth.

Berkeley gazed out the window, and a heavy silence fell upon the carriage. "I know that you have a manner of perceiving the world that is colored by your past. We all do. However, as an older brother, I must ask you to consider that perhaps these are Miss Haverford's actions alone. I do not have brothers, and I cannot imagine a world where I would have to compete with Serena. But I do know the terrifying responsibility of being an older brother. I have watched Coningsby with you. He is as stiff and formal with you as he is with everyone else. But you are always on your worst behavior when you are near him. And yet, he never chastises you. He never derides you. If anyone speaks ill of you in Coningsby's presence, he very formally requests an apology. He allows you to have a wide berth so that you may flourish."

Vincent had a million sardonic retorts, but Berkeley did not deserve to be insulted. It was remotely possible that Berkeley was even correct. Berkeley had no reason to lie to Vincent. But this measured objective tone, coupled with an unsettling revelation, strained Vincent's will. "You could be onto something, but I have tried to write him. I produced the most measured response I could by screaming at him with written words. He has not responded. Not one letter to simply tell me how foolish I am for believing Marlene. Not one word from him to refute my allegations. Not one word. If he is not happily fucking Marlene, then what could possibly motivate his silence?"

"I don't know. You have been travelling. Perhaps he has had an issue finding you? Coningsby tends to become a statue when he is under pressure. Perhaps he is unable to answer as he does not know the words to write to you."

"I hate how reasonable you are. Stop it. We hate Sebastian and will only speak ill of him." Vincent pouted resiliently. After all, this was a terrible bind. If Sebastian was the monster Vincent knew him to be, he would have anger in his heart forever. If Sebastian was not, then their mother's high praise of him would be somewhat vindicated—which was almost as bad. And Vincent would have to be vulnerable enough to forgive and reconcile. Ugh. This was sobering. There was a remedy at hand for that.

"Very well, you four-year-old. Coningsby fills his trousers and eats mud. Happy?" Berkeley asked.

"I am, rather. Actually…" Vincent laughed. He should not say this, but once begun was halfway done. "When Sebastian was twelve or thirteen, he became fiercely private, particularly in the mornings. I had assumed that he was wetting the bed, but finally he explained that it was something entirely more awkward." Vincent rose his flaccid finger to become erect and laughed.

Berkeley laughed as well. "Oh, good Lord. The

painful mornings of youth. When I began to enter manhood, Serena was only five or six. She thought the sun rose on my smiles and set on my frowns. Her favorite method of waking me was to jump upon my midsection. You have no idea of how sweet she was at that age and how in pain I was as I calmly asked her for some privacy."

Vincent briefly imagined a five-year-old Serena. She would have been adorable. Blonde bouncy curls and vibrant blue eyes. She would have been curious and precocious. He half wished that he had known her before. Before she was wounded by the world and loss of her parents. But the woman he loved now had been shaped by her experiences.

"I suppose there are benefits to having only brothers," Vincent offered.

"Oh, most assuredly. My God, I longed for brothers. I would say Adrian has been a brother to me. We roomed together in school and became brotherless brothers," Berkeley mused. He was lurching a little forward when emphasizing. He might be a little intoxicated.

"What of Lake? He has no brother, and he seemed close to the family." This was an earnest effort to not ask if one of Serena's former suitors would be lingering in her life. After all, Lake was a suspected member of the Shadow Society, and therefore must be investigated.

"I like Lake. Truly I do. He wanders, but I would welcome him back as a true friend. And though it might be Serena's...not fault, but it is because of her that he wanders, he seems to have thrived in his travels. He is an exceptional man. He spends time with the starving artists and pays their rent or for their wine in exchange for their paintings. He sends them to the Duke of Southampton or myself to preserve them. We both have more space than taste, you see."

Vincent chuckled. "I should very much like to see these works."

"Absolutely. You will most likely be adopted into our little clan as well. Serena and I have so little family, but I have always wanted a large, nay, tremendous family. I simply began collecting people. After all, the family you have is not always the family you need. I think you need us, Vincent." His confidence was again both comforting and annoying. "I honestly cannot explain why your family seems to disfavor you, but they do, and we cannot force anyone to love us. Whereas so many other people admire you and call you their friend. It is time to make a new family and let your old one become friends." Berkeley swayed a little from the uneven road.

Vincent considered Berkeley's words. Perhaps it was because Vincent had drunk far too much, but it made sense. He could let his family simply not matter. He did not live with them and could be as polite to his mother as to any other woman who judged him. Seraphina would of course be enraged that he pulled away, but he would be in another house and would be unable to hear it. And his father was a wonderful man, but he was not a man that defended his son against his wife. His brothers…well, he could maintain a relationship with Ralph and Lily. It was time to mature beyond the childish need for his family's love and approval.

"Indeed. I should be happy to join your happy band of brothers. But, Berkeley, is your longing for a tremendous family the reason you desire twenty children?" Vincent snickered.

"Oh, absolutely. I have the best idea. Truly remarkable. When we arrive in Louisville, we should get tattooed. To forever solidify our bonds as friends everlasting." Berkeley grinned like a schoolboy.

"A tattoo? Are they not simply meant for sailors?" Vincent asked and let the idea warm over him. He enjoyed pointless rebellion. It was the easiest type of rebellion, with the lowest stakes. A tattoo would not revolutionize the world, but it would anger his mother.

"You wear a wristwatch. Those are meant for soldiers. Let us dream of a world beyond restrictions that only some classes can have certain things. I want the poor to own homes and be educated. Therefore, I will steal tattoos for myself," Berkeley declared.

Vincent reflexively shook his wristwatch to gaze upon its glassy face. He simply liked the weight of it and hated pocket watches. Too often, they were stolen, and they caused discomfort in his pockets. It was also annoying to have the dead weight of time sitting in a pocket, a tiny albatross. "Absolutely. What will you get tattooed and where will you have it?"

Berkeley flashed a toothy grin. "A lion wearing a crown with a crescent moon. I was thinking of getting on my right shoulder. What will you get tattooed and where?"

"Why a lion wearing a crown with a crescent moon?" Vincent asked. Honestly, it was the most absurd notion.

"My mother's name was Regina, hence the crown. My father adored lions. And Serena has always enjoyed the moon. She used to say she would marry the moon. I suppose she loved the mystery of it and that it would provide light in the darkest hours. But, again, what will mark your body forevermore?" Berkeley asked.

"A black swan." The words came easily. "I think under my wristwatch is perfect. I can have it at the ready to shock people."

"A black swan is perfect for you. I love the idea. A swan is such a regal creature, but we usually define the anomalies as lesser creatures. The only exception being a black swan. Brilliant idea," Berkeley flattered as he fumbled with a basket, clearly looking for something.

Vincent struggled to tell Berkeley about the Black Swan. He was desperate to tell his close friend, a man who was ready to call Vincent "brother." He wanted to confess that there was a secret society who had committed the year of 1885 to the downfall of the Mandevilles. He wanted to discuss the trial and the conspiracies. He wanted a friendship, just one, that was without secrets or competitions. Berkeley was a wonderful friend, and he deserved to know everything about Vincent, especially if Vincent married Serena.

But there was the rub. If Vincent confessed his entanglements with lunatics that would try to destroy him, Berkeley would never allow him to marry Serena. Vincent had never considered himself a coward. Rather he was calculating. However, the idea of jeopardizing his future paralyzed him. It wasn't loyalty to the Black Swan or the vow he swore. No, it was an all-encompassing fear of losing Serena and to a lesser extent, Berkeley.

Berkeley tossed Vincent a cushion and quilt. "Rest. We will be in Louisville in the morning."

Vincent struggled to sleep but eventually felt the

heavy rest overcome him. Once he was married to Serena and returned home, he would convince the Black Swan to allow Berkeley and Serena to join. Of course, he also needed to adjust his attitude toward his family. And he must ready his home for Serena. There was a tremendous amount to do, but he wanted to end his bitter heart and replace it with a happy one.

The moon sang a bright and seductive song through the carriage window, and turning toward her brilliance, he caught his own reflection. So much of his identity was cast in the image of the rejected son, the outcast. What reflection did he want? Could he reinvent himself as a different man? What would fill that space within him? The lonely child had grown into an acrid man. But he had an escape, and her name was Serena. He could never let her be burned by the fire he frequently spat. Being Serena's loving husband was endlessly better than being Seraphina's spiteful child.

****

His wrist stung and reddened with the new black swan tattoo. He had never known a pain so sharp as the tattoo but kept comfort that it was temporary. He was a fool. The burn lingered so pointedly that he pocketed his watch rather than risk any more discomfort. He did not even want to close his cufflinks, but to walk about with one sleeve unfinished? What was he, a dockhand?

"It looks brilliant, Mandeville. Does it still hurt? Because I must confess that my shoulder does not feel altogether right." Berkeley grimaced.

"Yes, it troubles me. If we are still bothered in an hour, perhaps we should see a doctor," Vincent mumbled. He could not recall if anyone had died of a faulty tattoo.

"Certainly. It is most likely the permanent alteration of our skin. But let's find a pub and ease the pain with some bourbon." Berkeley surveyed three ladies walking and moved aside to allow them to pass. He tipped his hat with a cheeky grin. "Ladies, are your names Sunny, Star, and Luna? Because you have all made a dark morning very bright."

Vincent briefly wondered if Berkeley had been dying, would he continue to flirt? Absolutely. This was a man who would tease the nurse on his deathbed. The women smiled brightly and giggled as they continued walking.

"How do you always gain smiles from ladies? I am as pretty as you, but they never giggle at my greetings." Vincent preened to demonstrate his allure.

Berkeley laughed. "I have yet to meet a human being that does not enjoy a compliment without demands. I simply give kind words and do nothing after. Women are exhausted by a courtesy that is only given with the hopes of extracting something out of them. I am unique, and therefore they chase me if they so choose."

"And yet you are without a wife," Vincent argued.

"Indeed. Although I have only been seeking a wife in earnest for less than a year," Berkeley offered.

"What of Honoria?" Vincent demanded. She was Vincent's cousin; any good man would defend their cousin. And Vincent would too.

Berkeley reddened. "Damn. Listen, I need you to vow secrecy for what I am about to tell you."

"Certainly," Vincent answered. He had never seen Berkeley off kilter before. The man typically exuded an unflappable nature.

"Honoria approached me the first week she was introduced. She wanted someone to chase suitors away and hoped I might pretend to court her. I agreed on the condition that Honoria befriend Serena. I cannot allow Serena to know that one of her closest friendships began due to my meddling. Honoria genuinely loves Serena now, but I believe she would have overlooked Serena if I had not intervened." Berkeley silently pled with his eyes for Vincent's compassion.

Vincent nodded. If he had not wanted to see Berkeley, then he too would have overlooked Serena. She was fair to successful in obscuring herself. "I understand. But did you not propose to Honoria?"

Berkeley smiled. "Of course. She's a wonderful friend. While I do not love her, I would love to explore her. She has a quality to her that I find ravishing."

Even Vincent had to admit Honoria was a teasing little vixen. "Why did she not want suitors? Is that not the goal of being introduced?"

Berkeley shrugged. "She was in love with another man and will not marry anyone but him. I never pressed as I did not wish to know. Our marriage would have been unsuccessful regardless. The Percy curse and all."

"Curse?" Vincent asked, hopefully without sounding too enticed. Curses were nonsense but great fun.

"Ah, the Percys can only marry for true love. It cannot simply be love but true love. If there is any doubt by whatever enforces curses, then the marriage will not occur. Several debacles on the way to the wedding have terrified my family. A great uncle once lost his head the night before his wedding." Berkeley lowered his voice for the last bit so as not to shock any nearby ladies.

"Surely you don't believe such a silly idea, do you?" Vincent asked, although what he wanted to ask was "Does Serena believe in this curse?"

"No. It is helpful, however. My grandparents were very loyal to my mother because they believed she was my father's true love. And she was," Berkeley answered.

"And how does the curse define true love?" Vincent inquired.

"Ah, that is the question. Is it a pure love? Is it a love that will enlighten one? Is it alchemical? I honestly have no idea. My father described it as life changing. He told Serena and me that we would know our true loves when we saw them. That we were bound with an invisible string to always pull us closer to our home," Berkeley explained.

Vincent said nothing but walked in step with Berkeley. That was precisely how he felt about Serena. He found himself longing for her and meandering north to be near her. He missed her eyes most of all. He could not imagine ever growing tired of her or not wanting to make her smile. She was his moon, forever chasing the darkness away. He had to marry her. It was no longer an option. After all, the curse threatened her very life if she didn't marry her true love.

Chapter 15

Chicago is the city of the future! Rail and river meet here to serve the rest of America. There are buildings so tall they kiss the clouds. It is unlike any other city that I have ever visited. There is a simultaneous earnestness and consummate grift. I know they are absolutely picking my pocket, but I am simply too beguiled to care.

A Curmudgeon's Tour of America, October 1885

Vincent stepped off the train into the hard cacophony of Chicago. Berkeley had continued to speak of his sister, further aggravating Vincent. It was supremely irritating to hear about something he wanted with the simultaneous understanding that he was being deprived of it. He did not understand why she had to separate from them, but without her, the world was a bit lonelier. Finally, they were in the same city, and he would see her bright smile at breakfast.

"Mandeville, do me a favor please. I need companionship, but I fear Serena will hear me. Would you mind switching rooms with me during our stay in Chicago?" Berkeley asked.

Vincent smiled; a room closer to Serena would certainly make his life easier. "Of course. I am surprised that you have waited this long."

Berkeley smiled. "I am certain there are brothels in

Charleston and Kentucky, but I could not find them. Chicago has a reputation for sin, and I plan on taking advantage of all she has to offer. The Americans ask for a man to be far too chaste; he must unburden himself or become more aggressive."

Vincent shrugged. "Not that Britain is better, but they live in near endless war. However, like England, they build great things. Look at this city! I heard they have a building that has ten floors."

"I heard the same, and the city is especially impressive when you realize they had a fire just fourteen years ago. I recall my parents contributed to the rebuilding efforts, financially, of course. It is tremendously interesting how this nation forms itself. Chicago, New York, and Boston are ports for the Irish. Similar to the Italians, whereas the north welcomes the Nordic immigrants. An entirely new land, yet they cling to the old clans and narratives," Berkeley pontificated.

Vincent shrugged as he entered the carriage. "I cling to your family. This country is too large to be alone in. One needs a community, and from what I have read, Americans can be unwelcoming."

"Your statement is dripping with irony. America is exceptionally large, but they felt the need to make the Indians move to small pockets. This is not the Americans' ancestral home, but they are weary of immigrants. They are the man who beats his wife, so certain she will be unfaithful, but unappreciative of what he has. I would hope the Irish or Italian immigrants will recall these times and keep it in mind when refugees seek their help, but I have little faith. The human memory is terribly selective and short," Berkeley lamented.

"Ugh, you are far too maudlin. You need companionship; perhaps Melgum will join you on your quest to find a lady," Vincent offered. He needed the simple amenity of a hot supper and a recent newspaper.

"I doubt it. Benedict has never once accompanied me. You are welcome to shadow me," Berkeley invited.

"No, thank you. Serena does not wish me to have a mistress in marriage, so I doubt it will aid my courtship to visit a brothel." Vincent tried to sound aloof, but in truth, he was tired of his hand being his only companionship.

Berkeley laughed. "Our family is unusual. We believe in love, and a life without love is banal and not worth any gold. I will have a thousand children with my wife because, when I find one, she will have a faithful husband."

"I am unfamiliar with Chicago. What are some of the sights we must see?" Vincent asked.

"It is a pretty city," Berkeley claimed as he peered through the foggy window. "But it contains both the villains and heroes of America. I believe the labor movement is strong here. They have had a few strikes already. But the wealthy are unscrupulous here more than anywhere. A friend who rallies for labor told me that a cabal of businessmen are conspiring to purchase the newspapers and either shutter them or remove the labor section and replace it with a business section. Can you imagine the common man wanting a business section of the newspaper? It's absurd."

"No," Vincent answered honestly. What was the possible relevance to the working man, struggling to feed his family, of the esoterica of real estate or dividends? "Are you certain that they conspire or is it simply a theory?"

"I cannot say with abundant certainty. I fear the speed with which we are mechanizing labor. What will become of the workers? How many will starve? Without unions, there will not be anyone to speak for the masses. The poor have but one advantage—they are the many. If we do not wish to see our homes burned and our blood color the streets, we must see their plight. But my fear for America is that they are fooled by the pittance of representation. They vote, those incredibly lucky few that can, and therefore they feel that they own part of this society. Until they see that they own nothing, they will not rise up."

"So, what must be done?" Vincent asked.

"Personally, I annoy people because I can annoy the right people. I also give unions material support. Meeting houses, money, and the like. We need to reduce the amount of production that we expect from each person. There are women who work in factories for crumbs, who give their children opium so that they can work twelve hours a day. If a woman could work six hours a day, she would not have to saddle her child with a debilitation so her family may survive. If we had a society where childcare was a public good, where a woman could be paid by the state to mind children, that would solve a tremendous number of difficulties, including the high death rates of poor children. This is not an issue of merely improving the lives of the poor, although it should be. Sadly, this is a life-or-death issue for far too many people."

"Fuck," Vincent swore.

"Indeed. It's a heavy issue and often a depressing one. Let's speak of something more gay. I hope

Benedict's play was successful. You are a critic. What did you think of the play?" Berkeley asked.

That was unexpected, so Vincent stopped to think. The only consonant memory he had was his jealousy about Serena's suitors. "It was a terrific rendition of *Macbeth*. Why did Melgum choose the cursed play?"

Berkeley shrugged, apparently sharing Vincent's confusion. "I could not tell you. I have learned, long ago, never to question Benedict's decisions. The man confounds me, but he is a good friend and my cousin. It was assumed for most of our lives that he would marry the daughter of one of his neighbors, but he decided to move to America. I could not explain it, but it is none of my concern. It is his life and his happiness, and as his friend, I should simply support him."

Vincent chuckled. "I would not have been so kind. I would have pestered him until the cows came home, demanding to know why he would abandon his family, home, and title for the unknown."

"Perhaps I should have. But Benedict is full of angst. I have never earned his trust as to why he is so unhappy, but he will tell me when he feels I should know. His father is healthy and spry, so he has perhaps twenty years before Benedict inherits the title. Hopefully, he can sort out whatever keeps him from his home." Berkeley grinned. "Ah! At last, we have arrived."

Berkeley leapt from the carriage and into the hotel. After the room arrangements were sorted, Berkeley left to find women for companionship. Hopefully, it was just one woman, but who knew? Vincent ensconced himself in Berkeley's room. It was far more lavish than Vincent's usual accommodation, but Vincent was not a marquess, and hotels tended to bring out the fanfare for higher nobility. The further America grew from the governance of London, the more they strove to prove that they could be just as opulent. Vincent ordered supper in his room—roast beef with horseradish sauce—and began to unpack his clothing.

Afterward, he reclined in a simple chair and grasped the wafery, yellow sheet of the Chicago newspaper. How delightful, the foreign section said all eyes were on France. *The Mikado* was playing at the Chicago Museum, which was Vincent's favorite play. Apparently, the last baseball game of the season would be played on Saturday, Chicago versus Philadelphia. Perhaps he could take Serena and they could cheer for opposing teams as neither had any investment in the game or the teams.

Across the suite, a door allowed a small amount of light and vapor in. How intriguing. Either there was an adjoining bathroom, the closet was on fire, or had Berkeley snuck back in with a hookah and a harem? An en-suite bathroom was a luxury, so Vincent was curious to see if it had hot running water and a flushing toilet. Vincent was personally against the idea of hot running water in his own home, as it was bad for the art, but he did like the idea of having a hot bath after a long day on the train. From the vapor, Vincent suspected the water heater was overworking and went to investigate.

Beyond the door was another world, heaven truly. The pure white room was filled with steam and lit by gaslight. It was warm and smelled of flowers and spices. Through the haze, Vincent spotted Serena in the tub. He was nearly certain that this was a dream, but like all proper English ladies, she was wearing a shift.

Even in Vincent's wildest dreams, he would never have her wear a shift when she could be naked and wanting.

She lay in the tub with her head resting on the lip and her eyes closed. Her breasts bobbed out of the water, the shift unable to obfuscate the dark contours of her nipples. Vincent knew that her breasts were large; however, he would have to splay his fingers to fully grasp them. Her waist was impossibly small leading to endlessly long legs. His fate was sealed in that misty moment. He would marry this woman and make her his for the rest of their lives.

"Martha, enjoy the play! I will be fine, stop—" She stopped when she saw him and immediately curled to refuge in the tub.

"Berkeley and I traded rooms," Vincent said awkwardly, but unfortunately his grin gave away his true feelings.

She nodded, the ends of her hair falling into the water.

He needed to touch her, and fortune favors the bold. "Well, my lady, you are already ruined. May I assist you?"

She should scream or throw the heaviest object she could lift at him. After all, any other woman would have. "Very well, my lord."

He hesitated for a brief second as he loosened his necktie; he truly would ruin her. And he would have to marry her, forsaking all others for the remainder of his life. He crossed the threshold into the bathroom. After all, he'd loved her from the moment he saw her and wanted her to be his wife. He kneeled at the tub, lathering a washcloth. He applied the cloth to the places his lips longed to grace, beginning with her neck but heading for her collarbone.

"When we are wed, I should like to do this often. I will instruct the servants to hide your clothes and keep you naked all Sunday long." He used the cloth on her breasts now, teasing and stirring her dusk rose nipples to hard peaks. There were two layers of cloth between his hand and her breast, but he relished the supple flesh contrasting with the taut peak.

"Sunday is the day you go to church," Serena breathed. She seemed to be enjoying this, and he gave a little squeeze to her other breast with his bare hand. God, yes.

"Sunday is the day of rest. I think of a day spent in bed with you as restful." He moved the cloth to her stomach. He longed to kiss her everywhere. To feel her flesh with his lips.

"It is the day of worship." She giggled as he ticked her belly. Oh, she was ticklish. When he was not mad with wanting, he would relish causing endless giggles.

"Oh, I would worship you. I was convinced you were an angel when I first beheld you." He let the cloth float away as he held her mound in his hand, reveling in her gasp.

"This is better than my dreams." She moaned, squirming against his hand.

Vincent's cock leapt at this revelation, as though it were curious to hear more. He parted her lips, allowing the water to tease her. "You dream of this?"

"Of you…oooh." She cooed as he pressed the pad of his finger against her pearl and stroked upward. She blushed faintly as she seemed possessed by pleasure.

"Tell me," Vincent purred, thoroughly enjoying the show. Serena's blush deepened, and she shook her head. Vincent pinched her bud gently, soliciting another moan. "Tell me."

"I dream of you seducing me, every night," she gasped.

Vincent rewarded her honesty by plunging a finger inside her and working her jewel with his thumb. He continued for a few minutes while he savored the little show. Would she always be so eager? If there was a good God left in England, she would.

"You take me from behind and whisper depraved words in my ear."

Vincent leaned in to kiss her, wetting his shirt in the process. He loved her utterly; it was as if they were once one soul now broken into two. She soothed him, healed him, completed him. Vincent doubted she would ever understand how every day she proved more perfect for him than he could ever imagine. The idea that she dreamed of him warmed his heart and intoxicated him.

Vincent removed his finger from inside her and cupped her chin. "Time to go to bed. I wish to whisper depraved words to you."

Chapter 16

I believe in frequent bathing, but not daily during winter. Daily bathing in winter tends to dry one's skin and leaves one feeling uncomfortable. Of course, there are certain lotions and bath mixtures one can use to compensate for that, but it is still best during winter to bathe every other day.

Aunt Penny's Advice for Living, October 1885

Serena had lost her mind. As she stood from the bath, the cold air walloped some sense back into her. The shift rained water back into the tub before Vincent removed it from her, leaving her naked and cold. In the tub she had been warm and intoxicated by desire; now she was shivering and sober to reality. She was ruined, and her interior life, her privileged quiet—as it once was—was over.

Serena had decided to marry Vincent during their time apart, and hopefully he still wanted her. One should never allow a suitor to get so far without signed settlements. But it was too late now; she had behaved like a wanton, and her anxiety was not going to alter what had already occurred.

While Serena had been fretful, Vincent had wrung out her shift and hung it. He had a large white towel in his hands and wrapped it around her. "There was an item in the newspaper advertising that this hotel only

148

has Irish linens."

Her eyebrows arched in befuddlement; why did he continually speak of the oddest things while she was compromised? Would he compromise the linens next? Would she be panting and wanting only to have him discuss import taxes? "Are the Irish known for their linens?"

"I have no idea. Ralph and Lily would know; he would know where the most profitable linens are made, and she would know where the most fashionable come from." He mumbled as he lifted her, with one arm under her knees and the other supporting her back. Serena melted into him.

"They suit very well indeed," she muttered as he laid her on the bed. Her right hand held tight to the towel as though it would protect her modesty.

Serena watched as Vincent undressed. His body was exquisite. Serena had seen several of her brother's friends while they would swim, but Vincent put them all to shame. He was muscular without being bulging. Bulging was distasteful. He had little hair, and what he had acted as teasing trails to parts she wished to explore further. She adored his back, and she felt the bizarre need to lick and bite it. She could not stop staring at his cock. How would he remain so erect when she was molten for him?

"I know you wish for me to take you from behind, and oh God, do I want to, but I think face to face will be gentler for you. I want you to enjoy this. After all, this is how I will bribe you to have naked Sundays with me." Vincent walked over to her.

Vincent approached the bed and leaned over to kiss her, exploring her mouth with his tongue. He teased her sex with his fingers once more, and she felt herself open for him. She braced herself. He did not enter her; rather he kissed her neck. Serena moaned as he continued stroking and licked her nipples, taking her peak into his mouth. There was something coming. She could feel it with every moan and movement, and she began to quiver and quake. It felt as though electricity were running up her legs and eventually struck into her like tiny lightning bolts made of blindingly hot happiness, sending explosion after explosion.

Vincent entered her during her rhapsody; she was aware of the entrance but felt little pain. He merely remained inside her, and she stroked his back coaxing a little hum from him. He began to withdraw, and Selena wondered if the act was over and if so, why so many people made such a fuss about it. However, Vincent began to pump in a steady fashion, and Serena found herself trying to receive him further. Vincent pinched the folds of her, and she felt herself seizing and moaning once more. This time the lightning spread and stayed, coursing euphoria through her veins, and she felt his cock spasm in her again and again.

Vincent, still inside her, kissed her. "You will marry me, won't you? It is a moral shortcoming to deprive me of you. I would have to notify your vicar."

"Really, I am the immoral one? You are the real interloper here," Serena asked from deep within her reverie. She wanted to laugh and roll about, giddy in her bliss.

Vincent retreated from her and used the towel she was lounging on to clean himself. Serena moved to see the small amount of blood, and Vincent folded the towel. "Oh, yes. You see, I have decided to worship you, and therefore denying me my practice of worship is unethical. Marriage would allow me sanctuary with my savior."

Serena giggled. "I would hate to deny an earnest practitioner, but why must you continue to discuss these odd subjects?"

"You overwhelm me, you blonde fox. I must either babble like an idiot or profess my need to be buried deep inside of you. I choose the former. Will you marry me?" Vincent asked again. He was equal parts lust and potency, and he wanted an answer. And she had the power.

Serena felt utterly wooed at the notion that she could overwhelm the Malicious Mandeville. "Yes."

Vincent leaned over her to kiss her deeply. "Excellent, we have much to discuss."

"Allow me to ready myself for sleep first." Serena padded into the bathroom, where she used her bathwater to clean herself before donning her nightgown. She grabbed her hairbrush, so that she might try to tame her mane into place for sleeping.

"I read an article on the train about tight lacing. You don't do it, do you?" Vincent asked as he tried to sort out her corset.

"I do. There is a misunderstanding of tight lacing. Some women lace so tightly that it may cause health problems. I lace tight enough to define my waist, but one should never feel restricted by one's garments." She breathed patiently and sat on the bed. She began to comb her hair, counting the strokes in her head.

"You have a lovely waist without a corset, but I respect your prerogative as to how you wear your own underclothes. I cannot even figure how one wears this.

Oh dear, I think I ruined the stitching." Vincent frowned at the pink silk. He had not, but perhaps it would be fun to let him dangle a bit?

But instead, she walked over to him. "No, that is just the covering. The baleen is the expensive and difficult portion; the decorative cover is made to be changed."

Vincent kissed her. "I am glad that I didn't destroy it. We need to discuss our wedding. Once Berkeley approves, we can discuss our marriage."

Serena returned to the bed and tucked her cold feet under the covers. "Very well, what should we discuss?"

"Halloween is my favorite holiday, so perhaps we should have it then," Vincent offered.

Serena ticked off her fingers. "Halloween is my favorite holiday as well, but it falls on a Saturday this year. Saturday is an unlucky day to marry. Maybe the fourth of November instead? Besides, November is a luckier month than October for weddings."

Vincent groaned. "I hate to put off our wedding, but I need all of the luck I can get. I am marrying the devil's bride, after all. Although it does appear my luck has changed."

Serena smiled. "I like it. We will have great fun at Halloween, followed by our anniversary, and finally Guy Fawkes Day."

"Excellent. We will marry on November 4th in New Orleans," Vincent announced. He was still oddly fixated on her corset; maybe he was avoiding the tension by not looking at her?

"I may not have the entirety of my trousseau by then. I hope you will not think badly of me," Serena teased as she stroked her hair.

"Impossible. I insist you buy an unbearable number of dresses and whatnot before we reach New Orleans. You must buy more trunks and haul a year's worth of clothing across the continent and the Atlantic Ocean," he commanded. He was fixated on spoiling her, which was quite new.

Serena giggled. "You know, Frederick will realize his error in the morning and ask to have your rooms returned. I hope the brothels of Chicago are decent. If he sees one woman who appears sad or distressed, he will spend the balance of the evening attempting to rescue her."

"How often does that occur?" Vincent asked as he snuggled in her bed, her head on his chest.

"More often than I would like. Frederick despises brothels, but he has needs. When he cannot find a merry widow or a wife of an incredibly old man, he must go to them." She shrugged off such actions, and her shoulders lifted up in dismissive arcs. Poor Frederick hated himself the next day every time. What a terrible toll he paid for his baser inclinations.

"And Berkeley saves these poor prostitutes?" Vincent chuckled. "He's a bizarre saint."

"He's not a saint." She tried, but failed, to avoid rolling her eyes.

"No, he is. I was losing my mind with wanting. One more day, and I may have begun to get irritated, like a man deprived of coffee or tea who is forced every day to smell the sweet temptations and still go on until dehydrated. However, I don't believe Berkeley is as enticed by you as I am, so he may not be drowning in temptation. How am I going to survive the three weeks without your touch?" Vincent kissed her forehead.

"Once we are engaged, Frederick will be more diligent about my virtue. It seems absurd, but he will feel the need to finish his duty. However, we will have sleeping cars twice before we reach New Orleans. You can sneak into my cabin," Serena offered.

"Hmmm. Yes, I will, although I am mildly annoyed at Berkeley for being a decent brother. I actively aided Ralph's seduction of Lily. Of course, Lily is not truly my sister, and I knew Ralph would adore her whereas Berkeley does not have the same trust in me." Vincent trailed off as it became obvious he was struggling to remain awake.

Serena snuggled into his chest. She hoped to always have these talks after lovemaking. They were in a cocoon for two where a pink mist fell around them. Maybe they would share a bed most nights. How unexpected and joyful. Warmth enveloped her, and she could hear Vincent's heart beat so steadily. She had never felt so close to another soul in her life. As she drifted off to sleep, she began to slouch away from him, but even in sleep he pulled her closer.

Chapter 17

The greatest tragedy befell me in Chicago. I was asleep in the most beautiful bed, and by force of circumstance, I had to remove myself from its pillowy softness. This is clearly the worst thing that has ever occurred to anyone, and I truly hope that someone erects a statue to my misfortune. The injustices of the world are minuscule compared to my hardship. I shall persevere for your sake. Pray for me, dear reader.
A Curmudgeon's Tour of America, October 1885

Vincent had slept better than he had in years, even if it was interrupted by an unwelcome return to his own bed at four in the morning. Things were lining up for him perfectly. Serena would be his wife, and most surprisingly, she was a fantastic bed partner. Vincent had found proper ladies to be so afraid of pleasure that they froze and were therefore not worth pursuing. Serena, however, could not resist her own satisfaction, which would make her the kind of wife every man would envy. Not that he would kiss and tell. He had always wanted to be envied, but with Serena, he might tire of every man in London coveting her. However, it was a cross he was prepared to bear. He really was a righteous man.

Vincent entered the restaurant and immediately saw Serena. "Good morning, all."

"Good morning! Mandeville, I despise myself for being so whimsical, but we must exchange rooms once more. I had forgotten my room always adjoins Serena's, and it would not be proper," Berkeley greeted.

"What if I marry Serena and stay?" Vincent offered.

Berkeley's laughter sounded out lightly; he clearly did understand the gravity of Vincent's words. This would need to be restated in a serious voice.

"I am serious. Serena finally agreed to marry me."

Berkeley cocked his head toward his sister. His tone was neutral, and his eyes were level and exactly focused on her face, unmoving. Not a single twitch. "Is this true, pet?"

Serena nodded. "Vincent spoke to me of marriage in both Pittsburgh and Baltimore. I spent our time apart to consider the proposal and then sent word to his room. I am pleased it was delivered to him and not simply left in his room, or you would have known before he did."

Vincent smiled at her. "Yes. Of course, there is much to decide. And the settlements will have to be negotiated."

"Frederick, please convince Vincent to marry me in New Orleans. I cannot bear the notion of a large London wedding with all eyes upon me. Please, darling," Serena pleaded with her brother. What a proficient liar; she would make an effective wife. He required a woman who would be a bit of a puzzle on occasion.

"I will agree to such a proposition, with pronounced hesitation. I will require that I receive an adjacent room the rest of our trip." Vincent smiled at her.

"But, pet, people will assume that you have been ruined and slander you."

Serena sighed. "They may, but better to return a bride than foster the implication that Vincent had to be forced by his mother and father to do the right thing. Whenever two people marry without the years-long courtship and engagement, there is always suspicion of bad behavior. Only the four of us will know what happened in America, and simply returning married after a few months abroad will leave the possibility that we had a whirlwind romance. People love a romance."

Berkeley ruminated on this idea. That was understandable; it relied on the gossips' romantic tendencies to outweigh their ambivalence toward Serena and, worse, toward Vincent. "But what of Grandmother and Grandfather? It would break their hearts not to be at your wedding. And Aunt Louise and Uncle Benjamin."

"I would be saddened by their absence as well. Perhaps when we return to England, we will have a small party to introduce everyone? I have only met Vincent's family once, so a reintroduction will be necessary. Would you feel better if you put an announcement in the newspaper? We plan on November 4 in New Orleans. Simply wire the papers to announce the wedding. With so much of a delay, hopefully gossip will have abated by the time we return," Serena asserted, slightly overstating the best-case scenario.

"I believe that would be a decent compromise. You have to marry someday, and Mandeville cannot be worse than his reputation," Melgum offered with the pretension of a smug cat. Vincent wanted to throttle him; however, he was trying to help. In his own snide, judgmental way.

Berkeley sighed. "I suppose. I will wire the appropriate people to announce the wedding and get Rose to draw up the settlements. I must demand my sister's time for a couple of days, as I have made arrangements for some surprises."

Vincent smiled magnanimously; after all, he had won. "Of course, Berkeley. You know I value our friendship, and you will always be welcome to intrude upon us. I am not striving to steal your sister but to join your family."

Berkeley brightened. Apparently, that was the winning way of framing this hasty endeavor. "Well then, we need to research how one marries in America. The states have their separate laws, so perhaps we should consult with a lawyer. And we need your trousseau! I saw an advert for new winter fashions, but as we are headed to San Francisco and New Orleans, which are temperate cities, I did not see a need to purchase winter items. However, given Chicago's proximity to the fur trade, perhaps we should purchase some pieces for your trousseau."

Serena smiled at her brother. "I think that will be excellent, but I have no desire to haul an entire trousseau about. Perhaps we should send pieces to your home in London, and we can collect them upon our return."

"Brilliant as always, pet. We will call out the banns, metaphorically of course, and begin to shop for your trousseau," Berkeley offered.

Berkeley had spent much of his breath since learning of the engagement conveying how important this private time with Serena was to him. Although Vincent wanted more of Serena's time, he knew the fear and panic that occurred when one's closest friend was marrying. "I think that will be delightful. Lily would skin me like a cat if I married anyone without flawless fashion. If we meet with her approval, she will simply buy Serena the world. But nonetheless, please fashion my bride. I shall spend the day arranging for our time in Chicago. *The Mikado* is playing, and I will get tickets for that if everyone is amenable. Or even if not. And apparently, the last baseball game of the entire season is in Chicago, so I thought we could attend."

The quartet agreed, and after breakfast, they went their separate ways. Though he yearned to be close to Serena, Vincent reminded himself that a calm and measured engagement would earn him a wife and friends for life. Vincent had not met the Duke and Duchess of Wharton, but he was certain he would enjoy them as he adored their grandchildren (even Melgum). It was customary for the wife to leave her family and spend time with her husband's family, but Vincent hoped for the opposite. Although, he must spend time with Ralph and Lily as well. Perhaps they would divide their time between their families evenly.

Vincent had won the greatest prize on Earth. He had genuinely enjoyed his time in America. Maybe he should purchase a house in Chicago, and he obviously had to return for the World's Fair (hotels were always busy for the World's Fairs, and he could host his family). But traveling forever with Serena had an immense charm. They could be known as "The World-Traveling Mandevilles." It would be a brilliant method of avoiding society without appearing snobbish, and he could write a sarcastic series of travel guides for people fleeing double-crossing brothers and traitorous paramours.

As he aimlessly strolled, enjoying the foreign streets of the Second City, Vincent could hear a scuffle down an alley. It was rumored that Chicago was full of con artists, but not violence. The reality of it shocked his senses. A familiar face, contorted in strong anger, snarling behind a clenched fist. Melgum viciously set upon the other man. Dull, melancholy Melgum? Savaging a man? Drawing blood, breaking his nose? Vincent stealthily crept into the ally, desperate to know whatever could force maudlin Melgum to violence.

"Where is it, Cameron? You will make them whole again!" Melgum growled at the bloodied man.

"My lord, you don't understand. I was blackmailed to betray them. I only kept the twenty thousand pounds. The Shadow Society kept the rest of Lord Annandale's fortune. I am so sorry for my part, my lord. I thought perhaps you would marry Lady Penelope and rescue her," Cameron sniveled. He was not fighting back, which made his words that much more sincere.

What an unexpected revelation! The Marquess of Annandale was one of the oldest, wealthiest, and most powerful titles in all of Britain. The disparate facts began to weave together in his mind. Vincent knew that the Shadow Society had attacked a family before his and left them well-dressed paupers. If it became known that Annandale was penniless, it would crash the market—perhaps send England into a recession. The realization swept through him like light splintering in a broken window. The Black Swan's reluctance to bring the first family into the fold, Melgum purchasing ladies' items (clearly for Lady Penelope's introduction), and the reason Amesbury was promoting Annandale's whisky. Vincent couldn't blame himself for not noticing the pattern; it was as absurd as it was superficial. But truly, Melgum involved in anything interesting was farfetched.

"Very well, you will return the twenty thousand pounds and tell me everything you know about this so-called society," Melgum sneered. How grossly intimidating this little, dainty gadfly could be when he was angry!

"Well, you see, my lord, I had to spend a considerable sum coming to America and starting a business…"

"How much is left?" Melgum demanded.

"Twelve thousand. And I left Lady Penelope's dowry intact. I never wanted to hurt them, especially Lady Penelope; she was so kind to my mother. They threatened to kill my mother unless I stole for them. I am her only son! She needs me!"

"Who blackmailed you?" Melgum asked. He handed Cameron a handkerchief to clean the blood off of his face. Even in his rage, Melgum abhorred uncleanliness.

"I do not know; the Shadow Society uses code names. I am the Mouse. I only know of the Dragon and the Spider. I can give you everything I have from them. I fled to escape them. If you found me, they mustn't be far behind." Mouse was an appropriate moniker.

"Relax, no one knows where you are. I recalled that your mother was friends with my mother's maid. I read her mail to find you," Melgum said coolly. So Melgum was a criminal and a pugilist?

"I expect better of a gentleman! That is fraud! And illegal!" Cameron puffed.

Vincent felt the irony ooze into the cloying Chicago air while Melgum stared in contempt at Cameron.

"Yes, well, has the family recovered? Is Lady Penelope decent?" Cameron asked, and Vincent suspected Cameron might have formed an attachment for the lady.

"No. You stole nearly every penny from them; they are crushed. Lady Annandale is ill and unable to leave her bedchamber. Lord Annandale is laid low in melancholy. Penelope is twenty and has yet to be introduced. Did you truly believe she would spend her dowry on marriage while her family starves?" Melgum was getting angry once more.

"No, I suppose she would not." Cameron cowered.

"Of course not. No, she used her dowry to fulfill her family's obligations. You knew they promised a school and a hospital for the people living in the village. You did not put forth the money—you stole it. She had to fund them out of her dowry. There are precious few aristocrats who will give to the poor, yet you robbed the best of them. This robbery will not just hurt Annandale but generations of people whose lives would be changed by their generosity," Melgum spat.

Cameron began to weep. "On my life, I am so sorry. Please beg their forgiveness."

Melgum rolled his eyes and seethed, his breath exhaling pure fire and anger. "Penelope is a better person than I. *If* you give me everything, and I mean everything with nothing held back, I may be able to convince her to forgive you."

Vincent sincerely suspected Melgum was lying, but hopefully Cameron would believe the lie. Vincent sneaked away; he would inquire with Melgum later. The best way to get people to part with secrets was a feeling of security. Melgum's temper would be too short to investigate today. Not to mention the normally docile man would be wracked with guilt and unease with his actions for a few days. Vincent would have to wait. Patience was a virtue, not one he possessed, but a virtue nonetheless.

As Vincent returned to the hotel, the subtle quirks of fate that shaped destinies spun through his mind. If Marlene had not jilted him, he would not have come to America where he met Serena and discovered the first victims of the Shadow Society. After the betrayal, his life was poised to be infinitely better than the life he would have had with Marlene's doddering cow eyes and oily hair. Should he thank her for refusing him in the most humiliating fashion? Ah, that was ridiculous. The idea that Marlene or Sebastian would ever get a kind word from Vincent was as unlikely as a talking dog or the dead walking the earth.

Chapter 18

It is necessary to be moderately informed of subjects in which one has little interest. I truly find golf to be the dullest sport. However, my father absolutely adores it, and therefore I have learned enough to follow his conversations on the subject of golf. In turn, my brother attempts to inquire after my hobbies. It is merely good etiquette and kindness to take interest in our loved ones.

Aunt Penny's Advice for Living, October 1885

Baseball was duller than cricket. It was so trite that Serena began to mentally list the sporting events that she preferred in order; tennis, rugby, bowling, croquet, football, cricket, baseball, and finally golf. Sadly, that only required four minutes. And upon reflection, this might have actually been the most boring afternoon of Serena's life, including the afternoon she had a cold and spent her bedridden hours trying count stones in her grandparents' walls. If only she had brought a book to read. Even a treatise on wheat growth would be more interesting than watching grown men chase about after a ball.

Vincent leaned over to whisper in Serena's ear. "May I come to your sleeping car tonight?"

Serena nodded, and her whole body awakened at the prospect.

"Do you enjoy sporting life?" Vincent asked as he handed her a bag of caramels.

"Not inordinately. I support and cheer for Frederick, but I find sport jejune." Hopefully, using obscure language would avoid offending any of the other observers.

Vincent snorted. Why was he laughing at her boredom? "I will bear that in mind when I find things to occupy our time in the future. Or make the balls bigger and the men smaller."

Serena smiled. If she understood Vincent at all, she assumed there would be more sport in her life, or at least more games. "Thank you."

"There isn't much sporting in Norfolk. Although I do believe you will come to love Nightingale Lodge, once we freshen it up a bit." Vincent was leaning in close to her, speaking softly as not to disturb the others.

"I can imagine. I adore nightingales. Do you have many of them?" Serena asked. She felt lighter, as though she was sublimating, losing all solid form, to become a mere vapor in his presence.

"Not a one, but I too adore nightingales." Vincent caressed her hand, sending electricity through her blood. It was absurd; they had made love, but she was titillated by holding his hand.

"Perhaps we should build an aviary and stock it with nightingales. We could have midnight picnics in summer with them serenading us." Serena could envision them under the stars and moon, kissing, touching, making love.

"If you desire an aviary, I will happily comply. Pity we cannot teach nightingales to sing *Moonlight Sonata*. And you promised to plant a butterfly garden."

Ah yes, she had agreed to that at the bookstore. "Frederick mentioned that your estate had hidden rooms?"

Vincent nodded. "My house was once the vicarage on an estate. My brother and I bought it from the Marquess of Cornwallis and divided it into two. Poor Ralph was unfortunate to have the big house. The estate once belonged to the Viscount Bindon, a man who was by most accounts more pious than wise. He built a grand house for his priest but was miserly on his own home. He must have had a lot to atone for! The result was a gilded vicarage but a crumbling manor. During the age of Cromwell's terror, the priests built hidden caches to hide men and other such things. I have only found one, but I feel certain there are more."

Serena shivered with excitement. Maybe she would find the fantastic there! "Perhaps we could begin a rumor that it is haunted and host a Halloween party every year. A house party where guests will be too frightened to sleep."

Vincent smiled at her. "Yes, Bindon haunts because he is outraged that two heathens live in his home for priests. And if we do not find hidden rooms and secret passageways, we will build them to always give the servants a fright."

"If we frighten our servants, we will not have servants for long. Party guests and visitors are fair game. We could build follies to resemble haunted houses from literature—the house of Usher, Thornfield Hall, the House of Seven Gables, and Victor Frankenstein's house. Is there a forest or wooded area nearby? We could refer to it as 'the forest primeval,' " Serena mused. Oh, to feel the excitement of being frightened and then soon after the feeling of being safe. She could never tell if it was the fear or the rush of safety that she loved more.

"There is a small forest separating the big house and the vicarage. I cannot believe Ralph was so correct," Vincent said as he brushed stray stands of hair from her face.

Serena couldn't help but smile; his mind was so creative and odd, and so, given her embrace of unorthodoxy, she loved it. "Please explain."

"My brother would woo Lily with talk of his estate, as he grows lavender and saffron. I thought it was foolish to speak of crops when poetry could be recited, but he was right. We are planning and building our future. I am excited for it is all." His eyes sparkled like he knew what she was feeling and was bubbling over with secret joy.

Serena smiled and turned her gaze back to the baseball game. She was hopeful for her future; it grinned with possibilities that looked wonderful. She had long been an admirer of Vincent's wit and prose, but to discover he was also a handsome man was exquisite. She had been afflicted by the curse put on her family, to always find true love. She hoped it would not be a curse, but a blessing. But Vincent had never spoken of love to her, merely wanting and compatibility. It was troubling, but there were worse fates than being madly in love with your husband while he only liked you. Or maybe there weren't.

After the baseball game, they took a carriage to the train station where Martha was charged with instructing the porters to arrange their rooms. Serena happily ate a supper in her sleeper—less lavish than her family's private cars, but neither she nor Frederick had thought it prudent to ship them overseas. After her dinner, Serena washed and began to ready herself for sleep. Martha appeared to know what awaited Serena, applying perfume to her knees and in between her breasts. She was dressed in her most flimsy nightgown, and the lights were dimmed.

After an hour, Serena realized that Vincent had not arranged for a specific time. He simply sought permission. If she found him snoozing comfortably in a chair with a copy of the newspaper, she would be positively devastated. The books she had available for her would not aid in her mood later. One rarely read *Huckleberry Finn* and felt the urge to be a wanton. An adventurous raft down a river to be sure, but not to do a bit of business. Sadly, Serena was not skilled in womanly arts such as embroidery or crafts and could not use that to fill her time. She settled for watching the world swish by as she dreamed of her life with Vincent.

At exactly ten o'clock, a knock sounded at her door, and she leapt to answer it. Thank goodness for this welcome punctuality. Vincent sauntered in and grabbed her, running his hand around her torso. One hand snaked up her back to run his fingers through her hair, while the other cupped her bottom. He crushed her into him and kissed her deeply. It was as though he thought she was not close enough if they were merely touching each other, but instead, they needed to be one.

"I promise you endless conversation, I truly do, but tonight I need you," Vincent whispered as he broke their kiss.

"Mmmmm, yes." Serena moaned as he kissed her neck.

Serena began to undress him, needing to see his body once more. Every new patch of skin she uncovered was greeted with a kiss. Vincent, apparently impatient, began to shred his clothing before removing her nightgown. Both exposed, he lurched at her, causing them both to fall onto the small bed. Serena giggled as Vincent righted himself, his hardness caressing her folds.

"God, you are a paradox," Vincent murmured as he licked her nipple and nibbled at it. "I have to have you all to myself—I am a bastard that way...I barely tolerate you having family or friends. However, your body is stunning, and you should be famous for it."

Serena blushed at the idea of any other man viewing her in this fashion. "I think one famous Mandeville is sufficient."

"God, you would be the 'Mesmerizing Mandeville,' if I could bear for anyone else to see you. I absolutely cannot and will keep you as the best secret in the world, but know that you are so, so beautiful," Vincent purred.

Serena moaned and bucked her hips, desperate to get his cock inside of her, tired of being teased. Serena loved the feeling of his weight on her and wanted him inside of her, relishing the stretching she felt. Finally, Vincent appeased her and entered, filling her completely. Serena had thought it would not feel so intrusive after her first time and would be easier, but it felt as thrilling as the first time. Vincent merely remained inside of her, leaving Serena hungry for friction and movement.

"So tight," Vincent murmured as he lifted her leg to his neck. "And so wet, how did you become so wet?"

He had both of her knees at his neck and began to thrust. Somehow, he felt larger as he slammed into her, causing a mild smacking noise.

Serena's entire body grew more aroused than she had ever thought possible. Her lips longed to kiss him. Her breasts ached to be touched. Her bud felt as though it had grown to peek from its hidden realm, hoping to be touched by him. Overwhelmed by desire, Serena gave in to her body's demands and ran her hands over her soft skin to caress her breasts.

Vincent's eyes flared as he watched her. He lowered her legs to wrap around his waist, forcing him to be closer to her. Serena could feel the building of her release coming and began to stroke her jewel. Vincent kissed her as she moaned and pulsated onto his cock, her legs pulling him in close. Vincent groaned in her mouth as he withdrew from her and spurted on her thigh.

Vincent broke their kiss as he lifted himself from her. Serena became aware of how messy she had become; a light layer of sweat covered her, and there was something drizzled on her leg. Vincent took her hands and helped her stand. He led her over to the small area with the sink and shower. Serena did not trust showers; they were unpredictable and temperamental, hot at times they should be cold, icy when they should be scalding. But she trusted Vincent. As he turned the shower knob, icy cold water erupted, spraying both of them.

"Eeee! It's cold!" Serena cried as she shivered.

"I can see that." Vincent seemed transfixed by her breasts. "Careful not to get your hair wet. I would hate for you to catch a cold."

Serena pulled her hair to one side and allowed the still-cold water to wash her. "We do seem to find ourselves constantly hygienic, don't we?"

Vincent chuckled and turned off the water. "Indeed, although I prefer you in a hot bath."

Serena dried herself and retrieved her nightgown. As Vincent dressed, Serena snuggled into her bedclothes. She felt relaxed and warm, understanding how people craved this feeling. She could not understand those who created love without being in love, but she understood the need to be loved. Vincent had never said he loved her, but she felt loved, and Serena wondered if that might be enough.

Once dressed, Vincent came over to her bed. "I am sorry that I have to leave, but your brother is diligent. However, every night I sleep without you merely hastens the days until we are wed. During our return home, you will not leave our cabin as I make up for this time. I believe two nights in bed there for every one apart here is a reasonable return."

Serena's heart warmed, and she kissed him. "That is a pleasant viewpoint. I was simply thinking that we could not both fit in this tiny bed."

Vincent laughed. "Good night, my lady."

Chapter 19

Personally, I find Paris to be over-adorned.
London has become cluttered. New York is too
structured. But San Francisco is the most beautiful city
I have ever seen. The ocean floats right up to the city
and meets a gorgeous bay. There are hummingbirds
here. Creatures so beautiful that I almost mistook the
little bird for a fairy. It is truly magical.
A Curmudgeon's Tour of America, October 1885

Vincent hastened to the breakfast room of the
Palace Hotel in San Francisco. He had slept too deeply
and too long, but his bed was the most comfortable he,
or any person, had slept upon. The Palace Hotel was
reported to be the largest, costliest, and most luxurious
hotel in the world. While Vincent was not an expert in
the actuarial sciences, he certainly felt as though he
were in a palace. The hotel even had lifting rooms,
complete with a sofa, lamps, and plants, to lift you from
one floor to the other, although Vincent was not
confident enough to ride in them.

Berkeley waved him over to the table, grinning at
him. "Finally, Mandeville! We feared that you had been
shanghaied."

"Happily not. I am afraid my bed was too
enjoyable," Vincent returned, secretly wincing over the
fear that his poker face was not capable of restraining

his fulfilled smile. He had been with the Percys for over a month, but every breakfast was pleasant and a wonderful beginning to delightful days.

Serena nodded in agreement. "Indeed. I wonder if we would be able to purchase them to bring them home. I certainly understand why this grand hotel cost five *million* dollars to build. The maid told me that the hotel hired ladies to wash the coins so as to not soil my gloves. At first, I thought it was ridiculous, but then it occurred to me that it would provide employment for infirm women who must need money."

"It is exceedingly opulent, and I wonder if they are gilding the lily. This city is beautiful enough. Mandeville, I require a day alone with my sister, as I have a promise to keep," Berkeley requested. This humbleness was uncharacteristic of Berkeley.

"It is a dagger to my heart, but I cannot allow a broken vow on my conscience. Perhaps Melgum would like to visit the import shops with me?" Vincent invited. Surely that might create an atmosphere lending itself to honesty.

"Certainly. Perhaps we might find some Chinese silk. Or one of those Japanese robes," Melgum answered. Something soft for a man with a hidden rough side?

"Absolutely, I am given to understand that the Australians export to San Francisco. We may inspect a few jewelry stores for opals." Vincent winked at Serena, winning a smile and a pretty blush.

After breakfast they broke into their pairs for the day. Vincent grimaced at the idea of spending the day free of Serena, as he had grown accustomed to her smiles and charm. However, he needed to isolate

Melgum to inquire about the Shadow Society. Also, Vincent needed to get Serena a ring and some other gifts to overcome the guilt for proposing and bedding Serena without a ring.

Their first stop was a silk shop, where Melgum bought several bolts of scarlet silk. Vincent tried to stoke a conversation that might lead to the Shadow Society. "Beautiful silk. Is it a gift for the lady you bought the pamphlet for? Lady Penelope?"

Melgum nodded. "Penelope has ebony black hair and aquamarine eyes. Every shade of red gives her the air of a queen."

"You paint a ravishing picture. I had heard of a lady whose introduction was delayed because her family was betrayed. Oh, but you mentioned she has been caring for her sick mother. Let's shop in here." Vincent nodded at a shop.

The shelves he passed were lined without much care or consistency. He set about in curiosity, finding an abundance of items for Lily and her baby. He even found a few gifts for his mother. He stopped short for second in shock—how much had his resentment waned because of Serena's presence? For Serena, he had to be careful not to overindulge. She would be trying to fill her trousseau and might feel overwhelmed. Regardless, Vincent was fond of Japanese parasols and fans, so he would simply have to keep them until they returned to London.

As they shopped, Vincent watched Melgum carefully. Melgum purchased shrewdly, only purchasing items that would help a lady find a husband. Lady Penelope would have to have the dresses tailored, but he bought fashion plates and silks. It was clever;

with a luxurious wardrobe, no one would suspect that Lady Penelope was penniless. Only the suitors that made it to the settlements would be the wiser, and if they refused, people might not believe the jilted suitor of a beautiful woman.

"Mandeville, the lady you spoke of, what became of the family?" Melgum inquired as the left the shop.

Vincent shrugged, trying to appear aloof. "I am uncertain, although I am curious. The same collection of rogues attacked my family this summer."

"Are you certain? Who are these villains?" Melgum asked.

"From what we can gather, they are a conspiracy of people who desire revenge on some of the highborn families of Great Britain. I belong to an opposition group, if you can call it that. A collection of money, egos, and secrets is a better term for it. We know there has been another family ruined by them. However, that has been kept secret," Vincent explained. "Ah, my dear Serena needs a ring before we can wed. Will you assist me in choosing one?"

"Absolutely. Mandeville, I feel that you and I have a common foe. May I trust you as a confidant?" Melgum asked as he hastened to keep in step with Vincent. He dropped his voice so low that he had to keep close to be heard.

Vincent slowed his pace. "Of course. We are to be cousins after all."

Vincent congratulated himself internally. Huzzah for getting the secrets in a single afternoon! It was unnaturally simple for him to puppeteer everyone. People with secrets carried them like a burden and always were desperate to share. People were also prone to feel obligated to reciprocate. Therefore, share a secret to win a secret. Oddly enough this did not translate to favors. The trick with favors is to ask for a favor, and then people will feel invested in you and do more for you. Vincent had made a study of manipulation and was finally able to use it for the betterment of others. And for personal amusement. Either way.

Melgum exhaled. "Penny, Lady Penelope, is indeed the lady you heard of. Her father's steward was blackmailed to embezzle all of Lord Annandale's monies."

"Are you certain it was the Shadow Society?" Vincent tested. Once one broke a confidence, they were desperate to gain a trust. If you doubt them, they will reveal anything to convince you to believe them.

"Yes. Cameron, Annandale's steward, gave me everything he had regarding the Shadow Society. Also, the Shadow Society sent Lord Annandale a letter announcing their misdeeds, but Penelope intercepted it," Melgum explained.

"That is tragic. How much did they steal?" Vincent asked. If only Ralph were here; he had a better understanding of how upper-class men managed their money. Vincent believed that most men's wealth was valued by their land holdings, and they were extended credit based on their holdings. Few nobles had the majority of their fortunes in the bank.

"Around five hundred thousand pounds," Melgum answered as they crossed the street.

Vincent struggled not to react. Almost no man just had that much money lying around. Men with that sort of money invested it as his father did. "Annandale had that much to be stolen?"

Melgum shrugged. "It was opportunistic. Annadale had a return on investment of some sort and had the money to disperse. He had promised a school and a hospital for the area, and Penelope wanted to rebuild Annandale Hall."

Vincent considered the raven-haired beauty in a crumbling castle. It was the kind of story Serena would devour. "They left the family penniless in a house desperate for repair?"

"No! No, Annandale Hall has not been inhabited for two hundred years, and the tenants have pilfered from the house until it is an actual pile of bricks. Penelope convinced her father to rebuild the hall as a pet project. With the queen spending so much time at Balmoral, Penelope thought Annandale should improve every estate from the houses to the cottages."

"Indeed, the queen might not like to look upon downtrodden tenants with shabby cottages. How is Annandale faring with two estates and no capital?" This was a riddle. Estates could be profitable but often needed to be exploited to turn coin. It was why so many gentlemen needed to marry money, to maintain their estate, which was illegal to sell.

"Three estates. Annandale and the family live at Clova Keep, but there is Annandale Hall and Hartfell Castle. They are not thriving, but they are surviving. Penelope has an understanding of estate management that would rival any man's," Melgum answered.

"Why did Annandale not sell one of the estates or take on credit?" Vincent asked. Truly this was the simplest avenue.

"Penelope refused. She decided that the Shadow

Society was trying to either buy one of the estates or have power over Annandale through debt. Instead, she convinced my father and some of the other gentlemen in the area to invest in the school and hospital with her. The cottages were repaired but not as improved as she would have liked, but Annandale Hall remains in ruins," Melgum lamented.

"Where did she find the money to fund this?" Vincent already knew the answer, but it seemed the logical question to ask.

"Lady Annandale always dreamed of Penelope being a duchess and insisted on a dowry to purchase one. It broke her heart when Penelope spent her dowry on her family. Their estates are profiting, but I worry terribly for Penelope," Melgum mourned as they entered the jewelry store.

"From what you say, I think Lady Penelope is the one person you should not worry about. I will ask Lily to play matchmaker for her. Lily will outfit her well," Vincent offered before perusing the jewels. He had teased about opals, but there was too much choice to narrow his taste to just one gem.

Vincent had never been particularly good at buying jewelry, as his former mistress had informed him on every occasion. He tended to choose pieces that brought to mind the woman he was buying for, rather than the most expensive items. As Vincent surveyed the shiny rocks before him, he was unable to stop staring at a brooch. It was silver and diamonds, in the shape of a crescent moon with two silver stars. It was perfect for Serena. She was his moon and stars, so she was the only woman who could wear it.

"Mandeville, the rings are over here," Melgum

called. "I believe Serena would prefer a halo ring."

Vincent had no idea what a halo ring was, but he looked at the rings Melgum was gesturing toward. Vincent rather liked the idea of his angel with a halo. An atheist with a halo was also delightful. He knew instantly the ring he would have to buy her when he saw it. It was a white opal with blue and purple veins surrounded by diamonds and set in gold. It was ideal, not too ostentatious, but elegant, nonetheless. A happy medium of fighting excesses. Much like Serena.

After Vincent purchased a wealth of jewels for his lady, he and Melgum found a coffee shop to sit at. Vincent cast a leveling gaze at Melgum. "Alas, Melgum, is there anything more I should know?"

"I am certain there is, and I am certain I will forget to tell you some things. The letter intended for Lord Annandale instructed him never to allow Penelope to marry me. Penelope and I were never to wed; it was but a rumor," Melgum answered. How had Melgum not bought himself the silks after everything?

"The Shadow Society cared whether you married Lady Penelope?" Vincent asked. Why did the Shadow Society care so much about marriages?

"They wrote that if we wed, I would not survive the wedding day. We will obviously never wed. Penelope discovered Cameron, the steward that embezzled from Annandale, was in Chicago and asked me to find him. After some persuasion, Cameron gave me everything he had regarding the Shadow Society," Melgum explained evenly. Perhaps here there was enough privacy to speak in a gentleman's proper tone and volume.

"I assume he did not have the five hundred

thousand pounds?" Vincent asked, refusing to tip his hand.

"Twelve thousand pounds. Not even enough to cover Penelope's dowry. However, Cameron revealed that he'd sent the remainder to a bank in New Orleans. I hope to find a name or some clue to restore the family," Melgum said.

Vincent sipped his coffee and contemplated the irony of all roads leading to New Orleans. Serena believed her parents' murderer was there, and now the Marquess of Annandale's fortune might be there. Vincent felt that his whole life was leading to a small southern American city. He could finally defeat the man who threatened his family and be the beloved son once and for all. He could solve Serena's mystery and win her heart for all time. And he would wed Serena in New Orleans and be the most envied man in London. New Orleans held all his desires. How coincidental.

"Well, I suggest you pressure Berkeley to hasten to New Orleans," Vincent suggested.

"I will try, but you must understand how difficult this will be for him. For nine years, he protected Serena and cared for her, with almost no one else. I suppose it is the way a doting father might feel. If you spend a decade in one role, it is painful to see its end. Even the lifting of a heavy burden can bring the pain of its absence." Melgum frowned.

"I do understand," Vincent mumbled. Without Ralph to coax along, he had felt a bit rudderless.

"I think he is nervous about you specifically. Serena is anxious and constantly fears the disapproval and deprecations of others. When she was introduced, Lady Margret spread a rumor that Serena padded her corset. Which, if you have examined Margret's bosom, you understand was an immense irony. Serena cried in her room for days, and Frederick had to plead at her door so that she might eat. They have endured much and have learned that the only people they can ever truly rely on is each other," Melgum explained. What a terrible thing to learn.

"I would like to join them, not tear them apart. I will join Berkeley in his protection of Serena!" Vincent announced. Someday he would get Serena to write a list of every person that had wronged her, and Vincent would unleash his gift for insults upon them. There would be insults worthy of Chaucer. Rumors that would make the pope blush (even one of the interesting popes). After all, he would need somewhere to pour his reserve of derision.

Chapter 20

Yesterday I was inspired to have an autumnal picnic. I filled my basket with lovely goodies and set off to the nearest pond. I do love a picnic in spring and summer, but watching the leaves fall while eating spiced apples may be the cleverest idea I have ever had.
Aunt Penny's Advice for Living, October 1885

Mauve and pink butterflies danced above Serena's head as she twirled the parasol. Today was the most perfect day she had ever experienced. Even now, she lazily reclined in the idyllic rowboat while Vincent rowed them. The weather in San Francisco was so temperate it felt like May in October. Serena could not imagine a more beautiful place than this, and in this moment, she reveled in a found paradise.

Yesterday had been spectacular as well. Frederick had taken her swimming in the Pacific Ocean, which was so stunning a blue it felt unreal. After their swim, they rode a cable car around California Street and Market Street. Frederick hired a photographer to take their portrait atop Nob Hill, with the bay in the background. He ended the day by taking her for a lavish twelve-course meal and presenting her with a gadget cane, a gout stool, a grand jest.

However, Vincent knocked her up quite early this morning and presented Martha with a dress he had purchased and the adorable parasol. The dress was a fashionable cream color with a China blue pattern screened onto the fabric. Once she was dressed, Vincent whisked her to the Woodward Gardens to tour the aquarium, greenhouse, and zoo. They enjoyed a picnic in Golden Gate Park (where Serena ate more than she really should have, but Vincent had made her skip breakfast) before embarking on Lloyd Lake.

Serena noticed this was Vincent's first foray into the exercise of leisure boating as he would, on occasion, row as though he were in a race. It was endlessly endearing.

"Is there a lake on your estate?" she inquired.

"No, there is not. There is a river or creek; I cannot differentiate between them. There are a few ponds. Would you like a lake?" Vincent's blue eyes twinkled in the sun.

"Perhaps. I cannot recall a happier moment and may wish to recreate this." Serena sighed and gazed at a duck, trying to imprint every detail into her memory. It was truly rare to know the days you would always want to remember in advance of the hardships that demand such recollection.

"Truly? Well, I will have a lake perfectly made for you. We will row every day," Vincent declared with the confidence of man who genuinely believed in what he was saying.

Serena giggled. "We cannot *every* day. Winter would freeze the lake."

Vincent snorted. "Pshaw! We will merely have the groundskeeper set it on fire every morning it is frozen. Or buy a sled."

"People will think us mad!" Serena laughed.

"Nonsense. We are the wealthy descendants of dukes. We are the products of intermarriage between cousins for hundreds of years. Naturally, we are eccentric. Better this than inconstant religious warfare. Now, tell me which of the exotic creatures did you like best today?" Vincent grinned impishly at her. He was impossibly handsome.

"The otters. I adored the way they ate and swam. It was as though they are spending their entire lives staring at the sky." Serena sighed, thinking of the little furry beasts.

"I don't think I can buy an otter pup to bring home with us. Such a pity, I would like to give you a gift for our wedding day." Vincent frowned.

"I will be marrying a man who will purchase beautiful parasols and lovely dresses. What more could I ever want?" Serena asked.

Vincent's face darkened. "You deserve more. I am a terrible person, and I will hurt you. I have to make you happy."

Serena did not know how to respond to his statement. They were so alike, forever believing their critics but ignoring their admirers. Serena did not know the magic words to help him understand that she loved him and wanted him to be himself. She adored the Malicious Mandeville as well as the man trying to row a boat. However, if Serena knew how to unburden oneself from criticism, she would have healed herself years ago.

"Oh, Vincent. You will always find a way to make me smile." Serena attempted to flirt. "And if you cannot make amends, I suggest gifting me with parasols. You have a talent for finding ones I will adore. I am smitten with this one and fear I will damage it in overuse."

"Ah, I may have something less fragile. Please, hold the oars, but for God's sake, do not row! I would never live down the humiliation of having a woman row me about. Although, I would look fetching holding the parasol." Once Serena had the oars in hand, Vincent fished a black velvet box from his jacket.

"Oh, Vincent!" Serena cried when she saw the brooch as her hands flew to her face.

"Goddammit!" Vincent dropped the box to rescue the oars from falling into the lake.

Serena knew she should apologize but instead picked up the box and wiped away her tears.

"Oh, Serena, I am sorry I swore. Please don't cry."

"Oh no. Vincent, thank you! Did you have it made here? I did not think Frederick even remembered." Serena gazed at the brooch. This was a crescent moon with two stars set with diamonds. Her mother's had been a moon in sapphires with three stars made of diamonds.

"I am confused. I spied this yesterday, and it made me think of you. However, in your version I am immensely thoughtful, so please tell me what I've done." Vincent smiled as he pinned the brooch to her dress.

"My mother had a brooch like this, a gift from my father. After they died, some of her pieces went missing, most likely taken by one of the servants. None of the grand pieces, but some of the smaller ones my father gave her to make amends after an argument." Serena fingered the brooch and smiled at the memory.

"Your parents argued?" Vincent asked, amused.

"After every social event. I recall when I was

seven, some society matron discovered Frederick was 'a guest' at Mother and Daddy's wedding, and they ravaged Mother's reputation," Serena lamented.

"Scandalous, how old was he?" Vincent accidentally splashed a swan.

"Frederick would not be born for another six months from their wedding, but that is how our father phrased it. It was difficult for my mother, and she longed to retire from society. However, Father believed the heir to a ducal title should make his presence known," Serena explained as Vincent helped her from the boat to the small dock.

"Your father was most likely correct, but that doesn't make it right. It most likely pained him to have to humiliate your mother." Vincent offered Serena his arm. "Rest assured that I would never force you to attend anything you don't want to, unless my mother is hosting."

"I know you wouldn't and thank you again for this brooch. It means the world to me." Serena squeezed his arm.

"Even with the unpleasant memories?" Vincent asked.

"They aren't unpleasant. My parents always reconciled, and my father would buy my mother a piece of jewelry to demonstrate that the humiliation the ton inflicted only made my mother richer. In every way," Serena answered.

"I think that I would have liked your father," Vincent said, leaning in close to her as though they were sharing a secret.

"Oh yes! He was very much like Frederick; even his enemies liked him. Had he been alive to inherit the dukedom, he would have been a lion in Parliament," Serena recalled wistfully.

"Was he as progressive as Frederick? Equality for the Irish, votes for women, and better laws for laborers?" Vincent asked as he helped Serena into the cab.

"More so. Both he and Mother dreamed of a more progressive Britain," Serena said as he sat next to her.

"I hope they would have liked me."

"Mother would have *loved* you. You most likely would have embarrassed those hurting her. Father would have pretended to disapprove of you while allowing us to wed," Serena mused.

"Your father would have seen how I felt about you and hated me. He would be right to do so. Sometimes it makes me hate myself to think of such a proper young lady in such a way," Vincent whispered a little too loudly. But no one was around to hear except the two of them.

Serena wanted to ask exactly what her father would have seen. However, at that moment, Vincent kissed her, and the thoughts fled into the harsh winds. He kept her mouth busy until they returned to the hotel before leaving her dazed in a cloud of bliss. It was not until she returned to her room that Serena realized Vincent never said he loved her, or even that he liked her. Merely that they would suit. A man so verbose who would not speak his feelings was a bit queer. And of course, there was always the specter of Miss Haverford haunting her. At his heart, did he care, or was this an elaborate performance to secure her hand?

****

Sebastian Mandeville entered his mother's house at

ten to seven. Hopefully Ralph and Lily would be late for dinner. He had promised Ralph that he would speak to their mother about Lily's fragile condition. It was alarming now. Her ills were so palpable even her bravest face could not disguise them. Whereas most women spoke of a glow, Lily had a gloss of sweat. Sebastian could hear her being sick all day long. If she did not survive this pregnancy, the tragedy would rewrite Ralph's character overnight.

Mother was still in her bedroom, and Sebastian burst in the room. Mother immediately chastised him, but that was the most overdetermined outcome. "Good Lord, Sebastian! You nearly frightened Humphrey to death."

Sebastian nodded an apology to his mother's lady's maid. "Mother, at dinner you must be extremely nice to Lily. She is unwell."

Mother frowned. "What is the matter with her?"

"She is sick all day, and she sleeps to excess. Ralph is panic-stricken that she will not survive childbirth. We all must be kind to her and gentle with her," Sebastian pled. Perhaps saying we and not you would ease this criticism.

"When does the doctor believe the child will come?" Mother asked.

"He said they should expect the child around May," Sebastian answered, confused.

Mother ticked off her fingers. "The early stages of pregnancy are the most upsetting, but she should be over the hump. This is quite disconcerting, but we all must present a happy face."

"If I may, Your Grace, my mother is a midwife for our village," Humphrey spoke. "Lady Ralph is quite young and was…pure before marriage. They tend to have harder times but can recover quickly."

"Ah, thank you, Humphrey. I will try to make Lily's life easier, and we will all hope she recovers well. Shall we?" Mother stood and took Sebastian's arm. Her frown had disappeared, but she had hardly changed expressions. How much power there was in the sparse centimeters between a frown and an enthusiastic smile.

As they descended the grand stairs, the halls echoed with the boots and bustles of Ralph entering the townhouse with their cousins in tow. Ralph had been working closely with their cousin Adrian Rose, but why were Miss Rose and Miss Aurora Rose also present? It was poor decorum to simply pay a visit at a planned supper, unless there was an emergency. Sebastian's heart pounded loud enough to almost hear it. Could it be something with the Black Swan? If only people would simply wear signs announcing their problems.

Adrian Rose and Sebastian had always had an uneasy relationship. From the moment they met, years ago at Eton, they had been competitive. They competed on nearly every level. Adrian had a silver tongue and easy good looks. He was far more intelligent than any man Sebastian had met and twice as ambitious. In truth, if Sebastian had ever known that Adrian was his cousin, they might have been friends. But that was one of those things that his mother had chosen to hide from him.

Honoria Rose was a Gordian knot of a person. Sebastian had no idea which end to pull at with her. She was beautiful, even with her unfashionable bright red hair and smattering of freckles. But even her secrets had secrets, as far as Sebastian understood. She always wore too deep a smile, implying she knew your secrets too. How tragic that Vincent could not simply marry her.

The youngest of the Rose children was little Aurora. Aurora had chocolate brown hair and bright luminous eyes that shone like twin jade stars and took up the whole of her face. Like her siblings, Aurora seemed far too intelligent and pretty to trust. She was slated to be introduced this year. It was hard not to feel pity for her future suitors. Aurora would bat men about the way a cat might play with a mouse.

"Has Lily arrived yet?" Ralph demanded.

"No," Sebastian answered.

"Good, we can ease her into it. Vincent is getting married," Ralph announced. Oh, holy mother of God.

"What?" screeched Mother in a register that a studied soprano could barely meet. If Sebastian knew anything, it was that his mother didn't say the word "what." She also did not screech, though. Vincent would have enjoyed this level of irony more than anything in the world. How very unjust that he caused it but was not present to witness it.

Adrian sighed. "I received word from Berkeley that I should begin with the settlement process. He would prefer if we finished before the wedding. My sisters and I would like to attend the wedding and would like to finish this soon."

"Why did he not tell us?" Mother was aghast and seemed near swooning.

"There have been problems with the telegraph service coming from America to our home. Rose most likely got lucky," Sebastian explained. Hopefully that was the cause. The alternative was significantly worse.

"I had forgotten about the problems with the telegrams." Ralph smacked his forehead. "That explains everything. Well, then. Shall we begin negotiations?" Ralph gestured for Adrian to follow him as he left the room.

"When is this wedding set to begin? And to whom?" Mother asked as she rang for a servant.

"November 4, in New Orleans, to Lady Serena. The Duke and Duchess of Wharton will also be in attendance," Miss Rose declared. She was the heart of kind composure in this difficult moment and had not reacted to Mother at all.

"How did this even occur?" Mother wondered aloud, more a reaction to the absurdity of the situation than actually seeking an answer.

"It is so romantic that we have been waiting on bated breath for every letter," Aurora opined. Did this sweet little cat of a girl want to give Mother a spell?

"Do tell," Sebastian invited as he sat and gestured for them to follow suit.

"Well, Serena has been a long admirer of Vincent's writings and quips, but they had not yet been introduced. Then, in Philadelphia of all places, he found her handbag. From that moment on, they spent nearly all their time together. Vincent proposed in Pittsburgh, but Serena believed it was in jest. He then snuck into her room in Baltimore, before breakfast but after she had dressed, and demanded she marry him." Honoria spun the tale in a studied voice; she must do this sort of thing often.

"So romantic…" Aurora sighed.

Mother rolled her eyes and rested her head on her hand. For Vincent to propose marriage in such a fashion would upset her plans, a cardinal sin for which no indulgence could be bought.

"But Serena wanted time to think, as marriage is an incredible decision. Serena convinced Frederick to let her go to Chicago early and think on marriage," Honoria continued. She was closer and lowered her head a little so that Mother could look at her face.

"Because 'I cannot think in his presence, he simply renders me dumb with love,' " Aurora quoted.

"Yes." Honoria glared at her younger sister. "When he met her in Chicago, she happily accepted his offer. It's absolutely wonderful."

Sebastian smiled, infected by the sisters' happiness. "I would like to attend the wedding as well. May I travel with you?"

"Of course, my lord. Adrian will be handling our travel arrangements. We should be going, as Mother will wonder where we are. Lord Ralph insisted we announce the news of the wedding. It was lovely to visit, however." Honoria dipped a curtsey before pulling her sister out of the room.

"God help the man who marries either of those two," Mother mumbled as she drank her sherry. "Are you serious about going to America? What will I say to Miss Haverford about this wedding?"

"Of course, I am going. Lily will insist that one of us attends, and she is not well enough to do so. I suggest you invite Miss Haverford to tea and tell her delicately that Vincent is getting married. She will likely cut ties with our family," Sebastian answered.

"How kind of them to announce my embarrassment in a pack. It appears that our side of the family kept the money, but their side is rich with pettiness."

Mother was most displeased.

Chapter 21

America is far too large. I have spent too much time in trains rolling through deserts. My party has opted not to visit Texas, but from what I can see, it is much greener than I imagined.
A Curmudgeon's Tour of America, October 1885

Vincent strolled down the narrow corridors of the train. Practically living on trains and in hotels was exhausting, but he had never been happier. When one is forced to reckon with inconstant surroundings, one needs constant companionship. During his tour of Europe with his brothers, Vincent was miserable with the cramped trains and unkempt hotels, but Serena made the world beautiful in her wake. As they traveled from San Francisco to New Orleans, the view was dull and redundant of deserts with little to offer, but he had Serena to gaze upon. As excited as he was to have a longer place in New Orleans, he would miss the trains as they provided nights with Serena.

Their upcoming nuptials were terrifying. He was in love with Serena and wanted her at least fifty-nine seconds of every minute, but the Malicious Mandeville kept peeking out from behind the mask. He needed her, but she would grow to resent his barbs in time. Eventually, too soon for Vincent's comfort, they would return to London, and she would bear witness to the crimes of his rhetoric. The unfortunate mathematics of the situation were these: if provoked by his mother, he would be especially hateful, and Serena would flee. Sometimes he wished she would just tell him she hated him, then it would be over, and Damocles' sword would no longer hang over his head. He still couldn't live without her, so he would have to keep running from the worst version of himself and hope it would not catch up before their wedding.

Vincent entered the dining car slowly. Serena was sitting alone at the table, with just enough light and sound to make her a moving picture. Serena was most beautiful when she was near gaslight. Of course, she was beautiful all the time, but gaslight particularly highlighted her features. Vincent loved uncovering her bountiful secrets, no matter how sacred or banal. Which colors favored her best (Serena preferred blues and silvers, but she looked beautiful in white or pink) or the foods she loved (she appeared to love earthy flavors like chocolate and spices) occupied the same space as the great mysteries of the East. Every new discovery about her enticed him, but such revelations presented a bit of a paradox. Should he believe that the more he knew her, the less exciting she would become? But his heart still stopped when he saw her and slammed in his chest when he stood too near to her.

"Good evening. I hope you haven't been alone for too long." She made it impossibly hard to not kiss her as he sat. What a terrible vixen.

"Not at all. Frederick and Benedict have just gone off for a waylaid cufflink." Serena beamed at him, then leaned in dangerously close. "Will you come to my room tonight, around nine?"

"Wild horses could not keep me from it. I mean they could, but they would have to be strong, and I would have to be drunk. What I'm trying to say is I'm eagerly looking forward to when we can wed," Vincent said, his smile creeping too far onto his face.

"I feel the same. I am terribly excited to see your house," Serena confided. Oh good, she should know every detail of it before she set foot inside.

"Our house." This was a romantic correction, so hopefully she was not offended. "I am afraid that I have been derelict in furnishing the house and have focused on the acquisition of art and books."

"Of course, that is the most enjoyable part of decorative arts. I imagine you eat sweets before supper," Serena teased.

"Is there a man who wouldn't? He sounds dull, and you should avoid marrying him. I will delegate the remainder of decorating to you. We will need furniture and lighting. So, do you prefer gas, or will you be spending all of my money on candles?" Vincent teased her in return.

"Candles, but only until we can convince your brothers to wire for electricity with us. Apparently, we would have to build a generator in the village, so it would be wise to coordinate with nearby houses," Serena answered. "And I would like to discuss helping the villagers have electricity as well."

"Bah! I don't particularly trust electricity. Too much of a fire danger with all my paintings. But if you can find an electrician to convince me, I will be open to it. Why don't you want gas?" Vincent asked.

Serena shrugged. "Gas is pretty. I love to walk and see London by gaslight. However, I find it stains wallpaper, and I will get dizzy if I am in a small room for too long with gaslight. Perhaps I can offer a compromise. Darker wood-paneled rooms will have gas, but lighter rooms will have electricity. The greenhouse and the ballroom will have electricity. But your library and study will have gas."

Vincent smiled. "Wonderful. Now the house will burn down twice as quick! I jest, I love your offer."

"Good evening, Mandeville. Look, pet. I found it." Berkeley showed her an enamel butterfly cufflink, obviously given to Berkeley by his sister. One could always identify what Serena had given Berkeley as they were the items he cherished.

"Wonderful, I know they were your favorite." Serena smiled.

"Yes, and I could not see you wed without wearing them. On that subject, I have worked out a division of labor for the nuptials," Berkeley announced.

"Thank you! I was unable to sleep with the number of duties to accomplish. I will need a dress, one I like enough to wear often, and a bouquet. We will need a breakfast planned. And I have no idea of the legality of American marriages." Serena had clearly been anxious about their wedding day. Vincent had not given it much more thought than he would not have to hide his affection any longer.

"I have made a list. Benedict and I will find the church and…do they have vicars in America?" Berkeley asked.

"I believe they call them pastors or reverends or preachers. Unless they are Catholic; they are universally priests," Serena answered.

"Ah, well, Benedict and I will handle the legal

aspects of the marriage. I have arranged for one assistant but possibly more to help with the arrangements for the wedding breakfast, dress, and trousseau. And I task Vincent with planning our return to England, as it will be your honeymoon," Berkeley assigned.

"Huzzah! Serena, should we leave from New York or Boston?" Vincent asked.

"Hmm. Boston. We can pass through Manhattan on our way to Boston," Serena answered.

"Lovely, I liked Boston. Not as much as San Francisco, but perhaps I will like it more with you." Vincent smiled at Serena.

Serena blushed and sipped her wine. Berkeley rolled his eyes and began discussing the various religions in America with Melgum.

****

The train rattled and bumped over uneven tracks with a low noise like a dark heartbeat. Serena was a few feet in front of him and moved so quietly. This desirable ghost was all smiles merely minutes ago, but as soon as she had turned to walk to her private car, Vincent could not see her expression. He stole every chance he could to see her face reflected in the windows. The light danced and flashed too quickly. Every reflection was too impressionistic, too incomplete to be trusted.

If rumors were correct, women possessed a variety of reactions to engagement. Some took it as license to indulge and engage in what could gently be called "permitted but discouraged" intimacies. Some found titillation in the taboo of sex without the protections of engagement or marriage (or even in spite of it). And others met their marital duty with a sense of duty but not hedonism. Would Serena change now? There was not joy in her measured steps.

It was better to ask, even if it indicated insecurity in his new role as her fiancé.

A line of indulgent warmth beamed across his hand. Without a word, Serena had slowed for him and extended her unadorned, flawless hand behind her. She had not thrown a look to him or changed her expression; she reached with utter confidence and found him. This was unlike her.

And then there was the look. In a flash of orange and yellow brilliance, the sun blazed through the trees. It was the color and intensity it only had in the few moments before a sundown began. The last echoes of an adolescent star gave Vincent just enough light to see Serena's expression. A bee-stung bottom lip—bitten just a little in desire—and a crooked, lusty smile. Her gaze was fixed on the carpet. She didn't want the world to see what was in her eyes.

Did she have everything she wanted? Was that what this was? She turned the knob to the door carefully. Was she afraid a single pin dropping would ruin this moment?

He rushed through the door and grabbed her waist with his outstretched arm, slamming the door shut with his free hand. The room was bright, and the windows were unclothed, but he did not care if the world were looking in.

"Your excitement is…." Serena trailed off. "But you understand I have to get ready. It is not quite as easy as lighting a single candle for me."

Every nerve in his body clawed its way toward the

molten pleasure she had stolen from him and hid deep in herself. His hands were on her waist, and he could barely stop himself from tearing the wrapping from her. Her dress, her chemise, any cloth or lace, or embellishment in between his raw craving and her would be torn or shredded. He wanted to possess her, to make her feel like she would reside under him, receiving his desire, for the rest of her life, without another thought in her verbose brain.

"My dearest bride, I say this in perfect candor—make it easy."

Serena hastily pushed off everything covering her, but her lip was curled in lusty excitement, and her eyes were too intense. Was this regret? That would be terribly regretful. He grabbed the full curve of her gorgeous backside and crushed into her doubting lips. They looked redder than ever. Her eyes were light sea skies with faint clouds, blue and inscrutable. He kissed her, and she smiled a little. How could she be coy at a time like this?

He needed her to match his lust. His only mission was to make her as big a beast as he was. She could not entice him so without the same fire lighting her body. His tongue swirled in her mouth, meeting hers with force matching his ardor. This teased her the exact right amount—she matched his rhythm and glided and stroked in harmony. Her body crumpled heavily into his arm for just a second. His other hand had begun gently stroking her exposed breasts, tracing delicate circles around her perfect nipples.

For a few seconds, Vincent felt only the urge to arouse her, but his hardness roared back to the forefront of his mind. She was on the verge of her lust, but she needed a push. Her mind was still firmly in her head. It needed to be in her gorgeous body.

Quicker than she could react, his hand traveled to the taboo valley between her thighs. It was warmer than the rest of her. It was wet and felt welcoming, like lips craving the same overwhelming kisses that had been given to her mouth. His fingers glided into her, as if tasting her, until they met a small circle of delicate skin. Her eyes opened, and she stopped breathing for a second to moan. He gently stroked her, and she lay back. His fingers flowed up and down, teasing her and overwhelming her until her legs were spread. This was the greatest rush he had ever felt. To have exactly what he wanted—this flawless seraph, full of knowledge and restraint—aching and panting just like him, was his single greatest accomplishment. But she was possessed of a greater kindness than him, and so he recoiled for just a second. Was this what she really wanted?

"You overwhelmed me. I am sorry." He kissed down her stomach, stopping before his intended destination by just enough to allow her to refuse. "But I do not want to stop."

"I do not want you to stop, Vincent."

No further permission was needed. His tongue sank into her and licked the same elegant circle it had in her mouth, only harder. She flooded his senses, her perfect enticement filling his mouth, her hand on his head pushing him farther in. He could not have enough of her. She was his now. She moaned, and her hands were on her breasts, squeezing. Her legs quivered, and her foot was on his back, pulling him in. She moaned hard, then her body fell. She was a syrupy blonde mess and looked perfect. She glowed with innocence and devotion.

"I want you again."

Vincent braced his hands firmly above her head, desperately clawing at pillows so he would not have grabbed the edge of her bed, which would sharply bite into his fingers. His swollen manliness entered her as if under her control. The first seconds were the best, and she gasped a little. Sex was best when her pleasure led his or echoed it. As he thrust into her, her wetness clung fast, as though it was devouring him. It was the lightest of pressures but was seething with warmth and lust. As he pulled back, it clung greedily to him, and he felt as though he had to go back in. No part of him mattered anymore, just the throbbing center of his whole being, overwhelmed with the need to be in her. With every stroke, she kissed him, traced lines on his chest, or cooed. He could not stop himself. His body roared, and he gave her every drop of him. He could not move or breathe that well. Her sweet smile, blushing and large, was in his face, and although he had felt like a beast for her, he was a man again. Her man, perhaps for the rest of their lives.

He collapsed on the bed as soon as she rolled onto her side. The bed was not intended for two, so it was a tight fit, especially for those raised with the luxury of excessive and pillowy spaces before sleep. She was lightening the mood, which was fine. A whole night of heavy lusts might not have been the best way to cap their day. His brow wrinkled; this was his most vulnerable point. She had seen what she did, the power and desire she commanded. What was she thinking now?

"I am terribly tired, and I will be horrid in the

morning if I do not rest." She rolled over to look him in the eyes as the light faded outside the car. "I will always sleep better with you here."

"Then I will never leave." Could something so quaint and beautiful be his greatest happiness? His body raced with need at the sight of her backside and bare back in the gathering dark, but he was too tired to act on it. As his dreams sped toward him, he refused to move his gaze from her.

Chapter 22

Late October is when autumn turns from romance to mystery. With All Hallows Eve nearing, I like to think of the Banshees roaming the hills. And as the heavy fog rolls in, I swear there are spirits on it. I've often wondered, what do witches eat?
Aunt Penny's Advice for Living, October 1885

Frederick assisted Serena off the train. It was only eleven in the morning, but New Orleans was already balmy. Even in high summer, the heat of London had never been this humid, and Serena knew she would need linen dresses. As Frederick organized their luggage, Serena noticed her male companions were wilting under the oppressive heat as well. Of course, men did not have to wear corsets, stockings, or extra skirts. Perhaps they were the weaker sex.

After they settled in the carriage en route to the hotel, Frederick flashed the smile he only wore when he was scheming. "I do hope the assistant I have arranged for you will be at the hotel."

"I have never heard of an assistant for only weddings. Is it an American tradition?" Serena asked.

"I don't believe it is. The lady is not a professional. It is a favor, special for you." Frederick smiled.

Serena braced herself for whatever Frederick had planned. Frederick was impulsive and always well intentioned, but his surprises never went as planned. For Serena's seventeenth birthday, he whisked her off to Paris for a new wardrobe, only to realize he had failed to arrange accommodation for them. Two years ago, when Frederick was infatuated with the age of chivalry, he bought a falcon. Now they had to employ a falconer, and Serena occasionally woke to find adorable but dead hedgehogs on her floor.

The hotel Frederick had chosen to be their home for the next three weeks was the St. Charles Hotel on Canal Street. It was a massive white stone building with columns lining the front and a rotunda atop of it. It called to mind an exchange or bank or statehouse before a hotel. Yet it was a hotel, with marvelous views of the river and proximity to the American District. It was both strange and charming that New Orleans would have an American District. It was becoming obvious that New Orleans viewed itself as much a part of America as Boston viewed itself part of the English Empire, and that is not at all.

Serena walked into the hotel with her spine taut like a bride in her wedding march. But there, coiled like an elegant doll posed perfectly for that second, was her grandmother. Never had a kinder face ever graced the earth than that of Yolanda Percy. Even at the age of seventy-one, her hazel eyes sparkled, and her cheeks were still rosy. Over the years, Grandmother's auburn hair bore little silver invaders until she wore a halo of silver about her head. The happiness overwhelmed her, like waves of memory the exact golden color of the setting sun.

"Grandmother! What are you doing here?" Serena cried, and she ran and embraced her. There was a kind of magic to being held by someone who had loved her for her entire life. Serena was warm and comforted. After all, the word "cozy" was created to describe a grandmother's hug.

"My darling girl, we could not possibly miss your wedding." Grandmother stroke her hair. Though Serena was several inches taller than her grandmother, she seemed small and diminutive near her. "Frederick wired, demanding we rush to New Orleans, and here we are."

"I am so very pleased!" Serena laughed. She moved to let Frederick greet Grandmother before whispering, "Thank you."

Frederick responded with a good-natured grin and a wink.

"Where is Grandfather?" Benedict asked as he kissed Grandmother's cheek.

"He is in our suite with the tailor. He needed all new suits made. The heat is oppressive. One understands why the southerners speak with a drawl. The heat slows one down," Grandmother answered.

"Oh!" Serena exclaimed, suddenly recalling herself. "Allow me to introduce Lord Vincent, my fiancé."

Vincent walked forward to take Grandmother's hand, but she spoke quickly. "Oh, no. I know this man! We met at Lady Summerly's garden party. He told me that your grandfather was dull, insulted half the guests, and threatened to elope with me. It is of high interest that he has changed his affections so quickly. Be on your guard."

Laughter erupted, and the fear of disharmony slid out if the room. Vincent smiled warmly as he kissed the air above her glove, before announcing, with an unneeded southern accent, "If a man wishes to gaze upon the future of his wife, he must look to her mother and grandmother. Happily, when I have gone mad in my old age, I will still try to elope with her."

Grandmother smiled, the knowing smile of a cat with a friendly mouse in its jaws. "Not only a sharp tongue but a silver one as well. I very much approve of this match. One always desires a husband clever enough to talk his way out of a row. Serena, darling, why don't you change into a more appropriate dress so we might prepare for your wedding."

Vincent escorted Serena to her room. How terribly exciting to have her family present for her wedding! It was more solid and celebratory with her grandparents present. Their weight would fill, in small part, the gaping hole left by her parents' death. However, this new side of Vincent had birthed a thousand worries. Others would call them butterflies, but there was nothing light and airy about her prickly misgivings. His closest friends and family were not present. He had to feel lonely and left out. But perhaps it was her role as a wife to comfort her husband.

"Should I be jealous? Does my grandmother remind you of your precious Olga?" Serena teased.

Serena had beaten the cloud forming above his head with her parasol.

Vincent smiled brightly at her. "A little, but I must forget Olga as you want a husband to be faithful. And to wait for children. And me to treat you well. And not to beat you. It's fortunate you are so beautiful, or you would not be able to be so demanding."

Serena laughed at his jest. "Have we discussed

children?"

"Berkeley told me, you only wish for two and not for a few years. I barely want to share you at all, so I will agree." Vincent took her key and unlocked her room for her.

He never said he loved her, not once. He spoke like he loved her, almost tiptoeing around the words. All of actions indicated that he loved her. It was an elaborate ballet, choreographed to show intimacy, but where the partners never touched. On the one hand, it was impossible not to be happy he treated her well. On the other, it was trying that he had not declared his love. She wanted him to be the face frozen in time in her family portrait. It was as though someone had painted it, a lovely room, the sullen dogs, the carefully chosen dress, but the face was missing.

"Wonderful," Serena said as she entered her suite.

Vincent pushed her against the wall as soon as they entered and began to kiss her deeply. So, he was desperate to touch her, despite they had coupled just last night? Eventually, he released her. "I suspect that we will not have much time for stolen kisses before our wedding, and I needed one last kiss."

Serena caressed his brow. "I hope you are mistaken, but if not, we will have our lives together. Is my Vincent that impatient?"

Vincent emitted a sound between a groan and a sigh. He leaned his forehead to press against hers until his eyes became one, from her perspective. "Yes. I am impatient and greedy and selfish when it comes to you. I want you always, all to myself."

Serena kissed him. He loved her, so perhaps words were unnecessary. "You will have me for the rest of my life. I promise."

"Good. I am happy that your family is here. You should have help with arranging the wedding breakfast. Perhaps your grandmother will want to help furnish Nightingale Lodge as well. We also require staff," Vincent babbled.

"You don't have a staff?" This made her steam like an angry blonde kettle. An ancient house with no furnishings or staff was frustrating, and he knew it. It would be endless hours and a ton of work for Serena.

"Well, I may have fled the country before we could settle that detail as I was sharing a house with my brothers. Besides, I thought women liked having control over the house, and the staff will be loyal to whoever hires them." Vincent gave a smile she knew he must have worn before, maybe whenever he had vexed his mother. It was the face of a little boy who had stolen a piece of cake but was trying to convince his mother that it was for her.

Serena sighed, her air leaving her and the vacant space filling with resignation. Being angry wouldn't solve anything. "I am certain Grandmother has several ideas for how a house should be staffed. Perhaps we could hire an American cook or housekeeper."

"Outrageous! I love it." He pulled her into him and pressed their bodies together. She loved how solid he felt. He was not muscular but fit and defined, such as a statue might be. "I will miss our little talks, but I should go before anyone notices I am still alone with you."

Vincent left her, and Serena rang for Martha to help her change her dress. Serena was happy that men seemed to believe it required at least a half hour to simply change a dress. In reality, Martha could tidy her hair and replace a dress within fifteen minutes. But Serena enjoyed the time where she could use the toilet and have a few moments to herself. Honestly, she could change a dress in less than ten minutes if it were not for buttons or needing to change her boots.

At the dress shop, Grandmother paid close attention to Serena's night and dressing gowns. It seemed Grandmother was eager for great-grandchildren as she insisted Serena buy lace gowns that teased the senses the most. Grandmother apparently decided that Serena should be in fancy dress nightly but was unable to choose which fantasy. She adored Serena with items that resembled a lusty milkmaid, a buxom mistress, a wanton virgin, and Aphrodite. Serena bit her tongue from revealing that Vincent preferred her nude, with nothing between their skin.

"Grandmother, are you familiar with the Duke and Duchess of Bridgewater?" Serena asked as the shop girl zealously dressed her.

"Oh yes, the current duke took the title around the time Frederick was born." Grandmother was distracted by a fashion plate.

"The duke fought in Crimea, if I recall," Serena prompted.

"Both of the Mandevilles fought, as did your father. Grayson, the current duke, returned a hero." Grandmother easily sidestepped the fact that Serena's father had barely served as he had arrived near the end of the war. "It is odd to see history repeat itself."

"How do you mean?" Serena asked as the stockings were presented.

"Anson Mandeville was stiff and proper, similar to the current Coningsby. Grayson Mandeville was an intellectual with a hint of danger and mystery to him, much like your Vincent. The idea of a third brother is new to the Mandevilles."

"Am I similar to the duchess?" Serena asked.

"No. You are both blonde, but both doves and cattle can be the same color too. Seraphina Rose, now the duchess, always had an icy quality to her. Her father was a magistrate, so everyone felt the marriage between her and a duke's second son was well matched. When she became duchess, people wanted to believe it was a fairy story—a war hero and a majestic ice queen—but she was so hard it took away the magic. Then Llewellyn returned with your mother, and the proper fairy story was in place. I suppose Regina stole a bit of Seraphina's glory," Grandmother explained.

"I thought everyone despised Mother," Serena said. She was forever curious about her parents, so hopefully her grandmother would not be saddened by her question.

"It was fashionable to mock Regina, particularly in the beginning as her English had yet to be perfected. However, the more Llewellyn defended her, and as more people witnessed how passionately he loved her, it faded. Old snobs persisted, but in hushed conversations, I overheard many debutantes and a few married ladies speak of Regina with envy."

Grandmother soon became engaged by the seamstress. It seemed that a hemline was important enough to trail off about, but at least Serena had a second to consider these new details.

Serena sat still and watched her grandmother buy her trousseau. If only her mother were there. Even if her father hated Vincent or her mother was disappointed with Serena, it would be worth it. Whoever killed them had robbed Serena if not just this moment but of thousands of memories. She was in New Orleans not only to marry, but to solve her parents' murder. She had lost sight of this mission and needed to focus once more. Her happily-ever-after required more than just marriage.

Chapter 23

New Orleans is not to be missed. They seem to relish life as the French do, but without the pretense. To be sure there are grand mansions where the wealthy live as the wealthy in every country live, but in New Orleans, every man has access to the riches of the city. A cup of coffee is as delightful as a meal from the finest restaurant.

A Curmudgeon's Tour of America, October 1885

Vincent watched the bank of Louisiana as he sipped his coffee. The coffee was superb, on par with his visits to Vienna or Italy. The Duchess of Wharton was correct. The heat was oppressive, even in late October when the air should be chilling. The heat clung to him, as though the entire city were filled with an invisible steam. The city was haunted and mystical, even in daylight as he sipped his coffee.

"My apologies for my tardiness," Melgum said as he sat and dabbed his forehead with a blue handkerchief.

"Think nothing of it. I assume you were enjoying your grandparents' company?" Vincent signaled for another cup of coffee to be brought for Melgum.

"Yes, I never would have thought they would come to America." Melgum scowled at the hot coffee in the heat.

"Drink it. It should cool your scalding temperament. We will all have to return for your wedding. Is it a Percy tradition to cross the world for a wedding?" Vincent smiled, happy to make himself an honorary Percy.

"I would like that. What is that flavor?" Melgum gazed at his coffee cup, a weirdly agnostic glare on his face.

"Chicory, though I have no notion of what exactly chicory is. I suppose it is a nut or bark or, God forbid, animal that can be found nearby. And then I wondered which part of the animal. After we finish here, we will go to the bank. Our goal is to discover exactly where Annandale's money went or to whom," Vincent explained.

"I hope you have a plan. I would not do well in a Louisiana jail," Melgum retorted.

He actually could, though, considering what Vincent had seen in the alley. How bizarre to feign weakness. Maybe he was hiding something else—secrets traveled in packs.

Vincent sighed. "We are two English lords. We simply need to exploit that fact. I have observed Americans are dazzled by Europeans and especially the peerage. You will need to cash the check from Cameron and may be considering opening an account at the bank of Louisiana. Ask the banker to see the vault. Whilst there, ask every question you can think of."

"How will that get us answers?" Melgum asked.

"Banks are funny buildings. They focus all their time and attention on the money but relax when it comes to the real treasures, namely information. Alone in a banker's office, I can find the name or account that deposited Annandale's money." Vincent finished his coffee. Hopefully the flavor came from a nut and not a small woodland creature. He winced as he pictured a bright-eyed, bushy-tailed chicory. Please let it be more like a nut and less like a squirrel. "Shall we go?"

Melgum took a final swig of his coffee before tidying his clothing and standing. "I liked those pastries. Do you know what they were called?"

"Beignets, or at least that is what the chatty proprietor told me. Apparently, the Acadians brought them after their exile from Canada. Can you imagine anything more humiliating than being removed from Canada? He also told me that a risk of lobsters followed the Acadians from Canada, but by the time they arrived in Louisiana they had shrunk down to be crawfish." Vincent repeated the tall tales without embellishment. They were perfectly far-fetched without surplus myth.

"That is both interesting and absurd. Café owners never tell me anything." Melgum scowled.

"Try smiling at people. If it helps, imagine they have flowing blonde hair and a large bosom," Vincent teased.

"I don't often smile at Serena, but I take your meaning." Melgum climbed the stairs to the bank.

Why did all banks wear a uniform of banality? They all favored dark woods, be it walnut, cherry, or mahogany. Plain brass that did not require more polish than a gloved hand adorned the fixtures. The bankers themselves were mustachioed men wearing waistcoats, with the only deviance being spectacles on occasion. The building was a temple to greed, and the priestly garb was a set of false smiles of those eternally hungry for more. Vincent did not particularly care for banks.

Melgum and Vincent were being handled by a Mr. Jean Arnaud, the assistant manager. Arnaud was young, perhaps thirty with deep brunet hair and golden eyes. He was well dressed in a dark linen suit with silk tie and pocket square in red. Arnaud appeared eager and excited to help Melgum open an account at the bank and smiled far too much. Vincent had never been so happy to be right about human behavior.

"Now, will both of you gentlemen be opening the account jointly?" Arnaud asked as they took their seats in Arnaud's office.

"No, Lord Vincent is affianced to my cousin, and they will return to Britain after their nuptials. I am immigrating to America and am considering New Orleans as my home," Melgum elaborated, perhaps unnecessarily. But a margin of extraneous detail was not an issue.

"How fortunate for America to receive you. I am certain our bank can accommodate all of your needs." Arnaud spoke smoothly with a long drawl. He removed keys from a desk drawer. "Shall we have a brief tour?"

"Wonderful." Melgum stood.

Vincent began to stand and (purposefully but meaning to look accidental) banged his knee. "Ooooh."

"Oh dear, are you injured?" Arnaud asked.

"It is temporary, I am certain. May I remain here while you give Melgum the tour? He needs to see it, but I do not." Vincent winced and whinged as convincingly as he could. He was a critic, not an actor.

"Certainly, right this way, my lord." Arnaud escorted Melgum from the room.

Vincent began to search for the ledger, finally finding that there were numerous ledgers. As he examined the various numbers and shorthand, it was impossible to not want Ralph to explain what this nonsense meant. Finally, he found a notation for a check from Cameron for five hundred thousand dollars. (Vincent was not certain of the exact conversion of pounds to dollars, but it was around two hundred thousand pounds.) Vincent documented everything in the small notebook he kept in his breast pocket (where his best limericks and satirical drawings lived), especially the account number deposited to.

He hurriedly ransacked the file cabinets. His heart pounded in his chest, and fingers raced against the sullen, yellow papers in a drab white folder. Soon he would have a name to a real person inside the Shadow Society. He would know who had defamed his family. Who had jeopardized Ralph and Lily's happiness? Who had robbed Annandale of his fortune? Finally, Vincent's eager right hand flipped the right correct folder over in the cabinet, nearly fumbling the paperwork but deftly catching it as it fell the short distance between the drawer and the golden rug. The account holder's name was marked in eager and precise pen strokes: Mathew MacDonald.

Who the fuck was Mathew MacDonald?

How could a stranger, someone Vincent had never heard of, have a vendetta against his family? Vincent furiously scribbled every detail of the account, whose main holdings appeared to be a series of warehouses. Even Vincent, with absolutely no mind for business, could see that whatever the Shadow Society was doing in New Orleans was profitable. In two years, they had grown around twelve percent. Ralph had been quite proud when he achieved such a number. Never had

Vincent been so certain that he was the wrong brother for this task, but then again, Ralph might not have gone to New Orleans.

After Vincent replaced the file and ensured the office was returned to exactly the original orientation, he returned to his chair. He pushed the chair closer to the desk. If anything he looked patient but bored, as if the worst he had done was to critically examine the expensive pens that Arnaud had left behind. There were several explanations for why a man he had never heard of would have his name on the account. Perhaps the Shadow Society was larger than he imagined. Or it could be a false name. It could be a person who had been wronged that he simply did not know personally. After all, the upper class numbered thousands. It burned him to allow this choice fact, this mystery resolved, to burrow into him and not let it out. He had to do *something* with this information, but he was trapped in this ever-shrinking office that was quickly filling with his anxiety.

Finally, Melgum and Arnaud returned, but then they began the tedium of paperwork to open a new account. After they had finished, Vincent prompted Melgum. "We ought to go. One should never keep a duchess waiting for tea."

Melgum checked his pocket watch. "Yes, of course."

"My, my. So many royals in our fair city for a wedding? How remarkable," Arnaud observed.

Vincent resisted the urge to snark about the difference between royals, nobles, and the peerage. Instead, he simply smiled. "You should join us for dinner tonight. We are at the St. Charles Hotel. Will we see you at seven?"

"Why, wild horses could not prevent me from attending," Arnaud drawled.

Melgum was at Vincent's heels as they left the bank. "Why did you invite him to dinner?" he demanded, with a perfect scowl and eyebrows arched so angrily they formed little arrows pointing to his hairline.

"Because no one who had ransacked his office would invite him to supper. When people like you, they always want to give you the benefit of the doubt. As I was successful, we may need Arnaud in the future. If not, I am not bothered by making a new acquaintance," Vincent explained.

"I am nervous. What if he catches us lying?" Melgum frowned, returning to his natural position.

"We did not lie, Melgum. You opened an account, and I banged my knee. Tell me where we lied?" Vincent asked.

Melgum scowled as he searched his memory. "I suppose you are right. I reserve the right to my discomfort, though."

"That is understandable, you are new to…well, we are not spies or investigators. I suppose high-society busybodies loses some of the intrigue…regardless, you are new to this. Go have tea with your family and make my apologies for not being present. If you feel you will not be able to attend dinner, then make your excuses," Vincent offered.

Melgum nodded. "Very well, where should I say you are?"

"I have to go to the post office. Always be honest with people, but be vague," Vincent advised.

Vincent had to visit seven bookstores before he found one that carried a copy of Debrett's *Peerage and Baronetage*. How very reasonable, as why on earth would you need one in Louisiana? He bought the copy and one of Burke's as well and headed to a café. Vincent began searching, but unfortunately MacDonald was a somewhat common name in Scotland. Finally, Vincent saw the entry for Mathew MacDonald, Laird of Bladaire. According to the book, he owned a thousand acres in Scotland and a house called Bladaire Hall. He was a widower with a son named Braden, age ten.

Vincent stared at the entry, wishing they included pictures in lieu of the occasional sketch of a coat of arms. However, he now had a name, and MacDonald could be found and investigated. He could be hurt and exploited until the Shadow Society was finished. This one step was infinitely closer to his revenge, even if it was a stride across the ocean.

He had to relay this information to the Black Swan, but he could not telegraph. The mail was equally uncertain. He circled MacDonald's entry before writing on the first page *I found a man for your sister.* He mailed the package to Amesbury, with a note to Adrian Rose. If the Shadow Society was aware of their involvement, all was lost anyway.

Chapter 24

*In solidarity with all cooks everywhere, I implore
every lady in Britain to stop having puff pastry. I know
that it is fashionable to have it at every dinner party,
but please stop. The sheer amount of work required for
the delicate layers is nearing cruelty. For the time and
effort required to make a puffed pastry, one could
instead add another two courses to the dinner. Be kind
to your cooks, lest they poison your food.*

Aunt Penny's Advice for Living, October 1885

Serena loved the tiny hamlet of hedonism that was
New Orleans, almost as much as she had loved San
Francisco. San Francisco was paradise: sunshine, blue
skies, beauty wherever you looked. New Orleans
breathed deep darkness and exhaled mysterious
intrigues around every corner. Even the trees seemed
haunted with the pretty Spanish moss hanging from
them. And there was mysticism everywhere, with the
abundant voodoo queens, mediums, and black magic. It
was perfect for her.

It was surprisingly easy to plan a wedding for only
four guests, though Frederick insisted on the pretense
that ten guests would be present. Nevertheless, it would
be a small, simple affair. Martha was working tirelessly
on Serena's wedding dress, while Grandmother fussed
over the breakfast. Truly, Serena simply needed to

221

ensure her trousseau was in place and spent the remainder of her time visiting the voodoo sights and shopping to furnish Nightingale Lodge.

Serena had placed an advert seeking a cook three days ago, yet no one answered. Serena understood; leaving one's country and family must be a terrifying prospect. She had not specified the wages. In England wages were to be negotiated but generally fell in the fifty-to-seventy-pound-per-annum area. On the third day, Serena began to wonder if anyone would be adventurous enough to cook for a house in the wilds of Norfolk, England.

On the morning of the fourth day, a kind but very informal young concierge knocked firmly at her door. Finally, there was a girl who wished to see her, but she was not allowed to wait in the lobby. As Serena ventured down into the tedium of the hot air, she saw why. The young lady waiting near the service entry met her eyes and then looked away too fast. She was perhaps twenty with warm brown eyes and an infectious smile. She was also dark skinned, although she was dressed so properly, the only areas of exposure were her face and hands. That was certainly the basis of the hotel's policy in regards to her. What could be offensive about a face and hands, or any other part to be honest?

An issue (certainly not the most important, but the one Serena was facing currently) with those of African lineage who had been interfered with by Europeans (interference is of course a base euphemism for something worse) is that one never knew what to call them. She had heard people called black, negro, colored, and dark. Some were referred to as "freedman" or "Afro-Caribbean," but she lacked any reference to determine which nomenclature might be accurate. It would be shameful to display her ignorance and ask. So maybe simply opting to treat this young woman as she would behave with any other person seeking employment was the best course.

"Are you answering my advert seeking a cook?" Serena asked.

The woman smiled. "Yes! I am Loretta Thibodeaux, ma'am."

"A pleasure to meet you, Miss Thibodeaux. I am Lady Serena. I am soon to be wed, and we will be living at my fiancé's home in Norfolk. Do you have any references?" Serena asked.

"Yes, I have been working as my mama's kitchen girl since I was thirteen." Miss Thibodeaux offered a letter carefully and slowly. Her deliberateness seemed designed in response to Serena's own very stilted demeanor.

"How old are you?" Serena asked as she read the mother's letter.

"Twenty-two," she answered.

"Miss Thibodeaux, I have been contemplating what I want from a cook. You see, precision is a skill that can be mastered, but creativity is something one can never learn. Could you prepare two dishes for me to sample by noon?" Serena asked, before recalling the difficulty Miss Thibodeaux had entering the hotel. "We could meet at the park."

"I don't think I could have them done by noon, but I could have them done by two," Miss Thibodeaux offered.

Serena agreed happily. It was hard not to look

forward to an exquisitely curated late lunch. At two o'clock, she strolled in the balmy day and drank in the diverse conversations. She sat in the nearby park alone, with only a few bits of accented French wafting in the air to keep her company. She had invited her grandparents. However, being quite old, they preferred to nap. Martha was consumed by Serena's wedding dress and trousseau, quietly and exactingly obsessing over every detail. Vincent was spending an inordinate amount of time with Benedict, which was very odd, but she could not question. Frederick seemed to love New Orleans, and given his penchant for misadventure, he was most likely exploring the gambling dens or swamps to wrestle an alligator.

Miss Thibodeaux entered the park, carrying a picnic hamper. She was less embellished than earlier, but she had been working, and New Orleans offered no abatement for the heat. "Good afternoon, my lady."

Serena smiled. Someone had informed her of the proper greeting. "Good afternoon, Miss Thibodeaux. I trust your day went well."

"Yes, my lady. I have two dishes for you. The first is my mama's recipe for gumbo." Miss Thibodeaux opened the hamper and presented a dish of…brownish rice with unidentified bits in it. It had a savory aura that smelled like sausage and rich spices. It was heterodox in texture, but thick and rigid enough to resist shifting in the container.

Serena pulled the spoon from her picnic gadget walking stick. Of course, the primary reason was to show off her marvelous cane, but she was also so excited to use it. At first, Serena was repulsed by the stuff, as it was far too thick for stew. However, as the flavors and spices rolled over her tongue, she grew to like it. She even took a second bite. "Oddly delicious. How is it so...gravy like in texture?"

"Okra, but if you don't have any, then you can use a roux," Miss Thibodeaux answered.

Serena had no idea what either if those things were and nodded. "Will you be able to work with the ingredients found in England? We don't often have some of the items found here."

"Necessity is the mother of invention. Or as my grandpappy says, poor folk are crafty." Miss Thibodeaux brought forth another dish. This one was also a rice dish but darker brown with sausage. "Jambalaya."

The jambalaya was drier than the gumbo, and the spices had more heat to them. "I adore this! I hope you can make it often."

"Of course. I would like to make my own sausages and use my mama's recipe." Miss Thibodeaux grinned at the compliment.

"Now, Miss Thibodeaux. If you were to be my cook, you would have to live in England. You will be far from your family, and it is a slightly different culture. While my family and friends will treat you well, I cannot guarantee that you will always be treated as well as you deserve. Is that something you would be comfortable with?" Serena felt obligated to warn the woman of the possibilities.

"Yes, ma—my lady," Miss Thibodeaux answered.

"Very well. I would like to hire you at a hundred pounds per annum as well as room and board, of course." Serena hesitated and drew closer so she could speak at a low volume. "I will make you this offer, but please tell no one. If you should hate England, I will provide a return ticket to New Orleans for you," Serena offered, extending her hand.

"Thank you, my lady! You will not regret this!" Miss Thibodeaux shook Serena's hand with vigor and enthusiasm.

"I hope you are right. I am uncertain as to my fiancé's kitchen." Serena frowned. "Perhaps we should go and buy all of the equipment you will need. We will not be departing for England until after November fifth, so if your mother wishes to meet me or my fiancé, we can make arrangements."

"Should we go now, or should I make a list?" Miss Thibodeaux asked.

Serena opened her mouth to answer but instead heard "Pet!"

Serena turned to see Frederick cutting through the park, looking determined. "I believe we will have to go shopping on another day, as I am about to be absconded with very soon."

"Is that your fiancé? He's handsome." Miss Thibodeaux gawked.

Serena sighed, of course she would find Frederick handsome, but Serena would be hard pressed to think of a worse idea. "Frederick, may I present Miss Loretta Thibodeaux. She will be the cook at Nightingale Lodge. Miss Thibodeaux, this is my brother Frederick Percy, Marquess of Berkeley."

Frederick surveyed the pretty Miss Thibodeaux and clearly delighted in what he beheld. "A pleasure to meet you, Miss Thibodeaux. What a shame a gentleman never pursues a servant, or else I would be sending you flowers daily."

Miss Thibodeaux giggled as all women giggled when Frederick flirted. "Why can't a gentleman court a cook?"

"There are some that will, but it is never a good idea. You see, you exist at the pleasure of my sister. She could reduce your wages or overburden you. Therefore, I would always have more power over you than I would in a normal courtship. I prefer invitations over conquests." Frederick smiled and gestured to the dishes of food. "May I impose? I skipped lunch."

"Certainly." Serena handed him another fork from her cane, so pleased to be able to make use of the lovely piece.

"I love the food here. Much more flavorful than English cuisine. My God, Miss Thibodeaux! If you do not wish to work for Serena, please come cook for me. This"—Frederick gestured toward the gumbo—"calls to mind an Indian curry with the spices and rice. I shall be a frequent guest at my sister's house."

Poor Miss Thibodeaux positively bloomed under his attention. "Thank you, sir!"

Serena sighed. "We were considering shopping for Miss Thibodeaux's kitchen needs, but if you require me, I think we can delay until tomorrow."

"No, no. It is fine. I do need to show you something, but I think we will have until five o'clock. Allow me to escort you and help choose items," Frederick offered.

The next few hours were difficult for Serena. She had to balance being polite to her new cook and discouraging Frederick's natural flirtatious demeanor. Miss Thibodeaux clearly delighted in Frederick, but Frederick merely delighted in making ladies smile.

Serena found that speaking of Vincent dulled the happy chatter and allowed her to pretend to be concerned. She was thrilled not to know what he had and asked frequent questions of her cook. Frederick's friendliness had introduced Serena to most of her friends and her husband, but she would not sacrifice her cook for his compulsive need for feminine validation (which was the nicest way of putting it).

After they parted ways with Miss Thibodeaux, Frederick began leading Serena toward the docks. As they passed rows upon rows of warehouses, Serena felt a strange apprehension. "Where are we going, Frederick?"

"I saw a man, and I could not believe my eyes. I need you to confirm that he is who I believe that he is," Frederick elaborated awkwardly. The words trailed out of him, and his usual confidence hid under a deep coat of reservation.

Serena nodded. After all, she had dragged him across the continent, and Frederick had gone along with anything she asked. "Very well. Please tell me which man."

Frederick gazed at one of the warehouses. "I do not see him, yet. Bold choice with your cook, pet."

"Yes." Serena jutted her chin at him defiantly. "I must ask that you stop flirting. It is unkind to her."

Frederick grimaced. "I did not mean to flirt, but I will try to be more formal with her. Are you not concerned that she will have hardships in Norfolk?"

Serena shrugged. It made sense. She was extremely concerned for the woman, but she also knew that life anywhere was not perfect for Miss Thibodeaux. "I will be a good mistress to her, and I will try to insure a peaceful life. But do you really think America is better than England? There were race riots in Philadelphia, while we were visiting. There is a strong color line in this country. After all, they may have rebuilt much, but the Americans are only twenty-five years from owning *people*."

Frederick nodded. "But we taught them to enslave. We can judge in a lofty tower of piety as good English nobility, but we built this nation, and we own some of the responsibility for their greed and callous natures."

"Absolutely, as there is no perfect nation, and the British Empire has more blood on its hands that we can ever truly understand. However, we can effect change. Most distrust of the other stems from ignorance, so we must educate ourselves and others to promote a more equal ideology. Revise...and if our people are better, then we make the world better."

Frederick narrowed his eyes. "There...do you recognize that man?"

Serena looked toward the man leaving the warehouse. He was familiar to her, but she could not place him. It was as though she was trying to remember a dream. Her thoughts and connections did not seem make any sense. She kept seeing the man, much younger, with horses and with her father.

"Did he work for Father?" Serena asked.

Frederick exhaled a breath he had clearly been holding. "Yes! He was our stable master! He disappeared after Mother and Father died, and now he is here. I am shocked and hope you will accept my apology. I never believed we would find anything in New Orleans and hoped that you would end this search. As you observe, clearly I was wrong."

Serena stared at the man. She was overwhelmed by the reality that he was here. She was devastated by the implications of his existence. He could have had something to do with her parents' murder, and she was one step closer to resolving the mystery of their deaths. It was so rare and unlikely that Madame Olyenska had to be gifted. There was no legitimate way to detect this man, who had taken great pains to become invisible, without some gifts of deduction that far exceeded the boundaries of nature.

This was catastrophic. Mystics were real and legitimate, albeit rare. Did this mean God existed as well? If she had evidence, then she would believe in anything. The only thing she could be certain of was that Madame Olyenska was communicating with forces beyond Serena's understanding. She could continue searching for the evidence of God and the afterlife later.

As Serena and Frederick entered the hotel, she spied Vincent sitting in the lounge reading a newspaper.

He smiled as soon as he saw them. "Good afternoon! Where have you two been?"

Serena froze. She couldn't lie. Not to Vincent. And this was a lie that changed the color of her world.

"Serena and I walked along the docks. I am aware that it is not the safest avenue to walk down, but the wee bit of mist was surprisingly refreshing," Frederick supplied. Not entirely a lie, but certainly not the truth. The warehouse was adjacent to the docks by three blocks. So, a lie within three blocks of the truth.

"Ah, that is why you look so lovely today." Vincent grinned with a smirk she had only seen before he kissed her.

Serena smiled at the compliment, but her eyes

focused on a man approaching them. It could not be who she recognized. There was absolutely no possible universe in which the Earl of Coningsby was in New Orleans. However, the man perfectly resembled Sebastian Mandeville, except Serena had never seen the earl smile before. Perhaps he had come for the wedding. Perhaps he had come to stop the wedding, meaning she was ruined with no husband. Today was strange—maybe he was just an apparition.

"Vincent!" Coningsby called as he made his way to his brother. Their eyes met, and Serena could see the shock turning to fury in Vincent's eyes. Coningsby gestured to the Roses and their father. "We came for your wedding."

"How marvelous!" Serena placed a gloved hand on Vincent's arm, and her eyes silently pled with Vincent for peace. What little control he had hoarded (considering his other appetites were indulged) could stop an outburst, right? "It is lovely to make your acquaintance again, Lord Coningsby. I am delighted that you crossed an ocean, merely to support your brother. I am surprised that Lord and Lady Ralph Mandeville did not join you. I hope all is well."

"Sadly, Lily is unable to travel as being with child has proven difficult," Coningsby explained. His eyes narrowed on the empty air that should have contained his brother's warm greetings.

Vincent's face filled with anguish. "Is she ill? Why has no one informed me?"

"She is being cared for by Mother's physician. There is nothing to be done that is not already being done," Coningsby answered.

"Phhh. No one is making her laugh. I hear it is the

best remedy and one I excel at," Vincent muttered.

"Is she vomiting or is she having pains?" Serena asked.

"I believe the former," Coningsby answered dryly. Clearly, he found Serena's inquiry to be too bold.

Serena turned to Vincent. "Do not be concerned. Uncle Benjamin told me of this. If she had cramping or bleeding, there would be cause for concern, but she is not. Every child is different, but the common wisdom only applies for a select few. However, I am certain a letter from you would soothe her greatly."

Vincent nodded. "I will send it quickly."

Serena smiled. "I will leave you two to fret. I will see you at dinner?"

Serena was pleased to make a hasty exit from the tense scene. Did Coningsby not like or approve of her? She knew Vincent did not like his brother. For the life of her, why would a brother traverse the ocean to attend the wedding of someone he did not get along with to someone he disapproved of? Something was clearly missing. Whether it was that Coningsby was simply difficult to read and therefore her assumptions were wrong, or he was here as a saboteur.

Serena sighed. Her wedding was under a cloud. She needed to investigate her parents' murder. Vincent was acting out of sorts with Benedict. And now Coningsby had arrived. Her tightly fitted dress held in her urge to cry out, and her terror the wedding would not occur at all, and that the airy simplicity of their love was being vexed by revenge.

Chapter 25

Aside from the moors, I don't think there is a better place to spend late October than New Orleans. The Catholic iconography and voodoo worshipers lend an air of danger, though I am ensconced in a perfectly safe neighborhood. Every meal is spiced and warm. I am unsure if I will ever leave.

A Curmudgeon's Tour of America, October 1885

Vincent was aghast and afraid. To be sent reeling back a few months, into a former version of himself, gripped by intractable anger and an impulse to ratify his own loneliness with self-destructive behavior. It was a sensation that required copious whiskey.

Giving Sebastian a second chance was akin to giving him a second bullet after his first shot missed. However, Serena clearly wanted family harmony, and Lily was sick, so he needed to be mature, a first for Vincent. Marriage and maturity—this did require a drink. Even with offering Sebastian an opportunity, Vincent watched him like a hawk. If Sebastian so much as allowed his gaze to linger on Serena too long, there would be a war. Vincent had liked Marlene, but he loved Serena. There would be no place on Earth far enough away for Vincent to go if Sebastian stole Serena away. The haunting thought cooed in his ears like a petty ghost, and it made him paranoid.

Vincent had plenty to be paranoid about at present. After all, he was on his way to perform larceny on the building purchased by Mathew MacDonald using Lord Annandale's stolen money. Vincent was not a perfect citizen, but he had never actually broken the law before. Burglars tended to be hanged, and Vincent was rather fond of his neck. That was where he kept his ties, and one occasion, an elegant necklace (he would never again attempt such a fashion statement). However, he needed to know the body of this "Shadow Society," which was hard without more information. How strong were its arms, and how long was their reach? Did they cross oceans and move ships? Quite frankly, his curiosity was heavier than his care.

Vincent entered the cheap hotel and heaved himself and the suitcase up creaking, uneven stairs to room four and knocked four times.

Melgum opened the door, poking his head out and looking around. If he was trying to remain hidden, why would he poke his head out? "Did anyone suspect anything?"

Vincent pushed past him and into the room. "No. Serena was tired and retired early. Frederick had plans on a gambling boat or some such matter. He was very vague. The Roses, my family, and your grandparents were delighted to receive tickets to a play."

"Clever idea," Melgum complimented. "What is in the suitcase?"

Vincent smiled. "I have noticed a phenomenon whilst in America. They have a profound respect for authority but a distrust of government, which leads to private industry being treated like lords. In that spirit, I have arranged for us to have disguises."

Vincent presented two uniforms made to resemble the Pinkerton uniforms. In truth the Pinkerton detectives dressed plainly but with shiny silver buttons on their coat or vest, depending on the weather. That made them easy to emulate. There were a few shops with these buttons Vincent had found in their travels. He had purchased them as an amusement, but now they had purpose. He only owned four buttons, but truly they each only needed one at night.

As Vincent began to dress in the uncomfortable and plain clothes, he delicately folded his suit. Melgum watched him with surprising interest. "I know, I am very handsome, Melgum." Vincent had dressed in front of other men. Why did Melgum care?

Melgum reddened. "I have never seen another man take such care with his clothing."

Vincent shrugged as he hung his shirt carefully. "I cannot abide my clothing being mussed. My brothers had always teased me for it. But it is hard to ridicule from a position of wrinkles." Teasing Vincent for being a bit of a pettifogger would be unexpected but somewhat correct.

"Brilliant, now I have something to talk about with Coningsby. We have never been able to have an interesting conversation," Melgum grumbled.

Of course, they hadn't; Melgum was far too dour, and Sebastian was far too dull. However, this opened a door for Vincent to satisfy his curiosity. "Hmm. Is Sebastian getting on well with Serena?"

Melgum rolled his eyes. "Of course, you heard about that. I am certain it was nothing."

Vincent straightened, and in that rigidness, his stomach clenched. "What are you referring to?"

"Earlier, when we trekked to Jackson Square and they argued," Melgum answered.

Vincent had missed the trip as he needed time to find their uniforms. He was happy to hear that an argument occurred; it was tremendously better than a flirtation. "What was the argument over?"

Melgum let out an agitated puff of air. "Wealth disparity, the same tired issue Serena always argues; that is, if she is not arguing her right to be an atheist. It's incredibly vexing."

Vincent snorted. "Who was the winner?"

Melgum shrugged. "Neither moved the other. Serena accused the wealthy of only giving the poor enough bread and circuses so as not to have a revolt. Coningsby tried to explain that she did not understand economics and recommended that she read Adam Smith or Edmund Burke. Serena, familiar with both, called Coningsby a prig who is unsympathetic to mankind. She also corrected him that Smith himself would disagree with him, and said he needed to read *Theory of Moral Sentiments*."

Vincent chortled. God, he loved this woman. "I am certain that Sebastian will forgive her and merely blame Berkeley."

Melgum frowned. "Why on Earth would he blame Frederick?"

Vincent was confused. "Everyone knows he is the radical."

Melgum wore the face of a cat who had caught a particularly ignorant mouse. "Who do you think exposed him to such ideals? Serena attends these soirees and frequents coffee houses to be part of the left-wing intelligentsia. She is an acolyte of Engels and

Marx. She pestered Frederick to invest his money only in labor-friendly schemes. It has always been Serena influencing Frederick but not the other way round," Melgum explained.

Vincent had no idea. Vincent considered himself to be part of the more progressive intelligentsia, but in fairness, he had spent the two years previous touring the continent. "I assumed it was Frederick that had led Serena, but I am not bothered by the idea of my wife being so informed."

Melgum snorted. "Good luck to you. She gets these insane notions and convinces Frederick to follow them. Such as child labor—we passed laws dictating that no child under ten is permitted to work and after ten years of age they are limited to ten hours a day. But Serena, in her bleeding-heart madness, wants to educate the *entire* population to be ready for university. It is the height of absurdity. Only a woman who has never balanced a ledger would develop such a recipe for bankruptcy. And when you argue with her, she descends into more inane arguments. I tried to ask who would fund these schools, and she suggested raising taxes on the upper class—as though we do not pay enough. When I asked, 'What does a shoemaker need with an education? Why does he need to know the history of Rome?' she insists that industrialization will end most cobblers' jobs, and they will need an education to find clerk work. Finally, when I tried to illustrate that the poor need children to work so they can afford to live, she suggested raising wages in accordance with basic needs instead of the price that a laborer may accept for their work. She's mad, but I still love her as a cousin."

Vincent did not think they had the time nor attention to argue, but Serena was mostly accurate. Most of the gentlemen he knew did not use their education for anything more than to demean others. They would insult lower-class men to their faces in French and follow with a mere "Excuse my French." The best occupations required education or connection, with emphasis on family connections. But if one can gain employment by connection or nepotism, then why deprive the working class of an education? It was not a threat; it enriched the country and allowed success and mobility. Of course, Vincent needed to focus on breaking the law at present and not be distracted by child labor and education reform.

"Shall we be off, then?" Vincent asked.

The night fog had rolled in and hung in the air like an unwelcome guest who had drunk too much. Melgum and Vincent walked in silence as they made their way to the warehouses near the docks. In the distance, lit steamboats paddled up and down the river, their wheels creaking against the firm vibrations of nearby insects, reminding Vincent of how very far he was from London. His uneasiness began to grow with every step. After all, consider the possibilities that could unfold. They were foreigners in a city that had a history of hating the English, and if caught, there would be no indulgence for title or position. He could lose his family, his fiancée, or even his life. Vincent tried to control his anxiety by focusing on navigating the fog. He needed to be in control of himself now more than ever, but his worries were a new companion for the night.

With two blocks left to walk, Melgum spoke.

"How are we going to enter?"

Vincent was tempted to cut the tension by suggesting that he had no idea how to break into the warehouse but decided against it. Melgum was most likely as tense as Vincent was and would not respond well to a jest.

"Like banks, warehouses tend to focus on their cargo in lieu of the office. The office is up some stairs on the second floor with a private entrance. I assume as an escape in case of fires or a worker's revolt. I have purchased tools to pick locks and read a book on the subject," Vincent whispered before he started walking again. Reading a book on how to do a thing that their plan and personal safety depended on was surely enough to assuage any fears.

Melgum grabbed Vincent's arm tightly and demanded, "A book?"

"Relax. From what I have read, locks are a series of tumblers that need jostling. I spent the morning practicing on the doors of the hotel. I was able to see Serena sleeping this morning and Berkeley shaving." Vincent relaxed at the idea of his sleeping Serena. Her blonde hair was darker now, yet still flowed to cover her breasts like a well-wrapped gift. It was tempting to wake her for morning bed sport. However, who knows when her maid would have returned and observed their bedroom badminton. Being caught by a maid, morning indulgences—such things would titillate a lesser man, and so they also titillated Vincent.

Melgum frowned but released Vincent. Once again, they walked in silence until they found the correct red-brick building. There was no gas lamp at the top of the stairs, which made it dangerous, but also let him pick the lock with little notice. He held his breath and listened carefully for the little tinkles of the tumbler followed by the catch. Vincent smirked at Melgum as he opened the door and gave an actor's bow. Ta-da, you mysterious little man.

It was pitch black in the building, and so it made sense to wait for their eyes to adjust. Vincent carefully lit a small lamp near the door, moving slower than he wanted. The small bright thing was clearly meant for the first person in every day. His back tensed and fought the impulse to stop midway, but fumbling in the dark was not an option. The office was a tightly coiled bureaucracy, with everything set out just so. The clerks' desks were arranged neatly with a windowed wall separating the manager's office. Vincent handed Melgum the lamp and proceeded to unlock the office door with an almost imperceptible click. It was, of course, less difficult than the outer door. As surmised, they paid more attention to the profitable goods than the information. The filing cabinets slid open with a mild thud and the scritchy-scratch of wood dragging over wood. The files were barely lit under the glow of the lamp, their secrets barely coming into the orange light when a loud clatter rang down in the warehouse.

Vincent straightened as his fears become solid. He whispered to Melgum as he cupped the lamp as tight as possible, wrestling with the ephemeral glow. "Hide."

Chapter 26

Earlier that evening Serena had retired early, pretending to have a headache. She did not have any ailments but, rather, plans with Frederick to investigate the warehouse that employed their former stable master, Mr. Compton. Serena needed time to disguise herself as a man. Martha helped her tie her hair into a flat bun, like that a ballerina might wear. They tied down her breasts and dressed Serena in a man's suit followed by a heavy wool overcoat. Serena was far too warm in the ensemble, but it was less heavy than her winter dresses. Martha seemed to enjoy the process; after all, it was a respite from drudgery, and costumes were intrinsically amusing.

Frederick entered her room at ten o'clock and smiled. "Pet, you would be a disastrous man, as you are far too coquettish. I brought you a sailor's hat. Hopefully it will be enough to obfuscate your pretty face."

Serena donned the straw hat. "Better?"

Frederick gave a sympathetic smile that might have been truthful and sat next to her on the small settee. "Are you certain that you want to do this, pet? I will support you either way, but if you want to move past this and simply focus on your wedding and marriage, then we shall never look back. This is dangerous and reckless. Mother and Father have been dead for nine years; we could let them rest."

Serena rested her head on her brother's shoulder. "I know, but I must do this. Mother and Father were so good, and someone murdered them. I cannot live in this shadow. I cannot live in a world where that injustice is permitted. And the ton still mocks them. I once heard two men dismissively saying how Mother and Father 'wanted to make the world a better place.' As though that was silly or a bad idea. It wears on me, Frederick, the constant injustice. I am sick of seeing one class whose bright sunny hours are gardens and balls, and another who never see the sun at all. Who journey to their dangerous work before the sun rises and return home only after day has fled. Imagine only seeing your children, your family, in a world of darkness. If we all live in a world lit by the same sun, we all deserve the brightness of justice."

It hurt to say this. Her righteousness exceeded her joy, which was painful to her. "I feel as though I am tilting at windmills with my hopes for a more just world, but this! I can finally get justice now, and I need it. I just need to know that if one persists long enough, justice will be found." Serena blinked away her tears. She had never vocalized the mental exhaustion from fighting a battle that might never be won, of planting seeds of trees whose shade would never comfort her.

Frederick hugged her close. "I know, pet. It seems daunting and as if we will fight forever but never succeed. But we will win. There is mandated education until ten now, and they will be able to read the news and vote for men that better represent them. We simply must keep fighting, and more people will listen. You changed my mind, and together we will change more minds until even the poorest can sleep with a full belly at night. Now, are you ready to break the law for justice?"

Her laughter exploded from overheated steam, easing her tension. "Yes, I have a cane for you."

Frederick grinned. "Is it a bawdy art cane, like the one your fiancé carries?"

"No, and I am merely lending it to you. I have a ladder cane that we bought in Philadelphia, a torch cane that was once owned by a Chicago politician, and a sword cane. The sword cane is for you."

Frederick unsheathed the sword and demonstrated his skills. "I had always hoped we would make use of your canes."

"Happily, you have this cane and not the cane that helps give cow enemas." Serena grinned. "Shall we be off?"

As they walked to the warehouse, Frederick attempted to lift her mood by telling amusing stories from their childhood. They reminisced about their German nursemaid who would tell them fairy tales of hero knights and clever witches. Frederick had been in love with Snow White and would roam the woods on their estate seeking a charming cottage with a lost princess inside. Serena always wanted to be the king's magician, Merlin to an Arthur. Her heart filled with the powerful echoes of carefree days when the world was full of possibilities, and she was surrounded by love.

She had stopped paying attention to the dark, foggy street. Once they arrived at the warehouse, Serena tested the windows carefully with her cane, tapping inaudibly and pushing just enough to find a loose one. After she had tried most of them, she found one that was loose and could be forced open. She unpacked the cane to build a ladder and prepared to climb, but Frederick stopped her. It was absurd how beautiful the little invention was once it was built. The ingenious method for the little wooden bars interlocked, as if it were a puzzle, until a ladder appeared. Frederick grabbed the second rung firmly, climbed the ladder, and disappeared into the window before reappearing at the windowsill, pointing to the ladder, and waving her in. Serena climbed the ladder; it had worked better than planned. But as she looked inside, her breath caught, and she almost fell. She would need to land on a box roughly five feet lower, without noise. Serena sat on the window ledge and pulled the ladder up behind her. In the history of her bad ideas, this would truly take center stage. The elegant act of retracting the cane, holding her body on a thin ledge, and coping with the near pitch-black night was too hard for her ladyship. The hot air of the warehouse sailed around her as she promptly fell from the window face first. And of course, the ladder came tumbling after, striking her back and her head. Her only hope was that this would remain a private humiliation.

"Pet, are you hurt?" Frederick whispered as he lifted the ladder from her and steadied it against the crate she had fallen onto. Oh, what great joy—a wooden crate. If she had been wearing her normal dress, she would be adorned in scratches. But her disguise had cushioned her.

"No," Serena whispered. Her back, neck, and leg ached, but she was more or less intact. She climbed down the ladder and began to deconstruct it.

"How does one light the torch?" Frederick asked,

eyeing the cane.

Serena finished with the ladder cane before finding the compartment on the torch cane that held the matches. She struck the tiny match and held it fast to the torch. "It is an oil torch; be careful."

Frederick nodded, and the siblings began to make their way through the warehouse. Serena tried to read the crates and cargo, but the lettering was primarily in oriental languages (Serena was unsure if it was Chinese or Japanese) and a few Nordic languages. They found the stairs that separated the storage from the office, and the workers from management. The internal door was not locked, though it had a heavy door and solid lock. They moved beyond the desks and to the office door, which opened easily.

Serena struggled not to scream as two large figures stood in the darkened room and one of them rushed for her. The light glinted off a silver Pinkerton button. A pair of hands were on her, but they were not the rough hands of a Pinkerton. The dim orange light revealed two blue eyes, imperious as they were full of fury. But they narrowed, and the hands fell quickly. How could her love be here?

In his familiar but startled voice, Vincent asked, "What the bloody hell are you doing here?"

Serena wanted to apologize immediately, but Frederick spoke first. "What are *you* doing here?"

Vincent smirked. "Clearly this is the place in which Melgum and I have chosen to carry out our torrid affair. I hope you can forgive me."

"I think if you and Benedict were in love, that you might use his Christian name," Serena pointed out.

Vincent glared at her, but with a twinkle in his eye.

"If I were interested in men, I would simply ravish you in this outfit. I repeat myself, what are you doing here?"

Serena sighed. "A fortune teller told me we would find clues to our parents' murders here, and this warehouse is where Mr. Compton, our former stable master, is in the employ of the owner. What are you doing here?"

Vincent relaxed. "I find your explanation less likely than mine. My family was attacked by a secret society that purchased this building using stolen funds." He stopped and smiled halfway, like he had been tricked out of his hard-earned annoyance. "I would like to discuss this further, but not while breaking the law. I propose we search together and discuss this after we are safe from the law. Do we agree?"

Serena nodded and began to search the files. Even with her careful gaze, half the files seemed written in gibberish. Was this pointless after all? She was not skilled in business or accounting, so it was as though she were deciphering a drudging story written in hieroglyphs. They would need to get copies of the information and have someone translate it.

She had to cut to the quick; staying in a stale warehouse combing through financial apocrypha didn't help her. "This is silly. We need to convince Mr. Compton to talk to us. None of us know what we are looking for or what we are seeing, for that matter. The only person who can actually connect all the pieces is Mr. Compton," Serena explained.

Frederick nodded. "Correct, pet. But I did discover an outrageous amount of the profits are funneled to Sweden. Why on Earth would anyone in Sweden be involved in this tangled web?"

"We should have Adrian Rose look at some of these things, but for now, speaking with Mr. Compton and having us all working together is our best move." Vincent began to reorder the room so no one would know they were there.

Once everything was in the right place, Benedict opened a small door that Serena had not noticed. If her heart were not churning like an angry streetcar, she would have jumped. "Shall we be off, then?"

Frederick and Benedict started down the exterior stairs, but Vincent held her back. He took her torch cane and extinguished the flame so that only moonlight lit his face. His expression was one that Serena had only seen her father wear, a mix of fear, anger, and concern.

"Serena, we can't ever have this happen again. We must tell each other everything and help each other. When I think of the possibilities, how disastrous tonight could have been, I get palpitations. Please never commit larceny again; I don't think my heart can tolerate it," Vincent said. "Plus, you steal enough gazes and hearts, young woman."

Serena leaned in to kiss him. She was grateful that he had not lectured her on her bad behavior as some more patrician men might be wont to do. Rather, he recognized that they were both at fault, and so they both needed to do better in the future. "I promise to tell you the next time that I commit a crime."

Vincent smiled. "Thank you, but never kiss me again while dressed as a man. I would never stop laughing if we got away with breaking and entering, only to be arrested for buggery."

****

After breakfast, Serena surprised the Duke and Duchess of Wharton, as well as Vincent's father, with a golf expedition. This had been a hard-to-arrange secret and was nearly foiled by the weather. Which might have worked out just fine. Serena's shoulders and legs screamed in pure exhaustion. She and Vincent had remained awake until three in the morning discussing the Black Swan. She was vexed that he should be angry with her while keeping secrets of his own. What a hypocrite! But maybe the simplest explanation for the spat was their mutual frustration; neither behaved very lovingly. They had finally agreed to be honest with each other about any mysteries they were solving, and anything that might endanger them. How he felt about her was still a bit of a mystery, but the agreement to be truthful was always a wise idea.

After the older generation left the room, Vincent cleared his throat. "There will be a meeting of the Black Swan in Lady Serena's suite. Please move there now." How better to conduct a secret meeting than to announce it like an angry chamberlain.

Serena's suite had an adjoining sitting room where they met. The women sat on a settee in a row. Adrian Rose rested his elbow on the mantel above the unlit fireplace. Benedict leaned against the wall, seeming taller than everyone. Vincent sat in a wing chair with Frederick behind him. Coningsby sat on a tufted stool and looked rather silly and out of place.

Vincent stood from his chair. "Five months ago, I received a note warning me that my family had been chosen by a secret society called the Shadow Society. Apparently, by their terms, their organizing principle is revenge, and every year they have selected a major family to ruin. The Mandevilles were the second family chosen. The first family is being represented by Melgum."

All eyes went toward Benedict. How was the contrarian Benedict involved in all of this cloak and dagger nonsense? Maybe Vincent needed help and turned to Benedict; he seemed like he had his own secrets. Clearly, everyone else was confused but not for the same reason as Serena.

Benedict shook his head. "It was not my family, but that of a close friend who wishes to remain anonymous."

"And we will respect those wishes," Vincent continued. He paced seriously. "There is a counter group to the Shadow Society. We are known as the Black Swan. For the past weeks, Melgum and I have been tracking the stolen money, from its origin with the first family to entities here in New Orleans. And last night, we tracked it to a warehouse where we found two charming, but unskilled burglars." He stretched his arms toward the siblings with copious drama. "Berkeley and Serena would have never made it in a proper criminal organization."

Several eyes went to Frederick, who simply shrugged and tried not to flash a smug smile. "Most of you are familiar enough with my family to know that our parents were murdered. While trying to discover their killer, we discovered this conspiracy. It appears that whoever killed our parents is connected to the Shadow Society. What a weak name for a menacing organization. We stand ready to assist in any means we have."

"I am confused; do we think the Shadow Society

had the marquess murdered? How are they in America? And does this explain the telegram scheme?" Coningsby asked.

"What is the telegram scheme?" Serena asked.

Vincent waved his hand, batting away questions that could be answered better without their interruptions. "Foolish, really. I was trying to find your party but kept getting waylaid. And you may recall the silliness of the telegram you received from Miss Haverford."

"Oh, well, in light of everything, that seems fairly obvious as to why they would want to keep you from us," Serena said. Tiny butterflies were trying to take flight in the darkness of her body, starting in the depths of her stomach and flowing through her throat as she found her words. How bizarrely romantic that a shadowy organization had tried in vain to separate them.

A silence, gauzy and tired, descended over the room. Serena waited patiently, but no one seemed to understand. She could either feel rather stupid or try to explain herself.

"Oh, of course!" Honoria cried, and the two nodded at each other. Thank God for Honoria.

"I, for one, am lost. Please explain why they would want to keep Vincent from you," Rose asked. Well, perhaps this was her chance to articulate the terrible plot.

"If they have targeted only two families, they may know that Benedict would be privy to the details of the first family. It was never an attempt to keep Vincent from me. If he were with our party for long enough, he might discover everything that Benedict already has.

Our courtship was merely an annoying coincidence to the Shadow Society," Serena answered, but her voice wavered after the word "coincidence." But in her version, the tale where their love had defeated the shadows, and she and Vincent were heroes astride tides of history and passion, she was much happier. Such myth was much better fodder for her tired body and heart. And thus it was intrinsically more true.

"But what of your parents? Are they not victims of the Shadow Society as well?" Rose asked.

Serena shook her head. "I don't believe that the Shadow Society has been together for nine years. It is possible that they murdered my parents and then went underground, but unlikely. They are fairly brazen; they informed their victims of their plight, so a near-decade of silence seems unlikely. What is more plausible is that one of the members, most likely the founder, arranged for my parents' murders and formed a society with people who are ignorant of that fact. However, most of these questions will be answered this afternoon, when we go to speak with Mr. Compton."

"As far as the telegrams go, Vincent must have discovered that issue quickly. Since the rest of the party would not mention him in telegrams, the Shadow Society must have thought they succeeded. Until the wedding, of course." Honoria frowned. She had not finished her mental puzzle, and her gaze was far away, searching for the rest of the pieces.

"Truly? No one mentioned me? I am vexed and wounded at your lack of high regard. Am I so unworthy of praise and contempt?" Vincent joked.

Honoria shrugged. "Frederick only uses telegrams for business. Melgum is moving to America and most likely has nothing to say instantly to anyone in Britain, as the people he likes best are with him. And Serena had too much to say about you to put in a telegram, so she wrote letters."

"Oh? Serena had too much to say about me? Such as? What was in these lovely long letters?" Vincent asked.

Honoria raised an eyebrow, seemingly delighted with this turn of events. "Oh, I could never betray a confidence."

"Not even for your favorite cousin?" Vincent pressed.

"Not even for my favorite cousin," Honoria answered. Honoria was too good at this deception, even with those closest to her. What was she, to have such a practiced hand at a game she had not been playing long at all?

Vincent shrugged. "That is fine. Aurora will tell me."

All eyes were suddenly on Aurora, whom they had forgotten not to invite. She was not mature enough for Black Swan business or any of this. She was only seventeen, and so she did not know how to keep secrets. Serena knew Aurora well. She was too clever but spoiled enough to give away gold for pretty glass. She once ate pie for breakfast and did not bat an eye. How unnecessarily precarious this had just become. All of their secrets and weaknesses were in the hands of a delightful but imprudent lady.

"Oh, dear. I am so torn. I suppose were my need for pie met, I could or could not discuss such matters." She feigned a yawn and blinked with joy, holding her precious eyes shut too long. After she had decided her price, she opened them again, brimming delight. "I have also always wanted a pet bunny," Aurora said with a smile, her jade eyes still alight with mischief. Espionage was not a safe place for amateurs.

Chapter 27

Solitude may have a tendency to drive a man mad,
but the sudden appearance of family can send you right
to the madhouse. Of course, I love to see my father and
cousins, but the tension of ensuring that I do not offend
anyone in a quite large party is exhausting. I am
certain that I will not survive the next fortnight. The
only thing I have to look forward to is my wedding
breakfast. I truly love the food here.
A Curmudgeon's Tour of America, October 1885

Eight days. It had been eight days since Vincent
had felt true happiness, and the absence of it was
driving him mad. Of course, Serena was teasing him,
with her perfumes and occasional kisses. Sly little
minx. However, Serena was clearly not familiar with
men and might have no idea how badly he wanted to
bury himself within her silky folds. His wedding day
could not come fast enough. It would take a captain and
three shipmates to remove him from their cabin during
the ship ride home.

At present, she was forcing him to watch her
bustled skirts swish in front of him as she walked. She
was wearing a purple walking dress, silk and
reminiscent of irises. The air was heavy, but
occasionally the breeze would blow and smack him
with her perfume and memories of the times it had

lingered around him. The walkway clicked with her steps, and he yearned to see her boots and stockings. She gave a slight backward glance and offered a small smile at him. She even let her lip drop in a pleading gesture, as though she understood the mild misery she was leaving in her wake, along with the perfume.

Mine.

Thank God the road quickly led to the house of Mr. Compton. The neighborhood was decidedly middle class, a series of houses with pretty gardens, each too similar to be an accident. One could always identify a middle-class house, as the women tended to be house proud with flowery gardens. Mrs. Compton clearly liked butterflies; her garden was lousy with milkweed and cosmos erupting with pinks and yellows in front of the all-white house. The house itself was a charming Creole cottage, all in white that reflected the heavy sun, with pretty detailing atop the four columns that decorated the porch. Berkeley knocked on the wood near the leaded glass that adorned the door.

A woman who was clearly the lady of the house answered. Her chestnut hair was swept up into a bun, and she had nearly black eyes. She frowned and had a mask of fear the moment she looked upon Serena.

"*Madame Olyenska?*" Serena asked. Nothing could have prepared her for this revelation. The woman who had launched them on this course, with her convincing pretense of supernatural knowledge. What in the seven heavens and nine hells was she doing here?

"Greene?" Berkeley asked.

Vincent, who apparently did not enjoy being the odd man out, so he asked, "Mrs. Compton?"

"All three, I'm afraid. Please come in." Mrs.

Compton moved aside to allow them inside the house. She led them to a small parlor, silently and with her lips pursed and ready for a whisper. "It is the servants' afternoon off, so I apologize for not offering tea."

"Yes, Greene, by all means let us maintain the pretenses. This is surely not the most absurd situation. Cut to the quick—what is going on? You have spun a thick web of lies," Berkeley pressed.

"Of course, little Lord Lyons," Mrs. Compton began.

"It's Berkeley, now," Berkeley growled.

Mrs. Compton paled, visibly humbled as the realization of why Frederick Percy was not Viscount Lyons, but instead, the Marquess of Berkeley, dawned on her. It was a peculiarity of the aristocracy that when one's father died, the eldest son simply was called by his father's name. It was a permanent reminder that a man's success in life was a result of what he had been given. A jolt of gratitude raced through Vincent. In the sad event that his father died, Vincent would remain Lord Vincent.

"My tale is a long one, so please be seated," Mrs. Compton offered. Berkeley sat in an armchair near the back of the room, while Vincent and Serena sat on the rose-colored sofa on the wall near where they had walked in. Mrs. Compton lowered herself on to a cream settee, clearly positioned to gaze out the window. "Nearly ten years ago, I was Lady Berkeley's maid. I adored your mother, as all the servants did. She wanted so much to conquer her position, and she would always rise after being knocked down. We used to call her Lady Phoenix."

"The Phoenix is dead," Berkeley bit off.

"Yes. Henry—Mr. Compton—and I were desperate to be married. We hoped for a bit more money to have a little cottage where we could raise a family. One day, a Scotsman came to Henry. He claimed that Lord Berkeley would not hear out the problems of his people who had lost many in a train crash earlier in the year. Henry knew Lord Berkeley was a kind man, who cared for the lower classes, so he offered to help the Scotsman."

Vincent suspected that he knew the Scotsman's name, but he did not want to interrupt. Serena and Berkeley clearly needed to hear Mrs. Compton's tale. The Percys had waited so long to be whole again.

"The plan was to give the coachman—on that night it was John Smythe—a concoction to make him drowsy. Smythe would never drive at night while terribly sleepy, so he would pull over, and the Scotsman would arrive to assist Lord and Lady Berkeley. The Scotsman would have their ear for the drive home, and all would be well. Henry went out to find Smythe and recover the carriage. When Henry arrived, he saw the carriage was overturned and the Scotsman was murdering your parents." Mrs. Compton took a moment to lick her lips. The air tasted like lightning to Vincent. Poor Serena.

"Henry was terrified and raced to find me. He told me to get my things together, and we needed to flee immediately. I rushed to get my things before we ran on foot to the nearest docks, in hope of finding a ship. We found a ship to New Orleans, but we had to wait eight hours before it left. The Scotsman found us before then. I will never forget his face. He was plump with thinning orange hair, not ginger but orange. His mouth was pursed as though he had been sucking a lemon, and his eyes were ever squinting. There was a meanness to him, as though greed and stupidity took human form."

Vincent liked this woman. He immediately knew what this man looked like and who he was. Mrs. Compton clearly hated the Scotsman, and rightfully so. Vincent glanced at Serena, as she was still and calm to an alarming extent. Berkeley was fuming, his gloves tense on the knuckles as he clenched his fists. He never unclenched, only tightened them, until they were wound tighter than tiny cannonballs. Vincent felt uncomfortable being in a room with this much anger and acrimony, especially since none of this had anything to do with him.

"The vile man came to Henry and said words that I will never forget. 'It is by my grace that you will not hang. Never forget that. I own you now.' And he has owned my husband for nine years. Poor Henry must do this man's bidding. That is why I impersonated a fortune teller," Mrs. Compton explained.

"That is the piece I do not understand. Why pretend to be a medium and lead me here?" Serena asked.

Mrs. Compton sighed. "I have read about you both in the newspapers. My sister still lives near Roseland coast and has kept me up to date on both of your activities. I knew Lady Serena was interested in mystics and guessed that after New York, your party would head to Philadelphia. I discovered which hotel that you would stay at and bribed the concierge to recommend Madame Olyenska." Damn. This former maid was twice the spy Vincent could hope to be.

"Forgive me for pressing, Mrs. Compton, but you

predicted that I would marry Vincent?" Serena frowned.

"I most certainly did not," Mrs. Compton corrected. "I told you that you would meet a man with a heavy heart who was bitter from an event that had jaded him."

"To be fair, that sounds like me. Did you also say handsome and a giving lover?" Vincent added, happy to break the tension. Frederick stopped his scowling at Mrs. Compton and finally unclenched his hands— probably to strangle Vincent. "I am joking, of course." Better to lie than cause another crime, and in such a commendable little house.

"No, you told me that I would find great love," Serena pressed, making Vincent incredibly happy. "And that I would help him."

"I meant that you could help my husband overcome this shadow that has followed him for nearly a decade. I only said the bit about love because all fortune tellers promise love or fame or fortune. You are wealthy and shy, so you will be loved." Mrs. Compton shrugged.

Berkeley stood. "When can we speak with your husband? I will offer leniency, but only if he helps us find the Scotsman."

"He will be home tomorrow for tea. I want to return something, if you will wait one moment." Mrs. Compton left the room.

Serena stood and turned about the room. "This is a charming house. At least the Scotsman pays Mr. Compton a decent wage for his enslavement."

Vincent smiled at her. It seemed she was enduring this with grace. But she could be an ocean, flat on the top with vast conflicts under the surface. "Should we buy a little house in America? A great deal of the World's Fairs will be held here, and we could visit often."

Serena brightened. "Perhaps, maybe in San Francisco. We were so happy there, before the intrigue and conspiracies."

"They were there, pet. We were merely ignorant of them," Berkeley muttered. "Vincent, I will murder you for the lover remark. But I am gracious enough to wait until after the wedding." What an indulgence from Berkeley. Was he not merciful?

Mrs. Compton returned, carting a small case with the initials RP monogrammed on its fine leather. "When Henry found me, I was packing your mother's things as she wanted to visit your grandparents. I found this as I was unpacking in New Orleans and did not want to ship something so dear to both you and your mother. I believed we would return to England and simply held on to it. I hope this helps you."

Serena opened the case and gasped. Her hand flew to her mouth as tears walked in her eyes. "Mother's jewels!"

"Not her best pieces. She did not want to travel to Switzerland with them, but…" Mrs. Compton displayed a sapphire necklace shaped as a star. "Her ladyship wanted to give this one to her mother."

"Mother wanted to visit our grandparents in Switzerland?" Berkeley asked. Both he and Serena looked exceptionally confused. Finally, Vincent was not alone in the state of confusion.

"Yes, I was very excited to see the mountains. Her ladyship said she was no longer going to be separated from her own family by snobs. I believe that she was running away from something, and now I am certain. I hope this helps you, and that God may forgive me." Mrs. Compton absentmindedly touched her midsection. She might have felt maternal toward Serena.

Serena gave the woman a sympathetic smile. "Mrs. Compton, God knows what is in your heart, and I am certain he will forgive you. Thank you for this. I shall wear the star on my wedding day. It is old but new to me, and it was intended to be a gift for my grandmother. But I don't think she will mind if I borrow it, and it is blue! Thank you again."

"Yes, thank you. We should be going, but we will see you tomorrow for tea. I am Lord Vincent, by the by," Vincent introduced himself, realizing the Percys were too engrossed in their parents' death to maintain etiquette.

"I will carry those, pet. If we are set upon by a thief, Mandeville would throw the jewels and run away, or just try to insult his way out of it. I will at least take the jewels with me," Berkeley jested as he lifted the case from Serena. How had he regained his good spirits so quickly?

"I would! I am too pretty to fight, but I would devastate a mugger for wearing a belt if suspenders were clearly what his ensemble called for," Vincent volleyed. It felt good to joke after the awkward nature of the afternoon.

After their party left the house and had walked a block away, Berkeley turned to Serena. "I am conflicted. I am so enraged my world is ten shades of red. I want to kill this Scotsman with my own hands, but I have always been against such things. I don't know how to harmonize both thoughts in my mind."

Serena nodded. "I understand. The Comptons have endured enough. We must allow them to help us, and I believe they will feel better by doing right. However, we cannot allow the Scotsman to take more from us than he already has. We will still speak out against hangings, as we always have. But should the Scotsman hang, we will respect those laws. Enthusiastically respect them."

Berkeley frowned. "Does that not make me a hypocrite? That I want this man to hang? Hell, I want to choke the life from him until I see his death. Yet I have spoken endlessly about punishments being too severe. What kind of man am I?"

"It is easy to be righteous when life is easy but not when one is faced with this level of adversity. It is for that reason that we have governments, to be the calm actor when emotions are high. It is altogether too human to seek vengeance and to have bloodlust when one has been injured. But we are civilized." Vincent must be biting his tongue to the point of bleeding right now. "To be civilized is to allow others' judgments greater value when we cannot see beyond our own perspectives. If the Scotsman should spend the rest if his life locked in a tower, wearing an iron mask, I shall be grateful. But if he should hang, then I will continue to fight that no one else should. This man has taken enough from us. I will not allow him to take more by changing who we are." Serena had never sounded as forceful, and for the first time, Vincent understood that she was as much a lion as her brother.

After a few blocks, Vincent cleared his throat. "Serena, why did you tell Mrs. Compton that God had not cursed her? You don't believe in God."

Serena shrugged. "That poor woman has been a wife for ten years without a child. She must think that God will not allow her to have a child. People use God to prop up their agendas constantly. Why let a woman suffer when I can simply pretend to know what God thinks?"

Vincent did not respond, but her answer troubled him. If Vincent had noticed a woman who had inadvertently injured him was suffering, he would have pressed on. It was curious that the most thoughtful and kind person he knew would be assumed to be immoral. Maybe there was some grand revelation there, but he wasn't really interested in having a grand revelation. Vincent was exhausted. He had not slept enough and was simply tired of the Shadow Society. There was not time to rest.

Chapter 28

There is a certain liberty in the end of October. It is the only time of year where mischief and shenanigans are not only tolerated but encouraged. At no other time would I try to shape a turnip to resemble a monstrous visage, and yet that is exactly how I spend every October. At no other time would I welcome spiders or their webs, but I spin thread to mock the appearance. The most bizarre thing happened to me today as I wiped away a real cobweb only to decorate with a false one.

Aunt Penny's Advice for Living, October 1885

Serena was learning a great deal about herself. She had learned that when faced with people she had mentally villainized for years, she could show compassion. She learned she valued her ideals over her anger. She had learned that if given true evidence of the supernatural or spiritual world, she was open to believing. And she learned that she was engaged to a man involved in a secret society committed to battling another secret society, and he had failed to mention it to her.

Serena had seen every angle of Vincent's secrecy. Perhaps he had felt uncomfortable telling her unless they were married, or it was possible that he wanted to speak to the head of the Black Swan before introducing Serena to the concept. But would he have ever told her?

Men often viewed their wives as not deserving of information, other than the pittance of their household allowance, and there were men who even refused that. Serena had thought she'd chosen a man who would treat her as an equal. She still loved him, but this tiny sliver of doubt nagged at her as though it was a tiny shard of wood in her thumb, making her movements tender.

Serena unfortunately had to discover all this, as well as breaking and entering a warehouse, during her courses. She was far more tired than usual, but she needed to push herself and carry on. Typically, when Serena had her courses, she would lounge about eating chocolate and taking hot baths. She was surprised by her own ability to shuffle about a foreign city, unveiling secrets and pouting to rest long dead ghosts. Sadly, it would be inappropriate to ever discuss such things with anyone else, so Serena would have to hide how much more women could do.

They walked quietly to the Comptons' cottage for tea. So much had been revealed that it felt as though the heavy air was weighing everything down further. As though gravity had been made greater. Serena tried to cheer herself with the thought that Halloween was tomorrow, but sadly she had not planned anything and had no mask. Life felt quietly unsatisfactory, and Serena wanted to break free.

The housekeeper showed them into the cottage and into the parlor. Mrs. Compton had obviously warned her husband, as he stood but refused to meet their eyes and seemed oddly fascinated by Serena's hat. "Henry, I am certain that you recall Lady Serena and Lord Frederick Percy, the Marquess of Berkeley. Also, please meet Lord Vincent, Lady Serena's fiancé."

"Of course, please be seated. My wife has set the house to work for this tea; I hope it pleases you," Mr. Compton mumbled. His formality had not diminished, which made sense. Technically, he had never left service.

Serena surveyed the lavish tea with pastries so sugary that her teeth began to hurt. As she blinked at the sponge cakes and tarts, she felt her final tether snap. "It looks delightful, Mrs. Compton. However, I find myself weary of continuing the banal rituals while we are facing something so…extreme in nature. My parents were murdered. You know who murdered them, and he makes you work for him to this day. I want to know who he is. I want to know about his business. If you can provide this, I will speak to every magistrate, judge, and lord in the British Empire to ensure that you are not blamed for any part of this. Will you accept my offer?"

Mr. Compton's eyes filled with tears. "You don't want to see me hang, my lady?"

Serena's own eyes welled. She tried to remind herself to be strong, but she could not keep her feelings at bay. "Of course not. Frederick and I do not believe that is the proper punishment for anyone, but you have done nothing wrong. You were lied to. It is unfair for you to have to spend your life under a cloud because someone else lied to you. I forgive you, Mr. Compton."

Mr. Compton wept. Serena had never seen a grown man cry before, particularly not the stable master. However, it would be a tremendous burden to think that any false move could have you hanged. To live with that for nearly a decade must have been excruciating.

Hopefully he felt relief. There were no certainties left. No convenient truths could comfort her—those warm hearth fires had long burned out. She would have to keep her own fires burning from now on.

After a few moments of both the Comptons crying, they finally dabbed their eyes. "Thank you, my lady. I never hoped that I would be absolved for my sins."

Serena wanted to scream. They hadn't committed any sins! They were innocent, although naïve, victims in all of this. Somehow, they had been made to feel complicit in the murder of her parents, and if they had not, she might have known who to blame much earlier. The entire situation was endlessly frustrating, but Serena needed to calm herself. She wanted the Scotsman, and venting her anger would not get him in custody.

"Well, her ladyship has forgiven you as have I," Frederick said as he rose from his chair to place a hand on Compton's shoulder. "Will you please help us find the murderer?"

"Of course. His name is Mathew MacDonald. I run his business in America, but he has interests in China and Sweden. I will cooperate in every way I can," Mr. Compton answered.

Serena envisioned Mathew MacDonald breaking her parents' necks. She did not want to, but as she had discovered the bodies, it was unnaturally simple. Her mouth felt sticky, and her tongue felt entirely too large. She had wanted to know, quested for it, and now she felt sickened by the knowledge. When the picture was not complete, it was just a picture. This made it visceral, tangible, and horrifying.

"Mr. Compton, would you be willing to allow us to

make copies of the information at the warehouse and allow our solicitor to go over a few things? You see, Mathew MacDonald has stolen nearly five hundred thousand pounds from a peer, and I would very much like to return the money. Of course, catching MacDonald is my first priority, so we may wish to be very slow and discreet," Vincent spoke.

"Of course, my lord. I will do whatever I can to cleanse my soul of my misdeeds. The past nine years have been an unending hell," Mr. Compton agreed. He would have agreed to anything, though. Who in hell would not agree to a coup against the Devil?

Serena struggled not to roll her eyes; this was infuriating. "It could not have been all unpleasant. You were married to a woman you loved. Perhaps you should take a trip over Christmas. Have you been to San Francisco?"

"No, we have not felt brave enough to go anywhere, as we were afraid the Scotsman would have us arrested," Mrs. Compton answered.

"Well, he is not in America, and we will help with resolving that issue. We could pay for the trip if you would like. It's so beautiful there," Serena offered.

"Oh no, my lady. We cannot accept your generosity," Mr. Compton said quickly.

"You must. Serena is right. You will have to act as a double agent for a while. That will be distressing. The least we can do is offer a break in your 'unending hell,' " Frederick pressed.

"It would also be a strategically sound move. Until we can understand what MacDonald is doing, a brief halt in activity would be a boon," Vincent added.

"We accept!" Mrs. Compton cried. When her

husband gave her a shocked look, she replied, "They will keep arguing until we accept. You did not know Lord Lyons and little Lady Serena as children. I have never seen children build such cases for what they felt was right. I once saw Lady Serena quote two prime ministers and the queen in pursuit of a chocolate cake. We must yield."

"Mrs. Compton is correct. I will make arrangements for your vacation. We will go to your office on Monday to assess the situation. Thank you for the tea, Mrs. Compton. I have never seen such a beautiful service, not in America or Britain," Frederick flattered before they left.

After they had left and were walking back to the hotel, Vincent leaned into her. "Chocolate cake, eh? Can you be bribed that easily?"

Serena smiled. After all, she would always be charmed by him. "On occasion. Oh, dear. I hope Miss Thibodeaux can make a proper tea."

"She will learn if she cannot." Frederick rubbed his midsection. "Let's go to a café. I want beignets."

"Who is Miss Thibodeaux?" Vincent asked.

Serena covered her mouth quickly. She had completely forgotten to tell him. "I am so sorry. I forgot to tell you that I hired a cook. We both love the food here, and I thought we would like to have a cook from New Orleans."

"Oh, well, that is your domain. Is she any good at cooking?" Vincent asked. "If not, I assume Frederick chose her on the basis of her charms."

"Excellent! So delicious, in fact, I will be a frequent guest at your house," Frederick said cheerfully, as if he would not visit elsewhere. He had also artfully avoided the insinuation.

"Wonderful. We should find a fancy-dress shop to get some costumes for tomorrow. I saw a few events in the newspaper that we may wish to visit. Halloween is our favorite holiday after all. We should try to make our first one memorable."

"I'm concerned we won't have any good costumes. Halloween is tomorrow, and we cannot honor our pagan ancestry without the best fashion." Serena frowned. Usually, she would have Martha begin on her costume weeks in advance after choosing just the right fashion plate. A hasty purchase from a fancy-dress shop didn't feel right.

"Nonsense. I will be a ghost pirate, and you will be my ghost bride. True love bound us together forever. For after my ship sank, I would see you walking your widow's walk. But on Halloween, we are able to be together, this one night a year." Vincent told the easily made-up tale with appropriate spooky voice and vigor.

"And what shall I dress as?" Frederick asked.

Vincent considered the prospect. "Either my balding first mate or my parrot."

"Pssh. I shall dress as the British sea captain that sank your ship," Frederick declared.

Serena giggled. She was not where she had hoped she would be. Her parents' killer was still free, but she was happy. It was less than a week until her wedding. If she had tried to imagine this very moment a month ago, she would be shocked. The shortness of a month had transformed circumstances. Serena took a deep breath as the entered the café, smelling chicory and sugar. It was a blessing that the challenges of these days would soon be behind her.

Chapter 29

Having a fancy dress made from a fashion plate is always lovely. However, if you have received a late invitation or simply do not want a single-use dress, I have some creative ideas. An old red dress can become a devil's dress with the right alterations. A yellow dress could happily become a bee. By crafting some fairy wings, any dress can become a beautiful Titania.

Aunt Penny's Advice for Living, October 1885

Halloween

Serena was playing with fire. She held the lace to the flame and allowed it to singe the dress. She and Honoria had found a wedding dress in a store that would fit Serena, but the hardship was in making it look like a ghost's dress. It was bad luck to ruin a wedding dress so close to her own wedding, but she had never heard of anyone doing such a thing before. Perhaps fate would permit her this single indulgence.

"Shall we?" Honoria asked as she held a bottle of cannabis syrup.

"Yes, please!" Serena answered. She only partook in cannabis with Honoria, and she hoped it would unwind her tightly wound mind.

"May I have some too?" Aurora asked.

Honoria pursed her mouth. "You may have a little.

And do not tell Mother that I gave you anything. Ever."

Aurora's smile swallowed her entire face. She was seventeen and clearly ready to be considered a woman, but she still resembled the twelve-year-old that Serena had met pretending to be the bride of a somewhat bawdy sculpture. Aurora's guile had always been exceeded by her innocence and love of pie. Her green eyes were the largest Serena had ever seen. Her smile was so joyous that only a child could rival the brilliance. Serena worried for Aurora, as the suitors she might attract might only want her for her childlike traits and not the dazzling girl who held them.

Honoria stirred the syrup into a raspberry cordial and sauntered to Serena to offer the drink. Serena drank deeply and far too fast. "Thank you."

Honoria smirked and unbound her long red hair before sitting next to Serena. "I am terribly sorry that your wedding must be tainted by the Shadow Society. But it will be lovely, just as Lily's was elegant. I promise to beat back any troubles on your wedding day."

"It's quite fine. I simply had no notion of any of this, and as it happens, my close friends and fiancé were involved in a great mystery." Serena struggled to not feel offended by the secrecy.

"I was left out as well. I suppose because I was considered too young. Perhaps you were excluded because you were far away?" Aurora offered.

"Honestly, Serena, I hoped to never include you. It is an ugly business, and you have already suffered too much unhappiness. I simply wanted to see you happy ever after," Honoria offered.

Serena smiled. Honoria was always trying to keep

the unpleasant world from Serena. "I understand. And, in truth, there was not any reason for you to tell me. But Vincent truly should have mentioned that I was marrying into a family that was being targeted by an unhinged group."

Honoria nodded. "I agree. If I may defend him, I believe Vincent is terrified. Seraphina is...well, to call her cruel might be an exaggeration, but perhaps half cruel. She simply does not care for her second born. It appears that she will choose anyone over him. She still takes tea with Miss Haverford after she jilted Vincent. I cannot imagine Mother taking tea with a woman who did not like Adrian, much less one who had refused his proposal."

Serena agreed that it was unkind but failed to see how this anecdote related to Vincent keeping secrets from Serena. "Yes, I am aware that there is much strife in the Mandeville family."

"Strife is the perfect word for the dynamic. It is constantly unpleasant, but nothing ever so explosive as to cause an estrangement," Honoria agreed.

"She thinks we are a pair of idiots. She makes mention of it on every occasion when she thinks we cannot hear. I believe she is so covetous that she must insult everything she envies," Aurora muttered. The little pixie was under a cloud today, and it saddened Serena.

"I see that. She has three children who do not get along, and yet her brother's children always enjoy each other's company. However, I fail to see how any of this relates to Vincent hiding the Black Swan from me." Serena was finally beginning to feel the cannabis, and as always, she was more relaxed and bolder.

"Yes! I was making a point. Vincent loses everything. He was never wanted by his family. His best friend married his brother and will inevitably grow distant. His last romantic interest rejected him. Of course, we can see that he has many friends and is well liked, but he can only see the rejections. You are something that will be entirely his. You are not going to be easily captivated by his family as you are from a ducal family as well and will not find their world as enchanting as most women. You are shy and will not flit from social group to social group. You are not isolated as you have friends and a family that would travel the world for you, but you will cling to him. I believe that he is petrified of losing your affection and attention. He most likely did not tell you of the Black Swan as you might run away in fear or become wrapped up in the mystery," Honoria prattled. She never spoke this much, so perhaps the tea was too strong.

Aurora nodded, and Serena chewed a scone while she listened. "But should I not be concerned that he will persist in keeping secrets from me? The ideas you present are a lovely interpretation, but how can I ensure that he will be more forthright in the future?"

"Speak with him. Love is a constantly shifting promise, and you must consistently negotiate so that you are both happy. Simply explain that you understand why he kept this secret, but as his one and only, he must include you in future mysteries," Honoria explained.

"Thank you, Honoria. You are absolutely correct. Love is a constantly shifting promise?" Serena teased.

"Daddy used to say that. He was the lawyer, but Mother was his queen. They discussed everything for hours. He treated her as his partner in all things," Aurora supplied. Mr. Rose had died when Aurora was only eleven, so similar to Serena.

"My parents had the oddest habit of arguing about things they agreed about. They both agreed that people were generally rude to my mother, but they argued regardless. It was curious," Serena mused.

"Unhappiness is a contagion. It seeps and spreads. It's best to amputate the cause if you can," Honoria offered. "However, I am going to be the best witch this Halloween."

Serena giggled at Honoria's clumsy attempt to change the subject. "We were going to find an event to attend, but I think a little private party will be lovely."

"It can be your engagement dinner!" Aurora offered. "I think I should like a whirlwind romance. To simply see each other and know that you are meant for each other."

"It was not quite as romantic. I was haunted by Miss Haverford. If I am honest, and we all agree to keep secrets, I still am. Vincent wanted to marry her, and it was so recent. I feel nervous that he will regret our marriage." Oh no, that should not have been announced. To let one's insecurities linger in the air like soured wine was most unladylike. She never wanted to confess these feelings.

"Pssh. She was wrong for Vincent. Everyone but him could see how horrible she was. Lily is over the moon about your marriage. Apparently, she was scheming to introduce you and him, but Frederick decided to take you to America and waylaid her plans. Lily would be here if she could and would be talking Vincent's ear off about how wonderful your union will be. You have the absolute best allies for your marriage. Miss Haverford is merely pretty and matched his wit, but she did not love him. Love makes all the difference," Honoria lectured. Thankfully, Honoria was more intent on announcing her opinions than dissecting Serena's faux pas.

"Besides, he is marrying you. Miss Haverford be *damned*," Aurora swore and giggled with satisfaction at the taste of a forbidden word.

Serena nearly spit her second scone at Aurora's proclamation. "Well, thank you, Aurora. I should be less fearful of her. After all, Vincent told me that Miss Haverford prefers the Earl of Coningsby. It is difficult, as I want her to marry Coningsby so she will be ineligible for Vincent, but I do not want her to marry my soon-to-be brother-in-law. It is quite the conundrum."

The sisters exchanged glances.

"Oh dear." Aurora sighed.

"This is dreadful." Honoria rubbed her brow in frustration.

"I don't follow." Serena felt her anxiety rushing back to her relaxed body.

"The duchess is hosting a Christmas party. A grand fête that is to last over a fortnight. As Vincent's wife, you will be expected to attend. Miss Haverford is not only invited, but she has been helping to arrange the entire event," Honoria explained.

"And the duchess has been inviting Miss Haverford to tea at least once a week. We were concerned, but cousin Ralph said that the duchess was attempting to keep a friend. She also believed that Vincent was still courting Miss Haverford and was trying to help the courtship," Aurora supplied.

"If the duchess supports a courtship with Sebastian, then her behavior is explained," Honoria added.

Serena groaned. "What am I to do? I cannot avoid his family! Perhaps I can simply claim discomfort without Frederick's presence? I shall beg Vincent to cling to my family, as I am all Frederick has in the world."

"She might simply invite Frederick," Honoria argued.

"Yes. The duchess does seem to want Vincent around, although she never seems to actually enjoy his presence," Aurora noted.

"I suppose I shall have to quietly grin and abide this situation. I will simply have to hope that Coningsby and Miss Haverford do not suit," Serena offered hopelessly. What was the possible path forward that did not wind itself through this terrible thicket?

"Oh, but, Serena, you do not have to merely hope that they will not suit. We promise to ensure they will not suit. You know us well enough to know we are always ready with mischief," Aurora vowed.

"Wonderful idea, Aurora. We will be your little fairies creating devilry wherever Miss Haverford goes," Honoria promised.

"Nothing truly malicious, of course. Little jests should be sufficient," Aurora assured Serena. "And if those prove insufficient, then we always have this—" Aurora placed the singed wedding dress over herself and groaned like an angry, but somehow also aroused, ghost. What did Aurora think ghosts sounded like?

"Just enough to make the vein in Sebastian's temple bulge. As it did when we created champagne bowling." Honoria laughed.

"What is champagne bowling, and when did you invent such a terrible game?" Serena asked.

"It is not as frivolous as it may sound," Honoria began before seeing Serena's skepticism. "Very well, it is utterly harebrained, but it could have been worse. We arrange champagne bottles, the number does not truly matter, and then we use oranges as balls. The first person to knock down a bottle wins a point. After ten rounds, we open a bottle to drink."

"If you manage to knock a bottle with such force as to uncork it, you win the entire game. It's tremendous fun. We conceived of the notion whilst bored on the ship over. We can play on the return ship," Aurora offered.

"No, silly. Serena will be a married woman and will be kept abed for the entire ride home," Honoria chided her sister.

Aurora's eyes went wide. "Do you want that, Serena? Or would you like me to pester cousin Vincent so that you may have some freedom?"

Serena giggled at the girl's sweet gesture. If she were not over the moon for Vincent, the notion of several days held captive in his bed would be dreadful, but she was more excited for the idea than even her wedding. "Thank you, Aurora, but I believe I shall enjoy our return voyage."

Chapter 30

The morning after Halloween is a strange time. There are some Catholics who believe that it is All Saint's Day, but the majority of the world is merely tired after a party. The thrills of ghosts and goblins have fled, and all that remains is the cold light of a new day. However, the month of November holds much promise that I am eager to see.

A Curmudgeon's Tour of America, November 1885

The small Halloween party had been enjoyable but entirely uneventful. With Vincent's father and Serena's grandparents present, everyone had been on their best behavior. There was of course wine and plenty of food, but no one drank to excess. Serena played with the devil's cards for everyone. If Vincent were being critical (which he was), he would have called it dull (which he did on their return). However, he had missed seeing Serena smile, and the night held many of her laughs and giggles, so it was a pleasant affair.

As excited as he was for the wedding, Vincent missed the breakfasts he had become accustomed to. Instead of Serena and Berkeley, the breakfast table resembled a house party with people drifting in and out as part of their day. But this morning his angel was at the table waiting for him as she would for the rest of their lives. It was the perfect beginning to his day, and he hoped she would always be waiting for him.

Vincent sat next to her. "Good morning. Did you sleep well? I do not have to duel a ghost, do I?"

Serena giggled. "No, but if you did, you would have to wait an entire year to call him out."

"For your honor, I would easily wait a year and duel a ghost," Vincent assured her. He was losing his mind with wanting. He was worried he might take her on the wedding breakfast table in front of their entire party.

Serena leaned closer. Such intoxicating closeness in all things—the wedding, Vincent, secrets just out of reach. "We have permission to make copies in the warehouse but only after hours. How are we going to arrange to have your father and my grandparents not notice the large group of unmarried people sneaking off into the night?"

Vincent managed not to groan as he reached for a scone. Although in America they were referred to as biscuits. But if that was correct, what would biscuits be in America? He had hoped that they could simply make copies in shifts during the day, but if they were limited to the night, they would have to all go together. "Worry not. I will come up with something to distract them. Your grandparents are simple; we just have to eat heavy dinners, and they will go to bed early. As for my father…I could distract him right now if we wanted."

Serena smiled. "I am dying of curiosity to know how you could simply conjure forth a distraction. Do tell."

Vincent cleared his throat and began to speak loudly. "Truly, Serena? You wish to find books on local history and the voodoo practices? Very well, my dear, we shall seek a bookstore."

His father's head immediately perked. Grayson Mandeville closely resembled Vincent with the dark hair and slender build. However, being thirty years older, he was graying and less muscular. His father also had pointed tips to his ears and closely mirrored a Christmas elf when he was excited, as he was at present. If one were to place him close enough to Aurora, who also looked lithe and elvish, they could have quite a holiday menagerie. "I apologize for intruding, but did you mention voodoo?"

Serena beamed at Vincent before turning to his father. "Indeed, Your Grace. New Orleans is famous for its mystics. Marie LaVeau was said to be the voodoo queen, but she died a few years ago."

"Does mysticism interest you, my lady?" Father asked, clearly dying of intrigue himself.

"It does, but I have never discovered any truth to any of the claims. However, whenever I claim that the notion is false, believers simply tell me to keep seeking, so I do," Serena answered evenly. Vincent noticed that she avoided the idea of religion. Clever minx.

"Father, won't you join us for the morning? I know how you enjoy bookstores. And you can discuss mysticism with Serena. She is the most knowledgeable person I have ever met on the subject. Truly an expert," Vincent invited.

Father was obviously surprised as Vincent rarely heaped praise on anyone's intellect other than his own. "I shall be delighted."

"May I join this lovely outing?" Adrian asked. Vincent hadn't even noticed he was present, let alone close enough to hear. "I could use a respite from the gaiety of my sisters or the heavy nature of Melgum and others."

"You have those at cross purposes. Melgum is superlative in his gaiety. All happiness, with a laugh as varied as the colors of a rainbow." Vincent resisted the urge to laugh. Adrian's "others" meant Sebastian. "Certainly. We will have an expedition of the most learned in our party. Let's leave the others to twiddle their thumbs."

As they walked to the bookstore, Father peppered Serena with questions. Vincent was amazed at how well she managed him, whereas other debutantes merely humored him. Vincent could be happy, even with his family and hers surrounding them. She truly was his better half, and he needed to put in half the effort she was.

"How have you been enjoying America?" Adrian asked, pulling Vincent from his thoughts.

"It is difficult to assess. When I was alone, it was foreboding. However, the Percys have made it wonderful," Vincent answered honestly.

"I can imagine." Adrian gave a knowing smile.

Vincent chuckled. "Not merely my future wife, but Berkeley also has been a great friend, and even Melgum has been good companionship."

Adrian nodded. "Berkeley was my first friend at Eton. I can never thank him enough for his friendship, especially after I lost my father. If Berkeley declares you his friend, it is for life."

"Has anyone tested this bond? Not that I wish to be the first," Vincent asked.

"There are some I thought would surely fall away, but Berkeley persists in finding them and maintaining the friendship. One of our friends, Andrew Winters, simply disappeared off the face of the Earth, but Frederick hunted him down. Sadly, he had passed, so Frederick helps his widow, Mrs. Winters," Adrian explained.

Vincent bit down on his lip as hard as he could. How difficult Adrian made it to avoid a joke about a rake such as Berkeley "helping" a widow, but he seemed to take it very seriously and might not appreciate the jest. Ah, but Vincent could say it privately to Serena later. "How are you finding America?"

"It's pleasant. I am incredibly happy to get Honoria and Aurora out of London for a spell. The realms they have reached to stave off boredom have been exhausting. A trip abroad is perfect, and we should try to travel more," Adrian babbled. "Thankfully, Serena's wedding provided the perfect excuse."

"I did not realize that you were all so close as to traverse an ocean for a small wedding," Vincent mumbled.

"Not me personally, but Serena has been tremendously kind to my sisters. She truly helped them both after Honoria came out and Berkeley began courting her. You are marrying one of the best people in the world. Many congratulations," Adrian offered.

"Thank you. I am quite shocked that my brother and father arrived with you. I honestly cannot understand it," Vincent confessed.

Adrian shrugged. "I guess your father loves you, and maybe your brother does as well. I believe Coningsby is undergoing some form of revaluation of his life. He wanted to have the strangest conversation on the ship over here."

"Interesting. Do you feel like breaking a confidence?" Vincent pried.

"I don't think it was intended to be confidential by either personal means or professional means." Ever the lawyer. "He apologized for his poor behavior during the trial. I explained that solicitors and barristers see the very worst of humanity, as no one comes to us in a good state. He then explained how difficult it was to need me as we were competing for most of our lives. I was shocked. We have never competed. He will be a duke. I must work for my mother and sisters to have a decent life. He won at birth."

Even though he did not trust Sebastian, Vincent understood Sebastian. "Mother wants him to be prime minister. He had to be the best in every class. He had to view every man as competition. I believe you actually took firsts, and therefore he assumed you were trying to best him. Mother most likely pursued that thinking with him."

"Yes. We did discuss the duchess. Coningsby was quite curious as to why our families were estranged." Adrian looked to Vincent. "And now I suppose you wish to know. The entire ordeal is beyond foolish. My mother is the daughter of the Earl of Strange and should be called Lady Miriam Rose, but she eschews the title in solidarity with her husband. She did not like to be referred to as though she were higher than him rather than his equal. Your mother believed my mother thought she was marrying below her station and was insulting the family. The duchess and my father had a terrible row over it and stopped speaking. During their time apart, your mother became the duchess and began moving in more rarefied social circles. The tension came to a head when my brother died." Only Adrian would want to create a heavy story and announce it in a moment of levity.

Vincent knew it was just a tale, but it was a punch he had trouble bracing himself for. He had no idea there was a second-born Rose son. "I am terribly sorry."

Adrian waved his hand. "He was only two days old, and I barely recall any of this. However, during the funeral, your mother opted to attend a tea with several other elite ladies. Our grandparents were furious and disowned her. I want to be clear that I believe this was a decision made in grief and that everyone regrets their part to play. As far as your mother is concerned, I certainly see her side of this unfortunate situation. Funerals are not the best place to mend fences. However, she did apologize profusely at my father's funeral."

Vincent resisted the urge to point out the irony that his mother would apologize at her brother's funeral. "Your mother is very kind to have forgiven her."

"I suppose. My father and your mother were twins, and your mother's grief most likely matched my mother's. My mother made us vow to let the feud die with our father, which Aurora and I did." Adrian gave an awkward smile.

"Should I beware of Honoria coming for me with revenge in her eyes?" Vincent asked, half joking. The little redheaded demon coming for him with a knife in hand was far too easy to imagine. Far too easy. And she could probably pick locks.

"Not you, no. But Seraphina should sleep with one eye open this Christmas. In any case, it is fortunate that our generation is more sensible than to have vendettas with our siblings," Adrian prodded.

"Subtle," Vincent chided.

"Talk to your brother. Don't make me have to explain your regrets to his children," Adrian advised before catching up to Father and Serena.

Vincent found Sebastian in his hotel room. Vincent steeled himself as he entered the room. Sebastian was reading the newspaper and smiled brightly when he saw Vincent.

"Sebastian, I want—no, I need to know what you are doing here." Vincent was more forceful than he intended.

"Good afternoon, Vincent. How is the day finding you? Would you like some coffee?" Sebastian was clearly just being patrician to annoy Vincent.

"You and I are not close, and yet you traveled to a new continent to attend my wedding. Are you here to support my wedding or sabotage my marriage?" Vincent growled. He was not saying what he wanted to say. Are you here to steal Serena? But Vincent had always maintained the skill of talking around the truly deadly subjects.

"Support it, of course. Yes, we are not close, but I want us to be friends. I am your brother, and I love you. I am pleased to see you so happy and soon to be wed. I see how you are with Serena, and I am beyond myself with joy to see you so deeply in love. I want what's best for you," Sebastian pled. This was the best someone with his characteristic stiffness could do.

Vincent stared out the window to keep the tears from his eyes. He wanted to believe Sebastian. He wanted a harmonious relationship with his brother. But what was Sebastian's reasoning for his excitement over Vincent's marriage to Serena? Was it because Vincent was so happy and in love? Or was it because it cleared a path for Sebastian to marry Marlene?

"We may try again to be brothers on a few conditions," Vincent began.

"Anything. Anything you ask I will vow," Sebastian offered, standing at attention.

"Be kind but distant to Serena. I cannot bear it if another person prefers you to me. And promise you will never marry Marlene," Vincent demanded.

"Miss Haverford? Certainly," Sebastian agreed with such vigor it almost indicated an irritation.

Vincent blinked in confusion. Perhaps he was wrong. Perhaps Marlene had developed an attachment to Sebastian without encouragement. Perhaps she was mad, and Vincent was saved having a lunatic wife. "Very well. I hope we will be able to have a friendship that will grow in time."

"I could not be more delighted." Sebastian beamed.

Chapter 31

So many ask me how I always have the perfect methods for so many things. In truth, I was fortunate to have found a repository of notes from cooks and grannies all over Great Britain. The best skill I have developed is reading the handwriting of others. Ladies, practice your penmanship. The number of variations upon the letter Q has astounded me.

Aunt Penny's Advice for Living, November 1885

Serena sat in a warehouse on the eve of her wedding. For two nights, they had been copying the documents in the warehouse. Invoices and orders became a blur of numbers to her, not that any of it made much sense beforehand. Serena had never fancied herself a businesswoman, but this endeavor made her appreciate the mindset that could tolerate the tedium of numbers. She needed a diversion from this madness.

Serena decided to attempt a conversation with Coningsby. She had made friends with the duke, but she needed more support for their marriage if the duchess opposed the nuptials. "Do you mind if I sit with you, Lord Coningsby?"

Coningsby tensed. "Please join me, my lady. And as we will be family tomorrow, call me Sebastian."

"Then you must call me Serena. All I ask is that you not follow my brother's path of calling me 'pet.'

He does it out of a love of vexing me." Serena smiled.

"Truly? Berkeley always seemed to adore you. I cannot imagine him trying to vex you." Sebastian smiled. He seemed to relax in America more. Perhaps they shared the same unease in society.

"When he was fourteen, he adored frustrating me. We were at the beach, and I heard a man call his wife 'pet.' Being seven and what I believed a worldly and sophisticated seven, I pronounced the affectionate term as pedantic. Frederick hated it when I would act wise beyond my years. He wanted me to live in the carefree child's world forever, so he began calling me 'pet.' After our parents died, I stopped objecting to the name," Serena explained with a smile. "What was Vincent like as a child?"

"When he was incredibly young, before five, he was the best brother anyone could ask for. He always created the best games—pirates, knights, unicorn wranglers. My favorite game was exploring the house to find portraits of long-dead relatives, and Vincent would make up the most amazing stories about them. This is a king who could not walk, but only do ballet. This was a queen who honked like a goose when she sneezed. This was a knight who fought on a unicorn, so his peers laughed at him," Sebastian recalled.

Serena laughed. "That sounds exactly like how I would imagine it."

A loud smack erupted as Vincent slammed his work on the table. "Mind if I join you?"

"Of course not." Serena smiled. Vincent seemed cross, but she could understand. He could not know that she would only love him. "Sebastian was telling me of your youthful exploits. Do you recall any of the stories you used to tell? I would love to hear them."

Vincent softened immediately. "I do, and I promise to tell you all of them. Mother is hosting a Christmas party that I am certain we will be forced to attend, so I will tell you then. I really want to finish this work so that we may focus solely on our honeymoon."

Serena nodded. "I know, and you are correct. I was hoping Sebastian may have been restless enough to divulge all of your childhood misdeeds. Can you forgive my underhanded machinations?"

Vincent smiled. "Of course, let's get back to work."

As they worked quietly, the air simmered. Serena felt the tension rising with the balminess of the tight space. Hopefully, this would not be her entire future. Were dinners to be filled with strain and angst? Would parties be hours of snarky comments and subtle insults? On the other hand, Vincent seemed to want to lessen his contact with his family. It was possible that the acrimony would lessen over time with fewer interactions.

"Pardon me, but have I gone mad or is this gibberish?" Sebastian asked.

"Only you would say 'Pardon me' before asking if you've gone mad," Vincent mumbled before leaning over Sebastian's shoulder. "No, you have found something encoded. Where did you find this?"

"It was peeking out of that locked box over in the office," Sebastian answered.

Vincent immediately left to enter the office. Serena lifted her head. "May I see the paper?"

Sebastian handed it to her. "It is our alphabet but not any language I have seen."

Serena nodded. "I thought it might be a Nordic language as they ship to Sweden from here. However, this is nonsense. You should consult Honoria."

Sebastian frowned. "Does Honoria know many languages?"

Serena shrugged. "She is not fluent in a tremendous number of languages, but she studies language itself to find similarities. Honoria loves codes. It is a pity that we are not at war; she would have served the queen well as a spy. Everything she embroiders has a code within its art."

"What does her embroidery have to say?" Sebastian asked.

"Has Honoria ever embroidered something for you?" Serena asked as Vincent returned with the locked box.

"She has." Vincent pulled a handkerchief from his right pocket, as well as a set of tools.

Serena took the handkerchief from Vincent and pulled the lamp closer to her. She proceeded to closely examine the design of Vincent's initials with some flowers. "Do you see the white thread in the 'V'?"

Sebastian leaned on to see but was careful not to be close to Serena. There were two lines leading to four lines which led to six lines. On the bottom row, two of the lines had knots in them. "Is that a pyramid?"

Serena smiled. "No, the first two lines are your grandparents, then your parents, and then our generation. She has marked Vincent as her cousin and noted that they are both the middle children."

"What on earth are you two talking about?" Vincent asked as he tried to pick the lock. When did Vincent learn to pick locks?

"Honoria emblazons codes in her embroidery, and Serena is explaining what it means. What else is there?" Sebastian asked.

"Honoria believes that the left is what you are born with and the right is what you have made for yourself. So, on the left she has this rose with a tiny bridge over water. See the columbine? It is on the right side. There is a comedy mask in the center, but the crocus has a sad face on the left side," Serena explained in a most conspiratorial whisper. Secrets should never be revealed without amusement or drama.

"What does that translate to?" Sebastian asked.

"That I enjoy theater. Obviously," Vincent answered.

"No, it means he uses humor to disguise pain. You see, the comedy is a mask, but the sadness is a face. The snail's shell shows that he is a member of the arts club." Serena used the nib of her pen to point to the tiny insignia on the snail.

"Amazing! Why does she do this?" Sebastian asked as he looked for more clues.

"Honoria signs all of her work with a tiny vixen." Serena pointed to the red fox. "Foxes, I believe, pair bond for life. I think whoever taught her to do this is a man that she is faithful to even now."

Vincent frowned and took his handkerchief. "I cannot believe Honoria would be revealing secrets about us to some man. That seems ridiculous."

Serena shrugged. "She refused Frederick because she did not love him, and she has told me that she will only marry one man, who has rejected her overtures for not being of high rank."

"But why tell my secrets?" Vincent asked. "I

understand I am the most handsome and the most interesting, but me of all people?" Vincent was clearly not a man who used humor to deflect from his anxieties.

"I don't think she is telling your secrets. After all. I needed to closely examine the handkerchief to see the code. It is more like kicking someone on a train, a ploy for attention from the object of your desire," Serena teased. She had not, nor would she ever forget, his kicks due to his "polo injury."

Vincent grinned at her. She felt her stomach tighten with wanting. "Serena, would you help me look in the office for more locked boxes?"

Serena giggled and followed Vincent to the office. He closed the door and kissed her deeply. "Less than twelve hours until you are mine forever."

"Yes, I will be yours," Serena answered as she kissed him again. She hoped he would understand that she would only be his and that no man, especially not Sebastian Mandeville, could ever pull her away from him.

Chapter 32

I was once of the opinion that sailing across the ocean was quite dull. However, I have discovered that with the proper sport, the days of easy travel are quite fun. The simple idea is to find what you love and spend all of your time doing that activity. Suddenly you will find yourself sad that the long journey is over, and you must return to a life filled with people and responsibilities.

A Curmudgeon's Tour of America, November 1885

The Atlantic Ocean

Vincent's favorite aspect of married life was waking up every morning with Serena's bottom snuggled next to his cock. It was a warming, magnetic thing that was so round and full of forbidden promise he could not help but want more of it. Every morning he felt her silky hair on his chest and her soft skin against his, and it was paradise over and over. Serena was incredibly seductive in her sleep; she would caress him and emit little sighs. It was expected that they would have separate bedrooms, but Vincent could foresee himself spending nearly every night in her bed. Who would ever give up sleeping with an angel?

Their wedding was perfect. It was small, but flawless in its purpose—the union of Vincent and

Serena. Honoria was kind enough to take photographs to commemorate the day, and Vincent was planning on having a portrait painted to forever capture the best day of his life.

Their new chef, Thibodeaux, prepared the wedding breakfast with traditional Creole food. Vincent could not be happier with Serena's choice in chef, but he had not complimented her yet.

Serena, of course, was simply stunning in her wedding dress with a blush on her cheek. In the melancholy days right after he left his country, Vincent could not have foreseen the ecstasy he felt now. He was, after all, married to the person he genuinely loved, finally settled and happy for the first time in his life. And before Sebastian, which was quite a feather in his cap.

After their wedding, the Duke and Duchess of Wharton announced that they would spend the winter touring America. It was unexpected but understood that at their age, the duke and duchess might not have many more opportunities to explore the world. Melgum decided to settle in New Orleans, as he was rather fond of the city and he could keep an eye on MacDonald's business for the Black Swan. Besides, Melgum had made a friend in Mr. Arnaud, and Vincent reasoned that Melgum felt more comfortable in a city with one friend than a city without any friends. Though Vincent previously suspected Melgum would settle in Philadelphia, he was happy to have an agent in America for the Black Swan.

The party was now the Rose siblings, the Mandevilles, and Berkeley. As they made their way to Boston, Vincent had amused himself by playing tour guide. He was able to share with Serena the aspects of Charleston that he and Berkeley enjoyed, namely the barbecue and oysters. Asking proper ladies to enjoy a barbecue was always a source of amusement. And in Philadelphia, New York, and Boston, he and Serena shopped for their house. They parted from America with a bittersweet feeling, like a return to waking life from a cozy dream. It was a joy that rushed like new blood through Vincent—to be taking his bride home—but he had enjoyed his time in the new world. The only real comfort was that Nightingale Lodge would be littered with artifacts from the happiest time in his life, and he would look on them fondly.

However, this morning as Vincent opened his eyes, something was missing. They would be arriving in London today, and his time having Serena to himself would be over. Newlyweds were expected to visit nearly every person they knew and announce their new status. Serena blinked her lashes as she woke to the bright sunshine. She stretched, teasing him further, and sighed.

"Good morning, my sweet," Vincent mumbled as he pulled her closer by her bare shoulder.

"Mmmm. Good morning." Serena smiled at him. Maybe she could enjoy the socializing, even if he was quite bored of it even before it had started.

Vincent kissed her and began to slide his hand up her nightgown, but sadly there was a knock at the door. Martha entered and cleared her throat. Vincent hated referring to her as Martha—however Serena insisted. Berkeley insisted. Martha insisted. "My lady, we must dress you quickly."

Serena kissed his nose before rising and sauntering

from the room. Vincent bathed and dressed quickly before following her to the small dressing area.

"Please be calm, my lady. I can barely lace you when you breathe in this manner," Martha groused as he opened the door.

"I do apologize, but I cannot help myself. I am sick with nerves. What if she hates me?" Serena whined. Vincent had never heard Serena whine before.

"What insane bitch would hate you?" Vincent demanded. Those were strong words, but so was hate.

Serena exhaled to answer, but Martha took advantage of the moment and yanked on the laces causing an "Oof!" before she answered. And then she uttered the only answer possible, which was coincidentally the worst answer as well. "Your mother."

Vincent laughed. "Oh, wife! You are in an excellent position. If she hates you, then I will love you for all our days, even more than I do already. If she likes you, then you will be one of those lucky ladies that has a pleasant relationship with their mother-in-law. I predict indifference, however. We will have that in common."

"See?" Martha asked, far too loud and self-satisfied, as she snapped petticoats over Serena's bottom. "There is nothing to worry over."

"I suppose," Serena mumbled, staring at herself and far from convinced.

"Would a gift help assuage your fears?" Vincent offered.

Serena smiled seductively. "Perhaps. What gift are you offering?"

Vincent was tempted to take her, but she was

nervous, and they did not have the time. "I ordered this to be made in Philadelphia, but I became so caught up in our other intrigues that I put it to the side and forgot until last night. I hope you like it."

Vincent presented the cane he had made for her. It was beautiful with a black wood body and a silver handle decorated with mother-of-pearl butterflies. Vincent proceeded to demonstrate by unscrewing the handle and revealing a mirror. Vincent held the cane at an angle to allow the crystal teardrop perfume bottle, hair comb, and eyebrow comb to fall into his hand.

"You commissioned this for me?" Serena asked in disbelief. "It is so beautiful! I love it! I love you!"

Vincent tried to speak, but she was kissing him so vigorously he could not. When she finally released him to inspect her new prize, he quipped, "Well, now that I have a means to evoke that reaction, I shall be frequenting cane shops more often. Are all women so fond of canes?" But her worries were reasonable, and Seraphina was a whole bonfire's worth of judgments.

Vincent left her to tend to his own trunks. He had much to do when they arrived in London. Serena would help, but they would be busy, nonetheless. They needed to contact the Home Office about Serena's parents' murders and MacDonald's crimes. They also needed to staff their house so they could relocate there and not have to live in London. And finally, both Serena and Berkeley would have to meet the members of the Black Swan and be formally inducted.

A little before noon, they disembarked from the ship to an overcast London. With Serena on his arm, Vincent searched for a familiar face until he saw Ralph. Vincent's younger brother appeared aged and frazzled, his hair a little gray, his eyes fixed far beyond the crowd, as he made his way through the crowd. Lily was behind him, looking a bit pale and bloated. Nevertheless, Vincent was thrilled to see them. Perhaps pale and bloated was fashionable in London this year? He could ask.

"Ralph!" Vincent called, dragging Serena with him. "Lily! May I present my wife, Lady Serena Mandeville."

"We have already been introduced," Lily said as she embraced Serena.

"Pfft. But not as my wife, and that is much more important. Lily, you look ghastly," Vincent accused.

"I know!" Lily exclaimed good-naturedly. "This child is a demon! I would blame your influence, but you have been across an ocean."

Vincent leaned over to speak at her midsection. "Perhaps an honorific for me? Hello, baby Vincent?"

Lily groaned. "Absolutely not. It's bizarre and off-putting when people name their children after their siblings. Do you recall when Lord Carleston named his son after his brother? It was unsavory."

"I suppose Sebastian is unacceptable as well," Sebastian said as the rest of the party joined them.

"Absolutely! Welcome home!" Lily cried, and there was a general disarray of greetings and various handshakes.

"I see Mother, so we must be going. I promise to call tomorrow," Honoria announced before the Rose siblings left.

"Mother said she would greet your party, but I suppose that she is waylaid. I will fetch the luggage," Ralph said before whispering to Vincent, "She's lovely, and I have never seen you happier. Congratulations."

Lily smiled. "I am so happy to see you two united. And good morning to Your Grace and Berkeley. I did not intend to ignore you."

Father waved his hand. "Nothing is more exciting than a newlywed couple. It is pleasant to see you as well."

"Indeed. The duchess is planning a dinner party to celebrate your wedding and herald your return in three days hence. And I am having a tea tomorrow that Serena is invited to join. I was scheming to get the two of you together as I knew there was a destined marriage, but everything made it difficult. So, rather than being the matchmaker, I will simply be the person who can predict love." Lily grinned.

"I will gladly give you a matchmaking credit as the truth is far more absurd. Vincent stole my handbag as it suited him, and that is how we met." Serena seemed less shy around Lily, which made both women more lovely. It was a warm breath of relief to have a good woman for Serena to befriend again.

Vincent shrugged. "The handbag complemented my waistcoat perfectly."

"I would imagine…" Lily's voice drifted off.

Vincent followed her gaze to see his mother exiting his father's carriage. She turned to speak to Miss Haverford, who was following his mother's mannerisms perfectly. Vincent's jaw clenched, his eyes wanted to close, and his stomach tightened with anger. His hands balled up tight, making a fist to fight this terrible chain of events. What the fuck was Marlene doing here? And why was she with his mother?

Berkeley clapped his shoulder. "Now, I am aware

that you would like to go to your house, but I request that you and Serena stay the night at mine. Serena shopped extensively and sent everything to my townhouse, so it would be a boon for me."

Serena nodded. "I would like that as well."

Vincent did not want to go with Berkeley. It would be better to punch Sebastian and tell everyone what kind of whore Marlene was. Or to scream at his mother about how horrible he thought she was. However, Serena was present, and he did not want her to see that side of him. Besides, revenge was a dish best served cold. In three days, the duchess would get a much-deserved frostbite.

"Excellent idea. Lily, please make our excuses," Vincent said coolly as he led Serena away and followed Berkeley.

Vincent needed to plan his actions carefully. He needed to find the exact right words to inflict the most harm to those involved. Maybe inside he had not changed at all; he was simply acting the part of a typical lord. He would continue to hide his hideous true face from Serena, but in private, in dark corners, he would let himself be the monster he was. If there was a reason to leave home, one could probably never return.

Chapter 33

Bureaucracy can be frustrating. However, let us all try to remember that every person who helps us, from our servants to the postman to the shopkeeper, is a human being. Things may not always go smoothly, but behaving rudely to a stranger is not going to help anything. There is nothing more ladylike or dignified than treating every person with respect.
Aunt Penny's Advice for Living, November 1885

Serena waited anxiously in a bland, white office. She had envisioned that the Home Office would be full of dark wood walls and black curtains, as that was what she would imagine those who dealt with criminals would enjoy. However, this was pure dullness. White walls with chips in the plaster and ordinary maple desks. But maybe dealing with crime mitigated the romance of solving mysteries.

Serena had woken that morning feeling unbelievably sad. She felt heavy in her movements and exhausted. More than anything she wanted Vincent to put his arms around and tell her that he loved her, and that she would survive this. Except Vincent had been much preoccupied since seeing Miss Haverford. The entire situation made Serena want to cry, and she would sob as soon as she was able to.

Serena, Vincent, and Frederick were waiting for a

Lord Wyndam to meet with them. They had been waiting in an uncomfortable silence for twelve minutes. The room felt tense, and Serena hoped someone would speak. Why was everyone so quiet? Frederick hated silence but was mute for the first time in his life. Serena had grown accustomed to Vincent's need to express an opinion on nearly everything. Yet, still no one spoke.

"I do apologize for my tardiness; however, your allegations have caused a bit of a dilemma. My lady and lords, I am Lord Wyndam," announced a short, stout man who greatly resembled a mole as he entered the room and began shuffling papers in an obvious attempt to appear important.

"A pleasure," Frederick mumbled, with enough suspicion to convey his annoyance. "What appears to be the issue?"

"There are several, my good sir. Well, to begin with we separated Scottish issues to the Scotland Office earlier this year. Meaning our jurisdiction over anyone would be extremely limited. And in your accusation, you are targeting a laird, and so we are unsure if he should be judged by Parliament or by the common means. Finally, since MacDonald is a diplomat in Sweden, his role as a representative of Great Britain renders the aforementioned difficulties somewhat moot," Lord Wyndam meandered. He was throwing up every wall and gate he could avoiding the truth—he would not and could not do anything.

"I beg your pardon. How is it moot?" Serena asked. The rage crept up her neck. She was trying to contain it by shifting in her chair, but it was too much.

"Well, we cannot simply go to Sweden to arrest him. Have you ever heard of a laird and diplomat in service of the crown being laid low like that?" Wyndam seemed confused as to why Serena was hostile.

"I do apologize if I am mistaken, but are you telling me that MacDonald will not be prosecuted for bashing my mother's and father's skulls until they were dead because he is in Sweden?" Serena felt her voice get higher in her question until it ended with a high-pitched squeak. Her hands were tightly gripping her handkerchief and twisting it until it was a long string. "I assure you I could drag him here with these hands if necessary."

"Well, my lady, he is a diplomat to a very delicate country. Sweden is positioned between Europe and Russia. Therefore, it could interfere with trade to the eastern countries. And they are experiencing an industrial revolution due to King Oscar, who is widely regarded on the international stage. Rumor has it that MacDonald is to marry one of Oscar's closest advisors." Wyndam tried to declare these facts like brilliant shields against her argument, but to her, he just sniveled.

"Truly? And which country do I have to flee to in order to escape justice for the inhumane murder of a marquess and a marchioness? If I am rumored to be wedding a Romanov, could I murder you? Is a laird so above justice?" They would view her as shrill; however, she did not care. She wasn't shrill with irritation—she was a fury. "That is it! The difference between justice and injustice is who this *murderer* fucks?" She had gone too far. Good.

"No, my lady. Please calm down," Wyndam pled.

"Actually, I believe my sister is correct. We have waited for justice for nine years, and we—not you but we—found an eyewitness to the murders. But you feel the empire's relationship to Sweden is more important. We are an old ducal family, married into another old ducal family, yet we can find no justice." Frederick had not raised his voice yet. Something was coming. "How does the common man find justice? If I were the son of a farmer, you would not even meet with me. Serena is right to ask what lines are drawn for who gets away with murder. So please, explain why he still walks as a free man?" Frederick growled. Maybe he was restrained so she could continue unchained in her anger?

"MacDonald will be prosecuted. We will arrest him as soon as he enters the Empire. I ask that you be patient," Wyndam begged. He was not the master of this decision. Thus it was cruel to force him to defend it. But all there was left in the place of justice was cruelty.

"How do you propose to have MacDonald return? I hear Sweden is lovely, and he may have a new bride," Vincent inquired.

"His son is here, and if we become desperate, we can create bureaucratic reasons for his return, such as a tax issue. We are not without means, but we cannot sail to Sweden to arrest a diplomat. Please understand, Her Majesty believes in justice, but we cannot cause an international incident," Wyndam explained. "If it were revealed that our diplomat was a murderous, deceptive man, it may throw much more into question."

Serena was dissatisfied. She had waited for this moment for nine years, and now it was…nothing. All her rage, all her hours, all the things she deprived herself of, happiness she could never have, and she had knowingly foregone, flowed out with angry words.

They vanished in the empty air, in this sad, boring office. There was no trial and no declaration. Simply a bureaucrat telling her that she had to wait longer. The world was mired in stasis, and she felt a desperate need for something to change.

"You will keep us aware of what is happening, won't you? We still have other paths, such as the press or Parliament," Frederick said coolly.

"Oh, Berkeley, I am certain that the Home Office would not want us to take that route." Vincent's eyes sparkled with mischief. "The press would crucify them, and Parliament might be faced with the notion that the Home Office won't find justice for peers. It might cause a crisis. My family recently endured something of that nature, and so there is at least one lord extremely interested in the outcome of this situation."

Wyndam sighed. This broken little mole of a man must know he could not do more or less to help. "Yes, I promise to keep you informed. Please do not take either of those options as they would compromise our ability to ever find justice. I will discuss this case with my superiors, but I ask for you to be patient. I do understand that the process can be frustrating, but we must move carefully."

"Very well, we will keep silent for now," Frederick threatened. "Shall we go, pet?"

Serena nodded and stood. They left the building in silence, but once in the street, she could not stop herself. "I have never been so disappointed in all my life." This was no platitude.

"Come now, you said those exact words on our wedding night. I am beginning to think that you simply say that on occasion," Vincent joked. Of course, he joked; he thought to fight darkness with laughter.

Frederick chuckled. "I know it feels dark and daunting, pet. But we must carry on and fight. We have moved in our journey for justice. We cannot allow a minor setback to dishearten us. There is only one path—a forward path. We are dragging a mighty rock with us down that path. But the value of that rock is that, in dragging it, we have realized the weight that bears down on others. And if we drag it with us, its heaviness and breadth will widen the path we tread and deepen it for all who will follow us. That would make our parents happy. To fight not just for ourselves, but for others who we will never know."

Serena sighed and nodded. "I know, and you are right. I will allow myself to be heartbroken today but will try to put it behind me tomorrow."

"I have an idea that may please you. I have been thinking about what Mrs. Compton said about your mother. What if we journeyed to Switzerland to meet her family this summer? Would that be a fitting tribute to her?" Vincent asked.

"Brilliant idea, Mandeville! I shall leave you for the rest of the day and see you tomorrow at the Duchess of Bridgewater's dinner party." Frederick shook Vincent's hand and kissed Serena's cheek. "Try to enjoy the afternoon."

Frederick's carriage left, and a veil of bitter sadness fell over her. Her marriage had thus far been unusual as they had traveled with their family. Now, she was expected to live in Vincent's house and leave the only home she had ever known. Serena was nervous and a little scared of this notion. What if Vincent grew bored of her and locked her in the attic? Serena tried to beat down such an idea, as they would be living with Ralph and Lily and Serena was expected to attend Vincent's mother's events.

Vincent helped Serena into his carriage and sat next to her. He caressed her cheek. "I know you are disappointed, and I want to help you feel better. Perhaps, after tomorrow's dinner party we should go to Norfolk. We can arrange the art and furniture while enjoying Thibodeaux's food. The master suit has this enormous fireplace we can cuddle in front of and tell ghost stories."

Serena rested her head on his shoulder and sighed. He was entirely too lovable. "That sounds marvelous. I shall have Martha pack my things. I will have to insist that Martha try to find her replacement while we are in Norfolk, however."

Vincent frowned. "Are you terminating Martha? Whatever for?"

Serena shook her head. "Martha has always been more of a companion than maid. However, she wishes to open a perfume shop one day. I thought she could have a cottage on your estate and perhaps a greenhouse to grow flowers for her perfumes. Then she could open a shop in London or the village near your estate. She continues to find excuses as to why she should not leave service, but I will always support her. If she is not a success, then I will hire her as a companion."

"Hmm. She should speak to Ralph. He could advise her as to whether it would be wiser to grow her own flowers or import them. He could also help her discern the best location for a shop. I will ask him to research the endeavor," Vincent offered. That was remarkably thoughtful.

Serena kissed his lips. "Thank you, I really appreciate the effort."

Vincent kissed her deeply and ran his hands over her dress. "Mmmm. I am excited to have you alone. We can explore the house and maybe find hidden passages. Perhaps have an autumn picnic in the woods."

Serena giggled. "I am tempted to forget your mother's dinner party. After all, she did not invite us. Lily made the invitations. However, I worry that your mother would blame Lily, and I would hate myself for any disharmony."

"You are a perfect wife." Vincent kissed her once more, but the carriage stopped, and he pulled away. They were home, and Vincent swung the door open and helped her from the carriage onto a remarkably well-kempt stone entryway.

Once inside they were confronted by three men, or actually, three young boys masquerading as men. The tallest had dark brown hair and dark brown eyes, with a smooth, unblemished face and an impish grin. Next to him stood a man with a full beard and a rotund physique. Finally, stood a man Serena recognized, Mr. Oliver. He was a famous author, and Serena knew his spectacled face anywhere. All three grinned. She knew the expression of a cat who had found its mouse.

"Welcome home, Mandeville!" the tall and dark-haired man sang.

"Thank you, Osborne. Serena, allow me to introduce Osborne, Sutherland, and Oliver. They are my friends from the Arts Club. Gentlemen, this is Lady Serena Mandeville, my wife," Vincent introduced.

"Congratulations!" Sutherland cried as he hugged Vincent. Then, to her utter shock, Sutherland proceeded to hug her. Taking such liberties was quite new, but perhaps this was normal to Vincent?

"Yes, congratulations." Oliver shook their hands, with no pretense of a hug. Obviously, he was also uncomfortable with society and affection by the formal fashion he held himself.

"Ten columns and not one mention of a bride, Mandeville," Osborne chastised. "I am assuming that you met in Philadelphia?"

Serena nodded. "Yes, however did you know?"

Osborne shrugged. "Mandeville's writing became less surly around Philadelphia. By Chicago he was pleasant, and San Francisco had him waxing poetic. I was befuddled, but now everything makes sense."

"I do apologize, my lady, but we were hoping to abscond with Mandeville to the club for a proper homecoming. Would you be willing to part with him for the evening?" Sutherland inquired.

Serena did not want to be apart from him, but wives were expected to never mind when a man desired to be at his club. "Of course. Better tonight as we have dinner with the duchess tomorrow and are planning a retreat to Norfolk. Or perhaps I have that reversed—I do not know if he wants to see his mother or not. Have a lovely evening, dear."

After Serena watched them leave, she carried herself to her room. Maybe Britain held a curse for her, and she could never be happy within its land. She tried to cheer herself with the dear and new promise that she would not be denied justice forever. And Vincent would not go to his club every night. And once they settled in Norfolk, she would have a home of her own, and she would no longer have to live as a vagabond.

Even so, she wept out of loneliness and despair. There were days where even the pleasant parts could break you.

****

Sebastian paced in his mother's hall while he waited for her. Vincent had spent last night at Berkeley's house to escape him. Every time Sebastian tried to mend his relationship with Vincent, that pernicious twit Miss Haverford intervened. It was almost as if she were trying to keep the brothers from being friends. Sebastian bubbled like a teapot of fury, steaming even hotter when it seemed as though their mother was encouraging the estrangement.

"Sebastian, to what do I owe the pleasure of your company?" Mother asked as she greeted him. She was all light and airy, her blonde hair and blue eyes sparkling with an affect of happiness.

"Why was Miss Haverford with you yesterday?" Sebastian demanded.

Mother frowned. "She asked for a ride to greet you. She told me that you had telegraphed her and asked her to greet your party."

"That is senseless! I would not do such an imbecilic thing. In what fashion does that make sense? According to Vincent, she jilted him for me. Even if we go by her accounting of things, Vincent ran off in the middle of their courtship and married lady Serena. Why on Earth would she come to greet us?" Sebastian yelled. His mother was not a stupid woman, so surely she could grasp this.

"I have no idea why. However, we are hardly in a position to refuse kindness. Sebastian, we are trying to rebuild our reputation, and we must be kind to those who were kind to us." Her voice had cracked a little, potentially on purpose. Mother was near tears, and Sebastian had to remind himself that his mother had lost the most during the trial. She no longer ruled society with an iron fist. No one feared her any longer.

"I understand, but your kindness to Miss Haverford will cost us Vincent. He has a new family to cleave unto, and he may just stop seeing us altogether. Much akin to you with your family, and I do not want for my children or Vincent's children to pay that price. And if Vincent goes, Ralph and Lily may choose to follow him." Sebastian voiced his fears.

Mother sat. "Vincent would not leave us; we love him. I will begin to deny Miss Haverford, but she has invitations to the dinner party and the Christmas party. I cannot be rude to her, or the press will report my cruelty."

Sebastian sighed. How frustrating to see someone come so close to redemption and then pulling back. Miss Haverford should absolutely not attend any functions with Vincent or Serena. However, his mother was trying to compromise and rebuild herself. It was a horrible situation. "Very well, but not one other event after the new year."

"Of course. Now, sit and tell me of America and Vincent's wedding. Do they suit? Do you think he will be happy with her?" Mother asked. Was this genuine interest, or was she being a "good mother"?

"They suit very well. I like her a great deal. I have never seen Vincent so happy, as it is painfully obvious that he is madly in love. Serena is well informed in the subjects he is passionate about but is also interested in them. I believe that they will be happy if we can rid ourselves of Miss Haverford. You must know tomorrow will be awkward for Serena," Sebastian chastised.

Mother sighed. "I did not even think of her. I will try to make this debacle up to her in some way. Perhaps I will give her some of the family's jewels. What do you think would suit her?"

Sebastian shrugged. "Vincent gave her an opal wedding ring. I noticed he gives her things with butterflies on them. Do you have any butterfly jewels?"

Mother thought for a moment. "I know there is a dragonfly brooch from your great-grandmother's collection. I will fetch it and have it cleaned for her."

"Excellent. I am relieved that we might be able to have a peaceful resolution to this situation," Sebastian began, only to be interrupted by a knock at the door.

"Pardon, Your Grace, my lord. There is a Lady Olivia, Miss Hume, and Lord Amesbury here to see Lord Coningsby," the butler announced before moving aside to reveal the trio.

Sebastian stood immediately, feeling a rush of fresh affection for Olivia. He had missed her dreadfully, and she was as beautiful as ever. Possibly more so, as absence had made his heart grow fonder. "Good afternoon."

Amesbury bowed to Sebastian's mother. "I do apologize, Your Grace, but we must abscond with Coningsby."

"Of course. I shall see you tomorrow, Mother!" Sebastian began to leave before his mother could object. Once Sebastian had corralled them out of the house, it became harder and harder not to inquire. "What is the pressing issue?"

"Olivia discovered the method the Shadow Society

used to interfere with the telegrams," Miss Hume announced. Was it even possible she be more matter-of-fact in her delivery?

"Amazing! How did you discover this?" Sebastian asked.

Olivia blushed prettily. "I began to send telegrams from you to me. All of them went through but one. We then tested the agent twice more, to ensure that we were not mistaken, and he blocked both telegrams."

Sebastian nodded. "How tremendously clever. And we are *en route* to see this man now?"

"Yes. Her ladyship accepted an invitation to meet the man for a walk in the park. Apparently, he is smitten with her." Amesbury rolled his eyes. Although being smitten with Olivia was not terribly unbelievable.

Sebastian could understand but was rushed with jealousy. Olivia would most likely not marry a telegraph operator, but it disturbed him that in his absence, someone desired her in the same fashion he longed for her. "Anyone would be a fool not to be smitten with her ladyship."

"I think we should be gentle with him, as I believe he is simply a pawn. Hopefully we can find more information about the Shadow Society." Olivia sighed. "They are eternally bothersome."

Sebastian smiled at her. "I absolutely agree. They have interrupted both my brothers' weddings. I hope they will not interfere with mine." How laughable. Obviously Seraphina would string up every member of the Shadow Society by their fingernails if they interfered with the wedding she would plan for Sebastian.

Amesbury raised his eyebrows. "Are you getting

married? Found an American bride, have you?"

"No, no. I simply would hate to have to be investigating on the eve of my wedding as Vincent had been. Fortunately, Serena is truly kind and understanding." Sebastian held himself back with a practiced ease. Revealing the details of Serena and Berkeley's connection to the Shadow Society and the Black Swan should wait until they were all together once more. Then they could discuss everything at once and not rely on repeating voices to carry messages.

"I have not met Lady Serena Mandeville. What is she like?" Miss Hume asked.

"She is lovely and clever. I am not close in friendship with her, but she has been kind on every occasion," Olivia supplied. Well, at least the wives of the Mandeville brothers would be friendly.

"Ah, I worried about the woman Lord Vincent would marry. Either he would be less vicious with his wife, or she would have to be exceptionally strong," Miss Hume theorized.

"Vincent is kind to women he wishes to…court," he stammered, as he was with ladies and must correct his language.

Olivia smirked before approaching the man sitting on a bench. The man, most likely the telegraph operator, positively brightened at Olivia's presence. He was an overly thin man with auburn hair and large brown eyes. He was maybe twenty-four, clean as a suitor, and wore a brown suit that was slightly too small for him.

"Miss Hume, Lord Coningsby, Lord Amesbury, may I present Mr. Beasley. Mr. Beasley, this is Miss Hume, Lord Coningsby, and Lord Amesbury. We are here to discuss your crimes with the telegraph office in regards to the Shadow Society," Olivia announced.

Mr. Beasley paled instantly but remained calm and seated. "I knew this day would come. I have been on edge since they approached me."

Olivia sat next to him. "We are not angry with you personally, but we must know what they are doing. I propose two options; you can remain at your post and work for us, or you can tell us everything you know, with compensation, and take a cottage on my father's estate to retire to the country."

"I believe the latter is more in my interest." Beasley reached into his pocket to withdraw a notebook. "I am not certain how useful this will be; they use pseudonyms." This betrayal was transacted quickly. Apparently, the creed of the Shadow Society did not value loyalty.

"Any information will be useful, but more will increase your compensation. What are the code names?" Amesbury pressed.

"There is the Dragon; he resides in Sweden. The Spider was in London until a fortnight ago when he went to Aberdeenshire. The Cat remains in London. The Puma was in the south of France but is returned to London. The Wolf and the Fox are in Essex, but I do not believe either knows of the other. Most instructions went from the Dragon to the Spider, then the Spider would command as though he were in charge. I was the Pigeon," Mr. Beasley admitted. Mr. Beasley was too thin to be a pigeon, but maybe a sparrow or robin.

"What was the nature of the instructions?" Amesbury asked.

Beasley frowned. "For myself, it began with

keeping Lord Vincent from Lord Berkeley. Simply altering the times and places to frustrate him, providing a veneer of slight disinformation to separate them. They were also interested in the Lord Coningsby's love life and instructed me to interfere if he should try to woo any lady. Most recently, I have been informed that the Cat will be attending a house party in Somerset, near Wembdon."

"Interesting. What of the instructions for the others?" Amesbury pressed.

Beasley shrugged. "I cannot speak to that as they were written in gibberish."

Sebastian nodded. "Honoria is trying to decipher the Shadow Society's code."

"I kept copies of the telegrams, if you would like them," Beasley offered. This was less of an unburdening than it appeared. Mr. Beasley was withholding just enough to continue to acquire more from them.

"Absolutely, we would. Why don't you give me your address, and I will collect them tomorrow? I shall bring your compensation at that time," Amesbury declared.

Mr. Beasley nodded. "Very well. I want to thank you, my lady. You have been nothing but kind to me, and it gave me hope."

Olivia blushed and nodded. "Of course, Mr. Beasley. I will wire my father's estate manager today to arrange your cottage. I think you will like Leamington; it is better than Bath."

Amesbury, whose father's estate was in Bath, frowned. "Well, it certainly is more rustic, and you should not be bothered. Good day, Mr. Beasley."

Mr. Beasley began to leave the park, as did their party. As the gate grew closer and they were almost on the thoroughfare, Olivia whirled to face them. They were out of earshot of any interested interlopers or lusty couples who might be spying, and no one was on the street. "Has it not become obscenely obvious that Miss Haverford is in the Shadow Society?"

Sebastian frowned. "But she is a woman. And she is highborn."

"Yes, and she has been mucking things up for months. She has told me on several occasions that you are courting her." Olivia gestured at Sebastian. "However, Lily tells an entirely different story. She persistently connives invitations to the duchess's events. And if we are to believe Vincent's account, which I believe that we should, she jilted him in such a fashion that he felt the need to flee the country. Vincent is clever and was the person that would constantly bring us together. She must be the Cat."

Amesbury nodded, and his eyes darted around them with suspicion. "I am inclined to agree, but we cannot accuse her without more evidence."

Olivia shrugged. "Clearly the Shadow Society has an interest in who Coningsby marries. I suggest that he begin flirting with and courting—maybe Bella, Honoria, and myself—to test her reaction. I except Karolinda as she is in mourning, and Coningsby is known for his adherence to the social norms."

"I am not bothered to be left out of a false courting scheme," Miss Hume assured. Hume never had a spare second to invest in a romance.

This idea, like most good ideas, served two purposes. It would advance their cause, and it would allow him to court Olivia. "I will flirt and court the three ladies. Would you be willing to inform Miss Beauchamp and Honoria of the scheme? I would hate for Miss Beauchamp to have her feelings hurt by false pretenses."

Olivia grinned. "But Honoria can go straight to the devil?"

Sebastian returned her smile. "No, she spent nearly a month with me, and I did not flirt once. I believe it is safe to assume my cousin is not harboring hope for me as a husband. Miss Beauchamp is rarely flirted with, and I care for her enough not to simply use her."

"Very well. We will see you both tomorrow at the duchess's dinner party. Until then." Olivia dipped a curtsey before leaving with Miss Hume.

Amesbury shook his head. "That woman is a tempest."

Sebastian had to agree, but he had long loved watching storms and feeling their power.

Chapter 34

When hosting a dinner party, it is the host's duty to ensure the party mixes well. However, if one is to invite a shy person, one must be sensitive to that shyness. A shy person must come out of their own shell and never be forced. Trying to force a shy person to be sociable is akin to trying to force a kitten from a tree; it can be done, but you will have a few scratches.

Aunt Penny's Advice for Living, November 1885

Vincent sat in the carriage with Serena, Ralph, and Lily. The better outcome would be to let Ralph and Lily go to the dinner party while he fled to Nightingale Lodge with his wife. Since they had arrived in England, they had simply been too busy and had too much chaos to be intimate with one another, and Vincent missed her. He especially missed her smiles and sighs. He deeply missed how relaxed they were when they were able to be alone.

Sadly, they had to go inside his parents' townhouse. Vincent had not missed the immaculate façade of his parents' house or the constant dinners and parties. The same people attended the events, over and over again, but dressed up in different clothing. Tonight, as Vincent entered the townhouse, Vincent spied the members of the Black Swan and their relatives. And, of course, Marlene was present.

With several months to separate them, Vincent only held contempt for Marlene. She wore a slate-colored evening dress with black adornments. Everything about her seemed to be a generic version of Serena. Marlene's hair was a garish yellow, whereas Serena had honey blonde. Marlene had large brown eyes, without depth, but Serena had brilliant stars for eyes. Marlene was lithe and thin, but Serena's body was a replica of Venus herself. Vincent had never been so happy to have been jilted before but was suddenly grateful.

"Vincent!" his mother cried with what must be false happiness, her arms spread like an actress taking the stage. "I am so happy to see you! We have all missed you terribly. And this must be Serena! Welcome to the family, dear."

A tirade of insults sprang to Vincent's mind, but Serena must be seen to be accepted by everyone he knew. Even *Her*. So with a heavy heart, he smiled at his mother. "Thank you, Mother."

"Yes, thank you, Your Grace." Serena was shy once again, lowering her voice when she spoke. She was clearly uncomfortable with the attention, and his mother should back down.

"Oh, my dear, you must call me Seraphina. Please come and meet everyone. You will have to be a regular at our events now. As pretty as you may have bloomed, you cannot be a wallflower any longer!" Seraphina declared loudly as she whisked Serena to meet some of Seraphina's friends.

How hard would it be to grab his mother's pearls and strangle her with them? If anyone knew anything about Serena, it was that she was shy. Shy people didn't tend to be shy because they liked it, but rather because they were nervous or anxious about being in a crowd. Declaring the end of Serena's wallflower status and introducing her to the type of people that had ridiculed her was an unkindness. Serena was being foisted into the lion's den, and he should rescue her.

Vincent joined his wife and began to interject himself into the conversation. Out of the corner of his eye, he could see Sebastian speaking to Miss Beauchamp and Marlene. He was clearly flirting, and the sting of betrayal arose once more. How many times would he allow his brother to do this to him? How many more chances to be a good brother would he offer Sebastian only to find him stabbing him in the back? What more could he possibly do?

"Let us go to dinner," Seraphina declared loudly. "I know you are newly wed, but I want Serena to sit near me."

Vincent could see the terror in Serena's eyes and wanted to save her. However, he was unsure if it would humiliate Serena more to have a husband make a scene or to endure one uncomfortable dinner. Inevitably, he nodded and escorted Honoria into dinner, sadly taking his seat next to her.

"I am having trouble deciphering the Shadow Society's code," Honoria whispered. She never once broke her kind smile, even when she was talking about the shadows.

"What ails you?" Vincent returned.

Honoria shrugged. "It is not a book code, but I cannot crack it. It would have to be simple enough for several people to understand. However, it does not translate no matter what I do."

Vincent nodded. Nothing with the Shadow Society was simple or easy. "Well, let us contemplate the readers. They are British and most likely have some education."

Honoria brightened. "Perhaps it is in Latin or French. Almost everyone has a passing understanding of those languages. Also, that would explain the lack of single letter words."

"I beg your pardon?" Vincent asked.

"In the English language there are two common single letter words, 'I' and 'a.' I was searching for them as it is an easy beginning to understanding how a code functions. However, none of the documents contained a single letter word. So, you can see my frustration," Honoria whispered.

Vincent nodded. "I am planning a trip to Norfolk tomorrow, but perhaps I could help you. If you would like to visit us in a few days, we could try to sort this out together." Vincent wanted a few days alone with his wife, but Honoria was a friend to their marriage.

Honoria smiled. "I will need help. Have you heard? Amesbury found the telegraph operator who was interfering and purchased all of the telegrams. I now have to translate forty-two telegrams. I hope Amesbury gives me a very nice Christmas gift."

"Oh?" Vincent raised his eyebrows.

"If he is going to demand my time and effort, he can certainly buy me some sweets," Honoria clipped out.

"I will buy you something better than sweets for Christmas. Will you be my worker bee?"

Honoria laughed, and Vincent began to relax. They were two courses into a nine-course dinner, and afterward there would be cigars and brandy. He simply needed to survive for three, perhaps four, long, petty, and performative hours, and then he could have paradise. Unfortunately, there would always be another dinner party to attend or house party. Vincent needed to choose—happiness or having his family in his life. The choice seemed easy, but Ralph, Lily, and his father did not deserve to be severed along with Seraphina and Sebastian. In honesty, Vincent had always hoped that someday he would be able to get along with his mother and Sebastian, but walking away seemed like closing a door on that possibility.

Serena's laugh rang out, and it was the sound of the straw breaking the camel's back. Sebastian was flirting with both Serena and Miss Beauchamp. Vincent felt the panic in his chest, entirely new for him as he was accustomed to anger, jealousy, rage, cynicism, and frustration. Vincent had never had anything he feared losing before, but Serena was causing a panicked reaction. There was finally a cause for war between Vincent and Sebastian, and this is not one he intended to lose. He would destroy everything if it meant keeping Serena.

Vincent calculated the perfect words to destroy Sebastian. It would have to be a knockout, something Sebastian could never come back from. Yes, Vincent would lose Ralph and Lily. Yes, he would never be welcomed in his parents' home again. Yes, he might never be welcomed into society ever again. To be honest, that inveighed in favor of the insult. However certain things were worth this much loss, and he could not bear the pain of his brother stealing his wife. Sometimes the only option was the worst thing he could think of. After that he'd have to resort to violence.

Sebastian went upstairs to fetch the cigars, and Vincent followed. Once alone, in their father's private study, Vincent unleashed himself. "I often asked myself how many times I will forgive your misdeeds. And every time I grow more wary of you, and every time you persist in betraying me. But tonight, you flirted with my wife in front of everyone, and I cannot forgive."

Sebastian turned to face him, slowly. He was attempting to use his drollness to dismiss Vincent's justified anger. "I was flirting with Miss Beauchamp."

Vincent rolled his eyes. "Oh, you were flirting with Miss Beauchamp. Is that the reason why Marlene is here?"

Sebastian frowned at him. "No, and I can understand your confusion, but I am on your side."

Vincent laughed. "On my side? Were you on my side when you were flirting with my wife? Were you on my side when Marlene showed up at the docks? Your lovely lady coming to greet you on your long journey home? At what point were you on my side in your long march to steal the only woman I would ever love?"

Chapter 35

Take care with overhearing. You only hear the worst when you only hear half.
Aunt Penny's Advice for Living, November 1885

Serena had followed Vincent, who had followed Sebastian. This entire evening had been off-putting. Simply being the center of attention was uncomfortable. She was not a shiny bauble, and she did not need attention or validation. And navigating the Mandevilles' personal family politics turned out to be more difficult than an evening with the ton. Could someone have given her primer on who would be pleasant to her and who was a snake in the grass? Probably not, as they generally seemed to be the same people. The only three people she could really rely on were her husband, Lily, and Ralph.

The brothers had disappeared upstairs, and Serena wasn't entirely certain where to find them. Voices echoed down the hall—specifically, men arguing. Ah, she must have found them. Her stomach churned, and her mixture of feelings bubbled. On one hand, if Vincent and Sebastian were in a fight, she could go home early. On the other hand, disharmony so quickly forecasted a terrible conflict, and every time Sebastian and Vincent got together, tension filled the air. In all honesty, her husband needed to let some old pains go.

However, his mother and brother did seem to poke him a great deal.

"Were you on my side when Marlene showed up at the docks? Your lovely lady coming to greet you on your long journey home? At what point were you on my side when you stole the only woman I would ever love?" Vincent asked.

Wait, who exactly was the love he was speaking about?

As the word settled in the air, they stabbed her heart. It was as though someone had read her diary, knew her secret fear, and then arranged, in elaborate theater, for her lover to speak it out loud. She could not have heard what she heard. This had to be a great jest. She remained out of sight but listened at the door.

"For the last time, I did not steal Miss Haverford!" Sebastian roared.

"Truly? I do not believe you. All evidence leads to the conclusion that you are courting her. I do not understand why you would lie to me, when it is obvious to everyone. I know she's a good cocksucker, Sebastian, but is it truly worth losing your brother over?" Vincent sneered.

Serena wanted to vomit. The idea of her husband and his brother fighting over another woman made her sick. It felt so vile, that Vincent should commend her ability to suck his cock. He had never asked for that. Is that what would make him love her? The tears welled up in her eyes, burdened with her sorrow and rejection.

"I will not dignify this. I am not courting Miss Haverford. I have no affection for Miss Haverford. And should you not be more concerned with your wife? I don't think she'd like to hear that language," Sebastian stormed.

"Leave her be. Never speak to Serena again. As far as you are concerned, you do not know her. If you are bleeding, do not ask for her handkerchief. If you are burning, do not ask for her lemonade to put you out. Serena does not exist to you," Vincent growled.

Serena could take no more. He was in love with Miss Haverford. He did not want Serena to know his family. He'd never said he loved her. There was nothing left to do. There were no words to make this right.

Serena made her way down the stairs to a powder room and struggled not to sob. This was much like the death of her parents; the tears and screams could come later, but for now she needed to be strong for herself. She tried to breathe, unfortunately, a little more difficult in her tight-laced corset. She began to list all the things she needed to do.

She had to leave him, and they would have to get divorced. A small voice inside of her mind questioned if she actually needed to leave him. Maybe he didn't mean it; maybe he would learn to love her. But Serena had always wanted to be her husband's first choice. If Vincent wasn't enthusiastic about her, nauseatingly passionate, then there was no point in being wed. Love could come later, but enthusiasm had to come first.

Serena dug in her bag until she found the pretty silver pen she had purchased in New York. Her heart sank as she remembered the happy moments in her marriage. However, Vincent had vocally declared his love for Miss Haverford but never once to Serena. She would always be lost in this unrequited love and would forever know she was Vincent's second choice. She could not be a lonely and distant star when someone else was his bright sun. She needed to end this.

Serena wrote a quick note, so as not to be overly dramatic as she fled from her husband's mother's home to divorce him.

Vincent,

I overheard your argument with your brother. As you are in love with Miss Haverford, I will be leaving your home and pursuing a divorce. Please do not follow me or make this any more painful than it already has been. I hope you will be happy, but I cannot stay and bear witness to this.

Serena

Serena sighed at her note; it seemed too polite and nice. A small and patrician rebuff to a visceral wrong. However, she really did love Vincent and only wanted him to be happy. If she were bitter, she would have held on to their marriage and watched him wriggling like a worm with his hopes of marrying Marlene. But she was divorcing him so he could be happy and so she wouldn't have to stay around and watch. She still loved him, even though he would never love her. Part of her wanted to tear up the note and pretend she never heard any of that, but it would always be there haunting her.

Frederick walked into her as she left the powder room. "Pet! Where have you been?"

Serena stared at her brother. This horrible pageant was so much like when she was twelve, and the words would not come out. She needed to find her voice, and she pulled him into the powder room with her. "I just heard Vincent and Sebastian fighting over Miss Haverford. Frederick, it's dreadful. Vincent said he loved her—that she was the only woman he could love.

I want to go to Cornwall. Would you be willing to ask Adrian about a divorce?"

Frederick frowned. There was only so much you could say in a powder room at a party, but his dry mouth and creased brow said that he understood. "You may take my carriage, and I will send Martha and your things. I'll try to send a footman and a maid as well, but Stoney Breezes has no servants and is closed for the winter. And, pet, aren't you being a bit hasty? Most men love their mistresses, as well as their wives."

Serena shook her head. "But Vincent knew, he knew I didn't want him to have a mistress. He knew the idea upset me and that I wouldn't want him to love anyone else. Yet he married me anyway, and now no one will want me. Who would want a twenty-one-year-old divorcee? My life is over because he chose a temporary solution to his enduring love problem with Miss Haverford. He should never have come to me. He should never have proposed marriage to me. Every choice has been either been indifferent to me or rife with selfishness."

Frederick nodded. "Indeed, this is quite the conundrum. I will help you in any way you ask. I will always be on your side. We will get through this, I promise. For now, take my carriage. I will join you in Stony Breezes in three days. Will you be all right by yourself for three days? I cannot bear the idea of you taking a romantic but dramatic jump off a cliff. Promise me you won't do anything desperate?"

Serena wanted to be offended by the question; however, she had never been heartbroken before, and her brother couldn't know what to expect. They had both lost so much, so early, that the specter of another loss was constantly haunting him—and her. "I promise not to take any dramatic leaps off cliffs, you fool. I just wanted to go somewhere comfortable, where I can spend my days bawling and eating chocolates."

Frederick gave a wistful smile. "I am sorry you are going through this. You don't deserve this. What can I do to make you feel better? How can I help?"

Serena felt the tears drop on her cheeks. Her brother was her eternal hero, always ready to save her and everyone else from whatever ails them. "Martha and the servants. Perhaps in a few days you could retrieve Miss Thibodeaux from Norfolk. A great deal of chocolate sounds lovely. And if you could send some books."

"Servants, cook, chocolates, and books. I can easily arrange all of that. If you need anything, and I truly mean anything, even if you want me to find the Holy Grail, please send word. I would do anything for you, and it wounds me to see this pain in your eyes." Frederick seemed heartbroken himself as he spoke.

Serena embraced her brother. "Thank you. Thank you for always being my knight. I have always been better because I have had you. There is nothing I would not do for you, and you have proven that you will always be my champion."

For the first time in her life, Serena saw tears in her brother's eyes. She could see him struggle to stay stalwart in the face of his overwhelming devotion and strong rage. He quickly took the note from her and held it in front of his face, maybe to hide from her. "I will have the footman give this to Mandeville in an hour. That will give you a head start. I will have Rose take me home and privately speak to him about your divorce. Everything will be fine, pet. Do not concern yourself with anything but feeling better."

Serena kissed his cheek before peeking out the door. There was a clear path to the front door. If she needed to run to Frederick's townhouse, she could flee in a flurry of skirt and anguish. "Thank you. I shall see you in three days."

Serena left the Bridgewater townhouse with her head held high. Within twenty minutes, she was out of London and headed for Roseland. It began to rain, and she began to weep.

****

Sebastian's head pounded. He had absolutely no idea how everything has gone so out of control. He was practiced and well-behaved, but somehow everything was completely topsy turvy. Vincent had yelled at him, and maybe their relationship was truly unsalvageable. Sebastian had not blinked since their argument. Where had he gone so wrong? He must resolve this, in spite of himself and his brother.

Sebastian went to his room for a moment to simply be himself. He poured a glass of the apple brandy he had brought from Pennsylvania and sipped at it. Sebastian had always done the right thing, but his life was all wrong. He needed a plan, a path to find the way to make his life right again. First, he would square things with Vincent, then court and marry Olivia. Finally, he would destroy the Shadow Society once and for all. Taming a legendary curmudgeon and besting a globe-spanning conspiracy did not try his nerves, not even a little. Olivia would be the challenge. But first things first, he would speak to Vincent, and this time Sebastian would make his brother listen.

Sebastian stalked the landing to find Vincent, when he saw his brother sitting on the top stair. Sebastian and never seen his brother laid so low. Vincent looked broken. His eyes stared a league beyond the city and saw nothing. There was a certain stare a man had when he was looking at the empty parts of himself.

"Vincent? What are you doing?" Sebastian asked.

Vincent did not move. He was crumpled on the step and leaning against the railing. "She left me. She wants a divorce."

This was too shocking, even for Vincent. No one actually got divorced. It would be a scandal, and given the way Vincent was behaving, it might kill his brother. "But didn't you, not two hours ago, proclaim your love for Miss Haverford? With Serena divorcing you, you can marry Miss Haverford."

Vincent seemed as though he might punch Sebastian. "I was lying to hurt you. I don't love Marlene. She's a cow. I love Serena, and now I have lost her."

Sebastian sat next to his brother and rested his chin on his hands. "Well, I think you've learned something. When you wield words as weapons, to break glass egos and break down iron wills, the bitter shrapnel can have unintended consequences. In this case, I suppose Serena heard you say you loved Miss Haverford. We will go and find her. Women can be emotional creatures, and when she's calmed down, she may listen to reason."

Vincent eyes welled. "What if she doesn't? What if I have utterly lost her?"

Sebastian shrugged. "Then I will plead your case until she listens. Everyone could see how much you both loved each other, and how well suited you were as a match. But, Vincent, this must be the final argument in regards to Miss Haverford. I am not courting her. I do not love her or even like her. I wish to marry Lady Olivia."

Vincent raised his eyebrows. "You idiot. Do you realize how much time and effort you could have saved me by telling me this earlier?"

"I told you that I had no interest in Miss Haverford!" Sebastian exclaimed. In all honesty, had Vincent simply believed him, despite the acrimony, Serena would still be here.

"No, the bit about Olivia. If I had known you had your eyes set on Olivia, then I would have believed you were not courting Marlene," Vincent said simply.

"I am certain that you are using logic, but I fail to see it," Sebastian muttered. Why would Vincent have believed this, in spite of accusing him of being a dilettante mere moments before?

"You are not the type of gentleman to have several irons in the fire. If I'd known you were interested in Olivia, I would have relaxed." Vincent shrugged.

"I wish you could have trusted and believed me as your brother. I love you. I want us to be close, as close as you are to Ralph. Or Lily." Sebastian released the words he had never been able to utter before. It was easier than he had assumed it would be.

"I...never mind. I could go through every slight and prove how correct my actions were, but none of it matters now. If you want to be close as brothers, then we will try. My hubris has lost me my wife, but at least I can gain a brother." He reached out and gripped Sebastian's shoulder. Vincent seemed lost again, drowning in a sea of melancholy.

"Let's go find Berkeley and then Serena. I know we can convince her to return home." Sebastian stood and held out his hand for Vincent. To Sebastian's great surprise, Vincent took his hand and stood with him.

Within an hour they were in Berkeley's foyer. Sebastian had never been to Berkeley's townhouse before, but it was...warm. The walls were in a rich mahogany leading to polished and lustrous wood floors. It was warm in temperature and temperament, which felt nice coming out of the November cold. How could he make his own home so warm and inviting?

Though it was comfortable and inviting, there was a flurry of activity that distracted from the almost pastoral atmosphere. Large trunks were assembled near the front of the door, some marked for Cornwall. Maids shuffled by with chocolates addressed to Stoney Breezes. Though it was midnight, nearly every servant was working. Such a demand was unlike the marquess of the working class.

Finally, Berkeley thundered down the stairs. In a seamless blur, almost a sprint, he closed in on Vincent and punched him squarely in his face. Sebastian had boxed enough to understand this was an angry gesture, not one intended to maximize harm. Berkeley had not drawn back, leaned forward, or even put his body into it. Vincent was sent back a half step, but not knocked onto the gleaming floor. He did nearly collide with a box of confections and a trunk of gloves and parasols and hats. "What did I tell you, Mandeville? Did I not say that I would show you my skills if you hurt my sister? You are renowned for your cleverness, but you are not so clever as to not declare love for another woman in front of your wife?" Berkeley roared. His

335

breath quieted the air, and he stared at Vincent, waiting for a reason to pounce.

"Berkeley, I am sorry." Vincent began to straighten himself.

"Get out of my house!" Berkeley barked, before storming down the hall. Why such measured and hasty drawdown?

As quickly as Berkeley disappeared, a maid came forth with ice wrapped in a tea towel and a bottle of whisky. "His lordship wishes you to have this. I cannot stay, as I must be off to Roseland. I have never been there. I hope it is nice."

Vincent smiled at the girl as he pressed the ice to his jaw and plucked the bottle. "Tell Berkeley that I am grateful."

"Yes, my lord," the girl curtsied and ran off.

Vincent gestured to the chocolates. "Grab those, will you? Splendid chap, Berkeley."

Sebastian grabbed the chocolates. So, if this incident served as an example, if he punched Vincent, would Vincent call him a splendid chap? "I don't understand."

"Berkeley left notes everywhere to lead me to Serena without ever directly telling me. And there is this." Vincent held up the whisky bottle.

There was a small note, scrawled in haste and exasperation on the bottle.

Fix this, or next time I won't pull my punch.

Splendid chap, indeed.

Chapter 36

Vincent woke in the carriage with a pain in his neck. He had opted to travel to Cornwall by carriage instead of waiting for the train in the morning. He was immovable, heavy, and hopeless. He needed to get Serena to listen. His heart flitted between agony and fury. He could not see the rest of his life without his angel. But how dare she doubt his love for her when he loved her to the ends of the earth!

The worst aspect of this entire debacle was that it was completely of his own making. There was no one else to blame. If he had heard Serena utter the same words, he would have burned the house down, but she simply devastated him in the quiet manner she did everything. No, he chose his words and his actions and was suffering the consequences. Vincent had never been so angry with himself. This unforgiveable sin, born of rage, must be atoned for, and Serena was a vengeful goddess. He would never forgive himself if he could not mend this rift. He'd sworn to protect Serena, but he had been the one to hurt her more than any selfish prig of the ton, and that was unforgivable.

Vincent peered through the carriage window. Roseland peninsula was not the crowning jewel of Cornwall, not like a landscape such as Land's End. However, it held an idyllic charm with its rocky cliffs and pastoral farms. It was subtly beautiful and soothing.

This was a place designed for Serena, often overlooked but perfect. As the dawn began to break through the clouds, Vincent felt hope for the new day.

Sebastian began to stir. Vincent smiled and, for the first time, felt relief at the sight of his brother. Vincent never would have guessed that at his worst moment, it would be Sebastian to pick him up. Perhaps Vincent had misjudged his brother; perhaps being the golden boy was tiresome. After all, he seemed desperate for Vincent's friendship; it must be lonely to be perfect. If Vincent and Sebastian could be friendly after the years of competition, perhaps Vincent's wife could learn to love him once more.

"The nearest village to Stoney Breezes is Portscatho. Perhaps we should find an inn and get a room. I am starving." Sebastian yawned as he inspected the map.

Vincent nodded. He was not hungry, but he should eat. He felt as though he were a walking wounded heart, shedding bits of blood and gore about. He had no idea he could have so much pain, but Serena was the chink in his armor. He had never been cut so deeply and could barely move. Yet he needed to function, and food was essential to living.

While Sebastian arranged for a room and ordered breakfast, Vincent stood there, stony, scared, and feeble. It was as though he was haunting his own body and confused as to how it worked. Vincent shoved the breakfast into his mouth only understanding it was vaguely fishy.

"We should go quickly," Vincent mumbled.

"I have never seen you this way. Are you feeling well?" Sebastian asked.

Vincent shook his head. "No. I was happy, Sebastian. Now, I feel only darkness and cold. I can barely move, but I need my warmth back."

"We will find her and win her over. Eat a bit more; you need your strength. I will arrange for a lunch to take with us."

After an hour, they set off on horseback to Stoney Breezes. Stoney Breezes was a fortress of gray stone, imposingly square with octagon turrets at each corner. Large windows lined the two floors of the house and the three-story turrets. Vincent liked the house immediately, but unfortunately it held his beloved and seemed uninterested in letting him inside.

"Lovely home. I hope you do not mind if I visit often," Sebastian offered.

Vincent wrinkled his brow. "Why should I mind? This is Berkeley's home."

Sebastian chuckled. "Did you not read your own settlement papers?"

"Why would I? Is that not Ralph's arena?" Vincent asked. Reading, out of anything but an act of leisure, was for tenured bureaucrats or a judge. Vincent reading his own settlements would be like Sebastian buying art or Ralph becoming political.

Sebastian laughed. "Good God, man! This is your home. Berkeley gave it to you. Well, I suspect it was for Serena; he seems to enjoy her significantly more. But the charitable news is your wife has not left you. She simply is visiting a different house."

Vincent smiled sincerely for the first time in a day. "I believe that is an issue that can only occur amongst the upper class. We really have far too much if I can lose my wife because she is in one of my many houses."

Sebastian squinted his eyes. "Is that her lady's maid?"

Vincent followed his brother's gaze to see Martha riding out. "Yes, tie our horses to the fence post, and I will try to speak to her. Martha!"

Martha raised her hand to her eyes and spotted them. She nodded and slid off her horse in a quick and irritated fashion. After adjusting her bonnet, she walked her horse over to them. "I am not going to stand and converse with you. If you follow me into the holloway, I will not stop you."

Martha led them into the sunken lane and once beneath the umbrella of gossipy leaves, Vincent began to plead. "Martha, you must beg Serena to hear me out. I was a fool and trying to hurt my brother. I don't love Marlene, but I do love Serena. I cannot live without her. She is my sun, and I am in a dark night without her."

Martha nodded. "I thought as much. I will try to plead your case, but she is not thinking clearly. I have never seen her ladyship so aggrieved, nor have I seen her cry so much. It may take a day or two for her to see through her pain. Of course, we came to the house without a cook, so she is hungry as well as heartbroken."

Vincent felt a stab of guilt as he was the one to cause Serena such unhappiness. "I have some chocolates for her. And if I could speak with her, I know we can resolve this situation."

Martha nodded. "I am certain that you could. However, she is beside herself. Perhaps you could write her a letter, and in that small measure, you could explain yourself. In the meanwhile, I know she will love the chocolates."

The brothers allowed, separating from Martha and barely looking at her as she left. Martha managed to exit the holloway with her horse, and Vincent began to rummage through Sebastian's satchel. He finally found a meat pie and tore into it with his teeth, suddenly ravenous. "All in all, I am very optimistic."

"I often wonder if we are privy to the same conversations, as we seem to come to vastly different conclusions," Sebastian muttered as he fetched his own meat pie.

Vincent grinned. "There are few men suited to persuading Serena as I am in writing. And I believe that I have surmised the most romantic gesture in the history of England."

Sebastian sighed. "I hesitate to ask."

"I shall scale the wall and rescue my bride," Vincent announced and began to walk back to the house. Bards would sing of this day.

****

Serena was miserable. The question of whether she had made a horrible mistake rang out over and over again with the sort of pain that a church bell causes a hungover reveler. Vincent had followed her to Cornwall and written her several letters. Serena had yet to read the letters. Why would she when she didn't know if she wanted to hear his explanation? He was, after all, the Malicious Mandeville. He must be furious with her, but then again, perhaps he was apologetic. Curiosity and fear dueled in her, which was consistent with the rest of her daily life.

Coming to Cornwall was a mistake. Stoney Breezes might have been the place she felt safest, but it was cold and closed to her. The furniture was covered, and the cupboards were bare. Serena had gone off and run to a house with no food or coal. Even her house refused to love her, and Serena had never been so alone.

Serena was in her bedroom with a small fire and three small candles to light the room. The full moon shimmered on the sea, and Serena watched it wistfully. Serena loved the moon; it was her only constant companion. Frederick could leave or cavort, but the moon would never go for long. Tonight it was not quite full, but a warm yellow as opposed to the silver moon. Somehow the moon felt larger tonight, though she was not certain that the moon could get larger.

As Serena stared at the ocean, she ate a piece of chocolate and let it melt on her tongue. Suddenly a face appeared in front of her window. Her serenity broke, and Serena began to scream, or she would have screamed, if she had not had a mouth full of chocolate, so what came forth was a sort of fearful gargling sound. Vincent pushed open her window and hoisted himself inside, falling face down on the floor.

"What are you doing?" Serena hissed. There was a viper's nest full of how-dare-yous and the-sheer-gall-of-yous poised to strike this interloping man.

"Rescuing you," Vincent announced as he stood and began to dust his coat off. How confident of him.

Serena shook her head. Her husband did nothing in the traditional or expected manner. "Vincent, I don't need rescuing."

"Of course you do." Vincent grinned wolfishly at her and wrapped his hands around her waist. She missed this, but it was still all wrong. Did he understand this turmoil in her? Was he using it to silence her proper rage? "Some witch has befuddled you into forgetting that you love me."

Serena closed her eyes and sighed. "You know that is not what happened."

"Please come back to me. I will change, I promise." He sounded so sincere and hurt. She wanted to cry. But that was not who she was. She was the orphan who had tamed the world and uncovered a dark conspiracy. But in that moment, she was just a woman who wanted more from the man she loved.

"Oh, Vincent! I don't want you to be any different. I have always loved you for exactly who you are. I only wanted you to love *me*!" Serena cried.

"I do love you." Vincent moved to kiss her, but Serena wriggled free and moved to the fire.

"No, you cannot just say it now when you have never said it before. You still love Miss Haverford, and I refuse to be a second prize. The same way you would never be a second prize, Vincent." Serena sobbed the words that distressed her so much to say.

"There is a great deal to address in that statement. First, I do not love Miss Haverford. I never have. I was trying to make Sebastian feel bad. Surely you can trust in my venom?" Vincent was calm in his words.

"But I heard you say she was the only woman you could love. And how much you enjoyed her sucking your cock," Serena accused meekly. She desperately wanted to believe him, but she refused to be haunted by this.

Vincent blanched. Did he have a secret revulsion at his own conduct? "I did say that, and I truly regret my words. It was extremely disrespectful and rude. I was utterly wrong to have done it, and I apologize."

Serena found it difficult to be resolute in the face of a complete apology. "Very well, but that solves very little. I still want a husband that loves me."

"But I do!" Vincent cried.

Serena shook her head. "You have never said you love me until tonight."

Vincent frowned. "Are you certain? I feel as though I have declared my love for you."

"Yes! I have been waiting for those words every day! I have been trying to read them into your actions. I should not have to scry every sentence and gesture for hidden meaning. Love should not be a gilded puzzle to tease out." She wanted to say so much more, but it was not her job to educate this noble, vicious creature. "But not once did you ever tell me. I needed to hear you tell me that you loved me. I craved it as though I were drowning and those words were air." Tears began to roll down Serena's cheeks as she spoke. She sounded so pathetic and sad.

Vincent embraced her and rested her head on his chest. "I am so sorry. I fell in love with you from the moment I saw you. I was, in earnest, scared of frightening you away with how passionately I loved you. Do you recall the day in Philadelphia when we went shopping and bought the canes? That day, I wired Lily to tell her I was falling in love with you."

Serena began to cry again. He was saying the exact words she wanted to hear. She craved belief, trust, and comfort with Vincent. She wanted to trust him. However, allowing him near again after she had been so hurt? That was a hard thing. She did not know what to do and simply allowed herself to shed her tears.

"I have been thinking," Vincent began as he held

her closer, his embrace tightening around her, leaving very little distance. "You are a skeptic. Now, I know that I love you, but you are unsure. We must find evidence. Let's live together, happily married, and you will gather evidence as to whether I love you. If you conclude, at any time, that I do not love you, I will help you obtain a divorce. If we are unable to obtain a divorce, I will allow you to live here and take a lover."

The notion of Vincent allowing Serena to take a lover rang false to Serena. She gazed at him doubtfully. "I find it difficult to believe that you would be comfortable with me taking a lover."

Vincent shrugged. "Your lover may be me with a dashing moustache, and that is your only option."

Much to her chagrin, she giggled. "And if the divorce is granted?"

"Then I will woo you and marry you again, also with a moustache. I hope it comes in dark; dark hair with a light moustache would look terrible, but then again, we both know your taste in men is questionable." He stopped, proud of his jape at both of their expense. He held her chin fast so he could look into her tearful eyes. "I love you, Serena. It is an eternal and all-encompassing love. If I can think, I will think of you. Please, let me have another chance. It would be a supreme irony if I lost you because of something I *didn't* say."

Serena sighed. She was miserable without him, and she had nothing to lose by following her heart. "I love you, husband of mine."

Vincent pulled her to his chest and lifted her off her feet, spinning her around. After two spins he set her down and kissed her. "I promise to make you feel loved every day of your life. The world will know how much you mean to me. They will be sick of it. 'Mandeville truly loves his wife beyond the point of good taste,' they will say. But you will be utterly drowning in adoration until the day I die. To the point of sickness. You could even wear a dreadful bonnet, and I would refrain from mocking you. I swear this to you."

Serena laughed as he lifted her to carry her to the bed. "And I promise to discuss things with you before fleeing. That was badly done of me, and I truly apologize."

Vincent groaned, and he set her in her bed and began to slide off her dressing gown. "I was hoping you would not apologize, and I could bring it up the next time I made a misstep. Oh well, I suppose that I will have to stop being a person who holds on to slights to excuse my bad behavior."

"Tut-tut! I said that I do not want you to change." Serena cooed as he began to kiss her neck.

Vincent ripped her shift to expose her breasts. "And I promised to make you feel loved. I could write volumes on your breasts. They are perfect."

Serena moaned as he began to suck on her nipples. She stroked his hair and lolled her head back in ecstasy. This is where she belonged, with Vincent. In truth, they belonged to each other, having given themselves fully. This was love, trusting that they would care for each other and proving it with each day.

Vincent proclaimed his love repeatedly as they made love. After, he held her close, and she fell asleep on his chest. She slept deeply, the slumber one can only achieve by having one's fears assuaged after weeks of being tormented by anxiety. When Serena awoke the next morning, she felt as though she had slept a lifetime and could not recall her dreams. But Vincent's arms were still around her, and last night's fire still burned.

After Serena had relieved herself and washed her face, she went to warm herself by the fire and add more coal. As Serena picked up the shovel, she saw assembled bits of paper. There were six pieces of paper, as though someone had torn a letter. Serena pieced the letter together, and recognized Vincent's hand. He must had stayed awake after Serena fell asleep to write this but tore the letter for some reason.

Serena began to read:

Mother,

I forgive you. For far too long I have held closely to every rejection and injury. I assumed that you meant every word you said and withheld. However, I have hurt the person that I genuinely love and now realize how easily one can wrong someone, either in pique or negligence. Perhaps you could not see how greatly you favored Sebastian. It is possible that you never meant to make me feel unwelcome with our family, as though I were the black sheep. Therefore, I forgive the resentment from all the past.

I don't believe that I can simply pretend to be a happy son, but I am willing to try. I wish that you had, just once, realized how your actions impacted me. In fact

The letter ended there, as though Vincent realized he was in a quagmire. Serena was happy to see that Vincent realized that sometimes people are cruel without intending it. In truth, she wasn't certain that, without both parties trying, the relationship between Vincent and the duchess could ever be mended.

However, forgiveness was always less about the other person and more about refusing to allow the ghosts of the past to hurt oneself.

"Where are you? I love you?" Vincent mumbled, caught in the haze of sleep.

Serena tossed the letter into the fire and crawled into bed with Vincent. He immediately wrapped his arms around her and sighed. Serena snuggled in, happy to have finally been where she always belonged.

****

At dawn, Sebastian rode to Stoney Breezes. He had barely slept, as he had spent most of the night pensively rearranging himself in an unfamiliar bed and worrying about his brother. Vincent's plan to scale the house and surprise his wife was easily one of the stupidest ideas Sebastian could think of. Visions of his brother's crumpled body haunted Sebastian throughout the night. And when Vincent didn't return, it meant that he was either successful or dead or hurt. The strategy would either be written in prose or on Vincent's epitaph.

As Sebastian approached the manse, Berkeley began to exit his carriage. Berkeley looked as exhausted as Sebastian was, his face low and his arms drooping. Nevertheless, he gave Sebastian a smile and half a wave.

"Have they reconciled?" Berkeley greeted.

Sebastian shrugged. "Vincent decided to do what he felt was 'the Ultimate Grand Gesture.' So, he scaled the wall of your home to break into Serena's room. I have no idea if he was successful or if he broke his neck."

"Well, that is a grand gesture. In the vein of kindness, let's see if we can find evidence of his failure, so we can assume his success?" Berkeley walked to the side of the house and inspected the grounds. "I see no dead Mandeville, and therefore we can believe that they are happily reunited. A brother's work is never done, is it?"

Sebastian smiled. "An endless and thankless duty."

"Indeed. Come inside for a brandy," Berkeley invited. Sebastian barely heard him, deep in thought and close to feeling his longed-for relief.

They entered the house. Clearly this summer palace was closed for the winter. The chandelier and artworks were covered by drapes, like ghosts of happiness past. Berkeley led him into the library, a room that would have captured Sebastian's father's heart. Berkeley quickly removed the cloth covering two leather chairs and began to pour the brandy.

"Thank you," Sebastian said as he sipped from the snifter, a fine piece of cut crystal. Sebastian never drank spirits in the morning, but he was exhausted and cold. This was not his home, so he could be another person for a minute.

"As far as I can decipher, too many of our problems stem from the Haverford woman. What can we do to be rid of her?" Berkeley asked as he sat.

Sebastian could not repress a sigh. Her name evinced nothing but irritation. Miss Haverford was the eternal thorn in his side. "I've made my mother promise to be done with her after the Christmas party. We will be free of her soon."

"Why must she attend the Christmas party at all? She seems to be the most melodramatic conniver I have ever born witness to, and that is quite the accomplishment," Berkeley pressed.

"It is complicated. Over the years, perhaps rightfully so, the Mandevilles have seemed to be snobbish. After the trial, we are trying to rebuild ourselves and our reputations. As far as the public is aware, Miss Haverford has done nothing wrong. To cut her would seem cruel, and I worried society would blame Serena. If it is any comfort, Lady Olivia agrees with you. She actually believes Miss Haverford is in the Shadow Society," Sebastian explained.

Berkeley nodded. "Olivia is clever, far more intelligent than most of the men I know. How does she suggest we vet this theory? Our accusations carry weight, so I use them sparingly."

Sebastian reddened. "Lady Olivia believes that Miss Haverford is scheming to marry me and has requested that I court herself as well as Miss Beauchamp and Honoria."

Berkeley grinned. "Should I feel sympathy for that dark fate? There are worse things than entertaining three beautiful women, old chap. What can I do to help this? I hate feeling powerless when there's clearly something wrong. It is a bit of a compulsion."

"Well, we are awaiting Honoria to decode the telegrams that Amesbury purchased. However, there are Shadow Society members in Essex as well as Aberdeenshire. Do you have any connections there?" Sebastian asked.

"I do. My aunt and uncle live in Aberdeenshire, near Banchory. I imagine they would love to meet Serena's new husband. I could arrange a visit after Christmas, and perhaps take a trip to MacDonald's house," Berkeley suggested.

"Excellent. I believe we are close freeing the

Mandevilles of the encumbering scandal of this trial, but I worry for the next family," Sebastian expressed.

"Then we must unmask every member of the Shadow Society and expose their villainy. What do you know of Haverford? Why is she so old for her introduction?"

Sebastian frowned. They knew truly little of her but accepted her as one of them. "I know she hails from Northumberland, and she said she was delayed in her introduction due to caring for a sick aunt."

Berkeley snorted. "That is unlikely. If Haverford has an aunt, then I will marry Aunt Penny."

Epilogue

Marlene hurried to the tea house to meet her aunt. Marlene wore a scowl. She steamed hot frustration from her ears; tardiness was the mark of an unserious woman. And her aunt hated anyone that was late to an appointment. Of course, now that they were the Cat and the Puma, their relationship had changed. Gone was the illusion of a warm, loving aunt. A commanding harpy had come up in the night and replaced her. Not that her aunt was ever demonstrably loving to begin with, but the Mandevilles had made her that way.

Marlene moved to the table and took a seat across from her aunt. New wrinkles had set near her mouth, and she had aged a bit since Marlene last saw her. What was it, two years ago? Now fine lines encircled her eyes, which had once shown a brilliant copper, burning with vengeance, but were now more rust colored. Her strawberry blonde hair had lost its luster, and she looked ragged. Even her beauty had been stolen by the Mandevilles.

"I do apologize for my tardiness, Aunt. I am unfamiliar with Ramsgate, but I understand your unwillingness to go to London," Marlene excused herself.

Aunt made a dismissive motion. "How are you proceeding?"

Marlene's stomach churned. "Vincent married

352

Lady Serena."

Aunt glared at her. "Well, that was not the plan, now was it?"

"No, ma'am. I did not anticipate Vincent would go to America, which is where he met her," Marlene whimpered.

"How goes the seduction of Sebastian?" the Puma asked as she poured the tea.

"Not well. I have tried to be what he should want in a wife, but he will not give in," Marlene admitted. He was resistant to her physical charms, which had been quite potent against her other target.

"I am exhausted by your excuses, girl. I took you in. I raised you as if you were my own. You know what the Mandevilles have done to me. You must be Sebastian's wife. Or there will have to be a trial by fire. But either way the Mandevilles must suffer. Thieves do not deserve crowns, liars do not receive peace, and enemies should be given no quarter," Aunt growled.

"I understand! I...I do have an invitation to Seraphina's Christmas party. It is in a fortnight at Avebury Park. I promise, Sebastian will begin the year married," Marlene begged. She had offered herself, bodily, to this cause, more so than anyone. Why was she the only one being impugned?

"Be sure that he does. This may give you some ideas." The Puma slid a book across the table to Marlene. "You are excused."

Marlene rushed from the tea house, shaken. She was failing in the mission she had been groomed her entire life to fulfill. She had always been petrified of her aunt but knew nothing else. As she began to find her way back to the train station, almost losing the path and full of anxious daydreams, she looked at the cover of the book she had been given. Marlene had never read *Jane Eyre,* but the answers she sought surely lived within its pages.

A word about the author...

Christine lives in Elgin, Texas, with her husband, daughter Pandora, son Upton, and three cats. She studied Western Civilization in California and traveled in Europe before moving to Texas. When she is not writing, she is passionate about cooking, art, and her family.

Thank you for purchasing
this publication of The Wild Rose Press, Inc.

For questions or more information
contact us at
info@thewildrosepress.com.

The Wild Rose Press, Inc.
www.thewildrosepress.com